Samuel Richardson, Dress, and Discourse

Samuel Richardson, Dress, and Discourse

Kathleen M. Oliver
Assistant Professor, Department of English,
University of Central Florida

First published 2008 by
PALGRAVE MACMILLAN
Houndmills, Basingstoke, Hampshire RG21 6XS and
175 Fifth Avenue, New York, N.Y. 10010
Companies and representatives throughout the world

PALGRAVE MACMILLAN is the global academic imprint of the Palgrave Macmillan division of St. Martin's Press, LLC and of Palgrave Macmillan Ltd. Macmillan® is a registered trademark in the United States, United Kingdom and other countries. Palgrave is a registered trademark in the European Union and other countries.

ISBN-13: 978-0-230-57452-6   hardback
ISBN-10: 0-230-57452-1   hardback

This book is printed on paper suitable for recycling and made from fully managed and sustained forest sources. Logging, pulping and manufacturing processes are expected to conform to the environmental regulations of the country of origin.

A catalogue record for this book is available from the British Library.

A catalog record for this book is available from the Library of Congress.

10   9   8   7   6   5   4   3   2   1
17   16   15   14   13   12   11   10   09   08

Printed and bound in Great Britain by
CPI Antony Rowe, Chippenham and Eastbourne

To Charlie

struggling for control; the female body itself in eighteenth-century English society was highly problematic, as "the common law did not normally acknowledge the existence of any woman who was not under the protection of a man: father, husband, brother or guardian."[1] Last, Clarissa herself is tragically unable to distinguish between the two types of dress, natural and artificial, suggesting that distinctions are overly subtle, or, perhaps, that Clarissa herself somehow lacks discernment.

Again, Richardson appears to have recognized that meaning and signification in *Clarissa* remained unstable, particularly in terms of reader reactions to the characters of Clarissa and Lovelace. In a letter to Aaron Hill, one of Richardson's greatest and most vocal admirers, Richardson's frustration is clear:

> But I am very greatly mortified, that what I have so much laboured, as to make it manifest, that Clarissa, tho' provoked as she was … That this should be called, by such a clear Discerner; *a rash Elopement with a Man;* and that your Reasoning in this material Place, is built upon the Supposition of her voluntarily *running away from her Father's House, with a worse Man †than Solmes† of her own choosing!* I am very unfortunate, good Sir, let me say, <to be so ill-understood:> To have *given Reason, <I should say,>* to be so little understood.[2]

In *The History of Sir Charles Grandison*, Richardson achieves the seemingly unattainable goal of a stable language of dress, a system of ostensibly constant signifiers, which, I think, also stands for his desire to achieve some semblance of stable meaning within the novel itself. Yet, ironically, Richardson achieves stability in his depiction of dress only by eliminating all detailed descriptions of attire, with the exception of Harriet Byron's masquerade outfit, as his system of dress requires that all types of unruly or inappropriate dress be contained and confined under the heading of masquerade. Harriet's outfit, then, stands for all manner of inappropriate dress; the masquerade gown exists as the antithesis by which dress as tasteful and genuine expression of self may be compared, measured. Natural, tasteful, authentic dress becomes the province of Sir Charles, rendering him legible (or perhaps a more appropriate term might be transparent), yet this tasteful dress is never realized through detailed depictions, but exists only as general principles, much in the manner espoused by Mr. Spectator himself. By confining inappropriate (and unstable) notions of dress to the female, the feminine, and the feminized, Richardson finally achieves his goal of articulating, rendering legible, and stabilizing the meaning of "good" and "authentic" dress and, in tandem with this, the new domestic (feminine) ideal, paradoxically reconfigured as masculine. Yet Richardson's success becomes his failure, and his failure his success, as his employment of dress in *Grandison* renders highly conventional interpretations, such as were articulated in countless conduct books, poems, periodicals, plays, and more, while his use of dress in *Pamela* and *Clarissa* remains rich, dense, volatile, and deliciously unstable.

Analysis of dress in Richardson's novels reveals the novelist's sustained interest in and impulse towards the establishment of a system of dress where sartorial signification—and, by extension, all signification—becomes stable. Of interest is why Richardson felt compelled to devise such a system in the first place and what this means in terms of understanding and interpreting his texts. The most obvious reason seems to be the instability of Richardson's own texts, which took on meanings and interpretations that Richardson never intended. His attempt to control the language of dress, then, becomes expressive of his larger desire to control textual meaning. The study of Richardson's use of dress in the service of his writing allows us to understand the problems inherent in the craft of writing, and how one early proponent and practitioner of the novel set about solving them. The study of dress also hints at the enigmatic nature of creativity and art and that success in craftsmanship (in this case, the temporary stabilization of signification and meaning) does not automatically guarantee artistic outcome.

Another reason exists in Richardson's desire to render legible the sensible or sentimental body, in particular, as it relates to the body of the "new domestic woman," as Nancy Armstrong terms it.[3] The fact is that this desire remained, to a great extent, thwarted by the inherent instability of signification and the doomed nature of any project seeking to reduce all women or all bodies (or all of anything, for that matter) to a single set of socially desirable attributes. Jennie Batchelor has argued that this desire to render the female body legible is at the heart of sentimental literature, and that the seeds of sentimentalism's own demise resided in the nature of sentimentalism itself—"the fine line between virtue (affect) and its mere performance (affectation)"[4]—as well as sentimental literature's reliance on dress, an equally duplicitous or ambiguous signifier, as a primary means to articulate sensibility. Yet what remains most intriguing about Richardson's novels is that the sentimental body was indeed rendered legible, but this sentimental body was male, not female. This suggests the sheer unruliness of the female body, in terms of signification, but also that sentimentalism needed distancing from fashion, which the masculine provided. In *Grandison*, unruly, improper, or inappropriate attire is always associated with the female, feminine, or feminized body.

Curiously, what may be the finest articulation of the sentimental body in eighteenth-century English literature, *The History of Sir Charles Grandison*, identifies the perfect, legible, authentic sentimental body as a male one. What renders this body even more problematic is that this sentimental body, as a male body, is equally public and private, complicating both the definition of sentimentalism and the categories of "economic man" and "domestic woman," the yin and yang of bourgeois ideology. In Richardson's portrait of Sir Charles, we find those elements most highly esteemed in the domestic woman—modesty, industry, self-regulation, and active virtue.[5] Sir Charles's primary role is to instruct others in matters of domestic ideology and conduct; promotion of private, domestic life provides the impetus behind his public life. In addition, his male body enjoys an economic and a moral independence that no female body of the time could easily, if ever, lay claim to, making it possible to isolate, to stabilize, and to control the body's meaning. To whit, through the use of a male protagonist, Richardson was able to achieve what he could not with a Clarissa or a Pamela, a domestic ideal that could not easily be misread. By jettisoning the feminine, Richardson is able to create a portrait of ideal domestic virtue (and dress), and he is able to establish some control over signification, both in terms of dress and in terms of larger novelistic meaning.

Thus, while dress is but one way of entering into a text, and a small point of entry at that, analysis of dress in Richardson's novels provides us with insights into the nature of novel writing in eighteenth-century England; into the nature of Richardson's novelistic project of constructing a legible domestic feminine body whose signification remains stable; and into the paradox that Richardson's ideal, sensible (as possessed of sensibility) female body is ultimately coded as male. It also calls into question the whole construct of the "domestic woman" and what this construct means in terms of bourgeois ideology: Is the ideal domestic woman merely a man in drag?

Theorizing Dress in Eighteenth-Century Literature

In the past twenty years, increasing attention has been directed to material culture as represented in eighteenth-century texts, and, yet, the study of dress in eighteenth-century literature remains limited. As Clair Hughes notes, "An attention to dress provides, of course, only one way of looking at a text, but it is surprising that so few literary critics have

taken the trouble to give such attention in a systematic fashion."[6]
I would argue that the study of dress provides particularly rich insights
into eighteenth-century British culture, as clothing, more so than any
other material object produced during that time period, embodied and
performed cultural anxieties and desires, particularly those related to
gender, class, and nation. The fact that an article of clothing may be
interpreted in multiple ways does not lessen its potency as a signifier,
and, indeed, may serve instead to increase it.

Dress, both as material object and textual construct, may be interpreted in multiple, though interrelated ways—as symbol, as cultural
artifact, as commodity, as fetish, as performance, as discourse, and
more—and the study of dress engages with multiple disciplines—
"anthropology, consumer behavior, cultural studies, psychology, and
sociology,"[7] as well as social history, political science, the visual arts,
theater, and literary studies. However, some obvious differences exist
between garments fashioned from fabric and those constructed from
words. A silk umbrella owned by an eighteenth-century gentlewoman
possessed use-value (it sheltered her from rain or sun), commodity-
value (its existence had been brought about by exchange of materials
and labor for monetary compensation), as well as sociocultural value,
identifying the owner by social station, gender, nationality, and more.
In addition, the umbrella might make the owner appear more feminine (or masculine) in her own eyes or in the eyes of others, and it
might be something that the owner invested with fetishistic power (as
an object possessed of a certain social cachet).

The umbrella fashioned by Robinson Crusoe (who, in turn, has been
fashioned by Daniel Defoe) alludes to the material, cultural, and historical significance of the real, material umbrella. Crusoe has constructed
it in order to protect himself from the weather; his labor has brought
about the umbrella's existence; and its rough goatskin covering and
crudely constructed frame suggest social station, gender, nation.
Nonetheless, it is but an imaginative object, a confection of words with
no material presence or function. Yet, for all that, it resonates with
meaning in ways a real umbrella never can: It conjures up images of
resourcefulness, ingenuity, isolation; it becomes emblematic of the half-
civilized, half-wild man who labored week upon week to create it. The
umbrella, like the lone footprint, becomes a talisman by which the
entire text may be summoned in a single moment; one has merely to
think of Crusoe's umbrella and the complete narrative of the eccentric
character alone on his tropical island, with goatskin breeches and
floppy hat, with dog, cats, and goats as companions, with Xury in the

past and Friday in the future, immediately presents itself. Crusoe's umbrella simultaneously bears witness to eighteenth-century English culture and the existence of real umbrellas, but it also functions as a complex symbol through which culture and narrative become compressed and condensed. Crusoe's umbrella exists as one of the "dislocated images and forms," one of the "floating fragments" of myth, dream, and life that haunts the novel, in the words of Claude Lévi-Strauss.[8]

At its most basic (formalist) level, dress functions as symbol, regardless of whether it possesses material presence or written presence. For instance, the color of clothing has long held symbolic and emblematic meaning, and this symbolism pervades all cultural levels, from the sociopolitical, to the artistic, to the religious, to the literary. Yet color is only one small aspect of the symbolism associated with dress, as even the minutest details of an ensemble possess signification. In addition, specific signification associated with an article of dress may remain stable, or may fluctuate over time and place. A single article of dress may possess conflicting meanings, and several articles of dress, worn together, may communicate competing or warring messages. The wearer also contributes meaning to dress (for instance, body shape, posture, weight, age, gender, nationality, hair style, makeup, bodily alterations, and bodily adornment aid in interpretation), as does the person who views the wearer, as does the context in which the attire is worn.

Dress enters into eighteenth-century English literature, in periodicals like *The Spectator* or *The Lady's Magazine*, in sermons and conduct books, novels, plays, poems, and drama, precisely because it already possessed such rich and complex signification and meaning within English society. Clothing exists as cultural artifact, with all the sociopolitical meaning assigned to it, and most symbolism generates from the cultural context of dress. Nationality, class, gender, age, economic background, occupation, religion, morality, and more may be determined from dress, and information about how a society treats certain of its members, such as the poor, the aged, women, and gays, for instance, can often be gleaned from an analysis of the clothing worn by members of these social groups and the meaning which the society as a whole and the members of the group assign to this attire.

Clothing is political in nature, because it exists as a "text" that determines how individuals are viewed and treated within a society, and because access to particular types and modes of dress is controlled by the society, either through legislation ("indecent" dress, for instance, is frequently proscribed), through societal and cultural determination of what specific styles of dress mean (what "indecent" dress constitutes, for example), and through economics (certain articles of clothing are outside the economic reach of many members of society). Malcolm Barnard writes:

> Fashion and clothing are therefore not only ways in which social groups are constituted as social groups and by means of which they communicate their identity. It is another aspect of ideology that it ensures the functioning of a system of dominant and subservient positions within a social order. Fashion and clothing are ideological, then, in that they are also part of the process in which social groups establish, sustain and reproduce positions of power, relations of dominance and subservience. They are, moreover, part of the process in which those positions of dominance and subservience are made to appear entirely natural, proper and legitimate.[9]

Dress is also political because it functions as commodity, created by labor under specific conditions, which may or may not be advantageous to the worker; clothing is then merchandized and sold, purchased and worn. Dress is assigned a monetary value, an exchange value. It possesses intrinsic value, keeping the wearer warm, cool, or protected from the elements, but it also possesses extrinsic value, accruing significance from whatever meaning the culture assigns to it and the labor that produced it.

Because articles of dress are commodities, they also possess fetishistic value in capitalist societies. Marx, in a well-known excerpt from *Capital*, argued that, in a capitalist society, commodities function as fetishes, as these products are estranged from the labor that produces them, and, thus, "the social character of men's labour appears to them as an objective character stamped upon the product of that labour; because the relation of the producers to the sum total of their own labour is presented to them as a social relation, existing not between themselves, but between the products of their labour."[10] Social relations among human subjects and between workers (subjects) and the products of their labor are substituted with relations among and between commodities (objects). In a pre-capitalistic society, objects accrue value through their intrinsic nature (the inherent value of the materials used) as well as from their use-value, that is, from their use to the individual user, who is also the maker (worker). In a capitalist society, objects appear to accrue value solely through their relationship to one another, in essence, through their exchange-value, which is the object's worth in relation to other commodities. However, this exchange-value conceals the social value of commodities, which is the hidden "expenditure of human labour-power, of human labour in abstract."[11] The "secret" message that commodities relay is that of human social relations, and it is this which fetishizes the commodity and provides it with value, making the commodity a mediating object through which social relations can be expressed and enacted in a capitalist society. Thus, as Herbert Marcuse writes, "The people recognize themselves in their commodities; they find their soul in their automobile, hi-fi set, split-level home, kitchen equipment."[12] Of course, people recognize themselves in their clothing as well. To paraphrase Marcuse, people find their souls in their high-heeled shoes, baggy jeans, t-shirt, handbag.

If commodities function as the means through which modern cultures engage in social relations, then dress, as a commodity, can presumably alter social relations. It can do so in two ways: First, as Erin Mackie writes, "Fashion is a historically constituted category of commodity production and consumption, as well as of cultural criticism."[13] What is produced, who consumes it, and the cultural critiques (positive and negative) that accompany the production and consumption of dress— all participate in "a considerable tug-of-war between socio-economic and ideological forces."[14] Mackie continues, "*The Tatler* and *The Spectator* are part of a highly conscious and resourceful criticism that follows in the wake of British commercial expansion and the institutions of modern culture."[15] Cultural critiques of dress through discourse (magazines, novels, sermons, periodicals, conduct books, legislation, gossip) shape, define, and modify (or attempt to shape, define, and modify) social, sexual, and economic relations between specific groups within a specific society. These forces of production, consumption, and cultural criticism are not monolithic: Multiple items of differing cost, quality, usefulness, etc. are being produced, with multiple groups of differing gender, age, economic, and social status consuming them, and with multiple cultural critiques (positive, negative, indifferent) of these myriad productions and consumer groups in circulation.

If production, consumption, and cultural critique impose (or attempt to impose) some semblance of meaning upon particular items of dress which the public and, in turn, the individual comprehends and either accepts or rejects, then the individual or a group of individuals can attempt to utilize these meanings for himself, herself, or themselves, either by accepting the meaning associated with that dress, by modifying it in some fashion, or by challenging it. Thus, the second way that a commodity (such as dress) can function as a means of altering social relations is by the individual wearer using it to perform or to alter the identity associated with the clothing. All dress allows the wearer to perform some version of the identity associated with the clothing itself. Susan B. Kaiser notes, "Dressing and experimenting with appearance afford opportunities of exploring who we are. Information about the self may be gleaned from the responses of others, visual comparisons with others' appearances, and internal thought processes that lead us to attribute explanations to our own clothing choices and preferences."[16] When a particular style of dress is deemed "natural" to a wearer, it means that the dress is considered appropriate to the individual based on his/her sex, age, economic background, social status, occupation, bodily appearance, and more. Individuals frequently utilize dress to challenge these so-called "natural" meanings, or, if these individuals themselves do not fit into the prescribed notions of the appropriate wearer for a particular style of dress, they may use dress in an attempt to appropriate (successfully or unsuccessfully) a particular sartorial and social identity. Clothing fashions, or attempts to fashion, identity. Malcolm Barnard notes, "It is not the case that an individual is first a skinhead and then wears all the gear, but that the gear constitutes the individual as a skinhead. It is the social interaction, by means of the clothing, that constitutes the individual as a member of the group rather than vice-versa, that one is a member of the group and then interacts socially."[17] A change of dress changes the perceptions of others, and, in turn, alters social relations. Dress, then, both performs identity and can transform or alter identity.

Clothing and accoutrement are read, interpreted (rightly or not), and judgment of some sort pronounced upon the wearer. As Kaiser comments:

> The clothes themselves, as well as the ideas and images that surround them, circulate widely through cultural discourses. Cultural discourses are like conversations that involve working through ideas. Yet they operate visually and verbally, involving a circulation of objects, ideas, images, and values that form a kind of underlying logic for the social meanings we assign to our identities, clothes, and communities.[18]

In claiming that dress functions as discourse, as language, most sociologists (though not all) agree that dress does not function in the same manner as spoken or written language, but merely that clothing and accoutrement are "forms of non-verbal communication,"[19] of which the meaning is defined by a specific time period, place, culture, and context. Many fashion sociologists utilize the structural linguistic methodology of Ferdinand de Saussure, of the signifier (specific articles of dress) and the signified (the meaning or meanings assigned to them), and Roland

Barthes, in *The Fashion System*, has made admirable use of Saussurian structuralism, by applying it only to "written clothing," that is, to clothing as described in fashion magazines or books. As Barthes writes, "only written clothing has no practical or aesthetic function: it is entirely constituted with a view to signification"; "written clothing is unencumbered by any parasitic function and entails no vague temporality."[20] Terry Castle similarly treats clothing as a type of discourse:

> Modern semiotics has confirmed the force of the analogy: like language, clothing is after all a system of signs, and a means of symbolic communication. Like speech acts, different costumes carry conventional meanings; clothing opens itself everywhere to interpretation by others, in accordance with prevailing systems of sartorial inscription. Clothing inescapably serves a signifying function within culture; it is in fact an institution inseparable from culture.[21]

Yet some sociologists caution against treating clothes merely as a form of communication and particularly discourage the analysis of clothing through textual representation alone. As Joanne Entwistle wryly comments, "By textualizing fashion and dress these approaches can sometimes be reductive; if practices are reduced to texts, the complexity of fashion and dress and the way in which it is embodied is largely neglected."[22] In addition, Entwistle rightly notes that most studies of dress "tend to neglect the body and the meanings the body brings to dress."[23] Yet, when reading clothing that exists only in the form of words, as a description in a text, there are not only no clothes, but no naked emperor either. Reference may be made to real clothes, to real bodies, but the clothes and the bodies are merely written signs on a page. Nonetheless, clothing as described in the texts of a particular place and time provides tremendous insights into culture, allowing a momentary articulation of meaning.

The study of dress in eighteenth-century texts is particularly rewarding, as England was undergoing significant sociocultural change during the eighteenth century, and new genres, such as the periodical, the newspaper, the fashion magazine, and the novel appeared in response to this change, as did new forms of dress. Notions of gender, class, family, and nation were being altered and revised, and conflicting sociocultural and political models were enacted and performed through dress, as well as endlessly discussed, critiqued, and analyzed in print. Although the amount of critical attention directed to dress in eighteenth-century English literature still remains relatively slender, another study on dress in eighteenth-century literature, particularly one which focuses solely on dress in the novels of a single author, nonetheless must justify its place in the scholarly marketplace, addressing not only its unique contributions to the study of dress in eighteenth-century literature and culture, but also to the study of Samuel Richardson's novels.

In all of Richardson's novels (and, indeed, in a large number of eighteenth-century English novels), masquerade as event, dress, plot motivator, and trope is central. Characters attend masquerade balls, which, in turn, function as a means to propel the plot forward and provide the author with the opportunity to engage in social commentary. Pamela, once married to Mr. B., attends a masquerade ball, as does Harriet Byron, during her stay in London. Both masquerades produce disastrous results for the respective heroines: Mr. B. engages in an ill-advised flirtation with the Dowager Countess, creating disharmony and mistrust between himself and his pregnant Pamela. This lapse allows for numerous discussions on the sanctity of marriage, proper behavior for wife and husband, and the dangerous and wicked nature of masquerades, while serving to energize a heretofore enervated plot. Sir Hargrave Pollexfen abducts Harriet while on her return from a masquerade, again engendering discussion on the moral turpitude associated with masquerade, yet also allowing Sir Charles Grandison, as figurative knight on white horse, to enter into the narrative. Characters dress in masquerade garb, teasing readers as to the meaning of particular styles of dress in relation to the wearer's identity, such as the Quaker outfit worn by Pamela or the Arcadian shepherdess attire worn by Harriet. Masquerade also functions as a major trope (perhaps the major trope) in *Clarissa*, with Lovelace and his gang of rogues and whores engaging in elaborate masquerade, providing commentary on forced marriages and provoking comparisons to the Harlowe family. Thus, masquerade expresses itself as event, attire, and trope in Richardson's novels; it provokes social commentary; and it provides energy and impetus to the plot.

Of course, no work that engages in discussion of masquerade can avoid, nor should avoid, some mention of Terry Castle's seminal text, *Masquerade and Civilization: The Carnivalesque in Eighteenth-Century Culture and Fiction*. Castle's work provides important cultural and historical background on the masquerade in eighteenth-century England, and it argues for masquerade's destabilizing and ambivalent influence on the plot of eighteenth-century novels. For Castle, masquerade "is associated with the disruption, rather than the stabilization of meaning. Befitting its deeper link with forces of transformation and mutability, the masquerade typically has a catalytic effect on plot."[24]

Within the novel, the "masquerade episode serves as a point for narrative transformation—the privileged site of plot."[25] Castle also provides brief commentary on the masquerade episode in *Sir Charles Grandison*, as the means of achieving a comic, happy ending, as well as sustained commentary on the masquerade in *Pamela*, Part Two.

My own reading of masquerade in Richardson's novels utilizes Castle's sociocultural foundation and certainly acknowledges and builds upon her contributions, yet it also differs from Castle in significant ways: First, my emphasis tends towards cultural materialism, that is, I am interested in the material nature of dress, the body, and the relationship of body and dress to the display of virtue and the construction of the domestic ideal. Thus, when reading masquerade in *Pamela*, Part Two, in *Clarissa*, and in *Sir Charles Grandison*, I am most concerned with material elements associated with masquerade and their signification, rather than with the disruptive and subversive action of masquerade on plot and characterization.

Second, Castle concentrates on the destabilizing nature of masquerade and its ability to subvert "patriarchal structures," though, as Catherine Craft-Fairchild notes, Castle "neglects to stress that, to the extent that masquerade assemblies were tolerated, they had in some ways to conform to the dominant culture."[26] My interest lies in the dialectic created between masquerade, as model for all that is unnatural or artful, and a presumed naturalized and normative state, and the fact that this presumed normative standard cannot exist without its opposite, masquerade, to define it. In his discourses on dress, Richardson utilizes the metaphor of masquerade to include not only fanciful attire, but also all other categories of inappropriate dress, including the foppish, foolish, garish, or gender-bending. To whit, masquerade becomes a necessary foil or backdrop, against which Richardson defines and models his own interpretation of tasteful dress. Masquerade, in Richardson's novels, exists in opposition to all things natural, including suitable dress, appropriate behavior, and good taste, yet it is also required in order to understand and articulate these very things. In the end result, masquerade becomes a catchall for all things feminine and feminized, serving as a point of contrast by which a new form of patriarchal hegemony attempts to naturalize and normalize itself.

If masquerade is one of the narrative threads that weave through the corpus of Richardson's work, its dialogic complement, as previously mentioned, is the narrative of "naturalness." Richardson's discourse on dress engages, like *The Spectator* and *The Tatler*, in the attempt to create and sustain a culture of taste, based upon the belief that some sort of "natural" dress exists, which complements, articulates, corresponds to, and reconciles the inner and outer self. Richardson was highly influenced by *The Tatler* and *The Spectator*, and his desire to define and articulate a natural style of dress generates, in no small part, from his engagement with these two periodicals.

In *Market à la Mode: Fashion, Commodity, and Gender in The Tatler and The Spectator*, Erin Mackie examines the ways in which *The Tatler* and *The Spectator* attempt "to regulate and exploit" fashion.[27] As Mackie writes, "Quite simply, *The Tatler* and *The Spectator* register deep ambivalence about fashion, especially their own fashionability as modish lifestyle magazines. In them we find the logic of antifashion fashion: what is really stylistically desirable is defined against what is merely 'fashionable.'"[28] While I am deeply indebted to Mackie's work on the complicit relationship between fashion and literature, particularly to the notion that certain eighteenth-century texts, such as *The Spectator*, served to naturalize the norms of the bourgeois public sphere, my own interest lies less in how periodicals, dedicated to good taste and to the promotion of culture, seek to control and manipulate fashion, or even in how Richardson's texts seek to manipulate and control fashion, but how literary dress contributes to and complicates novelistic narrative and cultural meaning.

Richardson's dialectic treatment of clothing and fashion ("good" dress versus "bad" dress) is symptomatic of the novel of sentiment, and, indeed, of almost all eighteenth-century sentimental literature, including conduct books, periodicals, poetry, drama, and more. As Jennie Batchelor notes, in *Dress, Distress and Desire: Clothing and the Female Body in Eighteenth-Century Literature*:

> If sentimental literature suggested the possibility of a meritocracy ... then the fashionable, urban world represented its antithesis. Dress, as both the most immediate signifier of this world and most vivid symbol of its corruption, thus accrued a potent symbolism in sentimental discourse in which dress variously functioned as a rebuttal of the moral and financial excesses attributed to society's fashionable upper reaches, and was reclaimed as a symbol of bourgeois sentimental virtue.[29]

In Batchelor's argument, the sentimental, as expressive of bourgeois culture, reacts against and defines itself against the commercial (vaguely synonymous with upper-class and fashionable culture) through appropriation and reinterpretation of the "most resonant and pertinent symbol for the female consumer: dress"; however, in doing so, sentimental culture undermined its own project of social reform, as it, in turn, becomes associated with "fashionableness, speciousness and impermanence."[30] Dress, because of its volatile associations, signals the downfall of sentimental literature, once employed by and embedded within the novel of sentiment. Thus, Batchelor sees Richardson's "failure to convince his readers of Pamela's integrity" as stemming from "the novel's reliance on sartorial language and material signs."[31] This is an intriguing idea, as bourgeois culture repeatedly appropriated the symbols (dress included) of fashionable and/or aristocratic culture, revising or attempting to revise signification, and it is also true that bourgeois culture, taste, and dress required something against which to define itself. In addition, Richardson's descriptions of his protagonists' dress often excessively embellish what should, in essence, be simple attire. Last, as Batchelor notes, dress, like sentiment, may be affected or genuine; no stable marker exists to identify the one from the other. What, I believe, is most important about Batchelor's contribution is that she rightly acknowledges the centrality of dress in expressing sensibility, the importance of dress in sentimental literature, and the ambivalent messages created by an over-reliance on dress in terms of signification.

Yet dress does not make an appearance in all sentimental literature, nor does sentimental literature hold exclusive rights to detailed sartorial descriptions, nor is sentiment always viewed as potentially ingenuous. My particular project builds upon Batchelor's work, in that it acknowledges the instability of dress as signifier and the ambiguous nature of sensibility itself, but it diverges from Batchelor's study in claiming that it is the cultural ambiguity surrounding the female and feminine that exists as the originary source of unstable signification.

In Richardson's novels, dress and sensibility are in service of his attempt to render legible the new domestic feminine ideal. Nancy Armstrong, in *Desire and Domestic Fiction*, and elsewhere, has argued that Richardson's *Pamela* represents the first novelistic attempt to express the domestic feminine ideal, as first conceived in conduct-book literature. Armstrong argues that the new domestic feminine ideal, consisting of "a specific configuration of sexual features ... provided people from diverse social groups with a basis for imagining economic interests in common."[32] Armstrong writes, "narratives which seemed to be concerned solely with matters of courtship and marriage in fact seized the authority to say what was female, and that they did so in order to contest the reigning notion of kinship relations that attached most power and privilege to certain family lines."[33] To restate in a slightly different fashion, the domestic feminine ideal becomes the means (the secret weapon, so to speak) by which bourgeois culture achieved cultural hegemony. To me, Armstrong's argument is highly persuasive, yet its very persuasiveness raises two related problems: First, despite the fact that the domestic feminine ideal embodies a seemingly desirable set of cultural attributes, she (or her more modern counterpart, the domestic diva) has often been and remains the target of hostility and aggression. Second, despite the privileged position of the domestic feminine ideal in bourgeois ideology and culture, the culture itself was and remains patriarchal and, upon occasion, even highly misogynistic. What seems clear, upon examination, is that the domestic feminine ideal is nothing more than an artful (literary) construct under the guise of which one system of patriarchy displaced and replaced another.

With regards to Richardson, what I suggest is that, for all that Richardson admired his Pamela and his Clarissa, the representation of these characters also embodies long-held cultural mistrust of women; indeed, how could it not, when any text performs the culture in which it was created? If, as Batchelor notes, sentimental literature was in service of a "male fantasy of the legible female body,"[34] then this female body is one that inherently resists interpretation and whose representation simultaneously embeds anxiety and desire. If, as Robert Markley has asserted, sentimentality is "at least in part a masculinist complex of strategies designed to relegate women to the status of perpetual victims,"[35] then the domestic feminine ideal is the locus of such strategies, part victim, part legerdemain. Intriguingly, the ultimate legible body in Richardson's work is not female, but male—the transparent figure of Grandison—suggesting the resistance of the female body to reification, despite Richardson's determined efforts, as it is a body always defined in opposition to the privileged, known, knowable, and "natural" male body.

The attempt to render the body, female or male, legible relates directly to the desire to render the mind legible. The intense interest in eighteenth-century English culture in both body and dress generates from curiosity about the functioning of the mind, which Locke served to illuminate, and also the need to know, with some measure of certainty, the thoughts of others, two topics that will be discussed more fully in Chapter 1. Dress was presumed one indicator of the mind; the body, another. This need to comprehend the thoughts of others becomes particularly acute in times of great social and cultural change, when systems of signification are changing, as was the case in eighteenth-century England. As Juliet McMaster, in *Reading the Body in the Eighteenth-Century Novel*, notes, "Reading the mind through the body is an activity we are all involved in all the time. But during the eighteenth century, particularly, it was a highly conscious process, and the different languages of the body were not only being translated and analyzed by experts, but eagerly learned and interpreted by a growing population of keen and knowledgeable amateurs."[36] Through the related studies of physiognomy and pathognomy, eighteenth-century novelists attempted to make the body of their characters legible, and, in doing so, provide their readers with clues about the mind and spirit of the character, in much the same way that dress was utilized. McMaster writes, "[Eighteenth-century] Readers were alert to the mind/body connection, and took seriously the business of interpreting the one through the other. Far from registering the signals without thinking, like modern readers, they were thinking all the time."[37]

McMaster's book provides background on the body and bodily gesture in eighteenth-century English culture, discourse, art, and theater, with particular emphasis on its display in the eighteenth-century English novel; she engages in a fine reading of the body in *Clarissa*. McMaster's scholarly text provides an excellent accompaniment to any study of dress, as body and dress are inextricably entwined, in literature, in art, and in life. McMaster's book has subtly informed my own reading of dress in Richardson's novels. McMaster attempts "in some measure to recover the reading experience of the contemporary readers of eighteenth-century novels, by focusing on discourse on the expressive body that they knew very well, and following through the ways the novelists made use of them."[38] Like her, one of my goals is to "recover the reading experiences of the contemporary readers of eighteenth-century novels, by focusing on discourse" of dress "that they knew very well," and by tracking the varied use that Richardson, as novelist, makes of dress as discourse. While I do focus on the body, particularly in my discussion of *Pamela*, I do not focus on the interpretation of the physical aspects of body and face, nor on bodily gestures, as McMaster does. My own interest in the body generally relates to class and gender issues and their relationship to cultural perceptions of virtue.

Despite my desire to recapture a sense of how contemporary readers of Richardson's novels experienced and understood dress, it is a task fraught with some difficulty, as Aileen Ribeiro astutely notes:

When I read a literary text I "read" the dress, as I do when I "read" the dress in a work of art. This is sometimes difficult, since nuances perceptible only to those wearing and observing the clothes in the past are now lost to us and cannot be retrieved easily. Clothing can deceive and mislead, especially when represented in literature and art. It is therefore all the more important to have the *facts* of dress, the naming of names before we can understand how to decode this language; a caveat to enter here is the difficulty of pinning down the exact names of garments, fabrics and colours as they constantly change over a period of time, as understood by different people even within the *same* time span.[39]

No study of dress in literature can be accomplished without the work of costume and fashion historians, as they are the individuals who provide "the *facts* of dress," and many, such as Anne Buck, Anne Hollander, and Aileen Ribeiro, have provided informed, nuanced, and detailed readings of dress in art, literature, and culture. Although my focus is on dress as represented in literature, I am equally fascinated by dress in terms of culture, and my own methodology has been greatly informed by the materiality that scholars like Buck, Hollander, and Ribeiro bring to their study and interpretation of historic dress. However, as mentioned earlier, distinct differences exist between real historical articles of clothing and accoutrement and their fictional counterparts. While a real material article of dress, say, a hooped petticoat, may be defined both in terms of its materiality (size, fabric, shape, embellishment, use) and its cultural meaning (ambiguous sexual connotations, class associations, etc.), a fictional hooped petticoat must be read both in terms of its cultural meaning and its literary meaning, which may or may not be in agreement. The work of fashion historians allows the material nature of the garment to be known, as well as its cultural meaning, and the changes in both over time; this provides the basis upon which interpretations of dress in literature may be founded.

As Clair Hughes writes, "dress is not the hidden key to all mysteries" of fictional texts, but "an author's deployment of dress and its accessories can illuminate the structure of that text, its values, its meanings or its symbolic pattern."[40] Dress is but one way of entering Richardson's texts, yet, I believe, it is a highly productive way, due to the emphasis on dress in both eighteenth-century English society and in Richardson's own novels. Analysis of dress confirms older insights into the structure, values, meaning, and symbols of Richardson's novels, and it provides new insights into Richardson's work: His struggle to control meaning and contain signification; the ways in which he attempted to solve problems associated with interpretation and signification; his attempt (and failure) to render legible the new domestic woman, at least as woman. It also suggests the underlying misogyny of bourgeois culture;

even if, as Nancy Armstrong argues, "the modern individual was first and foremost a female,"[41] it is an individual constituted as something more than or less than female. The dominant social ideal remained male, though perhaps disguised in cap, gown, and petticoat.

This book is organized into four parts. Part I discusses the importance of dress in eighteenth-century English culture and literature: It begins with a discussion of Locke's ideas concerning the mind, in an attempt to uncover Richardson's own epistemology of the mind and its various discourses; it ends with a brief discussion of the increased focus on dress in eighteenth-century England and its implications for literary production. The remaining three parts follow the chronological order of Richardson's novels, with Part Two, analyzing dress in *Pamela*; Part Three, in *Clarissa*; and Part Four, in *The History of Sir Charles Grandison*. A brief conclusion sums up the major implications of this study in terms of Richardson's novelistic production and its relationship to the domestic ideal.

Part I The Body and Dress of Thought

Introduction

"For what are *words*, but the *body* and *dress* of *thought*? And is not the mind indicated strongly by its outward dress?"[1] So writes Samuel Richardson's young heroine Clarissa Harlowe to her friend Anna Howe. Clarissa has just met, for the first time, Lovelace's claque of libertines, consisting of Belford, Belton, Mowbray, and Tourville, and she has seen the men comport themselves freely with Mrs. Sinclair and Miss Partington. She refers in particular to Miss Partington, presumably a great heiress, though, in actuality, a high-class prostitute, and Clarissa's comments are made, not in relation to Miss Partington's attire, but to Miss Partington's "smiles and simperings," which encourage the men's licentious speech and which appear, at least to Clarissa's mind, inconsistent with "that purity of manners which ought to be the distinguishing characteristic of our Sex."[2]

This quotation from Richardson's novel is frequently cited as evidence of the eighteenth-century English belief that clothing functions as a kind of discourse, expressive of the mind of the wearer. As words spoken or written communicate the thoughts of the speaker or writer, so too do articles of dress provide evidence of the mind of the individual whose body they adorn. However, closer examination of Clarissa's observations on dress, words, and thoughts, as well as the context in which they are presented, render this a correct, yet an overly simplified interpretation, in several respects: First, if words relate to thoughts, as body and dress relate to mind, in what ways, if any, does the mind differ from the thoughts contained within? And, if difference does exist, does Clarissa's statement suggest that body and dress are equivalent to thought, that they exist as more immediate and direct expressions of the mind, than words themselves? Or, if no difference exists, does it mean that the physical body and the clothing in which it is adorned are, quite literally, the "*body* and *dress* of *thought*"?

Second, as Clarissa writes it, body and dress are treated as essentially the same thing; both are equivalent. If so, then the physical body of an individual and the dress in which that body is clothed speak equally about the individual, and both inform others as to the mind of the wearer. The body, as much as clothing, reveals the individual. Yet, while a person may change or discard her clothing, she cannot easily change the physiognomy of the body itself, so, in reading clothing, the body itself must function as an integral part of the overall message. However, does this indicate that clothing must always be read in conjunction with the body, in order to possess meaning? Does dress, by itself, function as an incomplete expression, or as an expression that the discourse of the body merely supplements or complements?

Finally, Clarissa does not say that the mind is strongly indicated by outward dress, but that the mind is strongly indicated by "*its* outward dress" [emphasis mine], and the text does not explicitly state what constitutes the outward dress of the mind. However, when placed in context of the entirety of Clarissa's letter, it appears that "its outward dress" refers not only to clothing and accoutrement, but also to body, gestures, mannerisms, deportment, words (spoken and written), and personal history. Clarissa's two-sentence commentary on words and dress is preceded by her disapproving remarks on the "indecent" (3:332) speech of Lovelace's cronies, and the subsequent encouraging, though nonverbalized, replies from Mrs. Sinclair and Miss Partington. Clarissa's observations are immediately followed by detailed descriptions of each of Lovelace's four friends, with particular attention paid to their "histories" (3:331), as previously provided by Lovelace, as well to the men's physical appearance, style of dress, mannerisms, and choice of words. But what is the reader to make of all these various discourses, of personal histories, body, dress, gestures, and words, particularly when they may provide conflicting messages? How is the reader to interpret the myriad messages transmitted by the mind when Clarissa herself concludes her missive to Anna Howe with an admiring, though cautious, evaluation of Lovelace in comparison to his friends? Notably, this letter to Anna Howe demonstrates Clarissa's largely accurate reading of "the *body* and *dress* of *thought*" exhibited by Lovelace's male friends, but her fatally inaccurate reading of the outward manifestations of Lovelace's mind. She writes to Anna, "On all these specious appearances, have I founded my hopes of seeing him a reformed man" (3:337). Although Clarissa realizes that appearances may be deceptive, she nonetheless determines her own course of action based upon the attractive messages transmitted by the "wit and vivacity" (3:336) of Lovelace's words, the "deceiving sweetness of his smiles and address," his "open" and "honest countenance," and the "natural dignity" of his deportment (3:337), privileging these messages over Lovelace's known history and ignoring those small, yet telling, indications of his perfidy.

It should be noted that, when revising Clarissa for the third edition, Richardson changed the original wording of Clarissa's observations on dress, in subtle yet significant ways. In the first edition, Clarissa writes, "For what are *words*, but the *body* and *dress* of *thought*? And is not the mind indicated strongly by its outward dress?" In the revised edition, the latter sentence was altered to read, "And is not the mind of a person strongly indicated by outward dress?" (3:332). First, Richardson changes "the mind" to "the mind of a person," a minor, yet nonetheless, noteworthy correction. The distinction between mind and "mind of a person" harkens to the philosophy of John Locke, who, in *An Essay Concerning Human Understanding*, takes pains to identify personhood with consciousness, which, in turn, represents the culmination and accumulation of experience. Thus, the "mind of a person" identified by Richardson is one that is already fashioned and formed. It is not the mind of an infant, or small child, but of someone in possession of memories and experience. Second, by removing "its" from in front of "outward dress," Richardson assures that the outward dress in question is, indeed, clothing and accoutrement, and not other outward manifestations of the mind. The context of the quote has not changed; the entirety of Clarissa's letter still addresses the clothing, gestures, mannerisms, words, and histories of Lovelace's cronies, but the emphasis has been changed, with dress now the focus, privileged over the other discourses of the mind. Yet, what can dress reveal that other discourses cannot? What is at stake if this discourse is falsified, as in disguise or masquerade? The subsequent two chapters discuss dress and its relationship to body, mind, and soul, as well as the importance of dress in eighteenth-century English life and literature.

1
Dress and the Discourses of the Mind

To understand the relationship between body and dress, and the connections among body, dress, thoughts, words, gestures, history, and mind, is to understand the epistemology that underlies Richardson's use of dress as discourse in his novels. And the place to begin understanding these relationships is by comprehending how the majority of eighteenth-century English men and women, in particular, Samuel Richardson himself, understood the relationship between body and mind and between mind and soul.

As Roy Porter, Christopher Fox, and others have demonstrated, numerous and often conflicting notions about the relationships among body, mind, and soul circulated during the early part of the eighteenth century, framed by religious, scientific, and philosophical debate.[1] However, Richardson's published writings and personal correspondence show compelling evidence of engagement with and admiration for the philosophical works of John Locke, as does Richardson's appreciation for *The Spectator*, among the first literary productions to advocate and promote Locke's ideas. Locke's treatises, then, serve as a base point for discussion, and, through an examination of those precepts of Locke's philosophy that Richardson embraced and those that he clearly rejected, Richardson's own philosophy regarding the mind and its outward expressions may be determined.

As any reader of *Pamela*, Part Two, can attest, Richardson had studied Locke's treatise, *Some Thoughts Concerning Education*, as Pamela comments extensively on the work and on Locke himself. Although Mr. B. "holds a very high regard for this Author," Pamela finds "some few things which I think want clearing up" in regards to Locke's treatise, and, indeed, she is able to find "fault with such a genius as Mr. Locke."[2] Yet Pamela's fault finding is over minor points and "little matters" (IV:224), not larger theoretical principles; she largely subscribes to Locke's thoughts on the education of children, though she offers small, yet sensible, modifications.[3] As Pamela notes, "... I thought it an excellent piece, in the main" (IV:217), and, from this, we may assume that Richardson himself approved of Locke's theories on education, "in the main." In addition, in *The Apprentice's Vade Mecum*, Richardson paraphrases Locke's thoughts on the soul, as articulated in *An Essay Concerning Human Understanding*, and some of the language of *Clarissa* vividly echoes *An Essay*, Locke's most renowned text.[4]

For Locke, the body, soul, and consciousness work in unison to fashion the individual. The body, consisting of "the cohesion of solid, and consequently separable, parts and a power of communicating motion by impulse," is "but a participation of the same continued life, by constantly fleeting particles of matter, in succession vitally united to the same organized body."[5] Locke's description of the body allows for aging, change, loss of limb, as it is "the same continued life" and "the same organized body." This physical body is animated by the soul. As Locke writes, "our idea of soul, as an immaterial spirit, is of a substance that thinks, and has a power of exciting motion in body, by willing, or thought."[6] George Cheyne, the celebrated Bath medical doctor, both friend and physician to Richardson, viewed body and soul in a similar, though rather more mechanical, way, with the body as some complicated piece of machinery, operated and overseen by the soul:

> the Human Body is a Machin of an infinite Number and Variety of different Channels and Pipes, filled with various and different Liquors and Fluids, perpetually running, glideing, or creeping forward, or returning backward, in a constant *Circle*, and sending out little Branches and Outlets, to moisten, nourish, and repair the Expences of Living. That the Intelligent Principle, or *Soul*, resides somewhere in the Brain, where all the Nerves, or Instruments of Sensation terminate, like a *Musician* in a finely fram'd and well-tun'd Organ-Case; that these Nerves are like *Keys*, which, being struck on or touch'd, convey the Sound and Harmony to this sentient Principle, or *Musician*.[7]

Within the brain, "the Intelligent Principle, or *Soul*" resides. Cheyne further notes that "the Intelligent Principle is like a Bell in a Steeple, to which there are an infinite Number of Hammers all around it, with Ropes of all Lengths, terminating or touching at every Point of the Surface of the Trunk or Case."[8] Thus, the soul or spirit animates, regulates, and directs the body. As *The Spectator* observes, the soul "remembers, understands, wills, or imagines."[9] This general understanding of the relationship between body, mind, and spirit was so ubiquitous that it entered into conduct-book literature of the time, appearing in *The Virgin's Nosegay* (1744) and Wetenhall Wilkes's *A Letter of Genteel and Moral Advice* (1740), for example. (Indeed, conduct-book authors appeal to Locke's theories with surprising regularity.)

To Locke, "the *idea of a man*" or human is "not the idea of a thinking or rational being alone ... but of a body, so and so shaped, joined to it."[10] Yet neither body nor soul truly constitutes the person for Locke, though both necessarily play an integral part in the creation of personal identity. No, consciousness alone is responsible for self-identity, though soul or spirit proves the animating force behind thought and action, and though the body provides the raw materials for consciousness and thought, through the five senses. Consciousness unites body and soul, "with the same personality."[11]

Locke likens the mind to a "cabinet," a "closet," or a "room," empty and dark at birth, with the bodily senses akin to windows letting in sunlight, and soon furnishing the darkened room with ideas gathered from sensation, which are, in turn, reflected upon and stored in memory.[12] For Locke, the mind is the storeroom of memory, the workshop of consciousness, where simple ideas become transmuted or refashioned into complex ones. The body and soul identify the individual as "man," or human, but consciousness identifies him or her as "person." Consciousness is personal identity, selfhood, and yet Locke still insists that "this consciousness is annexed to, and the affection of, one individual immaterial substance," that is, the soul.[13] Thus, personal identity requires both body and soul in order to operate, as the former provides sensory input necessary to provide the objects of thought, as well as the physical form necessary to be identified as human, and the latter initiates thought and animates the physical body; however, for Locke, consciousness identifies the person and always will, regardless of whether the individual changes his body or her soul for another. Specifically, Locke plays with the ideas that, if what constitutes consciousness enters into a different body, the person is still the same, though the physical body is different, and if the soul, after death, forgets the personal identity it formerly had, then it and the person with which it formerly co-existed are not the same. Locke does not worry about the afterlife of the soul, viewing mysteries of the soul as mysteries of God. Although Locke believes the soul is immortal, he remains skeptical about or perhaps indifferent to the soul's ability to remember its past consciousness or its need to reunite with a particular physical body at Judgment Day. The soul would be judged on its past, somehow or other, whether remembered or not, whether possessed of material presence or not. Locke's position on the soul and its relationship to the body presented many of his contemporaries with quandaries regarding the Resurrection, as scripture indicated that the physical body was necessary for reanimation at Judgment Day. So too did his ideas of the primacy of consciousness over soul and the possibility that consciousness could be transferred from soul to soul, as this suggested a separation between soul, the intelligent principle behind thought, and thoughts themselves.[14] Nonetheless, many individuals subscribed to Locke's general principles regarding human understanding, with some modifications and concessions made to accommodate the notions that some essential self existed, in the form of the soul; that the soul could be readily identifiable in another life and in the afterlife; that this soul retained consciousness after the death of the physical body; and, finally, that it was somehow capable of perpetual progression. Addison and Steele, and, later, Richardson himself, would be among this group.

Joseph Addison and Richard Steele, authors of *The Spectator*, were among the earliest literary proponents of Locke's work, and, while it is evident that Richardson himself had read Locke's treatises, many of Richardson's own interpretations of Locke's theories appear heavily influenced by *The Spectator*. In humorous fashion, *The Spectator* dissects a *"Beau's* Head" to find it stuffed, in the mode of Locke's cabinet or room, with "Ribbons, Lace, and Embroidery," "Billet-doux, Love-Letters, pricked Dances," powder and scent; "Fictions, Flatteries and Falsehoods, Vows, Promises and Protestations" and "Oaths and Imprecations"; and "a bundle of Sonnets and little Musical Instruments."[15] The interior of the beau's skull is described in terms of "Apartments" filled with "several kinds of Furniture."[16] Similar language is used in *Clarissa*, when Belford, writing to Lovelace, reminds Lovelace that "thou ... sayst, That we do but hang out a Sign, in our dress, of what we have in the Shop of our Minds," and he asks Lovelace, "tell me, if thou canst, What sort of Sign must thou hang out, wert thou obliged to give us a clear idea by it of the furniture of *thy* mind?" (6:403). The idea of the mind as shop also appears in *Pamela*, Part Two, in an exchange between Polly Darnford and an unidentified masquerader (IV:53). For Richardson, as for so many of his contemporaries, the mind is the storehouse of thoughts, where consciousness is housed and where personal identity exists.

Richardson's transformation of Locke's room, or *The Spectator*'s apartments, into a shop is suggestive, though, in fact, this particular trope became commonplace rather quickly, playfully alluded to in Swift's *A Tale of a Tub* (1704), wherein "the faculties of the mind were deduced" as follows: "embroidery was sheer wit; gold fringe was agreeable conversation; gold lace was repartee; a huge long periwig was humor; and a coat full of powder was very good raillery."[17] *The Connoisseur*, a mid-century periodical primarily authored by Bonnell Thornton and George Colman, taking its cue from Swift, devoted two issues to the discussion, with a pretend letter to the editor, inquiring, "But where, Mr. Town, can these people go to cloath their minds, or at what shops are retailed sense and virtue?"[18]

In Richardson's case, the choice of shop over room or apartment is deliberate, at least in *Clarissa*, as Richardson seeks to establish a link between the selling of merchandize and the selling of young girls on the marriage market. He may also wish to draw the reader's attention to Lovelace as salesman, falsely advertising damaged or shoddy goods. However, it also suggests that Richardson views the mind and the person in more social terms, possibly as a contractual obligation to represent oneself accurately. In addition, whereas personal identity and consciousness in Locke seem oddly isolated from social interaction, as the only entry into this "closet" of the mind comes from the physical senses, Richardson instead seems to feel that sympathetic minds can meet at some level, and, in *The History of Sir Charles Grandison*, he even imaginatively employs Locke's notion that the same mind, the same consciousness, can exist simultaneously in two different individuals. It is no wonder that Sir Charles, faced with two such "*Sister*-excellencies!" as Harriet Byron and Clementina della Porretta, is afflicted with a "divided heart."[19] Sir Charles repeatedly comments upon the seemingly identical nature of the two young women's essential selves: "You are Clementina and Harriet, both in one: One mind certainly informs you both" (3:191), he muses. To Harriet, Sir Charles remarks: "There spoke Miss Byron, and Clementina, both in one! Surely you two are informed by one mind! What is distance of countries! What obstacles can there be, to dissever Souls so paired!" (3:145). To Clementina, he approvingly comments, "Generous, noble Clementina! ... My Harriet is another Clementina! You are another Harriet!" (3:343). In Richardson's fictive worlds, kindred minds and souls will seek each other, as Anna Howe writes to Clarissa: "—But LIKE little souls will find one another out, and mingle, as well as LIKE great ones" (1:88).

Richardson also appears to have accepted, within limits, Locke's somewhat nebulous stance on the soul, at least in terms of human inability to comprehend the workings of God. For instance, in *The Apprentice's*

Vade Mecum, when confronting a world "over-run with Atheism, Deism, and Infidelity,"[20] Richardson argues for religious belief based on faith. He speaks of the "*Soul*, whose *Substance, Origination, Constitution, Operation*, and every thing of it, but that we know *it is*, and *feel* by its *Effects*, is altogether hidden from us."[21] He continues, saying, "Our coming into the World is totally a *Mystery*: No human Reason can attain unto it. And must there be no *Mystery* at all in our *Regeneration*, being born unto the never-ending World of Spirits? Is not the *other World*, is not *Heaven*, a Mystery to us? Do we *understand* it perfectly? Can we describe it?"[22] Thus, Richardson, like Locke, appears largely unconcerned with where the soul has been, prior to its inhabitation of the body; what form the soul will take, after the demise of the body; or even if a material body will attach itself to the soul at Judgment Day.

Yet, as anyone might expect from the author of *Clarissa*, Richardson, like most of his contemporaries, nonetheless required the assurance and comfort of an afterlife, where good was rewarded and evil punished, for where can such a tragic young creature as Clarissa find comfort, if not in her "*Father's house, Heaven*" (7:252). Once again, *The Spectator* offers a solution. Although Addison and Steele embrace Lockean philosophy, they refashion it in ways that ameliorate the Lockean soul, by suggesting that the soul of the departed retains consciousness of its earthly existence and that earthly deeds affect not only life on earth, but the afterlife as well. *Spectator* No. 90 muses on the Platonic notion that the soul, after death, retains the passions that enslaved it during life: "When therefore the obscene Passions in particular have once taken Root and spread themselves in the Soul, they cleave to her inseparably, and remain in her for ever after the Body is cast off and thrown aside." Punishment in the afterlife, thus, is a fitting one, in Dante-ish fashion: "In this therefore (say the *Platonists*) consists the Punishment of a voluptuous Man after Death. He is tormented with Desires which it is impossible for him to gratify, solicited by a Passion that has neither Objects nor Organs adapted to it."[23] And *Spectator* No. 447 assures its readers that they but plant the seeds of their afterlife while on earth:

> The Seeds of those spiritual Joys and Rapture, which are to rise up and flourish in the Soul to all Eternity, must be planted in her, during this her present State of Probation. In short, Heaven is not to be looked upon only as a Reward, but as the natural Effect of a religious Life.
>
> On the other Hand, those evil Spirits, who, by long Custom, have contracted in the Body Habits of Lust and Sensuality, Malice and Revenge, an Aversion to every thing that is good, just or laudable, are

naturally seasoned and prepared for Pain and Misery. Their Torments
have already taken root in them. ... They may, indeed, taste a kind of
malignant Pleasure in those Actions to which they are accustomed,
whilst in this Life, but when they are removed from all those Objects
which are here apt to gratifie them, they will naturally become their
own Tormentors.[24]

Certainly, one need only be reminded of the sordid deaths experienced
by Richardson's rakes and libertines, like Sir Hargrave Pollexfen and the
brutish Mowbray, or the horrific death of the wicked madam, Magdalen
Sinclair, to see how Richardson subscribed to this view of the soul, both
when housed in the earthly body and in its afterlife. Clarissa, in contrast, no doubt enjoys "those Supernumerary Joys of Heart, that rise
from ... the Prospect of an happy Immortality."[25]

Richardson also departs from Lockean philosophy on the issue of
whether or not the soul possessed "certain *innate principles* ... which the
soul receives in its very first being, and brings into the world with it."[26]
Locke begins Book One, Chapter One, of *An Essay Concerning Human
Understanding* by emphatically stating that it does not. While the soul is
necessary to Locke, as the animator of thought and action, it is never
viewed as possessing any innate qualities or traits that might be identified with personal identity. In contrast, with Richardson, as with *The
Spectator*, the soul is the essential self that is molded and modified by
lived experience. While Locke threw nature out, or, at least, devalued it,
in deference to nurture, Richardson, Addison, Steele, and, indeed, I would
suspect, most eighteenth-century English men and women preferred a
more balanced combination of nature and nurture. For instance, in a
letter to Frances Grainger, dated 29 March 1750, Richardson asks her "to
explain yourself on one sentence in your last letter," which apparently
is that "Human nature will sometimes give the lye to virtue."
Richardson responds, "and so it will, but it *ought not* nor *will* in a good
girl; in a girl who is good by principle. Such a one may err by sudden
impulse, thro' passion, or from persecution or provocation; but not
with deliberation if she have principle. Like a bow overstrained, she will
soon return to her natural bent, and be sorry for her error; and resolve
to do her duty to others, whether others do theirs by her or not."[27]
Common eighteenth-century usage of "principle," as defined in *OED*,
relates it to inborn traits or characteristics: "An original or native tendency or faculty; a natural or innate disposition; a fundamental quality
which constitutes the source of action." For Richardson, principle is the
"natural bent" associated with the soul, rather than with the conscious

mind. Thus, Clarissa is, by nature, "a good girl." Even Lovelace, thwarted in his efforts to "tempt her" (4:223), writes, "Then her LOVE OF VIRTUE seems to be *Principle*, native principle, or, if *not* native, so deeply rooted, that its fibres have struck into her heart, and, as she grew up, so blended and twisted themselves with the strings of life, that I doubt there is no separating of the one without cutting the others asunder" (4:224). Principles are "native," instilled at birth, part and parcel of the soul.

Lovelace, alas, is deeply flawed not only from a lack of early discipline, but is "wicked upon Principle," that is, his very soul is flawed.[28] To Lady Bradshaigh, Richardson writes, "... as shocking as his [Lovelace's] Actions are, they are but the natural Consequences of his Principles, as laid down at this very first Appearance in the Story."[29] Lovelace possesses innate character flaws, which early indulgence from an overly fond mother and a doting uncle have nurtured. As Lord M., Lovelace's uncle, sadly comments, "Indeed, it was his poor Mother that first spoil'd him; and I have been but too indulgent to him since" (4:119). Yet, through conscious and concerted effort, any soul may improve itself, as it is the natural inclination of the soul to seek virtue: This "perpetual Progress of the Soul" generates "From its Passions and Sentiments, as particularly from its Love of Existence, its Horrour of Annihilation, and its Hopes of Immortality, with that Uneasiness which follows in it upon the Commission of Vice."[30]

If the soul, then, possesses some sorts of innate qualities or principles, then it seeks housing suitable for its earthly sojourn, and, thus, the general belief in eighteenth-century England that physiognomy directly expressed the soul and mind housed within. As Juliet McMaster writes, during the eighteenth century, "The truth or otherwise of the doctrines of physiognomy—the study of the stable structures of face and body as indicators of lasting characteristics of the mind and soul—was hotly debated by laymen as well as by men of science and specialists in anatomy."[31] *The Spectator*, as is often the case, provides a succinct and elegant description of the overall debate:

> Whether or no the different Motions of Animal Spirits in different Passions, may have any Effect on the Mould of the Face when the Lineaments are pliable and tender, or whether the same Kind of Souls require the same Kind of Habitations, I shall leave to the Consideration of the Curious. In the mean Time I think nothing can be more glorious, than for a Man to give the Lie to his Face, and to be an honest, just, good-natured Man, in spite of all those Marks and Signatures

which Nature seems to have set upon him for the Contrary. This very often happens among those, who instead of being exasperated by their own Looks, or envying the Looks of others, apply themselves entirely to the cultivating of their Minds, and getting those Beauties which are more lasting and more ornamental.[32]

(Animal spirits were fine streams of fluids, connecting soul and mind to the various parts of the body, and, thus, might imprint a youthful, pliable face with those passions that predominate in the mind or soul.) Regardless, the soul somehow inscribes itself upon the body and the face, and a person must deliberately eschew his native bent in order to give "the Lie to his Face."

What then are readers to make of a Lovelace possessed of "a graceful exterior which belies his moral corruption"?[33] McMaster argues that "Lovelace's physical grace signals the good man he might have been, rather than the licentious reprobate he is,"[34] and, while this is indeed true, a rake, almost by definition, must possess a pleasing exterior. The devil takes many agreeable forms, as any eighteenth-century reader of Milton would know, and Clarissa allows Lovelace's exceedingly good looks to seduce her better judgment, at least initially. In addition, one might argue that Lovelace's handsome face and elegant form are the perfect abode for someone possessed of two primary vices, "Women, and the Love of plots and intrigues" (7:11). Like Dorian Gray, Lovelace's handsome exterior actually aids and abets his inward corruption. Yet, in virtually all other instances, the body and face of Richardson's characters conforms exactly to their mind and soul. From the "good" characters, such as Sir Charles Grandison, Harriet Byron, Clementina della Porretta, Clarissa Harlowe, Pamela Andrews, and even the naughty Mr. B., to "bad" characters, such as the bawdy Mrs. Jewkes, the loathsome Solmes, and the arrogant Sir Hargrave Pollexfen, to mixed characters, such as Colbrand, Belford, and Olivia, face and form mirror, not mask, essential character.

Together, soul, body, and mind express some sort of truth about the individual, as, while it is possible to refine or improve upon these fundamental elements, for instance, through education or religious practice, or through exercise and diet, the fact remains that, at least in eighteenth-century thought, the body, mind, and soul were difficult to falsify and impossible to alter in any real significant way. One cannot decide to lie to oneself, without being aware that one is lying, nor can one physically manipulate bone, tissue, and muscle in any substantial or meaningful way, in order to make the self taller, the bones finer, the lips fuller, or the nose smaller (at least not in eighteenth-century England). Yet, of all of these elements, only the physical body is clearly legible to others, and, even then, only the general outlines of the body and certain body parts, such as face and hands, were normally visible in eighteenth-century dress. Thus, in order to discover or interpret the soul or mind of another requires reliance upon other discourses produced by the soul and mind—words, gestures, personal history, and, what may seem odd at first to include in this listing, dress. While the soul, mind, and body are the primary components of selfhood, constituting both human and person, as Locke would say, all of the secondary discourses of mind, body, and soul are utilized when conducting social relations, and all may be used either to communicate with others or to deceive them.

These secondary discourses, though understood to be flawed or imperfect forms of communication, nonetheless were believed to reveal something of the thoughts housed in the "cabinet" of the mind, thoughts initiated by the soul. Facial expressions, gestures, mannerisms, and deportment were studied widely in the eighteenth century and earlier, and, as McMaster notes, the theater, painting, and the novel made lavish use of the art of pathognomy, "the study of passing facial expressions and bodily motions as signs of passing emotions and states of mind, such as anger or fear or shame."[35] According to McMaster, "the doctrines of pathognomy were less disputed than those of physiognomy" and "the process by which passion issues as expression and gesture, the mental motions being physically manifested, was read as good and satisfactory, whether or not the passion being manifested was approved of."[36] While it was acknowledged that an individual could consciously control or manipulate her gestures or facial expressions, yet, so it was thought, evidence of the true self would inevitably reveal itself, through involuntary impulses, such as a blush, a grimace, a shudder, or a shiver, particularly when confronted with events that provoked extreme passions. As discourse, it was pleasurable reading for eighteenth-century English men and women, a "familiar satisfaction in a comforting system of signs and correspondences."[37] The language of the soul and the mind is writ directly upon the body to be read and interpreted by others—or so it was believed.

Words, of course, were viewed as direct communications of thoughts: "For what are *words* but the *body* and *dress* of *thought?*" According to Locke, words function as "external sensible signs, whereof those invisible ideas, which his thoughts are made up of, might be known to others."[38] Or, to restate in slightly different fashion, "words in their primary and immediate signification stand for nothing but *the ideas in the mind of him that uses them,* how imperfectly soever or carelessly those ideas are collected from the things which they are supposed to represent."[39] Choice of words, style of delivery, topic, tone, and accent were all considered indicators of the relative refinement of the mind. Yet, again, the language of words is flawed, in several respects: First, words, either directly or perhaps even through their delivery, may be used to deceive. As Lord M. says to Lovelace, "And, to be sure, you have naturally a great deal of Elocution; a tongue that would delude an angel, as the women say—To their sorrow, some of them, poor creatures!" (4:242). Second, words, even if sincere and truthful communications of the mind and soul, nonetheless are merely words, which may or may not be acted upon. To quote the proverb-spouting Lord M. again, *"Words are wind; but deeds are mind"* (6:212). Or, worse yet, words may be empty of meaning. *The Connoisseur* writes, "It is supposed by *Locke* and other close reasoners, that words are intended as signs of our ideas: but daily experience will convince us, that words are used to express no ideas at all."[40] So words, whether spoken or written, whether truthful or not, require actions or deeds to give them credence, and this is where personal history enters in, as it is the record of an individual's mind and soul, as recorded through deeds or actions.

To recall an earlier point in this discussion, the soul is *"a substance that thinks, and has a power of exciting motion in body, by willing, or thought."*[41] Personal history perfectly integrates the soul, mind, and body, as the soul generates thoughts and initiates will, the mind houses the thoughts, and the body acts upon these thoughts. This is true regardless of whether or not an action has been planned or deliberated, or is spur-of-the-moment, based upon instinct or passion. While it is a commonplace that the early English novel engages consciously with the genre of history, partly as renunciation of the romance genre, partly to create an aura of verisimilitude, history is also important in that it was considered the most complete record of an individual's life, a recounting of her thoughts or his deeds, and it was thought to be the only way to record fully the interior workings of the mind. Of course, this is why "lives" of real individuals, whether historical personages, criminals, or saints, were read and studied, and this is precisely what the early English novel attempts to capture. As Sarah Fielding writes, "The Reader, like a Traveller, herein views the Manners of human Nature, and Customs of the World; the Intrigues of Policy, the Arts of Lovers, and the Exploits of Heroes; with the secret Springs and Motives of their Actions."[42] Thus, the full title of Richardson's masterpiece is *Clarissa; or The History of a Young Lady* and, thus, his final novel is entitled *The History of Sir Charles Grandison,* as personal history is a continuous record of the mind that can be traced, studied, analyzed, and utilized as exemplar. History is the sum total of experience, the very thing that Locke argues provides a person with "the *materials* of reason and knowledge,"[43] that is, the stuff of consciousness. As Lovelace exclaims, "What a devil does a man read history for, if he cannot but profit by the examples he finds in it?" (6:106)

Yet, like words and gestures, history may also lie. Although actions are viewed as direct indicators of "mind," as Lord M. reminds us, personal history (or any history, for that matter) may be falsified or distorted by the teller of that history (and, of course, Richardson's "histories" are fictions). Actions may also belie true thoughts, as when the individual feels she must act a certain way, regardless of her true feelings, or actions may only superficially indicate the depth or sincerity of the thoughts they express. *Spectator* No. 257 comments, "it is impossible for outward Actions to represent the Perfections of the Soul, because they can never shew the Strength of those Principles from whence they proceed. They are not adequate Expressions of our Virtues, and can only shew us what Habits are in the Soul, without discovering the Degree and Perfection of such Habits. They are at best but weak Resemblances of our Intentions."[44]

Thus, gestures, words, and even deeds are but "faint and imperfect Copies" of the thoughts housed in the mind, subject to falsification and misinterpretation, with gesture contradicting word, with word belying deed.[45] Yet, for all that, gestures, words, and deeds emanate directly from the mind, and they are communicated directly through the body, via the face, the hand, the mouth, etc. Clothing and accoutrement, in contrast, are material objects that exist outside the body, but that, nonetheless, rank equally with gestures, words, and actions as a discourse of the mind.

Dress, unlike other material objects, possesses certain attributes that permit it to function as one of the discourses used for communicating, understanding, and interpreting the mind and soul. First, its close proximity to the body, laying directly next to the skin and draped over bone and muscle, allows it to function as a second skin of sorts. In the eighteenth century, very little of the body was actually visible, even in the most private of circumstances, and, thus, clothing necessarily spoke on behalf of the body. It did so by providing a general indication of the shape of the body, its bone, fat, and muscle, and it drew attention to particular parts or aspects of the body, such as the texture of the skin, the tint and hue of the flesh, the shape of the face, or the size of the foot or hand. Second, while clothing may provide deliberately false or confusing messages about the body, with or without intent to deceive (for instance, by making body parts appear larger or smaller than they really are), these "false" messages nonetheless often provide some indication of what is going on in the mind, of the desire for the body to be something that it is not. Clothing not only speaks of the real physical body enclosed within, but of the ideal body to which the individual aspires. Third, for eighteenth-century English men and women, the individual's inner soul was believed to find expression in the choices made in dress. For example, *The Spectator* indicates that modesty is "a kind of quick and delicate *feeling* in the Soul,"[46] and modest dress would, of course, express this. In addition, clothing records memory and traces personal history, not only the physical growth, development, and aging of the human body, but events, mundane or momentous, in human lives. Last, clothing is above all a social object, with specific garments worn in deference to or defiance of social custom. However, despite all this, it is important to note that signification associated with clothing is inherently unstable, its meaning dependent upon and determined in relation to myriad other factors, many of which may be consciously manipulated by the wearer.

Let us return, then, to the questions raised by Clarissa's original statement and what they mean in terms of what Richardson attempted to accomplish through the depiction of dress: "For what are *words*, but the *body* and *dress* of *thought*? And is not the mind strongly indicated by its outward dress?" First, words are to thoughts, as body and dress are to thoughts, mind, and soul. Dress expresses consciousness, or personal identity, which is the content of the mind, the thoughts, and memories contained within; it directly engages with the body, which, in turn, bears the outward marks of the mind and the soul; and it also expresses the innate principles of the soul. Clothing, as much as words, is "the *body* and *dress* of *thought*," the outward manifestation of the inner self. Dress engages with conscious thought, as stored within the "shop of the mind," but also with innate principle, as associated with the soul, the initiator of thought and action, located within the mind.

Second, dress may be read by itself, but, for dress to function fully as discourse, it must always be read in conjunction with the body, as the body provides crucial information for interpreting the full implications of dress. Garments must always be read in the context both of the clothes themselves and the bodies that are covered by them, and context is always determined by culture. For instance, as will be the case in *The History of Sir Charles Grandison*, pink and yellow ribbons are coded as "youthful" and "feminine," and, thus, when they appear on a body that is old, or masculine, they suggest imbalance, a discrepancy between body and mind. This is an important point to note, for though body and dress are both deemed outward expressions of the mind and soul, they may be in conflict, with the body expressing one thing (for instance, age) and the mind expressing another (for instance, the desire for youth).

Finally, clothing and accoutrement, like any other discourse of the mind, may be manipulated or falsified, yet, when read in conjunction with the other discourses of the mind, with body, words, gestures, and personal history, indications of perfidy will ultimately and inevitably reveal themselves, no matter how clever and capable the artificer, or so it was widely believed in eighteenth-century English culture. This is always the case in Richardson's novels.

As will be demonstrated in Chapter 2, in eighteenth-century England, "The taste of the present age seems to be dress,"[47] and clothing and accouterment were objects carefully observed, studied, and interpreted by all, as indicators of the minds and souls of the wearers. The need to interpret correctly the minds and souls of others became increasingly important during the early eighteenth century, when social categories were undergoing destabilization and reinterpretation. In literature, particularly within the genre of the novel, which directly reflects and articulates the destabilization of social categories, as McKeon and others have demonstrated, the clothing choices of the characters could be studied in similar fashion, allowing readers to determine the messages that dress disclosed about the various characters and about the didactic purpose of the novel itself. It might be argued that the novel provided eighteenth-century English men and women with a primer as to the correct way to read the dress of others and how to clothe and dress themselves. In addition, with the novel's pretence of presenting the personal history of a particular character, as a written record of the character's thoughts and actions, it was a natural step to read the related discourses of mind and soul, as expressed through the character's words, looks, gestures, and dress.

2
Dress in 18th-Century English Life and Literature

In eighteenth-century England, the color of skin (for instance, ruddy or pale), physique, gait, and manner and style of dress were thought to proclaim one's social status and occupation: a ruddy-faced, sturdy-legged milkmaid from Devonshire walked, talked, and looked differently from a pale, delicate, society miss from London, or so it was believed. However, the social landscape of England—London, in particular—was unstable, with wealthy members of the middle station mingling with the nobility, aspiring and quick-witted young clerks becoming wealthy and respected city merchants, and naïve young country boys and girls rapidly acquiring city mannerisms and mores. Aileen Ribeiro notes, "It is a cliché, but none the less true for all that, that in England there were fewer glaring gulfs between the classes; a greater sartorial freedom produced—depending on the viewpoint—a kind of social anarchy, or a refreshing individualism. ... Foreign visitors to England often confessed themselves puzzled by the conflicting signals sent out by clothing."[1] Contemporary accounts confirm this view: As the author of *The Ladies Library* comments, "What Difference is there now between the Dress of a *Citizen* and a *Courtier*, of a *Taylor* and a *Gentleman*, or a *Servant* and a *Master*? The *Maid* is very often mistaken for the *Mistress*, and the *Valet* for *my lord*."[2] Similarly, as Eliza Haywood writes in *The Female Spectator*, there is "no difference made between the young nobleman and the city-apprentice, except that the latter is sometimes the greater beau."[3]

Second-hand clothing could be purchased in shops on Monmouth Street in the London parish of St. Giles-in-the Fields; in Houndsditch, on London's east side; on Rosemary Lane, near the Tower of London; and in towns throughout England.[4] The discarded silk dresses and petticoats, the Holland linens, and the buckled and embroidered shoes of the lady often adorned the body of her maid, while the cast-off waist-coat of the master was jauntily worn by his valet. A careful application of powder and paint could transform a woman's complexion, and, through careful observation, a countrified gait might soon give way to a citified stroll. Of course, what was considered the greatest imposture of all, for a woman to appear virtuous when she was not was the most difficult of all to detect. Anxiety and fascination with how to tell the "real" from the impostor is evident, finding its fullest cultural expression in the eighteenth-century preoccupation with masquerade and disguise, as the numerous novels, periodicals, criminal biographies, sermons, conduct books, and actual attendance at masquerade balls attest.

Fashion, false and fickle as it was deemed, nonetheless existed as the preeminent and preferred mode of expressing taste, culture, and refinement in eighteenth-century England. It was the ultimate consumer product, with an estimated twenty-five percent of middle-class income expended on articles of dress and accoutrement,[5] with the upper station outspending the middle station on dress in sheer monetary terms, and with the lower station enjoying a bountiful supply of recycled clothing. Dress was a commodity that could bestow immediate social cachet or instant ignominy upon the wearer.

Reasons for this avid and increased interest in dress are diverse, though interrelated. Sumptuary legislation, laws that restricted dress by social rank, had been revoked or had lapsed since the reign of Elizabeth I. Frances Baldwin has suggested that seventeenth-century legislators "seem to have recognized that acts like the statutes of apparel not only interfered too much with the daily life of the people and were burdensome, oppressive, and therefore liable to stir up discontent, but also that they might prove a positive hindrance and discouragement to trade and manufactures."[6] Although protection of English manufacture was purportedly the prime impetus behind sumptuary legislation, the truth was that, by the eighteenth century, English commerce greatly relied upon exportation of English manufactured goods to other European countries and to European colonies, and that importation of exotic goods was instrumental in creating a culture of consumerism in England itself. As Paul Langford notes, most social theorists living in England during the eighteenth century "agreed that they lived in a commercial age, an era in which the processes of production and exchange had dramatically increased the wealth, improved the living standards, and transformed the mores of western societies."[7] Commerce, to many eighteenth-century English men and women, "suggested a definitive state in the progress of mankind."[8] Daniel Defoe, in the introduction to *The Complete English Tradesman*, insisted

> that the trade of England is greater and more considerable than that of any other nation, for these reasons: 1. Because England produces more goods as well for home consumption as for foreign exportation, and those goods all made of its own produce or manufactured by its own inhabitants, than any other country in the world. 2. Because England consumes within itself more goods of foreign growth, imported from the several countries where they are produced or wrought, than any other nation in the world. And – 3. Because for the doing this England employs more shipping and more seaman than any other nation, and, some think, than all the other nations, of Europe.[9]

Trade brought prosperity to the nation and encouraged consumerism; with increased trade, once rare and costly items, including imported silks, cottons, and dyestuffs, became more readily available, less expensive, or both. To a great extent, the increased prosperity of those from the middle station drove the market for fashion consumerism; as Earle notes, "the regularly recurring demand for new clothes, especially by the men and women of the middle station, was one of the major factors keeping the economy going."[10] Many newly prosperous, and many not so prosperous, members of the middle station emulated the dress of the upper station, which, in turn, created a demand for new styles and fashions by the *haut monde*, as a means of reestablishing class distinctions through dress. In addition, an expansion in the print trade, in the numbers of journals, newspapers, periodicals, and novels published and promulgated, made information about the latest styles and fashions available to an increasingly wider range of individuals.

Because members of virtually all social stations possessed more clothing choices than in the past, whether through direct purchase, through hand-me-downs, or through the second-hand clothing markets, dress became an important means of determining individual character, of reading the mind and soul through outward dress. *The Spectator* commented that "there is a very close Correspondence between the Outward and the Inward Man" as revealed by "the Cast of his Visage, the Contour of his Person, the Mechanism of his Dress, the Disposition of his Limbs, the Manner of his Gate and Air."[11] Whereas style, color, fabric, and ornamentation of dress had previously allowed for identification of the wearer's social station or occupation (merely another indicator of social station), clothing and accoutrement now appeared to resonate with greater meaning: Dress still indicated wealth, status, and social station, to be sure, but also taste, modesty, and morality.

Thus, eighteenth-century English fashion appears driven by two seemingly opposing dictates: One the one hand, the need to emulate one's so-called social betters, to wear the latest fashions, as dressing "up" provided the wearer with increased social power, or, at least, the perception of it; on the other, the need to demonstrate good taste, refinement, and breeding, through simplicity and understated elegance. "Anti-fashion" pitted itself against fashion, with anti-fashion itself functioning as a form of fashion statement. As *The Ladies Library* argues, "Let Ladies, above all Things, consult Decency and Ease; never to expose nor torture Nature. Fashion is always aiming at Perfection, but never finds it, or never stops where it shou'd: 'Tis always mending, but never improving: A true Labour in vain."[12]

English fashions of the eighteenth century express the dichotomy between fashion and fashionable simplicity: For instance, ubiquitous male attire for those from the middle to upper stations was the three-piece suit, comprised of breeches, waistcoat, and jacket, yet this originally understated form of male dress could be glaringly ostentatious, in pink satin and green silk, with satin bows and silky ribbons. Fashion for most English women from the middle to upper stations was also driven by these competing impulses. French fashion, viewed as the epitome of "haute couture and high fashion,"[13] vied with the English taste for simplicity and informality, as expressed through the "Arcadian" style, with fashionable women donning "pseudo-rustic" attire, wearing more fashionable versions of the aprons and straw hats traditionally worn by rustic laborers.[14]

Dress, of course, has always possessed transformative power, and it is this aspect of dress that appears to have most fascinated and concerned eighteenth-century English men and women. As Jessica Munns and Penny Richards write:

> Above all, it is the *transforming* nature of clothing, the way that clothes do not fix but confuse issues of identity—such as status, age, gender, occupation, and nationality—that was focused upon. What may often be traced in the literature and visual arts of this period ... is an anxious discourse that adumbrates the power of clothing to alter appearance, alongside a complementary rather than a contradictory discourse that seeks to neutralize and contain that power.[15]

With more clothing choices available, with last year's fashions quickly passed down to servants or relegated to the second-hand stores, dress could be and was a means for the wearer to refashion him or herself. With the introduction of masquerades into England, early in the eighteenth century, the trope of masquerade became attached to the transforming nature of dress, used to describe anyone who had somehow altered his or her "natural" appearance and dress in any way, implying deceit or disguise on the part of the wearer. A tradesman dressed like a gentleman was in masquerade. As Defoe writes, "A tradesman dressed up fine, with his long wig and sword, may go to the ball when he pleases, for he is already dressed up in the habit; like a piece of counterfeit money, he is brass washed over with silver. ... In short, thus equipped, he is truly a tradesman in masquerade."[16] An individual from the middle station, dressed in upper-class garb, is nothing less than "counterfeit." A servant girl, dressed in her mistress's cast-off clothes, was similarly deemed something of a fraud. Masquerade was also closely linked to the theater, and, thus, to theatrical performance. Both the masquerade ball and the theater were associated with sexual licentiousness, with inversion of the social order, and, as such, were condemned in conduct books, periodicals, sermons, and novels. However, this did not stop these two fashionable forms of entertainment from being enjoyed by countless English men and women from all ranks of society, nor did it keep English men and women from viewing clothing as the agency by which they might perform, transform, or reform their lives.

Thus, most eighteenth-century English men and women, particularly Londoners, enjoyed the experience of shopping for new clothes, whether brand-new or merely new to them, reveling in their ability to pick and choose among countless fabrics and fashions, and proud that English enterprise had made this possible. They were attentive to what dress revealed and concealed (or, shall we say, to what they *thought* it revealed and concealed), to the potential that dress held to transform their lives and the lives of others, and the large majority understood that fashion could not be ignored, nor did they want to ignore it. Because the perception existed that clothing could be used, in a deliberate fashion, as a means to fool the casual observer, the typical eighteenth-century Londoner scrutinized the dress of others, with a careful eye for details and nuances of dress. And so Richardson, like most of his contemporaries, studied the clothing and accessories of others, seeking to decipher the clues presented by a green knot of ribbon, gaily perched atop a maidservant's cap, or by a muddied, worn pair of boots, or by a dirty hem of a rich silk gown.

Material objects that possessed resonance and meaning in everyday life entered naturally into literature, theater, and the visual arts as symbols and even as thematic devices. Thus, articles of clothing, foodstuffs, animals, money, and books, among other material items that possessed significance in the real lived world, emerged into the fictional realm of the novel and, in doing so, became a nexus between the fictional world described and the culture that produced it.

Literary depictions of dress generally fall into five or so primary usages, all of which may be employed simultaneously, with overlapping, complementing, or conflicting signification. First, clothing or accoutrement may function as symbol, intended to express something important about a fictional character, historical personage, or living individual, such as vanity, resourcefulness, or courage. For instance, the Wife of Bath's scarlet red stockings and Una's white gown provide readers with information that, in these instances, complements and confirms the reader's knowledge of the character. More complex examples include Crusoe's island outfit or Pamela's rustic attire, two ensembles that resist easy interpretation, yet seem to conjure up the character in his or her respective entirety. Second, clothing or accoutrement may be used as plot device, the most famous example being Desdemona's handkerchief, though Roxana's Turkish dress must be considered a close runner-up. Both articles of dress suggest certain things about character, yet they also become central to plot action. As Paula Backscheider notes, "A commonplace is that Roxana becomes her clothes. ... Her Turkish costume becomes the sum of her character and an identity so firm that Susan [her daughter] can use it to stalk her."[17] Thus, Roxana's gown functions simultaneously as symbol of character and as plot motivator. Cross-dressing also falls within this category, exposing character traits and disrupting plot narrative, though cross-dressing also destabilizes the plot in more complex ways, as Marjorie Garber has argued, by disrupting any binaries in place.[18] Third, dress may be used as thematic trope or device, perhaps suggesting that life is a masquerade, as in William Congreve's *Incognita*, or that all the world is a stage, as in Eliza Haywood's *Fantomina*. Fourth, dress may be used didactically, to educate the reader in the principles of good (or bad) taste, as is the case with *The Spectator*, *Sir Charles Grandison*, or Edgeworth's *Belinda*. Last, dress may be used merely to entertain, or even to titillate the reader, as occurs with Fanny Goodwill's near bursting stays or Fanny Hill's clothing (or lack thereof). As mentioned, an author may utilize dress in all its myriad expressions within a single text, and a single article of dress or accoutrement described may function as symbol, plot motivator, thematic device, didactic element, or entertainment contrivance, among other things.

In print, in paint, and on stage—dress employed in the service of artistic expression was available for Richardson to study. Many of the scenes in Richardson's novels, such as Clarissa in the sponging house, or Pamela in rustic garb, suggest Richardson's debt to theatrical tableaux and to painting, and these scenes translated particularly well into illustrations and paintings. As Janet E. Aikins writes, "Throughout his career as a writer, Richardson fancied himself a painter in words." Aikins argues that "Richardson's fiction is centrally concerned with the complexity of being a 'spectator' of both art and life," noting that "His novels offer a form of portraiture in that they attempt to represent imaginatively characters' physical features while also capturing the elusive qualities that transcend physical substance."[19] And as painter would with a portrait, Richardson carefully chooses the clothing in which his models will appear. The stage, too, must have had an enormous influence on literary depictions of dress, including Richardson's own. M. Channing Linthicum has studied costume in the Renaissance drama, not only its mention within the plays of Shakespeare, Middleton, and others, but also the fabrics, colors, and trim associated with the costumes worn on stage.[20] Certainly, there is no doubt of the importance of costume in theatrical productions, movies, music videos, and more, and Richardson and his contemporaries would no doubt have seen the visual connections to be made among character, clothes, and performance. Of course, it is a commonplace that Clarissa's white gown recalls similar gowns worn by the heroines of she-tragedies.

In print culture, fashion, dress, cosmetics, and women's vanity had long been popular topics: Conduct books, sermons, poetry, satire, periodicals, newspapers, plays, romances, business manuals—all weighed in on the topic of dress, particularly the relationship between women and fashion. A significant amount of this discourse on dress, particularly satirical discourse, was highly misogynistic. Tita Chico's investigation of the dressing room in eighteenth-century English literature suggests that satires on the dressing room and on dress itself focus on the "rhetoric of the fall" and the "association between clothing and the story of Adam and Eve": "From the reprimanding perspectives of these satires, Eve's hubris ruined the innocence and purity associated with the naked body and introduced the necessity for concealment." Chico notes, "Women's 'recourse to Dress' is both a means of deception and an effect of original sin, thus making every woman a descendant of Eve—at least to the satirists."[21] Richardson, as we will see, attempted to rewrite the satirical image of woman, partly through his depictions of women in "virtuous" dress, yet, from a cultural perspective, the overwhelming negative associations between women and fashion undermined the project.

Despite the relatively positive depictions of women in novels, particularly sentimental novels by women writers, it is important to remember that, in the literature of the time, women were often depicted as fault-ridden, duplicitous, and, even when virtuous, contradictory in nature. Two examples should, I hope, suffice: The following little ditty comes from *The Bath, Bristol, Tunbridge and Epsom Miscellany* (1735):

> A Woman's at best but a consummate Evil,
> She's All-Saint without, but within is All-Devil;
> And by her Good-will, as on all Sides confess'd,
> Her Tongue and Her Tail would ne'er be at Rest.

Alexander Pope's *An Epistle to a Lady* provides more elegantly and variously worded phrasing, but conveys the same essential message: "Nothing so true as what you once let fall, / 'Most women have no characters at all'" (1–2). Even a virtuous woman is suspect: "And yet, believe me, good as well as ill, / Woman's at best a contradiction still" (269–70).[22]

Richardson, however, eschewed the genre of satire, particularly after he himself became one of the most famous victims of it. Richardson's greatest literary influences, in terms of his depiction of dress, appear to be conduct books, *The Spectator*, Sir Philip Sidney's *Arcadia*, and the novels of Penelope Aubin and Daniel Defoe. From *The Spectator* and from conduct books, Richardson culled general principles of tasteful dress, which find fullest expression in his third and final novel, *The History of Sir Charles Grandison*. These principles of elegance and good taste were not just found in conduct books and Addison and Steele's highly popular periodical, but in virtually every lifestyle periodical of the time, so that Richardson's novels tend to be consistent with cultural norms regarding what constituted good taste, elegantly simple fashion, and appropriate dress.

From Aubin and Defoe, Richardson learned the efficacy of detailed descriptions of dress. Backscheider writes, "Aubin uses paragraphs such as one including fine details ('cherry-colour Silk Petticoat' with silver flowers, braided hair, and straw hat) in *Madame de Beaumont*. These descriptions always increase the heroine's attractiveness, indicate her economic condition, and harmonize with her mental state."[23] Similar descriptions occur in most of all Aubin novels, and Richardson admired Aubin's work. Defoe's richly detailed descriptions of clothing must also have resonated with Richardson. Crusoe's island attire, in particular, is described in great detail, from his goatskin breeches and vest to his goatskin umbrella. Crusoe, interestingly, designs, cuts, and sews his own garments, much like Pamela Andrews does. Defoe also utilizes dress as symbol, thematic trope, and plot motivator: Moll Flanders, after all, is named after a type of linen, marries a linen-draper, and gets caught stealing fabric, while Roxana's Turkish gown exists as a material expression of Roxana herself, provides her daughter Susan with evidence of Roxana's identity, and, ultimately, provides the initial impetus for Susan's murder.

Interestingly, both Pamela Andrews and Harriet Byron owe their most famous outfits—Pamela's rustic attire and Harriet's masquerade costume—to a romance, not a novel or periodical. Sir Philip Sidney's *Arcadia* provides several detailed depictions of dress, including that of the princess Pamela, dressed as a shepherdess, and that of the cross-dressing prince Pyrocles. Richardson appropriates both outfits for his own heroines, creating a textual *pentimento*: In *Pamela*, this textual layering confirms, complicates, and conflicts with Richardson's intended signification; in *Grandison*, it complements it. (Further discussion of Richardson's sartorial and literary debts to Sidney will take place in Chapters 4 and 10.) Richardson's obvious admiration of Sidney's *Arcadia* seems odd, to a great extent. Most famously, John Milton termed *Arcadia* a "heathen fiction," judging it "a book in that kind full of worth and wit, but among religious thoughts and duties not worthy to be named, nor to be read at any time without good caution, much less in time of trouble or affliction."[24] Yet, for all that, it is evident that Richardson very much admired Sidney's depiction of character and dress, so much so that he would borrow literary costumes from *Arcadia* to dress two of his virtuous young heroines.

Thus, eighteenth-century English life and culture provided a rich resource for Richardson's own depiction of dress within his novels. In sum, Richardson never strayed far from cultural ideas about fashion, taste, and style, though he did eschew the widespread tendency to depict women and dress in a negative fashion. In addition, he clearly was indebted to his literary, artistic, and theatrical predecessors in how he used dress within his novels. Yet, for all that, Richardson's use of dress is extraordinarily rich, diverse, and highly complex. Each of his three novels differs widely in how it depicts dress, due in no small part to Richardson's desire to stabilize the signification of dress, but it also shows willingness on his part to experiment, to try new things. As the following chapters will show, Richardson's use of dress provides fascinating insights into his works and into eighteenth-century English culture.

Part II Dressing for Success with *Pamela*

Introduction

A "little Hypocrite," an *"artful Creature,"* possessed of "Tricks and Artifices, that lie lurking in her little, plotting, guileful Heart!"[1] Thus is Pamela Andrews, the heroine of Richardson's first novel, described by her would-be seducer, Mr. B., and thus has she been described by countless readers, disparaging and admiring alike, throughout the novel's long history.[2] The charges of hypocrisy and artfulness leveled against Pamela generate, in some measure, from Pamela's numerous wardrobe changes, which suggest artificiality on her part and which serve to promote Mr. B.'s interest in Pamela, rather than discourage it. As the anonymous author of *Pamela Censured* wrote, "The Instruction here then is to the *Ladies*, that by altering their Appearance they are more likely to catch their Lover's Affections than by being always the same."[3] If dress provides direct evidence of the mind, then Pamela's widely disparate sets of clothing would seem to suggest either a singularly untidy mind or a mind actively engaged in deceit.

Richardson's first novel provides the most dramatic use of dress, yet it also proves the most challenging in regards to interpretation, as from the novel's first publication, multiple and disparate meanings have been assigned to Pamela's behavior and to her wardrobe. If the author of *Pamela Censured* condemned Pamela's rustic attire, others, like Aaron Hill, praised it, saying, "tho' she put it on with humble Prospect, of descending to the Level of her Purpose, it *adorn'd* her with such unpresum'd *Increase* of Loveliness."[4] Perhaps because of its inherent ambiguity, clothing in *Pamela* has received and continues to receive considerable critical and scholarly attention, unlike dress in *Clarissa* or in *The History of Sir Charles Grandison*.[5] Among other interpretations, Pamela's clothing has been viewed as performing the "contradictory aspects of the ideology of gender," in particular, the duplicity of femininity (Gwilliam);[6] as "a vital means by which Richardson tests and confirms the propriety of her social elevation" and "to figure the proximity of interiority and duplicity, of secrecy and sexuality" (McKeon);[7] and as encoding "the antagonism between dress, virtue and the legible body as it was played out in a range of sentimental novels, plays and non-fictional works" (Batchelor).[8] In almost all discussions of Pamela's dress, ambiguity, duplicity, secretiveness, and contradiction come into play. As McKeon notes, "The sartorial imagery of dressing up and dressing down, in particular, takes on a life of its own in *Pamela*, intimating a literally underlying secret that both those actions observe."[9] Similarly, Jennie Batchelor comments, Pamela's "dress itself constitutes a plot within the novel that gathers a momentum of its own and accrues meanings which diverge from the moral intentions proclaimed in the Preface."[10] However, both secret and plot have continued to elude, largely due to the fact that Richardson's novel, as William B. Warner, James Grantham Turner, and others have demonstrated, simultaneously employs the very strategies that it seeks to undermine.[11]

My own entry into the critical conversation on dress in *Pamela* centers on the nature of virtue itself, its relationship to "domestic woman," and the strategies that Richardson employs to articulate various kinds of virtue through Pamela's dress. The failure of Richardson's attempt to vouch unequivocally for the authenticity of Pamela's virtue and her lack of artfulness, I believe, originates from several sources: the hierarchical social system of eighteenth-century English society, which allotted to women and servants, a lesser or subsidiary portion of virtue; the forced marriage, officiated by scholars, between "domestic woman" and "economic man," when a more likely match would be between "domestic woman" and gentleman; and, finally, the borrowed literary attire in which Pamela Andrews appears, creating a textual *pentimento* that simultaneously augments and disrupts Richardson's intended meaning.

The following chapters explore Pamela's sartorial dilemmas in greater depth. In Chapter 3, the different types and levels of virtue available to men and women of different social stations and ranks are examined. This chapter also argues that "domestic woman" was originally intended as a portrait of the gentlewoman—not a portrait of bourgeois woman, though it perhaps later became so. It also argues that the male counterpart to domestic woman is the domesticated gentleman, not "economic man" (think Sir Charles Grandison, rather than Robinson Crusoe). If these claims are correct, as I believe they are, they provide important insights into Richardson's attempts to render legible the domestic feminine ideal, and his failure to do so when this ideal is configured as woman.

Chapter 4 analyzes the ways in which eighteenth-century English dress articulates virtue and bespeaks the moral nature of the wearer, through an examination of the contents of Pamela's wardrobe in *Pamela*, Part One. Different types of dress express morality and immorality, as do specific articles of clothing, and the same style of dress—indeed, the very same article of clothing—could be perceived as immoral or moral, dependent upon the social station of the wearer. Particular attention is paid to the "new Garb" (60) that Pamela herself designs (in reality, a copy of the Princess Pamela's outfit) and the problems attendant upon borrowing a literary predecessor's clothing.

Chapter 5 takes a look at Pamela in "high life," as Richardson termed it, exploring how Mrs. B., "our dear Pamela" (II:306), must still confront the inadequacies of her virtue, particularly after Mr. B. finds himself attracted to the "young Countess Dowager of —" (IV:80). Richardson's first deliberate use of masquerade occurs in *Pamela*, Part Two, when a very pregnant Pamela, dressed in prim Quaker attire, is jostled, teased, and tormented by a surfeit of masquerade monks, cardinals, and friars, with Pamela's swollen belly the subject of bawdy jests. Nervously searching the crowd of masqueraders for her errant husband, himself engaged in serious flirtation with a "fair nun" (IV:55), Pamela finds herself confronted by two fun-house versions of herself—the first, dressed in particolored clothes, mocking Pamela's "*linsey-wolsey*" self, "neither gentlewoman nor rustic" (IV:8); the second, in country dress, parodying Pamela's own rustic costume, in which she first fended off Mr. B.'s lecherous advances. Pamela's pregnant encounter, if such we may call it, highlights the ways in which virtue, for the non-patrician or non-genteel body, differs dependent upon whether the body is that of a maid, a married woman, or a married woman pregnant with child.

3
Ladies, Gentlemen, and Servants: Virtue and the Domestic Ideal

Virtue is an amorphous quality, based as it is upon culturally assigned and constructed notions of conduct and morality; however, several definitions of virtue were in circulation in eighteenth-century England, most of which depended upon the individual's class, sex, and religious belief, though other traits and characteristics could inform the type and level of virtue possessed. All definitions of virtue referenced, influenced, informed, and reinforced each other, yet all species of virtue, as articulated and understood in eighteenth-century England, were defined in relation to patrician virtue and Christian virtue. (When speaking of class, I employ it, as J. C. D. Clark does, to mean "rank, order, station, degree and calling."[1])

In terms of class, virtue and the virtuous body had originally been the sole province of the aristocrat, as Michael McKeon, in *The Origins of the English Novel*, writes:

> The traditional terms of social distinction in early modern England— "degree," "estate," "order," "rank"—are variously based on an idea of status derived from the personal possession, or nonpossession, of honor. And honor is a quality that points, through the crucial mediation of repute, both outward and inward. On the one hand, it is a function of ancestry and lineage; less obligatory, but likely to confirm the primary facts of ancestry, are other external circumstances like wealth and political power. On the other hand, honor is an essential and inward property of its possessor, that which the conditional or extrinsic signifiers of honor exist to signify. In this respect, honor is equivalent to an internal element of "virtue". The notion of honor as a unity of outward circumstance and inward essence is the most fundamental justification for the hierarchical stratification of society

by status, and it is so fundamental as to be largely tacit. What it asserts is that the social order is not circumstantial and arbitrary, but corresponds to and expresses an analogous, intrinsic moral order.

Virtue as defined by patrician ideology is based upon "ancestry and lineage,"[2] and it literally becomes embodied in the aristocrat. Someone from the middle or lower stations could not, under this definition, be in possession of virtue nor lay claim to a virtuous body, at least not to the full extent that the aristocrat could.

Yet the question remains as to what extent a female, aristocratic or not, could possess or participate in this type of virtue. While based on birth and ancestry, aristocratic virtue is, first and foremost, about masculine honor, relying as it does upon the systems of patrilineage, primogeniture, and entail, to ensure both the transmission of honor and its outward trappings, from one generation to the next; within such systems, the locus of female honor must always be chastity, as it is the only way to assure that male ancestral honor is maintained and lineage secured. In addition, aristocratic virtue was consolidated through and performed by external displays of wealth and political power, to which women primarily gained access through marriage. For women, virtue proceeded from their relationships with men, fathers and husbands, and this is born out by the fact that women took on the social station of the men they married, though with something of a nod to paternal rank. As Anne Laurence writes, "Women in early modern England were defined firstly by their sex, secondly by their relationship to a man, and thirdly by their class, or, rather, the status they assumed from their fathers or husbands."[3] Even the redoubtable Bess of Hardwick initially accrued and later consolidated and expanded her considerable wealth and power through a series of politically strategic marriages. Thus, a woman of noble birth could claim a larger portion of honor and virtue than, say, a woman of the lower orders, but her honor and virtue would always be subsidiary to and defined by the stock of virtue possessed by and through husband and father.

In many ways, the gentry were seen to possess virtue equal to or greater than that of the peerage. As Donald Greene writes, "If a peerage was generally testimony that its holder or some not very distant ancestor had been one of 'the new men'—a clever operator in business, land, or politics, or a professional man whose talent or luck had enabled him to climb the ladder of success—those who considered themselves the genuine old aristocracy of England, the backbone of the nation, the true hundred-per-cent Englishmen were the 'gentry.'" Greene further notes that "Even as late as the twentieth century, heads of such families proudly refused to accept peerages offered to them by a government anxious to secure their political support."[4] However, beginning in the late seventeenth century, there appears to be a growing sense that the squirearchy had somehow become debased, interested more in the pleasures of "Guns, Dogs, Horses,"[5] drink, and debauchery, than in virtue and duty. Richard Allestree's *The Gentleman's Calling* (1660) chides his gentleman readers, saying, "GENTILITY has long since confuted Job's Aphorisme, Man is born to labour, and instead thereof, has pronounced to its Clients the Rich man's Requiem, Soul take thine ease, eat drink and be merry. A Gentleman is now supposed to be onely a thing of pleasure."[6] The rank of gentleman, then, holds the greatest potential for the full expression of virtue—if the gentleman chooses; the rank of gentlewoman, as well, promises the greatest potential for the display of feminine virtue.

Virtue, as associated with the middling classes, both differentiated itself from and identified itself with patrician and genteel virtue. Those from the middle station sought to redefine virtue as "goodness of character" and as "demonstrated by achievement."[7] However, as Robert Markley notes, the "strategies" used to expand the definition of virtue did "not subvert, radically undermine, or fundamentally realign the hereditary bases of wealth and power but . . . [sought] to expand them."[8] J. C. D. Clark concurs, writing, "By the mid eighteenth century, increasing numbers of the middling ranks were able to afford the outward trappings of gentility, and (more expensive again) the inner dispositions. But although the ranks of gentlemen were expanded, this did not mean that the ideal itself was blurred."[9] In essence, the cultural ideals remained that of the aristocrat and the gentleman, and any inroads made by the middling sorts was viewed not as a challenge to the system, but rather a confirmation of it: "Although social mobility took place in the eighteenth century, the theoretical defences of the aristocratic code did not make many concessions to it. Mobility was chiefly seen as an experience of the lower or middle orders within their own ranks, or of picaresque adventure and wise Providence (or capricious fortune), not of challenge to or rejection of patrician hegemony."[10] Thus, virtue, as associated with the middling ranks, becomes a contraction of patrician virtue, as it is always something slightly less than and inferior to that virtue possessed by members of the aristocracy or gentry, as well as an expansion of patrician virtue, in that moral goodness, economic success, and social achievement allowed for slightly greater access into the ranks of the virtuous.

Using patrician virtue and Christian virtue as models, the middle stations likewise valued chastity among women, ranking it the primary and most highly valued aspect of feminine virtue. *The Virgin's Nosegay; or The Duties of Christian Virgins*, a 1744 conduct book, describes chastity in terms that indicate its indebtedness to aristocratic notions of virtue: It is "not only an Ornament to the Maiden State, but its Inheritance. Nor may you with greater Propriety call it by the Name of your Honour, than that of your Treasure, it being certain that you are not, nor cannot be accounted rich, but by its Possession, nor Poor but by its Loss."[11] Chastity guarantees "inheritance," not only of property, but of "ancestry and lineage." The possessor of it is "accounted rich" and owns "Treasure"; chastity, like wealth, confirms ancestry. Chastity may be called "by the Name of your Honour," and, as such, exists as a physical manifestation of virtue, and, for the female of the middling or upper stations, the principal attribute of feminine virtue. All other attributes associated with feminine virtue, such as modesty, meekness, temperance, obedience, and piety, are viewed as by-products of chastity. As James Bland writes, in *The Charms of Women: Or, A Mirrour for Ladies*, "*Chastity* she knows to be a Virtue of that excellent, and inexpressible Worth, that she looks upon it almost celestial. It produces congruous Effects of *Prudence, Piety* and *Devotion*, which never fails to check, subdue, and quite extinguish *luscious Thoughts, lascivious Words*, or *lustful Actions*."[12] Chastity assures patrilineal inheritance (or, in the case of the spinster, the possibility of Church inheritance) by regulating all other aspects of feminine behavior.

Clark argues that the continued acceptance of the "ideology of order" in eighteenth-century English culture was due in no small part to "the Christian language of hierarchy," promulgated through and sustained by the hegemony of the Church of England. Society is "pictured as an undifferentiated hierarchy, which owed its seamless gradations to Providential disposition. The belief that this hierarchy was not merely a contingent fact, but a divine ordinance, was its central guarantee. Human society was a hierarchy because the whole of Creation was a yet more vast hierarchy reaching down from God to the lowest form of life."[13] Of course, dissenting religious practice provided some challenges to this system, but this hierarchical system was deeply entrenched, even naturalized, within the society. In addition, while one might think virtue, as defined under Christian ideology, would be egalitarian, rather than hierarchical, this was clearly not the case: "'The Evangelical virtues of compassion, gratitude, and humility', argued [Bishop] Pretyman, 'can only be practiced where there is a diversity of ranks.'"[14] Even John Wesley thought in similar terms: "But those 'who are rich in this world,' who have more conveniences of life, are peculiarly called of God to this blessed work, and pointed out to it by his gracious Providence. . . . Being of superior rank to them, you have the more influence on that very account. Your inferiors, of course, look up to you with a kind of reverence."[15]

In many and in most ways, Pamela Andrews, a woman, a servant, and a daughter of a ditch-digger, possesses considerably less cultural credit in terms of perceived virtue than the "naughty" Mr. B., and, this, despite Pamela's chastity, her Christianity, and B.'s licentiousness. In addition, as servant, Pamela's chastity is of relatively little import, as it has little or no bearing on patrician (or middle-class) honor or inheritance. As Mr. B.'s Lincolnshire neighbor, Sir Simon Darnford, says, "Why, what is all this, . . . but that the 'Squire our Neighbour has a mind to his Mother's Waiting-maid? And if he takes care she wants for nothing, I don't see any great Injury will be done her" (122).

Yet, as Nancy Armstrong and others have noted, Richardson's little servant girl exists as the first novelistic embodiment of "domestic woman," that paragon of feminine virtue. Then how is it that Pamela may be perceived as both lacking [relatively speaking] in virtue, using the hierarchical model, and as epitomizing virtue, in terms of the domestic feminine ideal? The problem is threefold: First, "domestic woman" was originally intended as a model for women of the gentry, or, at the very least, for women from the wealthier segments of the middle station, not for servants and women from the working classes. Domestic woman's virtue becomes fully realized only within the rarified framework of leisurely household management, and domestic woman exists at a distinct level in the social and moral hierarchy, always ranked above the domestic servants that she supervises. Second, inherent within the portrait of "domestic woman" painted by conduct books is the belief in the overall frailty and frivolity of women, as a sex. Domestic woman achieves virtuous feminine perfection through eschewing and controlling what was perceived as innate feminine traits and tendencies: "Therefore a virtuous Woman is ever most careful to keep herself, as much as possible, I say, to keep herself out of the Way of Temptations; on which Account she sets a watchful Guard over all her Senses; and out of profound Reverence to her Soul, in purity of Thoughts, Word, and Deed, she looks most warily about her."[16] *Rambler*, No. 70, puts it rather more bluntly: "It may be particularly observed of women, that they are for the most part good or bad, as they fall among those who practise vice or virtue; and that neither education nor reason gives them much security against the influence of example. . . . it is certain, whatever the cause, that female goodness seldom keeps its ground against laughter, flattery, or fashion."[17] And, third, even if domestic woman enjoys a measure of virtue beyond that possessed by other women, her virtuous male counterpart must always lay claim to virtue in greater degree and in finer, fuller fashion, precisely because the culture privileged the masculine over the feminine.

Although many of the seven Christian virtues (chastity, humility, mercy, patience, temperance, fortitude or courage, and love of God, neighbor, and enemy) are gendered as feminine, it is nonetheless true that, in the eighteenth century, women were still considered the weaker spiritual vessels, thought to be easily beguiled by flattery, false promises, and fashionable pleasures. It was also considered part of the Providential plan that women were subordinate to men, as they were deemed physically, intellectually, and morally their inferiors. Thomas Gisborne speaks of "the characteristical impressions which the Creator has stamped upon the female mind; the leading feature, as such there be, by which he has differentiated the talents and dispositions of women from those of men." He adds, "It would therefore seem natural to expect, and experience, I think, confirms the justice of expectation, that the Giver of all good, after bestowing those powers on men with a liberality proportioned to the subsisting necessity, would impart them to the female mind with a more sparing hand."[18] And, for all that female conduct books insist that woman should not be considered Eve-like, that "in the sublimest part of humanity," that is, in her soul, she is man's equal, the virtues subscribed to her are modest enough: "native Softness and Gentleness," according to Allestree;[19] "quickness of fancy," "delicacy of sentiment," "warmth of affection," according to Gisborne;[20] vivacity and gentleness, according to the *Virgin's Nosegay*.

In the marriage made between "economic man" and "domestic woman," domestic woman clearly stands out as the morally superior partner, precisely because "economic man" possesses only a tangential relationship to domestic virtue: His realm is business; hers, the home. Yet, I would argue that domestic woman and economic man were not intended as partners, at least, not originally. As Amanda Vickery writes, "Some have built on the tale of woman's divorce from useful labour to assert that the 'new domestic woman' was the inevitable bride of the new economic man." However, Vickery suggests that "there is a certain confusion as to whether the new domestic woman was the epitome of bourgeois personality, or was an ornament shared by the middling ranks and the landed."[21] I believe the latter.

The more companionate marriage might be made between domestic woman and the gentleman, or between domestic woman and that "amphibious Creature, this *Land-water-thing*, call'd, *a Gentleman-Tradesman*,"[22] as Moll Flanders termed him. It seems clear enough, when wading through the sea of conduct book literature for women, that the original "domestic woman" was a member of the gentry, or, if of the middling station, certainly one of its more prosperous and upwardly mobile members, at least until late eighteenth century.

Ingrid H. Tague has identified Richard Allestree's *The Ladies Calling* (1673) as the conduct book that "most influenced the later development of the genre": "Not only were multiple editions published under its own title, but it was widely quoted (usually without attribution) through the eighteenth century."[23] Allestree clearly identifies his readership as members of the gentry: "if after a successful Attempt upon the more impregnable Masculine part of the Gentry, I now essay the Feminine."[24] In 1722, John Essex dedicates *The Young Ladies Conduct, or Rules for Education Under Several Heads* (1722) to three sisters of "Birth and Fortune," and, within the manual itself, he admonishes "Young Ladies of Quality" for their "Passion and Pride to the Servants," based upon "a false Notion of Superior Birth."[25] Similarly, Wetenhall Wilkes's tome frequently discusses situations in which "a profest Gentleman or Lady" may find him or herself.[26] Even as late as 1797, Thomas Gisborne, when discussing "the mode of introducing young women into general society," states: "I believe this picture to convey no exaggerated representation of the state of things which is often witnessed in the higher ranks of society," though he admits that "it is a picture to which the practice of the middle ranks, though at present not fully corresponding, bears a continually increasing resemblance."[27]

The subject and object of female conduct books during the eighteenth century is the gentlewoman. Certainly, because wealthy merchants and tradesmen could hope to gain entrance into the gentry, or, at least their sons and daughters could, a secondary audience would be women from the upper levels of the middling ranks, who would need to be knowledgeable concerning behavioral standards in order to gain entry into the ranks of the gentry. While no doubt wives and daughters of lower-level tradesman sought to act the part of ladies, it seems unlikely they could, in reality, live the life of "domestic woman." It may also be questioned as to whether or not a female mate really exists for "economic man," as his world is all business, never family. It is hard to imagine domestic woman on Crusoe's island. (Famously, Crusoe's unnamed wife is married, bears three children, and dies in the middle of a single sentence. Guy or gal Friday seems a more likely match for *homo economicus*.) Even in the case of the complete English tradesman, a wife who could be "seen in the counting house" or "behind the counter" was obviously the most desirable mate, regardless of her possible inclination to act the part of domestic woman.[28]

If the true counterpart to domestic woman is the gentleman, then it becomes clear that domestic woman's virtue exists as mere complement to that of her male counterpart. Interestingly, Allestree's *The Gentleman's Calling*, the companion book to *The Lady's Calling*, does not discuss masculine virtue in terms of emotional or affective qualities, as it does with feminine virtue, but in terms of "advantages," such as education, wealth, time, authority, and reputation, things presumed as innate and "natural" to the gentleman, as modesty and meekness are to the gentlewoman. Yet, through the possession of wealth, for instance, a man may exercise the Christian duties of charity, temperance, good works, humility, compassion, sobriety, and trust. In sum, virtue, in all its myriad forms, may be found in fuller and finer fashion, when in possession of the virtuous gentleman. The gentleman's virtue is viewed as active, public, and tested by trial, unlike that of his female counterpart. As Allestree writes, "there are many temptations to which men are exposed that are out of their [women's] road."[29] Gisborne confirms this view: "The sphere of domestic life, the sphere in which female exertion is chiefly occupied, and female excellence is best displayed, admits far less diversity of action, and consequently of temptation."[30]

To return to Pamela Andrews as a novelistic rendering of the domestic feminine ideal: Although Pamela enjoys most of the traits associated with domestic woman, such as modesty, "delicacy of sentiment," and a fierce interest in protecting her virginity, many of these attributes appear at odds with her status as domestic servant, primarily because they are largely rendered meaningless in terms of her social station (servant) and background (ditch-digger's daughter). In fact, it is those very attributes that define Pamela the "servant" as "domestic woman" that make her appear, if not artful, then at least ingenuous. Her patience (under severe trial), her mercifulness (to her seducer), her love of God and enemy (Mr. B.), and even her chastity—all are rendered suspect precisely because of her social status. Only when she marries Mr. B. and becomes elevated to his rank in society does her virtue take on cultural meaning, value, and credence. In addition, because domestic woman is, first and foremost, a woman, she continues to be viewed as lacking when compared to her virtuous male counterpart (think of Sir Charles Grandison). The construction of the domestic feminine ideal rests and relies upon the idea of an inherent inferiority and weakness in women, which conduct book literature only perpetuates and promulgates, through its insistence on women's propensities towards vanity, loquacity, frivolity, and the like, all of which must be fiercely controlled in order to achieve the status of virtuous woman. In contrast, the virtuous gentleman possesses no *innate* masculine flaws.

Thus, the character of Pamela embodies cultural paradoxes: of genteel virtue (a virtue that she claims, yet which she cannot be understood to possess in such a cultural milieu); and of femininity (in that a virtuous woman is always somehow less so than a virtuous man; in that a virtuous woman may only become so by eschewing innate feminine tendencies).

Pamela tells two stories, the first, that feminine virtue of the highest (genteel) order may be found within the person of a young servant girl; the second, that a debauched gentleman may be reclaimed and restored to his full measure of virtue. The question is which narrative is the dominant one? The one that disrupts the established social hierarchy, or the one that reinscribes it? Perhaps both. If we view Pamela, someone in the service of others, as text, as conduct book herself, something that the voluminous correspondence sewn into her underpetticoat suggests, then Mr. B. "reads" the conduct book of her person, and, in reading, becomes reformed, restored. Yet the fact that Pamela "authors" herself also suggests the ability to refashion self, to step up and over the hierarchical bounds, to become something different, someone "better." Both narratives are imbedded within *Pamela*, and both serve to complicate the narrative of dress.

4
"So Neat, So Clean, So Pretty!": Dressing Up Virtue

When Mr. B. first begins his active campaign to seduce Pamela, dispensing wet kisses and clumsily fumbling with her breasts, Pamela tearfully writes to her mother a confused and jumbled account of her reasons for not fleeing the B. household, all of which relate to dress:

> And so after I had dry'd my Eyes, I went in, and begun to ruminate with myself what I had best to do. Sometimes I thought I would leave the House, and go to the next Town, and wait an Opportunity to get to you; but then I was at a Loss to resolve whether to take away the Things he had given me or no, and how to take them away: Sometimes I thought to leave them behind me, and only go with the Cloaths on my Back; but then I had two Miles and a half, and a By-way, to go to the Town, and being pretty well dress'd, I might come to some harm, almost as bad as what I would run away from; and then may-be, thought I, it will be reported, I have stolen something, and so was forc'd to run away; and to carry a bad Name back with me to my dear poor Parents, would be a sad thing indeed! — O how I wish'd for my grey Russet again, and my poor honest Dress, with which you fitted me out, and hard enough too you had to do it, God knows, for going to this Place, when I was but twelve Years old, in my good Lady's Days!
>
> (36)

Part of Pamela's indecision stems from the fact that she is "at a Loss whether to take the Things he had given me or no, and how to take them away": The "Things" to which she alludes are the silk gowns and petticoats, the richly covered stays, the silk stockings, the elegant little silk shoes, and the brightly colored knots and ribbons that Mr. B. has given Pamela from his deceased mother's wardrobe. These rich garments present a moral dilemma for Pamela—"Temptations on one hand, or Disgusts on the other!" (38)—but she is equally dismayed by the difficulty of conveying her newly acquired treasures to her parents' home. If she leaves the B. household without permission, she leaves without a portmanteau in which to put these prized acquisitions, and without a carriage or cart to carry both her and portmanteau to her impoverished village, not only a physical necessity, but also something necessary to demonstrate her entitlement to these rich garments.

And, yet, even should she, ever so reluctantly, relinquish this rich and costly wardrobe, Pamela finds herself confounded by the problems that the "Cloaths on her Back" present to her escape. Her lady's maid attire, it seems, might encourage sexual improprieties from any bold footman or lascivious farmer she might encounter upon the two and a half miles and a by-way, and, equally dire, her servant's clothing might brand her as a thief, who must steal away from her master's house, as any servant conducting her master's business, or one traveling to new employment, would undoubtedly be riding in a proper conveyance. The only attire that Pamela believes she can safely wear for her escape is the "poor honest Dress" of a country miss, as if somehow this simple apparel imparts virtue to its wearer and renders her impervious to impertinences or worse. Because Pamela no longer possesses her "grey Russet" gown that she wore when "but twelve Years old," nor has she yet purchased homespun and made her own "honest" garments, she becomes paralyzed in her ability to act; she remains in "this Quandary, now considering, now crying, and not knowing what to do" (36).

Aileen Ribeiro writes, "clothes are not 'immoral' in themselves, but they become so when worn in inappropriate situations."[1] If Pamela leaves the B. household without permission, without the physical and symbolic protection of carriage and coachman, the attire of lady and of lady's maid prove equally inappropriate for Pamela; only by wearing the "honest" attire of a poor country miss can Pamela walk along the highway unmolested. Richardson, however, is not content to leave the issue of morality along the roadside, so to speak, but invites it into Mr. B.'s home and hearth. Specifically, in Richardson's novel, the dress of both lady and lady's maid suggest, if not moral corruption, then at least moral ambiguity when placed on Pamela's body, while the dress of a country miss is (or should be) unequivocal in its implications of virtue, innocence, and trustworthiness.

Prior to her lady's death, Pamela possesses only clothes suitable for an upper-level servant, a wardrobe commensurate with the position of housekeeper or lady's maid. This wardrobe consists of a "Silk Night-gown, Silken Petticoats, Cambrick Head-cloaths, fine Holland Linen, lac'd shoes, that were my Lady's; and fine Stockens!" (52); underpetti-coats of "Swan-skin and fine Linen" (52); a "French Necklace my Lady gave me" and "Ear-rings" (60)—all fine things, indeed. Yet, as lady's maid, Pamela also wears some humbler articles of dress, such as a "Calicoe Night-gown, that I used to wear o' Mornings," "a quilted Callimancoe" petticoat, "two old fine" shifts, "not worth leaving behind me"; and "two Pair of Shoes, I have taken the Lace off" (79). In fact, these latter items are simple and plain enough that Pamela intends to take them with her, no matter what, when she returns to her poor village, where she will reserve the calico gown for holiday or Sunday wear.[2]

The diversity of apparel worn by Pamela as lady's maid, the silk and the calico, speaks tellingly of the life of a lady's maid, whose various duties ranged from the genteel (providing companionship for her lady, reading to her lady, as well as singing, dancing, and playing the spinet for her lady's pleasure), to the humble, such as sweeping and dusting her lady's chambers, walking her lady's pet dog, carrying her lady's pack-ages, and picking lice from her lady's hair. By far, most of the duties of lady's maid, otherwise known as the lady's "'tire woman" (short for "attire") or waiting maid, centered around the care and maintenance of her ladyship's own person, as well as her ladyship's wardrobe: The waiting maid dressed and undressed her lady numerous times through-out the day; she pomaded, powdered, and perfumed her lady's hair; she brushed, cleaned, mended, and repaired her lady's clothing; she mixed up concoctions for her lady's complexion and cleaning agents for her lady's clothes; and she designed small articles of accoutrement for her lady, assuring that said lady was stylishly and fashionably dressed à la mode.[3]

Most readers tend to view Pamela as a particular pet of Mrs. B., caressed and cosseted, the recipient of Mrs. B.'s indulgent fondness, which allows the lowly born Pamela "to write and cast Accompts, and made me a little expert at my Needle, and other Qualifications above my Degree" (25). Indeed, Pamela effuses over her lady's goodness to her, exclaiming that "my Lady, now with God, lov'd Singing and Dancing; and, as she would have it I had a Voice, she made me learn both ... And I must learn to flower and draw too, and to work fine Work with my Needle" (77); in Pamela, Part Two, Mr. B. mentions that his mother provided Pamela with "masters to teach her to dance, to sing, and to play on the spinnet" (III:108). Yet Pamela, pretty and very young when she enters in Mrs. B's service, cheerful, healthy, and honest, has primarily been instructed in the basic requirements for the position of lady's maid for a woman of high rank; by teaching Pamela to read and write, to sing, dance, and play the spinet, Mrs. B., though undoubtedly kind, has merely created a perfect lady's maid for her own personal pleasure and comfort. It is also worth noting that Pamela has not received any wages during her entire three-year tenure of service— "I having no Wages as yet, but what my Lady said she would do for me as I deserv'd" (25)—though a lady's maid, by rights, should have been able to claim a salary of at least three to four pounds per annum, or more.[4] Pamela, however, perhaps because of her extreme youth, or perhaps because of the costs incurred in educating and training her, in clothing and feeding her, receives no pay in coin.[5] In contemplating leaving Mr. B.'s employ, she wonders if her years of unpaid service to her lady—and her unpaid care of Mr. B.'s own linen—will provide sufficient recompense for her education: "As to the three Years before my Lady's Death, do you think, as I had no Wages, I may be supposed to be Quits?" (80). Thus Pamela's only wages, other than room and board, are the clothes on her back and the skills that Mrs. B. has taught her, the latter of which are useless should Pamela return to her poverty-stricken village. In essence, the only visible remuneration that Pamela has received in her three years of service is her wardrobe.

The wardrobe of a lady's maid was similar to her lady's, as indeed much of the wardrobe was comprised of her lady's discarded clothes, refashioned and refitted for her maid's use. Because upper-level female servants (housekeepers, lady's maids) were often humbler, less financially fortunate relations of the master or mistress, or impoverished gentlewomen without other means of support (as is the case with Mrs. Jervis, the housekeeper for Mr. B.'s Bedfordshire estate), they wore the clothes of a gentlewoman. However, as Phillis Cunnington and Catherine Lucas have noted, the garments of a lady's maid (or housekeeper or companion) differed from that of her lady by "an avoidance of display."[6] If new, the gowns and petticoats of the lady's maid, though of a "fashionable cut," were generally constructed from less costly fabrics, and often of a darker, more serviceable hue, than those of her mistress; ornamentation of gown, petticoat, and accoutrement would be plainer, possibly with "an absence of lace on the neckerchief," or, more likely, without elaborate ribbons, bows, and knots; her coif would be lady-like, but less "smart"; her shoes of a fashionable design, but of lesser craftsmanship. And, although "it has always been the custom for the mistress to give her cast-offs to her lady's maid,"[7] it would have been the rare lady's maid indeed who received a gown that her ladyship still considered fashionable, or one made from extremely rich fabric, as the latter could be refashioned into something new for the lady of the house or her daughters—or perhaps even turned into "patchwork for screens, stools, cushions and the like."[8]

Yet, curiously enough, these silk gowns and petticoats that Pamela wears, that any female servant wore, were often considered immoral garments, and this despite the fact that these same garments, on her lady's back, would have possessed a distinctly different meaning. Indeed, dressed in the garments of an upper-level female servant, Pamela is bombarded with sexual overtures, from Harry, a servant, who grabs her, calling her "his pretty *Pamela*" (30) as he attempts to kiss her; to the elderly Mr. Longwood, who sighingly "wish'd he was a young Man" (51) so that he too could woo his "sweet little Mistress" (56); to Mr. B, her employer, whose constant kisses and fondling of her breasts are mere prelude to his future plans for seduction. As Pamela complains, a lady would not have to "bear an Insult of that kind" (54); a maidservant apparently did, particularly a young and pretty one, and lady's maids were frequently chosen for their youth, in part, because of the long hours required in the job, in part, because a young and fashionable lady's maid reflected positively on her mistress.[9]

The dress of an upper-level servant was often considered immoral for a variety of reasons, though the primary reason appears to be that servants themselves, upstairs or downstairs, back service or front service, were viewed as immoral. In particular, young female servants, by their very nature, were deemed "slippery in the tail" and "light of finger,"[10] as Daniel Defoe most famously asserted—to whit, maid servants engaged in whoring and thieving, the very things that Pamela fears she will be accused of should she leave the B. household surreptitiously. In *Directions to Servants*, Swift cautions waiting-maids against sexual liaisons with "my lord's eldest Son," for, if he is a rake, "you will get nothing from him, but a big Belly or a Clap, and probably both together," though, in regards to my lord himself, Swift urges that the lady's maid "take care to get as much out of him as you can, and never allow him the smallest liberty, not the squeezing of your hand, unless he puts a guinea into it."[11] In *The Apprentice's Vade Mecum*, Richardson chimes in with his own variation of this familiar song: "The present Depravity of Servants is a general Complaint in the Mouths of Families; and it must be allow'd, there is but too much Reason for it."[12]

Defoe, and many eighteenth-century English men and women, viewed the maidservant's wardrobe, comprised of the cast-off clothing of her mistress or of other "ladylike" items purchased or otherwise acquired, as indicative of her social ambitions: "Some more artful shall conceal their condition, and palm themselves off as young gentle-women and great fortunes."[13] The lady-like dress of the maidservant adds unneeded expense to the employer's household, as "printed linens, cottons, and other things of that nature, . . . require frequent washing," which called for the use of soap, an expensive commodity at that time; furthermore, it puts "our wives and daughters upon yet greater excesses, because they will, as indeed they ought, go finer than the maid."[14] The excesses of the middling stations, so it seems, could be directly attributed to the servants. This fancy dress worn by maidser-vants makes them falsely proud: it "sets them above themselves, and makes their mistresses contemptible in their eyes."[15] On a maidser-vant, fine clothes lead from "service to bawdy-house," "to whoring and thieving."[16] The maidservant's demands for ever higher wages; her lazi-ness, manifested in her refusal to perform none but the most essential tasks, and these with a huff and a grimace; her insolence, her sauciness, her pertness; her seductive flirtations with the master's apprentice or son; the petty pilfering of tea and sugar; the missing silver spoon or the lost pewter mug—all could be attributed to the maidservant's pre-sumptuous desire to dress the part of lady. Thus Pamela's attire as lady's maid marks her as socially ambitious, equally willing to trade sexual favors with the master or to steal the clothes from the mistress's back in her quest for social advancement.

Interestingly, the clothes of the upper-level female servant, who dressed only slightly inferior to her lady, and those of a prosperous woman of the middling station were virtually the same: In *The Complete English Tradesman*, Defoe describes the attire of the typical tradesman's wife, "she being a good honest townsman's daughter, . . . not dressed over fine":

> Her gown, a plain English mantua-silk, manufactured at Spitalfields; her petticoat the same; her binding, a piece of chequered-stuff, made at Bristol and Norwich; her under-petticoat, a piece of black callamanco, made at Norwich—quilted at home, if she be a good housewife . . .; her inner-petticoats, flannel and swanskin; her stock-ings from Tewksbury, if ordinary, from Leicester, if woven; her lace and edgings from Stony Stratford the first; and Great Marlow the last; her muslin from foreign trade, as likewise her linen, being something finer than the man's, may perhaps be a guilick-Holland; her wrapper, or morning-gown, a piece of Irish linen, printed at London.[17]

Pamela's "Silk Night-gown, Silken Petticoats, Cambrick Head-cloaths, fine Holland Linen," her underpetticoats of "Swan-skin and fine Linen," and her "quilted Callimancoe" petticoat are not unlike the attire worn by this imaginary shopkeeper's wife—and this, of course, presents a problem for those of the middle station. The "middling people" in eighteenth-century English society are those "who worked but ideally did not get their hands dirty," specifically, those "who had a stock of money, acquired by a paternal gift, inheritance or loan, which they continually turned over to make more money."[18] Like servants, those of the middle station were considered socially ambitious, as Peter Earle has noted, yet the middle station employed servants—they were not servants themselves—which explains much of the ire of Defoe's attack, particularly as he recounts a socially embarrassing tale of mistaking a "chamber-jade" for a woman of the merchant class.[19] In eighteenth-century England, the blurring of social station occasioned by dress affected not only the upper station, but the middle station as well. If those from the upper station were concerned about shopkeepers and their wives dressing like gentlemen and gentlewomen, like lords and ladies, then those of the middle station were concerned with servants dressing like shopkeepers and their wives.

In Joseph Highmore's 1744 painting of Mr. B. wooing Pamela within the confines of summerhouse, Pamela wears the clothes of lady's maid. The silk gown is a lovely shade of pale rose pink, worn over a pure white petticoat and adorned with a spotlessly white apron. Pale pinks and bright whites had been the sole province of the gentry and aristocracy for centuries, as fabrics dyed pale colors or bleached bright white stained easily (see Chapter 11 for a discussion of clothing color). The little mob cap perched atop Pamela's head is lace-trimmed and beribboned. It is an outfit that a young woman from the middle station could wear with pride, within the confines of her home. It bespeaks the fact that young miss does not have to perform any physically arduous or dirty tasks, like scrubbing pots or floors, yet the (spotless) apron suggests a love of domesticity. Pamela's allurements are manifestly evident in such an outfit (see Figure 4.1).

The other problem with the garb of lady's maid was its hand-me-down, cast-off nature. By contrast, the elegantly and fashionably dressed lady, the somberly yet richly attired gentlewoman, the prosperously appointed shopkeeper's wife—all had their clothes made for them and paid for by them; the maidservant did not, nor did many of the poor. The clothing of the servant always exists as a form of livery, as Jones and Stallybrass have noted.[20] In addition, for those on the lower end of the

Figure 4.1   Pamela and Mr. B. in the Summerhouse, from "Pamela: or Virtue Rewarded" by Samuel Richardson (1689–1761), published 1740, c. 1744 (oil on canvas) by Joseph Highmore (1692–1780). By permission of Fitzwilliam Museum, University of Cambridge, UK/The Bridgeman Art Library

social scale, the wearing of used clothing hinted at laziness on their part, and, by the end of the eighteenth century, Ribeiro notes, "it was increasingly felt to be morally reprehensible to wear old clothes instead of having the industry to make one's own";[21] no doubt, some of this attitude was already in place by mid-century.

In addition, hand-me-down clothes, particularly those given to servants, frequently found their way into the second-hand clothing markets, which, on the one hand, were associated with "sanctioned dealers," often pawnshop owners, and, on the other hand, with unlicensed, unsanctioned, "disorderly" dealers, who, most often, were either women or itinerants. As *The Connoisseur* remarks, "one of the first and chief resources of extravagance, both in high and low life, is the Pawnbroker's. I never pass by one of these shops without considering them as the repositories of half the jewels, place &c. in town . . . if we were to enquire, to whom the several articles in these miscellaneous warehouses belong, we should find the greatest part of them to be the property of the idle and infamous among the vulgar, or the prodigal and infamous among the great."[22] Yet, purchasing used clothes from a "disorderly" woman dealer was considered even worse. As Beverly Lemire notes, "Every effort was expended to quash the regrator or the unauthorized seller of wares, particularly those associated with women's household work. Indeed, offences were deemed particularly abhorrent when associated with women. Covert home-based production employing homely skills affronted the social order, it was claimed. Indeed, disorder itself held a particular association with the female sex."[23] Women and second-hand clothing become intimately linked with disorderliness. Of course, the wearing of someone else's cast-away clothes, no matter how rich and how stylish, has always been viewed somewhat askance, suggesting as it does, a relative state of poverty, the desire or need to emulate others, or the possible unsuitability of garment to wearer.

Thus Pamela's wardrobe of lady's maid proves problematic, as it relays ambiguous, even contradictory, messages: On the one hand, the attire is that of a gentlewoman. On the other hand, this same attire, when worn by a female servant, such as Pamela, becomes associated with immorality (whoring and thieving), as well as with social presumptuousness, the latter of which Richardson's young heroine has always been accused. Coupled with the fact that the non-aristocratic or non-genteel body was considered to be innately lacking in virtue, from birth, the potential for misreading Pamela's clothing—and Pamela herself—is enormous, as Mr. B. finds out. Thus, Pamela cannot continue to wear the wardrobe of lady's maid and remain virtuous, either in appearance or in deed, nor can these cast-off clothes of the lady, when worn by the lady's maid, allow Pamela to achieve some level of social parity with her would-be seducer, or garner her the respect she so desperately seeks.

Pamela cannot wear the garments of a lady, not just those unaltered garments that Mr. B has given Pamela, from his mother's wardrobe, a rich and silky bribe to soften Pamela's resolve, but the "four complete Suits of rich Cloaths" (166) that he offers her should she agree to become his mistress. Some difference does exist in the clothes that Pamela receives from the late Mrs. B.'s dressing room and those she already possesses as lady's maid. Pamela mentions that her deceased lady's "Clothes are fine Silks, and too rich and too good for me, to be sure" (30), and, while it is true that lady's maids frequently received the clothes of their deceased mistress, most often, the clothes were given with the understanding that they would either be sold, for cash, or altered in some fashion to befit the lower social station of the maid.[24]

Among the gowns that Mr. B. gives Pamela are "a flower'd Satten, that was my Lady's, and look'd quite fresh and good, and which was given

me at first by my Master" (266) and "rich white Sattin Night-gown, that
had been my good Lady's" (287). (Appropriately, the satin nightgown
will later become Pamela's wedding gown.) Other articles of dress from
her good lady's wardrobe include "half a Dozen of her Shifts, and Six
fine Handkerchiefs, and Three of her Cambrick Aprons, and Four Holland
ones" (30) and, later, "Two Suits of fine *Flanders* lac'd Headcloths, Three
Pair of fine Silk Shoes, two hardly the worse, and just fit for me; for my
old Lady had a very little foot; and several Ribbands and Topknots of all
Colours, and Four Pair of fine white Cotton Stockens, and Three Pair of
fine Silk ones; and Two Pair of rich Stays, and a Pair of rich Silver Buckles
in one Pair of the Shoes" (31). Finally, Mr. B. later offers Pamela diamond
jewelry (a necklace, rings, and earrings) should she comply with his plans
for seduction. Most of these articles of dress are accoutrement, rather
than gowns and petticoats, and it is precisely through accoutrement (the
ribbons and top-knots, the stockings and stays, the aprons and shifts, the
earrings and necklaces) that the lady clearly distinguished herself from
her maid. Even as late as 1861, Isabella Beeton could still write, "*The
Chausserie*, or foot-gear of a lady, is one of the few things left to mark her
station."[25] All these lady-like items, some intimate, some not, all rich and
costly, would outwardly identify Pamela, should she wear them, as a
lady—yet issues of immorality exist for Pamela should she adopt the
attire of a lady, as she clearly understands.

To begin with, Pamela is not a lady and wearing a lady's clothes, when
she has not been born or elevated to this social station, would clearly
mark her as a high-class whore to those familiar with her social pedigree
(though not necessarily to those unaware of her background). It would
also, in Defoe's terminology, mark Pamela as "counterfeit money" or
decked out in "masquerade."[26] It is a servant's body, relatively lacking in
virtue by definition, that would be wearing these garments, and the
clothing, in turn, becomes classified as non-virtuous. Again, clothing
worn by the "right" sort of person confers morality; by the wrong sort
of person, immorality. Pamela, of course, views whoredom in terms of
physical chastity and Christian morality, and, thus, she returns the
clothing that Mr. B. has offered her from his mother's wardrobe, saying,
"So they were to be the Price of my Shame, and if I *could* make use of
them, I should think I should never prosper with them; and, besides, . . .
if I would not do the good Gentleman's Work, why should I take his
Wages?" (80). The four suits of rich clothing are similarly rejected, as is
the diamond jewelry:

> Your Rings, Sir, your Necklace, and your Ear-rings, will better befit
> Ladies of Degree, than me: And to lose my best Jewel, my Virtue,

would be poorly recompensed by those you propose to give me. What should I think, when I looked upon my Finger, or saw, in the Glass, those Diamonds on my Neck, and in my Ears, but that they were the Price of my Honesty; and that I wore those Jewels outwardly, because I had none inwardly.

(166)

Although these items represent the garb of a lady, they nonetheless function as a sign of servitude, a form of livery, for they are wages for services rendered.

For Pamela, another problem with the dress of a lady resides in the fact that virtue, in the form of physical virginity, cannot be determined by this type of dress, as, of course, the same clothes that adorn a high-born lady also bedeck the high-class mistress. For the lady, the innate virtue of the aristocratic or genteel body transforms the clothing into an emblem of virtue; for the mistress, the body again determines the meaning inherent in the clothes: If the body is non-genteel or non-aristocratic to begin with, then no dress can make it so. If the body of the mistress is genteel or aristocratic, it has lost some measure of its innate virtue, because it has discredited its role in assuring inheritance of property and title. In this latter instance, the body has become un-virtuous precisely because it has placed itself outside the aristocratic system that confers virtue through "ancestry and lineage," by producing illegitimate offspring. Thus, Pamela's physical chastity, the locus of her claim to virtue of the moral sort, would be undermined by the dress of a lady. As physical chastity cannot be viewed outwardly—Pamela's intact hymen cannot be worn upon her sleeve—dress must necessarily function as the outward symbol of inner virtue. Because upper-class dress did not distinguish the virtuous woman of the upper station from her un-virtuous counterpart (and, presumably, the dress of other social stations did), the clothing and accoutrement of a lady cannot provide evidence of Pamela's physical chastity—and, indeed, it would do the exact opposite. Only when other outward markers (the public announcement of the engagement, the witnessed wedding ceremony, the public display in church the Sunday after the wedding) establish the fact of Pamela's marriage to Mr. B., a time when Pamela assumes some of the honor and virtue attendant upon her husband, does she dare wear the morally ambiguous dress of lady.

Interestingly, at one point, Mr. B. even offers Pamela a legal contract, almost identical to the articles of settlement, should she become his mistress. The articles of settlement detail property issues and inheritance, but also clothes, jewelry, pin money, and dowry for the wife.[27]

Mr. B.'s *"ARTICLES"* (164) address all the requisite items, with the added clause that Pamela "shall be Mistress of my Person and Fortune, as much as if the foolish Ceremony had passed" (166), and Mr. B. even offers the possibility of marriage to Pamela "after a Twelve-month's Cohabitation" (167) should he feel so inclined. Despite Mr. B.'s unnecessary and rather offensive contractual asides, the marriage articles for upper-class wife and Mr. B.'s articles for mistress are remarkably similar; however, Pamela rejects this contractual arrangement, one by which "virtue" is conferred through property and wealth, precisely because she recognizes that this definition of virtue holds little or no credence whatsoever, when applied to someone from her social station. As McKeon notes, wealth and property merely "confirm the primary facts of ancestry";[28] in and of themselves, they cannot confer virtue of any sort.

If the garb of a lady's maid, and the garb of lady, present themselves as morally ambiguous or even decidedly un-virtuous, when on the body of a servant or kept mistress, then Pamela must find alternate means of expressing her virtue, her honesty, and her personal independence through dress. When she weeps in frustration that she no longer possesses her "grey Russet," she expresses her exasperation with the insufficiency of her current wardrobe to represent her, its inability to communicate accurately about herself. Anne Buck notes the significance of the russet cloth for Richardson's young heroine:

> Pamela is recalling her childhood and a village girl's clothing, but the term russet is evocative of more than this. A grey or brown cloth, it was one of the few cloths allowed to labourers by a fourteenth-century sumptuary law, repeated in the reigns of Henry VIII and James I, and by this time it was not only the actual wear of country people but had become synonymous with rustic innocence and simplicity. Because it was an untreated cloth, it also had the image of honesty and plainness.[29]

Deprived of her "grey Russet" gown, Pamela must create a new outfit for herself that outwardly speaks of her inner worth and virtue, of her "rustic innocence and simplicity," of her "honesty and plainness." Significantly, Pamela fashions this outfit herself; it is not made off from the hand-me-downs of her lady. Pamela's outfit, purchased with her own wages and created with her own hands, also asserts her independence, implying that she cannot be bought, that she is not a servant, wearing her mistress's clothes or her master's livery. As Gwilliam notes, "In fact Pamela is making a claim for self-definition and self-representation."[30] From top to bottom, from undergarments to outer-garments, Pamela's new outfit announces her morality, her virtue, her moral self-sufficiency, and, equally important, her desirability.

Next to her skin, she wears a newly made shift of "pretty good *Scots* cloth" (52) with black ribbons encircling the sleeves. Shifts worn by those of the middling to upper stations were made of linen, a fabric woven from the fibers of flax, while "*Scots* cloth" or Scotch cloth, a fabric associated with the lower classes, was woven from the fibers of nettles. The sleeves and sometimes the necklines of shifts and other undergarments were exposed, and the cleanness and whiteness of linen was felt to be a distinguishing mark of upper-class dress. (The wealthy possessed more changes of linen, as well as more servants and soap to keep the linens clean.) Pamela's shift, because of its newness, is clean and white, and the black ribbons accentuate the whiteness of her shift. The pristine nature of her linen associates Pamela with the upper station; the plainness and simplicity of her cloth, with the lower station. In addition, Pamela's clean, bright linen suggests purity and moral cleanliness as well, as it is in the eighteenth century, that cleanliness first becomes associated with godliness.[31]

For her gown and petticoat, Pamela chooses a "good sad-coloured Stuff," a homespun woolen fabric of dark hue, usually blue or brown, with "Robings and Facings of a pretty Bit of printed Calicoe" (52). As Caryn Chaden remarks, "Pamela's selection of materials—homespun wool with calico trim for her dress, and camlet, a combination of wool and silk for her 'coat' (what we would call a petticoat, not an overcoat) — clearly mark her as a country girl."[32] Yet, as Chaden also notes, this is not everyday working dress; Pamela writes that it is clothing that "will serve me . . . for a good Holiday and Sunday Suit." The cloth from which Pamela's gown is fashioned indicates industry and honest labor: "Farmer *Nichol's* Wife and Daughters" have spun their own wool (52), most probably from their own sheep, and most certainly have woven and dyed it themselves; and Pamela had designed, cut, pieced, and sewn the gown herself. The gown would most probably be a nightgown of sorts, which fit closely around the waist, a sign not only of morality—loose clothes suggested moral slackness and easy access to the body beneath—but which would also show off a slim waistline. The somber color of the gown speaks of rustic simplicity and lack of undue pride, while also accenting the brightness of her linen and the newness of her printed calico robings and facings. The fact that it is a "Sunday Suit," Pamela's Sunday best, hints slightly at Pamela's religious nature, but it also takes the gown out of the realm of true rustic attire: It is rustic clothing at its very best—new, scrupulously clean, with no patches or mends or tears. Into the bodice of her gown, Pamela wears a "plain Muslin Tucker" (60), a white fabric fringe around her neckline; around her waist, an apron is tied, presumably also of muslin. A black silk ribbon encircles her neck, in lieu of a necklace, contrasting with the pristine whiteness of tucker and the soft whiteness of skin. Unlike most typical country misses, Pamela possesses "fair soft Hands, and that lovely Skin" (71); indeed, her skin is of lady-like fairness. Her hands are covered by "a Pair of knit Mittens, turn'd up with white Calicoe" (53). Her legs are encased in "ordinary blue Worsted Hose, that makes a smartish Appearance, with white Clocks" (53); her feet are shod in shoes of Spanish leather. Perched atop her head is a "pretty enough round-ear'd" (52) cap with "a green Knot" (60) of ribbon on it. In her gloved hand, Pamela carries a "Straw-hat" with "two blue strings" (60) to tie under her chin. Her "sad-coloured" gown and petticoat would be either a dark blue or reddish-brown wool, with woolen gloves of the same dark blue as her "blue Worsted Hose." The white of her shift sleeves, tucker, apron, and cap would contrast sharply and charmingly with the dark hue of the gown, as would the white clocks with the blue of her stockings, and the white edgings with the blue of her knit mittens. The black ribbons on her sleeves, the black silk necklace, the blue ribbons in her straw hat, and the green knot on her cap present an elegant, even playful counterpoint to the somber hue of her gown. However, this is not an outfit to wear while milking cows, scrubbing pots or pans, or even sewing plain-work. Caryn Chaden reminds us that Pamela's "worsted hose with white clocks (embroidery sewn at the heel and ankle) . . . are a step up from the plain yarn stockings common to women of the lower classes" and that other articles of Pamela's so-called rustic dress "mix class markings," such as her shoes (made of Spanish leather instead of "Neats-Leathern") and the "pretty good" quality of her shifts, gown, and petticoat.[33] We might add, as previously noted, that Pamela's fair skin and white linen are also incongruous with true rustic attire.

Also, as both McIntosh and Chaden have noted, the small unique touches that Pamela adds to her dress are sexually charged. The blue ribbons with which she ties her hat, her black silk necklace, the black silk ribbons which gather the sleeves of her shift, and green knot of ribbon flirtatiously perched atop her little white cap—all display her desirability. As Chaden sardonically writes, this is "hardly the appropriate attire for a girl who claims she wants to stop her suitor's advances."[34] Certainly, the anonymous (and still unidentified) author of *Pamela*

Censored, a pamphlet published in April 1741, thought Pamela's rustic dress highly provocative, and took Richardson to task over it:

> your Skill in Intrigue is most apparent, [when] you contrive to give us her Picture in simple rural Dress . . . She, who could charm so much in a loose Undress on the Floor, must doubtless keep the Ardour still alive, dress'd in the unaffected Embellishments of a neat Country Girl. And tho' the *Servant Maid* might fail to please, the *Farmer's Daughter* must inevitably catch the *Country Squire;* yet how artfully is this *Masquerade* introduced![35]

Desirability is an essential part of Pamela's rustic attire, and Mr. B. remarks on this, when he accuses Pamela of duplicity: "and so you must disguise yourself, to attract me, and yet pretend, like an Hypocrite you are—" (62). Mrs. Jervis admiringly remarks, "I never saw you look more lovely in my Life, than in that same new Dress of yours . . . I believe truly, you owe some of your Danger to the lovely Appearance you made" (66). Yet this outfit also provokes other responses, as well. Mr. B. pronounces Pamela, in her new attire, to be a "pretty neat Damsel" and a "tight prim Lass" (61). He teases her, saying, "Whose pretty Maiden are you? I daresay you are *Pamela's* sister, you are so like her. So neat, so clean, so pretty! Why, Child, you far surpass your Sister *Pamela!*" (61). Pamela's new clothes (so neat, so clean, so tight, so prim, so pretty, and so provocative) express everything that Pamela desires: They tell the world, in a tale woven of cloth and ribbon, that she is industrious and hard-working; lacking in social ambition; unpresuming and unpretentious; honest and moral; independent; and, yes, desirable (because, of course, virtue should be desirable).

Having demonstrated Pamela's virtue, through her dress, in terms of her rustic social station and lowly rank, Richardson must also establish her merit and virtue in terms that express her worthiness to be elevated into the ranks of the gentry, and he does this by associating Pamela Andrews with her literary antecedent, the virtuous princess dressed as a shepherdess, in Sir Philip Sidney's *Arcadia*, who wears "shepherdish apparel" made of plain "Russet cloth."[36] At first glance, aligning Servant Pamela with Princess Pamela seems a stroke of sartorial genius on Richardson's part, as it allows Pamela to display virtue as identified with the lower classes (humility, honesty, innocence) as well with virtue as identified with the aristocracy.

In Sidney's *Arcadia*, Pamela is the eldest daughter of Basilius, Duke of Arcadia (and, yes, she really is called the Princess Pamela). In order to avoid the fulfillment of a prophecy, Basilius sends Pamela to live with an ignorant goatherd and his family; Pamela must dress in the garb of an Arcadian shepherdess. Richardson's intimate knowledge of Sidney's *Arcadia* is evident in the appellation Pamela, a unique and unusual name at the time; through Pamela's country dress; through reference to Mr. B. as "Musidorus" (the Princess Pamela's lover) in *Pamela*, Part Two; and through Harriet Byron's masquerade gown (see Chapter 10 for a more detailed plot synopsis of *Arcadia* and for a full discussion of Harriet's outfit). Unjustly imprisoned at one point, Sidney's Pamela utters the following famous lines: "Let calamity be the exercise, but not the overthrow of my virtue. . . . but, O Lord, let never their wickedness have such a hand but that I may carry a pure mind in a pure body."[37] Of course, Richardson's Pamela might easily have spoken these same words. In addition, Princess Pamela's innate virtue and nobility belie her rustic appearance, yet her desirability in this outfit is evident: "But believe me, she did apparel her apparel, and with the preciousness of her body made it most sumptuous."[38] The same occurs with Servant Pamela. By linking Pamela Andrews with Sidney's princess, Pamela accesses the Arcadian princess's heady mélange of moral goodness, Christian stoicism, physical chastity, beauty, desirability, and aristocratic virtue.

In Joseph Highmore's painting of Pamela in her rustic attire (Figure 4.2), the color of Pamela's "sad-coloured" gown is a russet brown, linking it to the Princess Pamela's russet gown and Pamela's own childhood attire. Pamela's linen and her apron, in color and coarseness, look hand-bleached and hand-woven. The blue ribbons on her hat provide a bright, yet inexpensive note of color. Interestingly, this style of straw hat, known as the "milk-maid" or bergère style, was originally inexpensive rural attire, yet became an integral element of faux rustic attire worn by fashionable ladies. As the *Ladies Library* writes, "Is not a lady as proud of her *Straw Hat* and *Country Habit* as the *Park* and *Play-dress* . . .?"[39] The straw hat was also an integral element of one of the most popular masquerade costumes in eighteenth-century England—that of Arcadian shepherdess.

Yet this literary borrowing of old clothes is not without its problems, not the least of which is that Sidney's *Arcadia* is a romance, an aristocratic genre, while Richardson's *Pamela* is a novel, generally considered a bourgeois genre. Sidney's text promotes aristocratic ideals, expressed through courtly love, knights, fair ladies, and the restoration of aristocratic order. Richardson's text advances bourgeois values, by suggesting that someone from the lower or middling ranks may possess virtue

Figure 4.2 Joseph Highmore. English (1692–1780). *Pamela Preparing to Go Home* (1743–4). Oil on canvas. 63.5×76.2 cm. National Gallery of Victoria, Melbourne. Felton Bequest, 1921. By permission of National Gallery of Victoria, Melbourne

equal to or greater than those at the top of the social system and by celebrating domesticity (though, of course, the novel also allows for the restoration of the gentleman to his former virtuous glory).

These conflicting ideologies are also articulated through the dress of the respective Pamelas. In order "to show an obedience" to her father, Sidney's Pamela has "taken on a shepherdish apparel which was but of russet cloth cut after their fashion, with a straight body, open breasted, the nether part full of pleats, with long and wide sleeves." However, while she dons the garb in compliance to her father's wishes, she despises the circumstances attendant upon it: "The fair Pamela, whose noble heart ... doth greatly disdain that the trust of her virtue is reposed in such a lout's hands ..." as the goatherd, Dametas.[40] The shepherdess attire simultaneously signals her filial obedience, yet also suggests the foolishness of her father, who denigrates himself and his daughter through his actions. Princess Pamela's dress shows the temporary denigration and decay of aristocratic virtue. In contrast, Servant Pamela's rustic garb suggests her humbleness, appropriate to her station; filial obedience, as Pamela makes the outfit in order to return to her father's home; and the simplicity and innocence of rural life. The overlay of one set of values over another creates textual tensions.

Other problems are attendant upon Servant Pamela appropriating the apparel worn by Princess Pamela. First, the outfit of the Princess is a disguise, meant to keep away a specific type of unwanted suitor. The question of the authenticity of Pamela Andrew's outfit is rendered even more problematic, through its association with the inauthentic dress of the princess. Second, the outfit worn by Sidney's Arcadian princess/shepherdess was one of the most popular masquerade outfits of the eighteenth century, adding yet another claim for the argument that Pamela Andrews's outfit is sheer masquerade dress. Finally, the idea that some sort of deceit is being perpetrated becomes compounded when one remembers the accusations of plagiarism associated with the Princess Pamela's captivity speech. *Eikon Basilike*, published upon the death of King Charles I, was purported to contain his private and intimate thoughts while imprisoned (though the text was most probably written by John Gauden, Bishop of Exeter). In it, without attribution, is the Princess Pamela's captivity poem, presented as King Charles's last words, before his removal to the scene of his beheading. John Milton, in *Eikonoklastes*, expressed outrage at "a prayer stolen word for word from the mouth of a heathen fiction praying to a heathen God."[41] In sum, instead of solving the problem of Pamela's sartorial dilemma, the textual *pentimento* created by dressing Miss Andrews up in the borrowed clothes of Sidney's Pamela further complicates the issue of the little servant girl's authenticity in dress.

Although Pamela's rustic attire seems highly aligned with masquerade attire (and borrowed masquerade dress, at that), Richardson would nonetheless have it taken that these clothes represent a genuine expression of who Pamela believes herself to be, and, one might reasonably argue, it is the only way that Pamela's complex virtue can be sartorially expressed within the novel. On the one hand, this refashioned and refurbished rustic dress articulates the virtues generally associated with idealized rural life: simplicity, honesty, thrift, innocence. On the other hand, it refers obliquely to aristocratic virtue, through its allusive link to Sidney's Arcadian romance. Of course, Richardson's ingenious strategy doesn't quite work. The meanings behind Pamela's body, dress, and virtue remain in constant flux, a dialog without end, without conclusion, precisely because Richardson attempted to show that a servant girl could possess the same type and level of virtue as that of a gentlewoman (or a princess!).

5
Quaker, Rustic, and Fool: Masquerading with Mrs. B.

In *Pamela*, Part One, Mr. B., as a member of the gentry, possesses virtue based on lineage and heredity, yet his overall stock of virtue is diminished by his own lack of physical chastity, moral goodness, and Christian belief. Pamela, in contrast, evinces the respective (and conflicting) attributes of virtue as associated with the gentlewoman and the country miss, though she clearly lacks the necessary birth, ancestry, and related trappings of wealth. However, once married to Mr. B., Pamela gains in overall terms of virtue, as she can now legitimately lay claim to virtue, based on heritage and lineage, not because she herself possesses an aristocratic or genteel body, but because she is allied to one, and her own body, through the production of heirs, becomes an instrument of service in the reproduction of aristocratic virtue. Mr. B., too, accrues virtue upon marriage, in terms of moral goodness and physical chastity, regaining the full measure of virtue associated with a "good man," in particular, with a virtuous gentleman. Thus, marriage for Mr. B. and Pamela allows for an increase in the quality and quantity of virtue identified with each spouse.

Yet all is not well at B. Hall. *Pamela*, Part Two, again, addresses the issue of virtue. Pamela's non-genteel body, now enormously pregnant with son and heir, nonetheless continues to demonstrate a lack, or so it seems. And Mr. B. still has a long way to go on the path to moral redemption. As Pamela recounts to her parents, during the early days of her marriage: "There was but one thing wanting, my dear parents, to complete all the happiness I wished for in this life: and that was the remote hope I had entertained that, one day my dear Mr. B—, who from a licentious gentleman became a moralist, would be so touched by the Divine grace, as to become in time more than a moral, a *religious* man" (IV:280). Yet Pamela's "charming hopes" for Mr. B.'s complete transformation are dashed by "a nasty masquerade," which sends Mr. B.'s "sliding feet"

down a "slippery path" (IV:282) into presumed debauchery and dissolu-
tion, a rejection of his newly acquired morals.

Terry Castle has written, brilliantly and at length, on the masquerade
scene in *Pamela*, Part Two, yet my interest is not in the re-carnivalization
of Pamela, as Castle puts it, but in how Pamela's body, dressed once
again in disguise, embodies and displays multiple forms of virtue. I am
particularly interested in how religion informs the debate on virtue, and
in a particular moment at the masquerade ball, when Pamela, dressed
as a Quaker, confronts several masquerade versions of herself, a widow,
a rustic, and a fool.

To recap, Pamela and Mr. B. have journeyed from Bedfordshire to
London, to await the birth of their first child, and for Mr. B. to attend
the sessions of Parliament; they are soon joined by Miss Darnford, the
eldest daughter of one of B.'s Bedfordshire neighbors, Sir Simon
Darnford, the same man who formerly had thought so little of Pamela's
virtue, as lady's maid. Sir Simon, an old rake himself, is concerned for
his daughter's safety in the B. household, as who would "trust such a
sprightly girl as Polly in the house with such a fellow as that!" (III:56),
and Sir Simon's concern is prescient, as Mr. B. still, it seems, has a bit of
the rake left in him.

After the normal rounds of London entertainment, such as the theater
and the opera, Mr. B., Pamela, and Miss Darnford attend a masquerade,
with Pamela in grudging attendance: "But finding Mr. B— chose to have
me go, if, as he was pleased to say, I had no objection; I said, I *will* have
none, sir, I *can* have none, when you tell me it is your choice; and so
send for the habits you like, and that you would have me appear in, and
I will cheerfully attend you." Mr. B chooses the costume of "a Spanish
Don, and it well befitted the majesty of his person and air"; Miss Darnford
wears that of "a young widow" (IV:52). For Pamela, Mr. B. chooses the
costume of a Quaker, which, she feels, suits her well, "for I thought I was
prim enough for that naturally" (IV:53), though Terry Castle finds the
very pregnant, Quaker-clad Pamela "an image of festive contradiction—
a walking double entendre."[1]

Although Mr. B. had assured his pregnant Pamela that he will "have
me always in his eye," yet, immediately upon his arrival, Mr. B. is
"singled out by a bold nun" (IV:52) and the two disappear, "out of sight
in a moment" (IV:53). Pamela thus spends the majority of the masquerade in the company of Miss Darnford, and they soon meet two
other masqueraders, who like themselves, are always together, always
"having something to say to everybody" (IV:55), and always followed
by a crowd: "Two ladies, one in a very fantastic party-coloured habit,

with a plume of feathers; the other in a rustic one, with a garland of flowers round her head; were much take notice of for their freedom, and having something to say to everybody. They were as seldom separated as Miss Darnford and I, and were followed by a crowd, wherever they went" (IV:55). Clearly, this encounter is filled with purpose. All four masquerading women—pregnant Quaker, young widow, be-flowered rustic, and parti-colored fool—represent a Pamela of sorts, and all four costumes interrogate different aspects of Pamela's virtue.

During the masquerade, Pamela's virtue, in the sense of chastity and Christian morality, is constantly called into question, because of the seeming incongruity expressed by dress and body. One masquerader quips, "I hope, friend, thou art prepared with a father for the light within thee?" (IV:53). The parti-colored masquerader calls attention to Pamela's snug-fitting gown, which emphasizes her pregnant form: "Friend . . . there is something in thy person that attracts every one's notice: but if a sack had not been a profane thing, it would have become thee almost as well" (IV:55). The sack, or *sacque* dress, was a style of gown introduced from France, "which flowed unrestricted from pleats at the shoulder to the hem",[2] and the loose nature of the sack was viewed as an invitation to sexual immorality, by many English. Quakers did not wear the *sacque* gown, as it was considered immodest, primarily because it could hide the results of sexual indiscretion, in the form of pregnancies; a nightgown, which fit tightly around the waist, was worn instead. However, Pamela's pregnant body emphasizes her sexuality, as Terry Castle has noted.

Problems exist with the costume itself, but also because Mr. B. has chosen it for Pamela. As both Marcia Pointon and Jennie Batchelor have demonstrated, Quaker plain dress was interpreted in widely different ways—as an indication of moral and physical cleanliness, as deliberate deceit, as social leveling, or as anti-social behavior. Like many of the other costumes worn by the masqueraders, Pamela's Quaker outfit proclaims religious affiliation, but it does not designate her as a member of the clergy, a leader of a congregation, but as member of a society where all are considered equals who have learned to walk "in the light." Pamela, unlike her fellow masqueraders, alters her speech to fit her outfit, and her language is sprinkled with "verily" and "thee" and "Friend." Both dress and speech of the Society of Friends demonstrated social egalitarianism. As Rosemary Moore writes, "Quakers did not care for personal titles, because they indicated social distinctions. . . . 'Thou' was the normal Quaker address to a single person"; in addition, "Quakers would not give customary greetings, for they said that only God, not humans, should be so honored."[3] Quakers also do not doff their hats as a sign of respect to those of the upper ranks. In addition, among many other traits, Friends believed in "absolutely right conduct," refusal to pay tithes or take oaths, "strict ethical standards that put much of the responsibility on the individual," "complete equality as regards the ministry, as least in theory, between men and women," and, of course, "their peace witness."[4] Thus, Pamela's dress suggests radical resistance to the hierarchical social system in place in eighteenth-century England. Yet does the Quaker garb express something about Pamela herself, or, instead, what Mr. B. thinks about her? Is Mr. B. fearful that Pamela is engaged in "a Levelling project, of robbing him of his Birth-right, of degrading him from those priviledges, which belong to his quality"?[5] Is this Richardson's coy way of confronting the accusations of leveling that accompanied the reception of *Pamela*, Part One?

The primness of Quaker dress and mannerisms could also be viewed as either too singular or potentially duplicitous. While the *Ladies Library* (1714) extolled simplicity in dress—"Look on the Simplicity of the Ancients"[6]—the strikingly distinct nature of Quaker dress seemed to contradict its very simplicity. As Pointon writes, "in eschewing things of the world—Quakers could appear so peculiar that they became greater spectacles than their fellow humans, no matter how elaborately dressed and be-jewelled."[7] In addition, as Batchelor notes, "Like sensibility, Quakerism focused intensely on, indeed revered, the body," and, like sensibility itself, could be read variously as genuine or artificial expression.[8] Batchelor also points out that both John Wesley and James Fordyce found "Quaker simplicity a form of artfulness."[9]

The ambiguity associated with Quaker dress becomes expressed in Defoe's *Roxana*. The eponymous heroine of Defoe's novel, avoiding discovery by her daughter Susan, takes lodgings with a Quaker woman and her family. The authentic Quaker, "a most pleasant and agreeable lady," is honest, friendly, loyal, and moral. However, as part of Amy's "Scheme" to avoid detection, Roxana herself soon takes on Quaker dress and mannerisms. Roxana professes an interest in Quaker dress to her landlady: "I pretended, after I had been there some time, to be extreamly in Love with the Dress of the QUAKERS, and this pleas'd her so much, that she wou'd needs dress me up one Day in a Suit of her own Cloaths, but my real Design was, to see whether it wou'd pass upon me for a Disguise." In sum, "I pass'd for a QUAKER among all People that did not know me."[10] As Clair Hughes writes, "her Quaker dress now conceals a whore."[11]

Mr. B.'s choice of Quaker attire for Pamela's masquerade gown suggests a high level of ambivalence towards Pamela, not unlike the response generated by Richardson's own readers. When confronted by Pamela about his presumed liaison with the "bold nun" (IV:52), in reality, a widowed Dowager Countess, Mr. B. retorts by expostulating against Pamela's "tears and grief," arguing that he had reason for "apprehending that your temper was entirely changing" (IV:163–4). It would seem that the married, pregnant Pamela is a different Pamela than the one whom Mr. B. had married, a fraud. (Of course, Pamela only acts differently *after* Mr. B. has entered into his intrigue.) Alternatively, if Pamela exists as "conduct book" wherein Mr. B. may read his duties and responsibilities, then surely Mr. B.'s choice of Quaker garb for his pregnant wife suggests a surfeit of moral advice on his part. He has had his fill of reformation, thank you. Didacticism without some measure of entertainment, so Mr. B. as reader informs us, is not worth having. Give us a romance instead.

Religious garb also highlights Mr. B.'s fall from a state of moral goodness. As Paul Langford notes, "Religion was in some measure a matter of class" in eighteenth-century England,[12] and Richardson utilizes religion as a mask for class. Specifically, religion exists as the medium through which Richardson recreates the hierarchical and ideological tension over what constitutes virtue.

Although the usual assortment of masqueraders appear, the Quaker Pamela is most disturbed by those dressed in Roman Catholic ecclesiastical garments: She questions "the liberties of expression and behaviour taken by some of those who personated bishops, cardinals, priests, nuns, &c.?—For the freest thing I heard said were from persons in those habits; who behaved with so much levity and indecorum" (IV:56–7). Those in Roman Catholic clerical attire (such as the nun and the cardinal) reveal themselves to be members of the upper station—aristocrats, to be precise—by their fluency in foreign languages, their noble carriages, and, most of all, their immoral behavior. Mr. B., as Spanish don, aligns himself with aristocratic corruption—and fun.

The reasons why Richardson chose to associate Roman Catholicism, at least in masquerade form, with the upper station are uncertain, though they can be guessed at. First, Catholics, at least in England, were viewed as supporters of hereditary rights and hierarchical religious and social systems. As E. I. Watkin writes, "For Catholics were Jacobites giving allegiance to the exiled King and later to his son. But they were suffering, not for loyalty to the Pope at the expense of loyalty to their Sovereign, but for their loyalty to their King by hereditary right."[13] Second, charges of moral laxity had been garnered against the Catholics since the days of Luther, and moral laxity is something that Richardson and many members of the middle station associated with the aristocracy. Finally, Pamela complains about the "showy part" of Roman Catholicism and all the "fine pictures and decorations in the churches" (IV:291), and the many middle-class complaints lodged against elaborate religious display were the same as those against the elaborate and ostentatious dress of the upper station. Thus, through their masquerade costumes, chosen by Mr. B., Pamela and Mr. B. represent widely disparate views concerning merit, virtue, and worth, and, as Castle notes, this invigorates a largely enervated plot.

And, in the topsy-turvy world of masquerade, more than one Pamela may appear—and does. Polly Darnford, in her costume of widow's weeds, becomes a masquerade version of Pamela, as Mr. B. has metaphorically widowed Pamela. When Mr. B. reappears after his first dalliance with the Dowager Countess, dressed in nun's attire, Mr. B. acts "as if he had not known us" (IV:54). Pamela feels isolated from her husband: "we appeared not to know one another" (IV:54). When Mr. B. later recounts his version of events to Pamela, he informs her that the false nun had inquired about Pamela, saying to Mr. B., "That fair quaker yonder is the wit of the assemblée: her eyes seems always directed to thy motion: and her person shows some intimacies have passed with somebody: is it thee? (IV:147). Mr. B., with linguistic sleight of hand, suggests his unfamiliarity with Pamela or her unborn child. In Peter-like fashion, Mr. B. denies his Pamela thrice (IV:146). The masquerade turns Pamela, at least temporarily, into a "young widow," the identity that Miss Darnford, the dark shadow always at Pamela's side, has chosen.

As if Pamela were not having difficulties enough with an errant husband and a flirtatious nun, she soon encounters two fun-house versions of her former self. The boldest of the two wears "a very fantastic party-coloured habit, with a plume of feathers" (IV:55). When the parti-colored masquerader satirically comments on the incongruity between Pamela's Quaker dress and her pregnant body, Pamela responds in kind, saying, "I thank thee, friend, . . . for thy counsel; but if thou hadst been pleased to look at home, thou wouldst not have taken so much pains to join such advice, and such an appearance together, as thou makest!" (IV:55). Pamela, of course, is mocking the parti-colored habit of the masquerader, but, on a different level, this may be read as a critique of the uneasy appearance that Pamela herself makes as part-gentlewoman, part "awkward country girl" (IV:9). It may also be seen as interrogating the two modes of virtue, that of the gentlewoman and that of the rustic, as being inconsistent with each other, as incongruent as Pamela's body and dress.

This parti-colored costume of the masquerader hints at the married Pamela, whom Sir Jacob Swynford, one of Mr. B.'s relatives, refers disparagingly to as "*linsey-wolsey*" (IV:8), suggestive of Pamela's status as "neither gentlewoman nor rustic" (IV:8), and neither "Christian or Pagan" (III:213). As Sir Jacob puts it, she is "half one, half t'other" (III:213). Pamela's problem becomes one of consistency: How can someone be genuine, when she is neither one thing or another? Similarly, how can two competing versions of virtue exist within the same body? Does one cancel out the other? In order to convince Sir Jacob of the worthiness of her social elevation, Pamela must put on the disguise of Lady Jenny, which involves changing the size of her hooped petticoat and pretending to be the unmarried daughter of a Countess. In essence, she must perform as Lady Jenny in order to be accepted as Mrs. B. She thus erases or renders invisible the virtue associated with her self as ditch-digger's daughter and honest rustic, and performs virtue as defined solely by aristocratic ideology.

Pamela ultimately solves the problem of her *"linsey-wolsey"* self by deciding to become an "original," sidestepping the issue entirely: "instead of being thought neither gentlewoman nor rustic, as Sir Jacob hinted (*linsey-wolsey*, I think, was his term too), I may be looked upon as an original in my way; and all originals pass muster well enough, you know, madam, even with judges" (IV:8). But the parti-colored masquerader, also an original, does not pass muster with Pamela herself. This odd encounter suggests that Pamela's incorporation of various modes of virtue works only for her, and, even then, always with some sense of being, as Defoe described it, "counterfeit coin," a masquerader, or, worse yet, a fool. In the nightmare world of masquerade, the country-born Pamela, now married into the gentry, is an object of ridicule, a clown, a "butterfly" (IV:55), a fool.

Pamela, next, turns to the "country girl" (IV:55), a parodic version of an earlier Pamela, when outfitted in her "poor honest Dress," with round-eared cap. This masquerader wears "rustic" dress, with "a garland of flowers round her head" (IV:55). The Quaker Pamela questions the rustic Pamela, demanding "if she has not weeds in her heart to disgrace the flowers on her head" (IV:56). Virtue in this instance concerns only moral goodness; there is no indication that this rustic costume alludes in any way to that of Sidney's Arcadian shepherdess, nor does any other co-opting of aristocratic virtue seem in evidence. This false Pamela makes no response, yet the reader is left to wonder if Mrs. B. questions the motives of her earlier self, seeing herself through the eyes of the various satires upon and criticisms of her earlier, youthful self, or if she is attempting to deny others the right to claim multiple versions of virtue. This brief encounter either rewrites Pamela's earlier self, or it attempts to claim that only one Pamela, the "original," may achieve some semblance of social parity and participation in the patrician mode of virtue. The masquerade version of the rustic Pamela remains oddly mute in response to Pamela's interrogation, and Pamela herself offers no further commentary, leaving the reader to provide any answers.

In its entirety, the masquerade episode explores the different definitions of virtue available in eighteenth-century England, and the encounter between the four masquerade versions of Pamela suggests a reevaluation of the different versions of virtue available to someone from Pamela's background. Mr. B., the Dowager Countess, and others of their social station, possess patrician virtue in full measure, yet they lack moral goodness and chasteness, or initially seem to, though their full measure of virtue is restored to them by the end of the novel. The gentry and aristocracy, so it turns out, merely look unvirtuous to undiscerning outsiders. Pamela, as rustic, possesses (one hopes) moral goodness and physical chastity, but nothing more, and even this appears to be in question. This becomes a representation of the unmarried Pamela, and, in turn, the non-aristocratic, non-genteel body, lacking the virtue that comes with noble birth and ancestry, whose own access to virtue as moral goodness cannot be ascertained by the flowers on her head or the dress on her back. The "*linsey-wolsey*" Pamela, dressed in parti-colored clothes, seems in partial possession of virtue as defined in terms of gentility and of country simplicity, but, as "butterfly," she flutters between the two modes, part fraud and part fool. This is the married Pamela.

Yet, it is the pregnant Pamela, dressed as a Quaker, who claims the right to full possession of virtue in all its myriad forms, and this despite the fact she may be somewhat of a fraud. With her pregnancy, Pamela's body has become completely absorbed into the system of ancestry and lineage; her chastity, as wife, may be read in terms of patrilineal inheritance. As a pregnant Mrs. B., Pamela's body has been transformed into the genteel, virtuous body. Her body is no longer the site of ideological struggle, but has been subsumed into an older model of virtue. The Quaker costume, then, in its moral ambiguity, allows Pamela to play it both ways, to retain at least the appearance of humility and simplicity, while fully engaged in the project of sustaining the hierarchical status quo. What occurs, then, in *Pamela*, Part Two, is the inversion of *Pamela*, Part One, with Pamela's body and dress engaged in endless ideological dialectic.

Part III Window-Shopping the Essential Self with *Clarissa*

Introduction

Belford writes to Lovelace, "thou . . . sayst, That we do but hang out a Sign, in our dress, of what we have in the Shop of our Minds. This, no doubt, thou thinkest, is smartly observed: But pr'ythee, Lovelace, tell me, if thou canst, What sort of Sign must thou hang out, wert thou obliged to give us a clear idea of the furniture of *thy* mind?" (6:403). The analogy of person to shop was commonplace in eighteenth-century England, but in *Clarissa*, its use is particularly apt, as it articulates two different, though related themes of the novel: One, that the inner person, the conscious mind and soul, can only be known through outward signs, through window-shopping, so to speak, a particular risky venture for a young woman in the market for a mate. Two, that the female body is often treated as goods to be sold in marriage, or cheapened, by rakes or libertines, and it is a body whose ownership may be contested. These themes extrapolate onto the larger issue of government, both of self and of others.

Richardson employs the debate regarding art versus nature, in order to reveal the signs by which the real versus the artificial may be known, how the exterior may provide indications of the interior.[1] In essence, he provides a didactic shopping guide for his readers, on how to examine the signs hung over the door and to inspect the goods displayed in the window, in order to evaluate the unseen contents found within "the Shop of our Minds."

Art versus nature was but one of many related subtexts in the great cultural debate over the ancients and the moderns, itself part of an "even older argument about the relation between the humanities and the sciences."[2] The argument over the ancients versus the moderns arose early in the seventeenth century, became particularly heated during the Restoration, and continued unabated throughout the eighteenth century.

This debate influenced and informed virtually every field of intellectual pursuit: architecture; gardening; literary production (translations versus original creations; the battle of the books; and more); languages; painting and sculpture; archeology; and, of course, the humanities and the sciences, in general.

Nature was associated with native genius, with originality, with taking inspiration directly from nature. Art was that which was learned and studied; it was considered imitative, if only due to its reliance on what had come before. For Edward Young, in *Conjectures on Original Composition* (1759), that which is based on nature "*grows*, it is not *made*," while "*Imitations* are often a sort of *Manufacture* wrought up by those *Mechanics, Art*, and *Labour*, out of pre-existent materials not their own."[3]

In terms of the larger cultural debate, nature was most often associated with the ancients, whose literary productions, architecture, etc. appeared to have no antecedents, or, at least, no known antecedents, though even the ancients were parceled out into groups of "originals" and those authors who were known to have taken their works from the no longer extant works of others. In "The Battle of the Books" (1704), Swift's spider, representing the moderns, "displays to you his great skill in architecture, and improvement in mathematics," the only things "genuine that the Moderns may pretend to . . . unless it be a large vein of wrangling and satire." The spider spins his web—a creation of poison and dirt—out of his own entrails, that is to say, from the works of other modern (or ancient) writers. The bee, representing the ancients, has "come honestly by my wings and my voice; for then, it seems, I am obliged to Heaven alone for my flights and my music"; the bee goes directly to nature to make creations of "sweetness and light."[4] Yet there could be modern geniuses as well, such as Shakespeare and Milton, and nature could also inspire individuals of lesser talents. In his ode, "To the Pious Memory of the Accomplished Young Lady, Mrs. Anne Killigrew" (1685), John Dryden writes of the deceased young woman:

> Art she had none, yet wanted none;
> For nature did that want supply:
> So rich in treasures of her own,
> She might our boasted stores defy:
> Such noble vigour did her verse adorn,
> That it seemed borrowed 'twas only born.[5]

In *Clarissa*, clothing, as language, as signifier, becomes split into two opposing discourses—the discourse of art and the discourse of nature—in order to provide a guide for determining the artificial from the real. The discourse of nature, that is, dress as the natural expression of the wearer, is one where the exterior and the interior are in agreement and harmony, where the outward expresses the inward truth. Clarissa Harlowe is mistress of the natural world. In dress, "her choice of *natural* beauties set those of *Art* far behind them" (4:74). Her outward dress, unstudied yet distinctive, is described in painstaking detail by Richardson. It expresses not only her innocence, her elegance, and her unique sense of style, but the depth of this expression; by disclosing the intimate details of her dress, Richardson demonstrates that her outward appearance is neither artificial nor superficial, but one which is unique to her and which naturally springs forth from her inner being. Strip her of her clothing, show her in *dishabille*, yet she is always the same—pure, innocent, and lovely. The progression of her dress, from rich, elaborately decorated suits to simple gowns, lacking ornamentation, functions as a system of symbols, reflecting her journey from the material world to the spiritual world, a gradual casting away of earthly concerns, and it also records the way in which different individuals, including Clarissa herself, seek to lay claim to her body.

In contrast, the discourse of art is the language of the world of carnival and masquerade, where dress serves to disguise the wearers, making them appear the opposite of who and what they really are. The discourse of art—dress as a studied or deceitful expression by the wearer—is the language spoken in the topsy-turvy carnival world in which Robert Lovelace reigns supreme, "where Art (or *Imposture*, as the ill-mannered would call it) is designed" (6:83).[6] It is a dual world, where the exterior conceals the interior, where the inner and the outer are forever at odds. In this case, clothing is both superficial and artificial, described by Richardson in little detail, as it serves solely to cloak and to conceal, lacking in-depth meaning and expressing nothing of the true nature of the wearer. Indeed, beneath the seemingly respectable costumes of Lovelace and his band of rogues and whores, "one of Swift's Yahoos, or Virgil's obscene Harpyes, squirting their ordure" might be glimpsed (8:51–2), as well as the occasional cloven foot. The clothing of Lovelace and his confederates, carefully studied yet stereotypical and prosaic, is painted with broad strokes of the brush, in order to reveal its artifice, as clothing that conceals character lacks the personal, individualized touches that indicate a unique person. The progression of dress that Lovelace and his minions wear—from one disguise to yet another—reflects only Lovelace's love of *and need for* deception.

Tragedy occurs because these two opposing worlds and discourses come together, leading to the misreading of clothing and of wearer. Clarissa knows nothing of carnival and masquerade—until she is horribly raped. Then she too learns the art of disguise and uses it to flee from her tormentor. For Lovelace, carnival is truth, and he assumes that once Clarissa is disrobed, she will be like all the others, for "every woman is a Rake in her heart" (3:106).

Although there are two separate discourses of dress—one of art and one of nature—the danger lies in their *appearing* the same. Clarissa cannot tell the difference, and, thus, is tragically raped. Yet is there a way to tell the difference? Richardson, in how he depicts the clothing of Clarissa and the clothing of Lovelace and his confederates—the former as unique, the latter as imitative—is suggesting perhaps that it is through the details of dress (the blue knot of ribbon here, the hand-embroidered violets there) that we can tell the authentic from the imposter: The dress of the genuine person reveals something of his or her personality, of soul and mind, while that of the imposter shows only what the viewer *expects* to see. While dress as natural expression is indeed unaffected and in harmony with the wearer, it is also as refreshingly unique as the wearer herself.

It should be noted that, in attempting to articulate the difference between the virtuous and the unvirtuous through the deployment of the debate over art versus nature, Richardson creates a concept previously unheard of—that of personal style. While it is commonplace today to associate style with a unique fashion sense, this concept did not take hold in any significant way until the latter part of the eighteenth century, when Marie Antoinette, under the direction of her *marchande de modes*, Rose Bertin, became "a leader in the realm of fashion."[7] To be sure, there had always been those who reveled in extremes of dress, such as the fop or the "amazon," but personal style as something to which every individual might subscribe and aspire was something new and, to the best of my knowledge, first finds expression in the novels of Samuel Richardson. Thus, although I use the terms such as "distinctive style" or "personal touch" in describing Clarissa's dress, it should be remembered that this notion is a relatively new one. (It may be that Richardson's novels have had a greater influence on fashion than originally thought. For instance, the embroidered robings on Clarissa's gown, Harriet Byron's "white wedding," and Clementina's della Porretta's flowing black gown—all make their literary appearance prior to their historical popularity.)

In addition, in evaluating dress in *Clarissa*, it must be noted that three of the most highly detailed descriptions of Clarissa's dress come directly from Lovelace, which begs the question: Is this Lovelace's view of Clarissa, or is this the "true" Clarissa, as Richardson wants his readers to interpret her? Perhaps both.

Lovelace attends to the "*minutiæ*" (3:185) in all things. He is concerned with the details, as befits a man fond of contrivances. He is able to make subtle distinctions in the hue and tint of a yellow silk gown ("primrose-colored") and identify the stone in a seldom-worn ring ("rose-diamond"). He studies Clarissa's dress as an indicator of her character, which will provide him with the clues necessary to woo her, to con her, and to seduce her. He does not misread her dress so much, as misread the relationship of dress to mind and soul. For him, regardless of external signs or outward coverings, "One woman is like another" (3:228). Clothing, to Lovelace, merely indicates the petty vanities of his prey, revealing individual weaknesses that will contribute to their fall, as fall they inevitably must, according to his philosophy. The fault, then, lies not with Lovelace's description of Clarissa's dress, but with his misreading of women in general (and Clarissa, in particular). The descriptions of dress provided by Lovelace still allow readers to decipher Clarissa's wardrobe in the way that Richardson intends, as an outward and honest expression of her mind and soul, even as they provide insight into Lovelace's own mind and soul. Clarissa, notably, never provides the reader with any detailed descriptions of dress, either of her own clothing or the clothing of others, perhaps to demonstrate her own modesty and lack of calculation in regards to personal dress, but also to provide evidence of her relative naivety in evaluating the dress of others. Despite her fashion sense, Clarissa demonstrates no real interest in dress *per se*, protecting her from the cultural cliché of conspicuous female consumption. In addition, Clarissa's generalized descriptions of the dress of Lovelace and his confederates are consistent with the way in which the attire of these individuals is described by themselves and by others, confirming Richardson's intention to make dress that is in any way contrived remain nonspecific and impersonal.

The three descriptions of dress provided by Lovelace are noteworthy in other respects as well. Lovelace only divulges the details of Clarissa's clothing when he is at the point of capturing her—or losing her. With peculiar and precise attention to detail, Lovelace describes, after the fact, the outfit in which Clarissa elopes against her will. It is a gleeful and triumphant recounting, as befits someone who has pulled off a nearly impossible feat, savoring each and every detail. In addition, Lovelace rewrites the details of Clarissa's ensemble in such a way as to justify his own role in the elopement—she is the "rogue" (3:28), not he. He also describes Clarissa in dishabille, after he has touched her "almost disrobed body" (4:366) and lifted "the half-lifeless Charmer" (4:367) onto the bed, a prelude to rape in the eyes of the reader, a prelude to seduction in the eyes of Lovelace. Again, although Lovelace is the writer of this passage, readers draw a startling different conclusion than he does, from the events recounted. And, finally, Lovelace relates the particulars of the outfit in which Clarissa first escapes from Mrs. Sinclair's house. This account of dress is highly succinct, lacking his customary exultant tones; in fact, this precise, concise description holds underlying tones of desperation and hysteria. However, once again, Lovelace's words shift blame onto the victim, rather than the perpetrator: Clarissa has robbed Lovelace "of the dearest property I had ever purchased"; she is a "hypocrite," a "traitress" (5:17), a "Cruel creature, and ingrateful as cruel!" (5:29).

Lovelace's descriptions of Clarissa's dress invoke simultaneously two distinct and widely disparate "readings": one reading reveals Clarissa's innocence, fear, and desperation; the other, Clarissa's complicity, hypocrisy, and scheming. Lovelace becomes the reader whom Richardson hates, the one who views a Pamela Andrews as a Shamela or a Syrena Tricksy. Lovelace represents those members of the populace who insist that no woman can ever possess true virtue: "This plaguy Sex is Art itself: Every individual of it is a plotter by nature" (4:20). Indeed, Lovelace terms Clarissa's virtue "a Wind-mill Virtue" (5:17), as much an illusion (or romantic delusion) as Don Quixote's giants. For Richardson, Lovelace's interpretation of Clarissa's actions and dress functions as metaphor for all those readers who, through the debased nature of their own minds (or so Richardson would think), turned Pamela and her virtue into frauds. Any reader who makes the similar mistake of "misreading" Clarissa and her clothing must also face the uncomfortable knowledge that his point of view is the same as that of a rapist. To a great extent, it appears that Richardson attempted to forestall the problems of signification inherent in Pamela's rustic garb by providing, upfront, two opposing readings of Clarissa's various outfits and, by doing so, attempting to control interpretative outcome. Nonetheless, interpretation of Clarissa's wardrobe must always be complicated by the fact that it is Lovelace who supplies the evidence of Clarissa's "authentic" and "natural" dress, while simultaneously arguing for its inauthentic and false nature.

One additional point regards the emphasis on masquerade that I make and will make when reading the dress of Lovelace and his band of rogues and whores. Although the trope of masquerade by no means fully addresses the complexity of Lovelace, it is nonetheless a highly useful metaphor for describing the activities of someone whose self-described vices include "the Love of plots and intrigues" (7:11). The profession of rake, if such we may call it, requires deliberate and self-conscious fashioning. In a letter to Lady Bradshaigh, Richardson describes "the dress and address of the rake":

> The rake is, must be, generally, in dress a coxcomb; in address, a man of great assurance; thinking highly of himself, meanly of the sex; he must be past blushing, and laugh at those who are not. He must flatter, lie, laugh, sing, caper, be a monkey, and not a man. And can a good man put on these appearances? We have heard that the devil himself has transformed himself into an angel of light, to bring about his purposes; but never an angel of light borrowed a coat and waistcoat of the devil, for any purpose whatsoever.[8]

A rake puts on "appearances." As James Grantham Turner has noted, the rake or libertine is driven by competing and paradoxical impulses, in that he must imitate, but appear original while doing so. Turner writes, "The goal of the court wit or *libertine honnête homme* . . . was to be 'inimitable' without being eccentric, to seduce by recombining the polite conventions into a wholly original effect, 'brilliant and incomprehensible.'" The rake's concern is "with the quality of imitation, with the *reproduction* of behaviour in a way that must be wholly methodical and yet wholly devoid of mechanism."[9] More pointedly, the trope of masquerade is precisely what is revealed when studying the dress of Lovelace and his associates in *Clarissa*; their dress is studied, contrived, and artificial.[10]

The trope of masquerade is useful in other respects. Lovelace turns the brothel into a masquerade version of Harlowe Place, with his various minions playing the roles of Harlowe and Lovelace family members: Patrick McDonald, as Captain Tomlinson, becomes a stage version of Uncle Antony; Sally Martin plays the role of Arabella, and Polly Horton, that of Cousin Dolly; Dorcas takes on the supporting role of Clarissa's maid, Hannah; while Bab Wallis and Johanetta Golding play the roles of Lady Betty Lawrence and Miss Charlotte Montague, respectively. Together, they perform a parody of a play that might be entitled "The Marriage Market," where Clarissa is forced to give herself, against her will, to a suitor determined by her guardian. In this mock marriage plot, Lovelace functions both as guardian and as suitor, playing the combined roles of Clarissa's father and Solmes. The middle-aged madam, Mrs. Sinclair, becomes a bloated and perverse conflation of Clarissa's mother and her Aunt Hervey, intent on forcing Clarissa into an unwanted liaison, one that requires consummation through the sexual act.[11] Richardson asks his readers to compare the characters in each act of Clarissa's drama. While, admittedly, differences exist, so too do striking similarities.

Lovelace's deliberate choice of brothel, as the site for his deceitful and despicable performance, urges further comparisons with Harlowe Place. The brothel, in essence, is a shop that sells female flesh. Lovelace is both a regular customer of the brothel, which functions as a kind of second-hand store for the purchase of female bodies, and he is a regular purveyor of "goods" for the brothel, which he helps to stock with his discarded, cast-off mistresses, those women "who made themselves too cheap to him" (3:238). Prostitutes become property circulated among men, yet the world of the brothel mirrors the so-called normal world, where young girls are sold as property to the highest bidder (Solmes, for instance), with parents and relatives acting the parts of pimps and madams. The difference is merely one of the relative value placed on the female body: The marriage market sells new, "undamaged" goods; the brothel sells second-hand, "used" goods, recycling them endlessly until such time as all worth and value have been eradicated. Neither market (marriage or prostitution) values the soul or mind, merely the body and its relative worth as a source of profit or pleasure. Of course, Richardson valued the institution of marriage, yet abhorred the aristocratic model of marriage, where alliances and wealth take precedence over mutual esteem and friendship. As Mr. B. states, in an aristocratic marriage, "Convenience, or Birth and Fortune, are the first Motives, Affection the last (if it is at all consulted)" (366). The Harlowes move beyond the aristocratic model of convenience to the violence of a forced marriage, and, in writing *Clarissa*, Richardson had it as "one of my Two principal Views, to admonish Parents agt. Forcing their Children's Inclinations, in an Article so essential to their Happiness, as Marriage."[12]

By utilizing the trope of masquerade, Richardson creates two parallel worlds, both of which indulge in a form of masquerade: At the brothel, madams, prostitutes, rogues, and rapists play the part of respectable citizens. At Harlowe Place, Clarissa's respectable family members play the parts of madams, prostitutes, pimps, and rogues, with their chosen suitor, Solmes, designated the role of legally sanctioned rapist. Clarissa's experiences at the hands of Mrs. Sinclair's "family" and her own are remarkably similar, and it strongly suggests that marriage against one's will is a form of rape, and that parents who arrange such marriages are engaged in the act of prostituting their daughters. As Leslie Richardson notes, "A forced marriage would be simply a socially acceptable form of rape."[13] The extended metaphor of masquerade and "unnatural" behavior calls attention to the unnatural behavior of Clarissa's family, not only to Lovelace's own artful nature.

Thus dress, in *Clarissa*, utilizing the debate concerning art versus nature, articulates and advances the themes of the (un)reliability, yet necessity of outward signs and the tendency of society to reduce the female body to a form of saleable goods, through forced marriage. It also provides a critique of governance that extends beyond the immediate domestic concerns of the novel. Clarissa writes, "All young creatures, thought I, more or less, covet independency; but those who wish most for it, are seldom the fittest to be trusted either with the government of themselves, or with power over others" (1:124–5). Clarissa's tragedy paradoxically stems from the lack of wise governance on the part of her family and the reluctance of these same individuals to allow her some measure of self-governance. As Richardson writes, during this last year of Clarissa's life, "her Parents and Uncles" were "despotic, arbitrary, tyrannical."[14] Lovelace, similarly, proves himself an unsuitable guardian for this young girl. If Clarissa had married him, this would have been his legal role. As is, she is "a poor creature who has no protector" (4:369) but him, and the results are disastrous. Michael McKeon writes, "Manifestly not a veiled allegory of public events, *Pamela* derives a great deal of its critical edge from the metaphorical concretion by which a signifying politics invests its amatory signified with socio-ethical weight. If Mr. B. and Pamela are not actually tyrant and rebel, their characters are subtly inflected by these political types."[15] If *Pamela* provides a critique of political and class-based tyranny, then *Clarissa* cautions equally against patriarchal and familial tyranny. For Clarissa, both forms of "government" may prove tyrannical, in that they hold the potential for usurping and trammeling the rights of society's most vulnerable populations, women and children, and Clarissa reacts accordingly.

The following chapters examine dress in *Clarissa*. Chapter 6 begins the discussion, by analyzing two articles of fashionable dress worn by eighteenth-century English women—the hooped petticoat and a pair of stays. These two garments speak for the female body as both chaste and sexual, and Richardson uses them to indicate sexual threat, as whenever Clarissa is sexually threatened, her stays are loosened or cut, and, after her horrible rape, her hooped petticoat is discarded. Chapter 7 discusses Clarissa's clothing, five outfits of which are described in the course of the novel; each outfit is examined in regard to what it says about Clarissa in general, to what it reveals about each particular stage of her travails, and to what it discloses about the governance of her own body. Chapter 8 treats the disguises of Lovelace and his confederates as artful expressions designed to conceal their inner baseness; as will be demonstrated, their dress is closely linked to the topsy-turvy world of carnival and masquerade, which, in turn, reveals that the occupants of Harlowe Place indulge in a form of masquerade as well.

6

Virtuous Stays and Sexual Hoops: The Social Self

In the 1740s in England, the decade in which *Clarissa* was written, fashionable attire for both sexes was at an extreme: The female figure was flattened and compressed above the waist, yet with ruches, ruffles, and ribbons adding some bulk to the flattened surface. From the waist, all the way to the ground, the female silhouette billowed out to an enormous width. Peeping out from beneath the massive umbrella-like skirt, tiny feet could be glimpsed, encased in exquisitely decorated slippers of brocade or kid, with high heels and pointed toes. Masculine attire mimicked the general outline of feminine fashion. From neckline to waist, the male figure was also flattened, yet be-ruffled and be-ruched with fine laces and linens. Over form-fitting knee breeches, a long buttoned waistcoat was worn, which fell to mid-thigh. A coat, cut relatively close to the upper body, flared below the waist, reaching its greatest width at the hemline, just below the knee. The legs were tightly encased in stockings; the feet, in buckled leather shoes.

Despite the rough similarities of form in masculine and feminine attire—a smooth, flattened upper torso; a flaring silhouette from waist to hemline; and small neat legs and feet—a significant difference can be seen: Masculine attire smoothly and gently flows in one continuous line from shoulder to below the knee; the rough outline of the male body is always evident. In contrast, the lines of feminine dress radically separate and sever the upper part of the body from the lower, minimizing the female form above the waist, and greatly exaggerating it below; the natural shape of the female body is largely concealed. The two garments responsible for making feminine attire substantially different from masculine attire of the time are a pair of stays and a hooped petticoat. These two garments convey certain messages, albeit often contradictory messages, about issues of class, age, virtue, sexuality, and gender in eighteenth-century English society.

A pair of stays was a tightly laced bodice, which fit snugly around the torso, over the shoulder blades and under the armpits, covering the lower half of the bosom, and extending below the waistline in a v-shape. The foundation of this garment was made of stiff, coarse fabric, such as heavy linen or canvas, stiffened with glue or paste. Into this foundation, running from top to bottom, closely stitched rows were sewn, into which busks—ribs of cane, steel, or whalebone—were inserted. A pair of stays laced either in front or back, the design determined by the rest of the outfit: Front-lacing stays were used in conjunction with a stomacher, a decorated piece of fabric, which was either inserted behind the laces and in front of the stays, or which entirely covered the stays; because front-lacing stays, with the exception of the laces, were not visible, they were generally covered in serviceable fabrics, such as cottons or linens, with the stitching between busks readily visible. Back-lacing stays, an integral part of the total ensemble, were normally covered in richer fabrics, such as silks, satins, and brocades that matched the gown and petticoat and were often exquisitely embroidered; however, back-lacing stays required that the wearer seek assistance when dressing.[1] William Hogarth, in *The Analysis of Beauty*, rhapsodized about the formal beauty of a pair of stays and the perfection of the waving line produced by a pair of whale-boned reinforced stays: "for the whole stay, when put close together behind, is truly a shell of well-varied contents, and its surface of course a fine form; so that if a line, or the lace were to be drawn, or brought from the top of the lacing of the stay behind, round the body, and down to the bottom peak of the stomacher, it would form such a perfect, precise, serpentine-line."[2] A well-made pair of stays boasted beauty of line, rich fabrics, elegant embellishments, and fine stitching.

The hooped petticoat was worn over a white shift or chemise and an underpetticoat, a narrow, tubular garment, which tied around the waist with cloth ribbons or tapes, reaching to the calf. The hooped petticoat was also tied around the waist with ribbons or tapes. Three to six hoops of metal, wood, cane, or whalebone, "increasing in circumference from the waist downwards,"[3] were either sewn into a petticoat of stiff, coarse material, perhaps of linen, canvas, or horsehair, or suspended on tapes. The widest of the hoops fell somewhere around mid-thigh to knee. In the 1740s and 1750s, the hooped petticoat was bell-shaped, wide at the sides and flat in front and back; it was also at its widest circumference, between six to eleven feet for formal occasions.[4]

Both a pair of stays and the hooped petticoat are obviously garments that had little to do with comfort or ease, nor were they terribly practical garments. However, they were potent signifiers. At a very basic level, they were indicators of social position. Although English women of all social classes wore stays, those made for working women were usually fashioned from softer materials, such as leather, and were frequently half-boned or lacking busks, allowing the women to move about and to bend more freely.[5] In contrast, stays for women from the middle to upper stations, with their stiff coarse fabric, full-length busks, and extended v-shaped bodice, "impeded women from bending too far forward, and made crossing the legs, except at the ankles, slightly uncomfortable."[6]

Hooped petticoats were also impracticable for working women to wear, again precluding easy movement. Women of the middle to upper stations were the primary wearers of the hooped petticoat; as such, the hooped petticoat becomes indicative of class.[7] The size of hoops also had meaning: The more formal the occasion, the larger the hoop. Of course, those highest up the social scale attended the most formal events. It is surely no coincidence that the largest hoops were worn for Court wear, where the upper-most members of English society displayed themselves in all their finery. Countrywomen generally wore smaller hoops than city dwellers. Those on long journeys wore smaller hoops than otherwise. At home, in the intimacy of family, small to medium hoops were worn, or no hoops at all. Thus, a hooped petticoat made those from the middle to upper stations readily identifiable from their lower-class sisters, and the size of the hoop further ranked individuals along the social scale.

A pair of stays and a hooped petticoat were also potent signifiers of virtue and sexuality, the stays signifying the virtue of the woman and the hooped petticoat, her sexuality.[8] Significantly, although their stays were equally stiff and as tightly laced, older women appear to have worn smaller hoops than younger, unmarried women. When Anna Howe's hoop keeps Mr. Hickman at bay, Mrs. Howe urges him to "sit down by *me*: I have no such *forbidding* folly in my dress" (2:168), suggesting that her hoop is considerably smaller than her daughter's, or, perhaps, that she is not wearing one at all. As a widow and an older woman, Mrs. Howe can avoid the "folly" of current fashion. She also does not need to be as "forbidding" in her attire as her young daughter, nor does her sexuality need advertising, as her status as a widow already proclaims it.

For a young, unmarried woman, stays and hoops proclaimed that she was a chaste, yet sexual being. To succeed in the eighteenth-century marriage market, a young girl's virtue and sexuality needed to be advertised. Of course, she could not speak outright of her chastity nor of her potential to prove a companionable and procreative wife; instead, these messages had to be articulated in an alternate fashion—through her conduct, through her body, and through her dress.

All women, regardless of age, were urged to put on a pair of stays prior to leaving their chamber, unless pregnant or severely ill. The Reverend Wetenhall Wilkes, in *A Letter of Genteel and Moral Advice to a Young Lady* (1740), intones:

> Never appear in Company, without your Stays. Make it your general Rule, to lace in the Morning, before you leave your Chamber. The Neglect of this, is liable to the Censure of Indolence, Supineness of Thought, Sluttishness—and very often worse.
>
> *The Negligence of loose Attire*
> *May oft' invite to loose Desire.*[9]

English women, more so than their Continental sisters, prided themselves on their tight lacing.[10] To be "straight-laced" was to rigidly uphold virtue. (The very nature of the garment rendered its wearer somewhat impervious to touch, and anyone inclined to touch would no doubt be put off by this busk-stiffened armor.)

Within Richardson's novel, the association of stays with virtue is supported. At Mrs. Sinclair's deathbed, Belford is disgusted to find seven of the prostitutes "All in shocking dishabille, and without stays" (8:51). Clarissa, in contrast, never leaves her room without her stays, much to Lovelace's dismay:

> could I but have gained access to her in her hours of heedlessness and dishabille [For full dress creates dignity, augments consciousness, and compels distance]; we had been familiarized to each other long ago. But keep her up ever so late; meet her ever so early; by breakfast-time she is dressed for the day; at her *earliest hour*, as nice as others dressed. All her forms thus kept up, wonder not that I have made so little progress in the proposed trial.
>
> (4:145)

While a tightly laced pair of stays was synonymous with virtue, the hooped petticoat appears to have been directly associated with female sexuality, possibly functioning as an emblem of sexuality for those who were unable to display their sexuality outright—women of the middle to upper station, particularly young, virginal females of those classes. The hooped petticoat simultaneously concealed, occasionally revealed, and always encircled, enclosed, and exaggerated (an "o" within a considerably larger "o") the female sexual organs. As such, it was regarded with mixed emotions by eighteenth-century English men.

On the one hand, the hooped petticoat appeared to allow greater access to the female sexual organs, something which men either delighted in or found profoundly threatening. According to Elizabeth Ewing, the hooped petticoat was "liable to be blown about (and even turned inside out) by the wind or sudden movement or an unwary step. The provocative effect of the exposed ankle or leg was made much of and the plight of the lady whose hooped skirt was swept upwards was the theme of gaily ribald jests among the men of the time."[11] The September 24, 1712, edition of the *Spectator* reported a popular new recreation among young ladies and gentlemen—the age-old game of swing with a new twist:

> They [the young ladies] get on Ropes, as you must have seen the Children, and are swung up by their Male Visitants. The Jest is, that Mr. Such-a-one can name the Colour of Mrs. Such-a-one's Stockings; and she tells him, he is a lying Thief, so he is, and full of Roguery; and she'll lay a Wager, and her Sister shall tell the Truth if he says right, that he can't tell what Colour her Garters are of. In this Diversion there are very many pretty Shreaks, not so much for fear of falling, as that their Petticoats should unty: For there is great Care to avoid Improprieties; and the Lover who swings the Lady, is to tye her Cloaths very close together with his Hatband before she admits him to throw up her Heels.[12]

Of course, if her "Petticoats should unty," the hoop would billow out and provide an unhampered view of the young girl's underpetticoat or worse. To put it quite bluntly, as A. D. Harvey does, "it was easier even than today to get unimpeded access to a woman's pudenda. Stockings were secured by coloured garters above the knee, but otherwise nothing at all was worn beneath the shift."[13]

Yet the hooped petticoat's blatant association with sexuality often rendered it a source of great uneasiness to eighteenth-century English men, as Erin Mackie, in *Market à la Mode*, argues: By wearing a hooped petticoat, "women get some control over their sexuality not simply because ... it guarantees successful seduction but also because the hoop can serve as a shield to hide illicit pregnancy."[14] Kimberly Chrisman notes, "the hoop became a symbol of female sexual autonomy and artifice, or, alternately, of male anxiety about those threats."[15] The hooped petticoat was also associated with women as public, rather than private, domestic beings: "The hoop, the patch, the party-colored caps are tokens that buy women access to public discourse and social territory out of the bounds of the legitimately feminine."[16]

Yet, at the same time, the hooped petticoat was paradoxically seen as protecting female sexuality against male assault. As early as 1711—when hoops were relatively small—the *Spectator* lodged the following complaint:

> The hooped petticoat is made use of to keep us at a distance. It is most certain that a Woman's Honour cannot be better entrenched than after this manner, in Circle within Circle, amidst such a Variety of Outworks and Lines of Circumvallation. A Female who is thus invested in Whale-Bone is sufficiently secured against the Approaches of an Ill-Bred Fellow.[17]

In Richardson's novel, Anna Howe uses her hoop to keep Mr. Hickman an appropriate distance away. She says, "I desire my hoop may have its full circumference. All they're good for, that I know, is to clean dirty shoes, and to keep fellows at a distance" (2:168). Clarissa herself feels violated when the loathsome Solmes intrudes on her hoop space: "He took the removed chair, and drew it so near mine, squatting in it with his ugly weight, that he pressed upon my hoop.—I was so offended" (1:93). In either respect, whether as an instrument allowing easy access or as an instrument of deterrent, the hoop was associated with female sexuality.

Finally, both a pair of stays and the hooped petticoat speak of gender issues. Despite the real discomfort of both garments, it appears that many women *chose* to wear them. In 1731, the male editor of the *Weekly Register* noted, "The Stay is a part of modern dress that I have an invincible aversion to, as giving a stiffness to the whole frame, which is void of all grace, and an enemy of beauty; but, as I would not offend the ladies by absolutely condemning what they are fond of I will recall my censure."[18] While a pair of stays undoubtedly made some women appear more attractive—an overweight body looked slimmer and sagging breasts looked firmer and higher—it would also seem that the garment satisfied some psychological need. As Anne Hollander comments, "generations of ordinary women in their long skirts and stiff bodices could feel supported and enabled by them, fully armed and well presented, attractive and considerable as women and as persons, their secrets intact."[19] She continues:

> Most corsetting simply gave a neat line to the figure, and supported the correct fit of the bodice and the right hang of the skirt rather than primarily imposing an unbearable grip around the body. The grip was firm, rather; and since it produced both elegance and countenance, it was often more reassuring than troublesome, in the days before muscle-training was fashionable. By suggesting a certain self-respect,

it had a protective character. In the erotic mode, it provided a dynamic difference between the sleek dressed figure and the soft nude body.[20]

Similar motives might explain eighteenth-century women's infatuation with the hooped petticoat. Kimberly Chrisman comments, "While the hoop petticoat's portrayal as an obstacle to sex and a passport to promiscuity may seem contradictory, these criticisms are firmly rooted in a single, revolutionary principle: female sexual autonomy. The wearer alone determined whether the hoop acted as a barrier or an invitation."[21] In addition, Susan B. Kaiser, in *The Social Psychology of Clothing*, states that "studies indicate that males occupy more space in terms of bodily position as compared to females. Males are more likely to spread their legs apart or fold their arms behind their heads."[22] Yet, in eighteenth-century England, women of the upper to middle stations, wearing their hooped petticoats, took up the largest amount of space by far. Erin Mackie observes that the hooped petticoat "takes up a lot of space, public as well as domestic. It demands accommodation. ... To make way for the hoop, wider staircases were put in houses; coaches were redesigned so that hooped ladies might ride in them."[23] It is during the eighteenth century that women were bombarded with texts urging their confinement to the domestic sphere, and the hooped petticoat, as a garment that requires a huge consumption of space, as an article of public dress, as an article of female sexuality, resisted easy incorporation into the domestic sphere. Significantly, it was those women who were the primary targets of the campaign for female domesticity—women from the middle to upper stations—who were the primary wearers of the hooped petticoat. As women were increasingly urged to confine themselves to home and hearth, the hooped petticoat stood as a garment of resistance. As Henry Fielding astutely noted, "Of all the Articles of Distinction the Hoop hath stood the longest, and with the most obstinate Resistance. Instead of giving Way, this the more it hath been pushed, hath encreased the more."[24]

If a pair of stays speaks of feminine virtue, command, and self-respect, and, if a hooped petticoat tells of female sexuality and feminine resistance, it is surely significant that Clarissa Harlowe, one of the most fully formed fictional representations of the new domestic feminine ideal, loosens her stays after her rape and discards the wearing of a hooped petticoat after her final escape from Mrs. Sinclair's brothel. As will be shown in the next chapter, Clarissa's provides a rich fabric record of the events in the final year of her life.

7
"Of Her Own Invention": Revealing the Self

Dress functions not only as societal expression, but as personal expression. Clarissa, in particular, is noted for her unique style of dress. When Clarissa attempts to attend church in London, Lovelace fears she will be discovered, as she is "Known by her cloaths!" (3:317). Yet Clarissa's clothing is also seen as a natural extension of who and what she is. Her mother writes to Mrs. Norton of her younger daughter's "elegance in dress; for which she was so much admired, that the neighboring Ladies used to say, that they need not fetch fashions from London; since whatever Miss Clarissa Harlowe wore, was the *best* fashion, because her choice of *natural* beauties set those of *Art* far behind them" (4:73–4). Lovelace himself expounds at length on the naturalness of Clarissa's dress, when he tells Mrs. Smith of Clarissa's fashion sense:

> That she gave the fashion to the fashionable, without seeming herself to intend it, or to know she did: That, however, it was pleasant to see Ladies imitate her in dress and behaviour, who, being unable to come up to her in grace and ease, exposed but their own affectation and aukwardness, at the time that they thought themselves secure of a general approbation, because they wore the same things, and put them on in the same manner, that *she* did, who had everybody's admiration; little considering, that were *her* person like *theirs,* or if she had had *their* defects, she would have brought up a very different fashion; for that *Nature* was her guide in every-thing, and *Ease* her study; which, joined with a mingled dignity and condescension in her air and manner, whether she received or paid a compliment, distinguished her above all her Sex.
>
> (7:95)

Dress, then, as the natural expression of the wearer, must be easy and unstudied; it must complement the face and figure of the wearer; and it must be unique to the wearer, as it is supposed to reflect the wearer's unique self. It is not just the clothing, or how it is worn, but how the clothing itself exists as a harmonious extension of the wearer, how it *speaks* for and about the wearer.

Edward Young, in *Conjectures on Original Composition* (1759), notes that nature "brings us into the world all *Originals*: No two faces, no two minds, are just alike; but all bear Nature's evident mark of Separation on them. Born *Originals*, how comes it to pass that we die *Copies*? That meddling Ape Imitation, as soon as we come to years of *Indiscretion* (so let me speak), snatches the Pen, and blots out nature's mark of Separation, cancels her kind intention, destroys all mental Individuality."[1] Most unusually, Clarissa seems to have retained her unique nature and originality in a world filled with imitation, and this is expressed through her dress.

Throughout the course of the novel, Richardson describes, in varying degrees of detail, four suits of clothing owned by Clarissa. Three of the suits are worn by the heroine for weeks on end without change, evidence of their symbolic nature; one is never worn at all. While each outfit is a testament to "her elegance in dress" (4:73), all differ widely in color, style, and ornamentation, providing a fabric record of the significant changes in this final year of Clarissa's young life. In addition, in one scene, Richardson describes Clarissa in *dishabille*, foreshadowing the rape that will take place a mere five days later. The fabrics, colors, and ornamentation of her gowns and petticoats; her hoops and her stays— all reveal her transformation from the most beloved daughter of an extremely wealthy family, one whose youth, virtue, and innocent sexuality combine to make her the glory of her family and a prize on the marriage market, to tragic young girl, one who has physically lost her virtue and who has subsequently rejected her role as a sexual being. In addition, as a fabric record of Clarissa's young life, dress also articulates the way in which ownership of her body is claimed and contested.

Clarissa describes the first outfit as a "gown and petticoat of flowered silver of my own work; which having been made up but a few days before I was confined to my chamber, I never wore" (8:102). This outfit is first mentioned during her confinement at Harlowe Place; again, while she is residing at the Smith's; and, last, in her final will and testament. Mrs. Harlowe makes the first reference to the dress, when she relates the negotiations with Solmes to Clarissa: "Your Father intends you six Suits (three of them dressed Suits) at his own expence. You have an entire new Suit. ... As the new Suit is rich, if you chuse to make That one of the six, your Father will present you with an hundred guineas in lieu" (1:281). This first mention of the gown proclaims this outfit as part of a financial exchange between the Harlowes (in the form of Clarissa's gown and her person) and Solmes (in the form of his marriage offer). The gown is viewed in monetary terms, its worth assessed at "an hundred guineas," suggesting that the body enclosed within the gown is viewed in similar monetary terms.

Clarissa herself mentions the gown next, when, in order to alleviate her family's suspicions of elopement, she makes the impudent Betty Barnes perform a periodic inventory of her clothing: "but to employ the wench now-and then in taking out my cloaths, suit by suit, on pretence of preventing their being rumpled or creased, and to see that the flowered silver suit did not tarnish" (2:148). Again, the gown becomes a proxy for Clarissa herself—if the gown is physically present, then Clarissa must be as well, and, indeed, when she elopes with Lovelace, the gown is sent after her, signifying the Harlowes' disowning of their daughter. Later, when lodging with the Smiths and the Widow Lovick, after her escape from Lovelace, Clarissa attempts to sell this same suit and one other: "she had requested them to find her a purchaser for two rich dressed Suits; one never worn, the other not above once or twice" (6:306). Belford's efforts to purchase surreptitiously "the richest" of the suits, presumably the flowered silver suit, backfires when Clarissa mistrusts that he is the "advancer of the money; and would not let the cloaths go" (6:326–7); however, she later is able to sell the second suit of clothes to a gentlewoman "for half their worth" (6:395). The attempt to sell the gown may be seen as a way to regain ownership of her body, as the monetary transaction accrues directly to her, not to others, or it may acknowledge the Harlowes' complete renunciation of their younger daughter. Either way, Belford's attempt to purchase it merely signals a continued lack of personal agency and control over her own body, by Clarissa, which must, in turn, be thwarted by her. Ultimately, Clarissa's costly silver outfit is willed to her "kind and much-valued Cousin Miss Dolly Hervey" (8:102).[2]

Little description is given of this suit of clothing, other than its material ("flowered silver"), its value (100 guineas), and the fact that Clarissa has somehow "worked" it, no doubt with embroidery. The relative lack of detailed description in regard to this particular outfit most probably stems from the fact that this suit is more a reflection of the Harlowes than of Clarissa herself. However, it does say a great deal about her position within this family, and, despite the poverty of description, sufficient information is given to recreate the outfit in more precise detail. According to Anne Buck, in *Dress in Eighteenth-Century England*, this dressed suit, worth approximately £100, was "the range of dress worn by the nobility."[3] Silver cloth and gold cloth were exceedingly expensive, as finely spun strands of silver and gold were woven into the fabric; silver cloth—as Clarissa notes—really could tarnish. Because of the great expense, these rich fabrics were worn most often by royalty and nobility, most notably for Court wear or as wedding attire.[4]

The costly nature of the fabric establishes that Clarissa's outfit is full dress, to be worn at balls and assemblies. By the 1740s, the *sacque* or sack-back gown had replaced the mantua as the most popular gown for formal dress occasions, except for Court dress, where the mantua still reigned supreme. The *sacque* was an open-robed gown, the most popular style of gown for formal and informal wear for middle- to upper-class women at mid-century. For formal wear, the *sacque* opened from bodice to floor, revealing an elaborately embroidered stomacher—a triangular piece of stiffened fabric which covered the stays—and a matching or complementary-colored underskirt, known as the "coat" or petticoat, worn over large hoops from six to eleven feet in width.[5] The *sacque* had loose and flowing lines, with double box pleats of fabric gracefully falling from the shoulders down the back. Robings, sewn-down revers, edged the opening of the gown from the bodice to the waist. The gown, stomacher, and petticoat would be richly trimmed with silk and lace and ribbons. The *sacque* had elbow-length sleeves, from which snowy white linen, elaborately embroidered and trimmed with fine laces, would have appeared.[6]

The fact that Clarissa refers to the fabric as "flowered silver"—rather than silver flowers on a white ground or colored flowers on a silver ground, the most common way of referring to flowered silk—suggests that both ground and flowers are of silver. Floral designs could be woven into the fabric, painted on top of the fabric, or embroidered onto the fabric. As the outfit is a "suit," her gown and petticoat would have been made "of the same or complementary fabric."[7] Because Clarissa remarks that the flowered silk is "of her own working," and, as she is noted for her great skill in needlework, the outfit has undoubtedly been embroidered by Clarissa herself, a not unusual accomplishment for a woman of gentle birth. At a minimum, the stomacher and cuffs would be embroidered; however, as the fabric itself is termed "flowered silk," it would appear that the entire length of fabric itself has been embroidered rather than simply elements of the gown, the petticoat, or the stomacher. The leisure available to Clarissa for such a painstaking and time-consuming task demonstrates her social station and familial wealth; the embroidering of her own suit also provides evidence of her patience and her domestic abilities, as well as allowing her to invest the outfit with her own distinctive style and to establish some sort of ownership, over her dress and her body.

Despite the great wealth of the Harlowes, this suit is an extraordinarily expensive one for a young middle-class girl living in relative seclusion in the country. This rich outfit attests to her family's wealth and desire for upward mobility; it would be suitable for attending balls and assemblies, for meeting members of the aristocracy, and for attracting suitors of the highest rank.

All those who view this outfit, other than Clarissa herself, see it as material evidence of her family's wealth and social standing. For her mother and father, the dress has been reduced to its cost, something to barter and to bargain with in their negotiations with Solmes. For the Smiths and the Widow Lovick, the silver-flowered suit makes them revise their opinion of Clarissa's social station: "And the richness of her apparel having given them a still higher notion of her rank than they had before, they supposed she must be of quality" (6:307). Yet, for Clarissa, the outfit exists both as a symbol of her original standing within her family—the most beloved and precious of the Harlowe children—as well as material evidence that the family's favor has been lost and that she is no longer beloved, particularly by her father. As she mournfully states, *"My Father loved to see me fine"* (6:268). When she considers selling this or any other article of dress, she repeatedly returns to the fact that "her Sister, and other relations, were above wearing them: That her Mother would not endure in her sight any-thing that was hers" (6:306) and that "None of my friends will wear any-thing of mine" (7:207). The suit functions as a symbol of the life that Clarissa was intended to have—one of wealth, privilege, love, and special care—and that she has lost. Her virtue, her sexuality, her special charms, and the wealth of her family should have entitled her to a courtship with and a marriage to one worthy of her both in fortune and virtue. Nonetheless, there is something cold about the outfit, not only in its color, its metallic shine, and its formal nature, but its clear associations with money and property transactions. It is clothing that expresses the Harlowe's ambitions, as well as asserts their ownership over Clarissa's body. Ultimately, the silvery ensemble is willed to young Dolly Hervey, the closest of the Harlowes to Clarissa in sensibility and spirit, and, indeed, the only Harlowe who unconditionally loves Clarissa; however, based upon the ambiguous nature of the outfit, it is uncertain what possession of this outfit portends for young Dolly.

The next outfit is the one in which Clarissa elopes, albeit reluctantly, and it is described by Lovelace in exquisite detail:

> Her head-dress was a Brussels-lace mob, peculiarly adapted to the charming air and turn of her features. A sky-blue ribband illustrated that. But altho' the weather was somewhat sharp, she had not on either hat or hood ...
>
> Her morning-gown was a pale primrose-coloured paduasoy: The cuffs and robings curiously embroidered by the fingers of this ever-charming Arachne, in a running pattern of violets and their leaves; the light in the flowers silver; gold in the leaves. A pair of diamond snaps in her ears. A white handkerchief wrought by the same inimitable fingers, concealed—Oh Belford! what still more inimitable beauties did it not conceal!—And I saw, all the way we rode, the bounding heart (by its throbbing motions I saw it!) dancing beneath the charming umbrage.
>
> Her ruffles were the same as her mob. Her apron a flowered lawn. Her coat white satten, quilted: Blue satten her shoes, braided with the same colour, without lace; for what need has the prettiest foot in the world of ornament? Neat buckles in them: And on her charming arms a pair of black velvet glove-like muffs, of her own invention; for she makes and gives fashions as she pleases.—Her hands velvet of themselves, thus uncovered the freer to be grasped by those of her adorer.
>
> (3:28)

The outfit described is a morning gown, and from its description, most probably a version of the nightgown, a closely fitted open-robed gown, worn widely for informal wear, its edges bordered with robings, revealing stomacher and petticoat.[8] As informal attire, it would be worn with small to medium hoops and a silk or satin petticoat, or with small or no hoops and a thick quilted petticoat.[9]

Clarissa's gown is primrose-colored paduasoy, a rich heavy silk fabric; her petticoat is of white quilted satin. According to *The Female Spectator* (1744–6), the yellow color of Clarissa's gown is the "colour so much the mode in England at present."[10] In addition, pale pastel colors were normally worn only by young ladies, rather than older matrons.[11] Over the white petticoat, an apron of sheer "flowered lawn" is worn, which further distinguishes it as informal, domestic attire, though the apron is largely decorative in nature. Around her neck and shoulders Clarissa wears a handkerchief, presumably white, and fashioned by her as wearer, as was typically the case. On her head, Clarissa wears a mobcap, a style of cap worn indoors and for undress; hers is a confection of white lace and blue ribbon. Her slippers are relatively thin, made of blue satin, rather than leather. The pale yellow gown, the sky-blue ribbon in her cap, the blue-violet of the embroidered flowers, the blue shoes—all affirm her sense of style and her attention to detail.

Figure 7.1 shows Francis Hayman's painting of the abduction scene, though, in Hayman's panting, Clarissa's dress has been somewhat changed: Instead of a nightgown, she wears a *sacque*, her petticoat is embroidered, not just her robings, and her robings extend to the hem of the gown, rather than to the waist. In addition, she lacks her apron and her black velvet glove-like muffs; her mobcap is barely visible, topped with a red, not blue, ribbon; her shoes are ivory satin, rather than blue. Yet, despite the inaccuracies in dress, Hayman's painting

Figure 7.1   Robert Lovelace preparing to abduct Clarissa Harlowe, from "Clarissa" by Samuel Richardson (1689–1761) by Francis Hayman (1708–76). By permission of Southampton City Art Gallery, Hampshire, UK/The Bridgeman Art Library

nonetheless invokes the spirit of Clarissa's dress, in its pale primrose color, embroidered violets, and its overall air of delicacy.

Clarissa's outfit, though lovely, assures the reader that Clarissa had little intention of eloping with Lovelace. The gown is the wrong style for traveling—a riding habit, or a loosely fitting, informal version of the *sacque* would have been an appropriate traveling wear in the 1740s[12]— and the wrong color and fabric, as pale yellow silk easily stains and soils. Her slippers are too thin. She has neither cloak nor hood nor hat. As Lovelace mentions to Belford, it is "unsuitable dress upon the road" (3:50), and Clarissa later bemoans the fact that "I have no cloaths fit to go any-whither, or to be seen by any-body" (3:146). Yet the outfit is also suggestive of youth and demure sexuality. Its bright Spring-like color is fashionable and youthful, its embroidered flowers and flower-like color indicating Clarissa's own blooming youth. Lovelace's mention of "this ever charming Arachne" embroidering these violet flowers, suggests that Clarissa weaves a web of attraction, snaring the unsuspecting male with her skill and charms. Not coincidentally, the elopement scene occurs in the Harlowe's garden and just outside the garden gate, in Spring. Clarissa's outfit intimates that she is the most attractive element in the garden. All in all, this outfit pleads both Clarissa's innocence in eloping as well as her Spring-like, flower-like allure.

Two aspects of Clarissa's outfit appear somewhat unique in terms of English dress in the 1740s: the "curiously embroidered cuffs and robings" of the gown, and the "black velvet glove-like muffs of her own invention." The robings of her gown are richly embroidered by Clarissa herself with silvered blue violets and golden-tinted leaves. However, robings were rarely embroidered prior to 1750, except for Court dress[13]—the countrified Clarissa appears to be at the vanguard of this fashion movement.

But, by far the most curious aspect of Clarissa's outfit is the "black velvet glove-like muffs of her own invention." Gloves were worn to keep the arms and hands white as well as warm. Muffs provided warmth, both indoors and out, and they also existed as a fashion statement, a fashion accessory. Muffs were designed in cloth, feathers, or fur, dependent both upon the current season and the current fashion.[14] From paintings of the period, it appears that a single, larger muff was worn with a pair of gloves. Smaller muffs or "muffettees" came in pairs and apparently in two varieties: One version, made of black silk or velvet, covered only the wrists, providing warmth and protecting the ruffled sleeves of the wearer's linen. The other version was like "large closed mittens just covering the hand, with a separate compartment for the thumb."[15] However, Clarissa's invention appears to be a version of fashionable mittens: "From the seventeenth century to the early decades of the nineteenth, women wore plain and decorated, elbow-length mittens of kid or fabric. These left the ends of the thumbs free and did not enclose the fingers; they were, however, usually cut with peaked flaps over the knuckles."[16] Her creation must have looked similar to the above-the-elbow chamois mittens worn in Jean-Auguste-Dominique Ingres's *Mademoiselle Caroline Riviére* (1806), shown in Figure 7.2, though Clarissa's gloves are of black velvet, rather than chamois and most probably extend in length only to mid-forearm, rather than above the elbow. These "glove-like muffs" would protect Clarissa's hands and arms from the sun, while allowing her hands freedom of movement—to pluck a flower, to feed her prized poultry, to write notes to Anna Howe while in the ivy summer-house. The black velvet would disguise any soiling from dirt, or from ink, while emphasizing the whiteness of her skin. Thus, it is both a sensible as well as a fashionable garment.

Richardson provides an extraordinary amount of detail about this outfit. This outfit, more than any other described in the course of the novel, is meant to reveal the real Clarissa, her innocence, both in eloping with Lovelace as well as her moral innocence, as well as her allure, her sense of style, her uniqueness, and more. The entire ensemble confirms that she had no intention of eloping, though Lovelace takes the unsuitability of her outfit as evidence that "she seems to have intended to shew me, that she was determined not to stand to her appointment. Oh Jack! that such a sweet girl should be a rogue!" (3:28). The outfit also emphasizes her youth, her beauty, her special charms. The "curiously" embroidered cuffs and robings of her gown demonstrate her skill with her needle, her domesticity, her wealth, as well as her creativity and unique fashion sense. Her black velvet muffs are both fashionable and highly sensible, like Clarissa herself. By providing such a detailed and complex account of Clarissa's quite lovely outfit, Richardson argues her inward complexity and her inner loveliness, the many pleasing facets of her personality; in addition, his detailed description suggests that such an unique and intricately fashioned outfit can never be anything but the natural expression of its wearer.

This outfit is perhaps the finest expression of Clarissa's own personality, of her mind and soul, and it is an outfit that asserts Clarissa's claim to her own body and person, though Lovelace, through his gleeful, gloating description of her dress and person seeks to assert his own claim. (A discussion of the implications of Lovelace as the source of information regarding Clarissa's dress and accoutrement may be found in the introduction

Figure 7.2 Jean-Auguste-Dominique Ingres, *Mademoiselle Caroline Riviére* (1793–1807). Musée du Louvre, Paris, France. Photo credit: Erich Lessing/Art Resource, NY

to Part III.) Although she wears this ensemble when imprisoned within Harlowe Place and within Sinclair's brothel, it nonetheless shows Clarissa's "signature" style in every element, with little or no indication that Clarissa's body, mind, or spirit have been compromised, and, to a great extent, they have not at this point, though she is admittedly under great duress. Clarissa wears this ensemble from the day of her forced elopement, April 11, until the remainder of her wardrobe arrives from Harlowe Place, on May 4, a period of slightly more than three weeks, during which time, however, she somehow manages to appear "to such advantage, as if I had a different suit every day" (3:147).

The next outfit of Clarissa's is no outfit at all, as Clarissa is described in *dishabille*. In the early morning hours of June 8, Lovelace has arranged for a small fire to be set in Sinclair's house in order to gain access to Clarissa when she is most vulnerable, that is when just awakened from sleep and wearing only her bedclothes. Lovelace, pretending to be urgently concerned for her safety, rushes to her chamber: "When I had *flown down* to her chamber-door, there I beheld the most charming creature in the world, supporting herself on the arm of the gasping Dorcas, sighing, trembling, and ready to faint, with nothing on but an under-petticoat, her lovely bosom half-open, and her feet just slipt into her shoes" (4:366). Although she begs permission "to hide herself from the light, and from every human eye" (4:368), Lovelace nonetheless continues to gaze upon her with avidity. He carefully notes:

—Her bared shoulders and arms, so inimitably fair and lovely: Her spread hands crossed over her charming neck; yet not half concealing its glossy beauties: the scanty coat, as she rose from me, giving the whole of her admirable shape, and fine-turn'd limbs: Her eyes running over, yet seeming to threaten future vengeance: And at last her lips uttering what every indignant look and glowing feature portended.

(4:368)

Clarissa, like many women in early to mid-eighteenth century, sleeps in her shift, not in a nightdress; she also sleeps in her underpetticoat, something that appears to have been more a matter of personal choice for women, rather than custom. On her head, with her hair tucked in, Clarissa wears the ubiquitous nightcap, standard nighttime garb for both men and women.

The shift or chemise was a loose gown made of linen, cambric, holland, or lawn, frequently decorated with embroidery. White in color, it fell just below the knee. It had a rounded or square neck, laced with a drawstring, and sleeves that extended below the elbows. Under daytime attire, the shift showed at the bodice or neck, as well as arms, and was visible to the public. As a shift differed from a sleeping nightgown only in length—the shift was slightly shorter—many women slept in their shifts, exchanging them in the morning for a new, clean shift, or, if clean enough, leaving it on.[17] Clarissa also sleeps in her underpetticoat, a narrow, tubular garment, tied around the waist with ribbons, and falling to the calves; wearing her underpetticoat to bed is indicative of her innate sense of modesty.

In this outfit, Clarissa's legs would be visible from the calves to her feet. Her breasts would be unconfined, no longer flattened by stays, nor hidden beneath a handkerchief, though "her charming tresses," falling free when "her night head-dress" (4:369) comes off in her struggles, soon provide her with some welcome concealment. Her waistline would be revealed, as well as her hips. In contrast to daytime attire, which concealed the female body beneath rigid stays and hoops, Clarissa's natural body shape and softness of skin would be shockingly apparent. In addition, Lovelace has dared to touch her, clasping her in his arms with "ardour" (4:366), lifting her onto the bed, and "incircling the almost disrobed body of the loveliest of her Sex" (4:367). Eighteenth-century English men and women were rarely completely nude and rarely saw others in a state of complete nudity, even if married.[18] (In the 1740s, bathing the body was a rarity and primarily done only for health reasons; sex could be and was performed with some clothing on, at the very least, a shift.) For Clarissa, then, being seen in her shift and under-petticoat is akin to being seen completely naked.

Richardson uses this scene to demonstrate two seemingly contradictory things: First, that Clarissa, *sans* outer dress, is as lovely and innocent as she appears on the surface, and, second, to suggest that ownership of Clarissa's body has been fully claimed by Lovelace. Some contemporary readers charged Richardson with "indecency" in writing this scene, yet Richardson responded to this claim, by saying that "the Passion I found strongest in me, whenever I supposed myself a Reader only, and the Story real, was *Anger*, or *Indignation*: I had too great an Aversion to the intended Violator of the Honour of a CLARISSA, to suffer any-thing but alternate Admiration and Pity of her, and Resentment against him, to take place in my Mind, on the Occasion."[19] However, the scene's titillating elements, if such they may be called, nonetheless show both Lovelace's violation of Clarissa's body, his gaze prying into the secrets of her body, and also the purity of this body, as external representation of the mind and soul. In this novel, *dishabille* reveals the true person (as confirmed by the later horrific vision of Mrs. Sinclair and her whores in *dishabille*). In addition, this scene not only foreshadows Clarissa's rape, but is a sort of rape itself, as Lovelace has seen and touched what no man, except Clarissa's husband, should ever have seen or touched.[20]

Most significantly, Clarissa is without her stays, the garment symbolic of virtue. She realizes Lovelace's intentions, and, rather than be raped, she is willing to stab herself with a pair of scissors: "she protested, that she would not survive what she called a treatment so disgraceful and villainous; and looking all widely round her, as if for some instrument of mischief, she espied a pair of sharp-pointed scissors on a chair by the bed-side, and endeavored to catch them up, with design to make her words good on the spot" (4:368). In this sole instance when Clarissa is without her stays, and whenever the laces of her stays have been cut and the garment loosened, the threat of some penetrating object is always evident. It is no wonder then that Clarissa feels the urgent need both to conceal herself from Lovelace's eyes and to escape from his presence. She later writes to Anna Howe, "He extorted from me a promise of forgiveness; and that I would see him next day, as if nothing had happened: But if it were possible to escape from a wretch, who, as I have too much reason to believe, formed a plot to fire the house, to frighten me, almost naked, into his arms, how could I see him next day?" (5:50).

Later that same day—June 8—Clarissa does effect her first escape from Lovelace, while wearing a "brown lustring night-gown" with a "quilted petticoat of carnation-coloured satten":

'She had on a brown lustring nightgown, fresh, and looking like new, as every-thing she wears does, whether new or not, from an elegance natural to her. A beaver hat, a black ribband about her neck, and blue knots on her breast. A quilted petticoat of carnation-coloured satten; a rose-diamond ring, supposed on her finger; and in her whole person and appearance, as I shall express it, a dignity, as well as beauty, that commands the repeated attention of everyone who sees her.'

The description of her person I shall take a little more pains about. My mind must be more at ease, before I can undertake that.

(5:27)

Lovelace describes this outfit, not because of its peculiar charms, but rather because Clarissa has fled from Sinclair's in it, and he must use a description of her person and clothing to recapture her. As she has escaped from Sinclair's with "no cloaths but those she had on!" (5:24), this is necessarily the same outfit in which she is returned to the brothel and raped.

This outfit is noticeably more somber and practical than the Spring-like outfit of her elopement, yet Richardson again provides a few intimate details, such as the black ribbon around her neck and the rose-diamond ring, in order to demonstrate the expressive nature of Clarissa's dress, despite the fact that this outfit is a deliberate attempt to remove the marks of her uniqueness. Like the gown of her elopement, this gown is also a nightgown, a tight-bodiced, fitted, open gown with a full skirt, appropriate for walking in or for informal, indoor wear, dependent upon fabric and ornamentation. No doubt, Clarissa wears this "practical" gown with small hoops under her silken petticoat. The fabric is lustring, "a summer season taffeta with a glossy sheen."[21] The gown lacks embroidery or any elaborate ornamentation, other than some simple blue knots of ribbon at the bodice. The style is plain; the color, serviceable. There is nothing particularly youthful about this gown; even the most somber matron could wear it with impunity. On a practical level, the dark brown color is less likely to attract the attention of others, though the style of gown is unsuitable for travel. Her accessories—the black beaver hat and the black ribbon around her neck—provide a fashionable, yet melancholic accompaniment to the dark brown gown. The carnation-colored petticoat covering the lower portion of her body is the only real spot of color, pink, in all its different hues, being the most popular color for eighteenth-century female attire.[22] However, in this instance, the carnation-color is somewhat ominous, the word carnation deriving from the Latin word for flesh. The *OED* defines "carnation" as "the colour of human 'flesh' or skin," "a light rosy pink, but sometimes ... a deeper crimson colour as in the carnation flower."[23] Whether the rosy pink color of flesh or the crimson color of blood, her carnation-colored petticoat ominously foreshadows her rape. Perhaps even more portentously, when the false Lady Betty and the false Miss Montague return her, four days after her escape, to Mrs. Sinclair's house, Clarissa becomes faint, and the two women insist, "You will faint, child—We must cut your Laces" (6:166). Her pair of stays, that garment synonymous with feminine virtue and self-respect, is loosened against her will. Shortly after, she is raped.

This ensemble is notable for what it is not: It lacks the direct and ostentatious displays associated with the Harlowes' desire for power; no ownership claim of theirs is connected with the clothes or the body housed within. The outfit lacks and, indeed, deliberately seeks to avoid any assertion of ownership by Lovelace; it covers the body he would claim and does claim, and, in its somberness and plainness, seeks to remove the body from him forever. The outfit also lacks the many distinctive elements that define Clarissa's normal attire, if we take the Spring-like outfit as indicative of who Clarissa had truly been, in the recent past. Yes, the black ribbon around the neck, the rose-diamond ring, and carnation-colored petticoat provide glimpses into her personality, but, overall, it is an outfit that attempts to subdue the most unique elements of dress and person. It is, above all, an outfit that seeks to avoid the claims that others have made over the ownership of her body, though this attempt fails.

Although Clarissa never again wears the outfit after her rape, she does effect her second escape by having someone else wear it. She promises the unwitting servant, Mabell, the gown for "Sunday wear," once it has been altered by a seamstress, and a quilted petticoat, presumably the carnation-colored one: "I will give you … a quilted coat, which will require but little alteration, if any; … But the gown I will give directions about, because the sleeves and the robings and the facings must be altered for your wear, being, I believe, above your station" (6:92). When Mabell is wearing "her *Lady's* clothes" (6:94) for alteration, Clarissa escapes by throwing Mabell's gown, petticoat, cloak, and hood over her own white gown. With a great sense of poetic justice and irony, Clarissa leaves her tainted garments behind at the scene of her rape; Mabell, too, fearing violence from Mrs. Sinclair, makes her escape, leaving Clarissa's gown and petticoat behind.

After her rape and until her death, Clarissa wears "a white damask night-gown"(5:321)—as everyone knows. Lovelace mentions her wearing it when she encounters him the first time after her rape. It is mentioned again, during her second escape, and it is mentioned, in passing, throughout the remainder of the novel. John Belford gives the most detailed description of the outfit, when he finds her at Rowland's on July 14:

> Her dress was white damask, exceeding neat; but her stays seemed not tight-laced. I was told afterwards, that her laces had been cut, when she fainted away at her entrance into this cursed place; and she had not been solicitous enough about her dress, to send for others …
>
> … the kneeling Lady, sunk with majesty too in her white flowing robes (for she had not on a hoop) spreading the dark, tho' not dirty, floor, and illuminating that horrid corner; her linen beyond imagination white, considering that she had not been undressed ever since she had been here.
>
> (6:274)

Again, this outfit is a nightgown, though possibly a closed robe version of it. It could be semi-formal or informal wear, and, according to Belford's observation, this particular gown was intended to be worn with a small- to moderate-sized hoop. The gown is white damask, a silk fabric with a raised pattern of flowers woven into the cloth.[24] As many scholars and critics have mentioned, the white gown is the garb worn by the heroines of stage tragedies. It also symbolizes her innocence and purity, as she has in no way contributed to her rape.

She is hoopless and her stays are loosened. Without a hoop, the gown would likely have trailed on the ground, yet there is no stain upon it. As she refuses to remove a single piece of clothing from her body while at Rowland's, she had apparently attended church services, whence she was picked up for confinement at Rowland's, without a hooped petticoat. In discarding the hoop, she has removed herself from the constraints of fashion, as well as denounced her sexuality and announced her ruin. Her laces have been cut from her fear of sexual assault. Conducted to Rowland's by *"Men* only" (6:250), Clarissa expects Lovelace and even perhaps other men to rape her there. The whores Polly Horton and Sally Martin warn Rowland and his wife to keep "out of her way any edged or pointed instrument; especially a penknife; which, pretending to mend a pen, they said, she might ask for" (6:269). Again, the cutting or loosening of the laces of her stays is always accompanied by the threat of some penetrating device.[25] Iconographically, her "virgin white" (7:412) gown proclaims her as the pure and innocent victim of tragedy; her loosened stays and cut laces speak of her loss of virtue and self-respect; her discarded hoops tell of her renunciation of, and her ruin through, her sexuality. In many ways, this white gown renounces all claims that have made upon her body, even her own, as does the starved body itself. Her white gown is a page wiped clean, a *tabula rasa* that attempts to erase experience.

The last suit of clothing that Clarissa will wear is her "burial-dress" (7:313), or, as she terms it, her "wedding garments." Clarissa writes:

> My wedding garments are bought—And tho' not fine or gawdy to the sight, tho' not adorned with jewels, and set off with gold and silver (for I have no beholders eyes to wish to glitter in); yet will they be the easiest, the *happiest* suit, that ever bridal maiden wore—for they are such as carry with them a security against all those anxieties, pains, and perturbations, which sometimes succeed to the most promising outsettings.
>
> (7:373)

It is significant that Clarissa's clothing becomes less elaborate, less costly, more plain the closer she gets to her death. Each successive outfit allows her to come closer to renouncing worldly possessions and cares. She is no longer the daughter of the wealthy Harlowes, begowned in flowered silver, nor is she the young lady who allured suitors with her flower-like attractions. She has literally cast off the dark gown and flesh-colored petticoat of her despair and her disgrace. She has dispensed with her hoops, symbol of her sexuality; her virtue no longer needs the outward mark of tightly laced stays. She has even exchanged the white garments of earthly hope and heavenly expectations for the nebulous garments of the grave.

Clarissa uses the language of dress to tell a story of seduction and rape that, despite the more than one million words in the novel, is often difficult to express in words. Her clothing, more so than her words, pleads her innocence in eloping with Lovelace. Later, her loosened stays and discarded hoops clearly express her lost virtue; they state the word "rape," a word which Clarissa herself never uses. After the richness and intricacy of her former outfits, which spoke clearly of and about her, Clarissa's plain white gown acts like a blank page, telling us not only of her innocence, but that she lacks words to describe the horror of the rape, that her story has essentially ended, that she will soon die.

8
"Where ... Art is Designed": Concealing the Self

Lovelace displays a curious and contradictory attitude towards dress: On the one hand, he purports to say that clothing is an outward display of the inner person, an assertion of which Clarissa is living proof. Yet, on the other hand, he appears not to believe this entirely, thinking that everyone, even Clarissa, conceals something beneath his or her outer garments. As an astute observer of dress, he delights in his power to cloak the inner corruption of individuals, including himself, under the attire of respectability—and, in his case, exquisite taste.

In his personal correspondence, Samuel Richardson writes, "The rake is, must be, generally, in dress a coxcomb"[1], yet he takes pains to assure that Lovelace's personal attire is not foppish. Anna Howe, furious at Lovelace's brazen public appearance after the rape of Clarissa, nonetheless takes a moment to admire his dress: "So little of the fop; yet so elegant and rich in his dress ... no mere toupet-man; but all manly" (6:416). Clarissa, as well, views Lovelace's dress in positive fashion: "But he is so graceful in his person and his dress, that he generally takes every eye" (4:67). It would seem that Lovelace, in his person and dress, provides the masculine counterpart to and complement of Clarissa. Like Clarissa, Lovelace possesses "so happy an ease" (1:279) in dress; his attire is elegant, rich, and seemingly natural.

Yet indications exist that something is slightly awry with Robert Lovelace's wardrobe. At one point, Clarissa notes that Lovelace is "too proud of" his dress (3:335). Another time, she writes, "one may see, that he values himself not a little, both on his person and his parts, and even upon his *dress*" (1:279). Pride in dress suggests the opposite of natural expression, as it betokens conscious superiority in relation to others, rather than a largely unconscious expression of self. One need only think of the cunningly disheveled curls or the starched, "carelessly" tied cravats of George Bryan Brummell to comprehend the art underlying this casual elegance of dress displayed by Lovelace. (Brummell's toilette reportedly took over two hours to complete.) The fact is that Lovelace's elegant attire is carefully studied, as he himself admits to Belford: "the gracefulness of dress, my debonair and my assurance?—Self-taught, self-acquired, these!" (1:199). Thus, on one level, Lovelace's dress is artful, in eighteenth-century parlance, because it something learned and studied, because it is not innate and natural.

In addition, Robert Lovelace, "so elegant and rich in his dress" (6:416), "so graceful in his person and his dress" (4:67), reveals little of himself through his clothing. The seamless perfection of his attire discloses no small eccentricity, no foible, no folly; this very perfection suggests that his dress is like the costumes he fashions for his confederates—attentive to the minutiae, yet lacking the mark of the personal. This lack of impersonality in dress suggests deceit of some sort, as it demonstrates an unwillingness to reveal the full self to others. The elegant and exquisite, yet superficial, nature of his dress argues more persuasively than words for the duplicity and falseness of rakes. When Lovelace mocks Belford's attire, Belford retorts, "As to *my* dress, and *thy* dress, I have only to say, That the sum total of thy observation is this: That *my* outside is the *worst* of me; and *thine* the *best* of thee" (6:391). A rake who does not dress like a fop or a coxcomb conceals his "thinking highly of himself, meanly of the sex"[2], and, thus, deceives his unwitting victims by his outward appearance.

The real masquerade begins, however, once Lovelace begins his elaborately contrived plot for stealing Clarissa's virtue. He makes his associates don costumes and personas, and he himself alternates in his own disguises, wearing either the attire of a gouty old man, or a metaphorical domino and mask. At Sinclair's brothel, Lovelace comments, "I must make all secure, before I pull off the mask. *Was not this my motive for bringing her hither?*" (4:128).

Perhaps because of his extensive study of dress, Lovelace understands that it is the details that make an outfit convincing. Lovelace proudly notes, "I never forget the *Minutiæ* in my contrivances. In all matters that admit of doubt, the *minutiæ* closely attended to, and provided for, are of more service than a thousand oaths, vows, and protestations made to supply the neglect of them" (3:185). Lovelace is aware how thoroughly, yet how unthinkingly, people rely on clothing to evaluate others. According to Susan B. Kaiser, "It is hard to imagine how clothing could be more relevant to everyday life, more concrete as an illustration of basic social processes, or more visual in terms of impact. Yet we are accustomed to thinking about clothes in a fairly routine and matter-of-fact, almost unconscious, way. Only when our attention is drawn to them do we actively realize that we analyze clothes."[3] Lovelace understands that, in order for dress to deceive convincingly, every article of clothing and all accoutrement must be perfectly consistent with the character portrayed; even a small item may alert the viewer that something is not quite right, and, thus, make he or she pay closer attention to aberrations in behavior, mannerisms, and speech.

Through his attention to the minutiae of dress, Lovelace makes fine ladies out of prurient whores; a retired army captain out of an unscrupulous rogue; and a gouty, crippled old man out of a youthful seducer and rake. Although Clarissa knows deep down that the looks, behavior, and actions of these individuals somehow belie their outer garments, their outward appearance is so convincing that she believes that they are who and what they say they are, against her better judgment. Adding to Clarissa's confusion is the fact that the disguises of Lovelace's confederates mimic the everyday attire and personas worn by the inhabitants of Harlowe Place.

Yet, despite Lovelace's convincing use of dress as disguise, Richardson refuses to allow Lovelace to beguile the reader in the same fashion, and so provides only superficial descriptions of the dress worn by Lovelace and his band of rogues and whores, thus, suggesting the superficial nature of dress as artful expression. Dress as artful expression conceals the mind and the soul. In contrast to Clarissa's silver-flowered suit, woven of real silver threads and hand-embroidered with silver flowers by Clarissa herself, dress as art is merely "tinsel dress," to borrow a phrase from another of Richardson's heroines, Harriet Byron.[4] It contrives to look like the real thing, and often does look it on the surface, but it is, in reality, either a cheap and tawdry imitation or a studied attempt to portray oneself as something that one is naturally not. In addition, because dress as costume seeks to conceal, rather than to reveal the nature of the wearer, it lacks those small details that make it expressive of the wearer. While dress as costume, as artful or deceitful expression, focuses on the minutiae of dress, in order to assure that each item of dress and accoutrement is consistent with the character portrayed, it lacks spontaneity and individuality, and that is how, so Richardson would teach us, one can tell the real from the artificial. Thus, some indications, however small, exist to indicate the false natures of those individuals whom Clarissa meets while at Sinclair's brothel.

Every reader of *Clarissa* is familiar with the disguises of Lovelace and his myriad confederates. Margaret Anne Doody states that "The sheer number of disguises used or alluded to throughout *Clarissa* is astonishing. Lovelace, himself, the master of metamorphosis, a perfect Proteus, seems the center of all disguising."[5] From the time Clarissa first enters Mrs. Sinclair's brothel until just hours before her rape, she is living in an elaborate masquerade world, albeit a *reverse* masquerade world, constructed by Lovelace to confound and confuse Clarissa. Terry Castle writes:

> the masquerade projected an anti-nature, a world upside-down, an intoxicating reversal of ordinary sexual, social, and metaphysical hierarchies. The cardinal ideological distinctions underlying eighteenth-century cultural life, including the fundamental divisions of sex and class, were broached. If, psychologically speaking, the masquerade was a meditation on self and other, in the larger sense it was a meditation on cultural classification and the organizing dialectical schema of eighteenth-century life. It served as a kind of exemplary disorder.[6]

Amidst members of the middle to upper ranks of society, dressed as dominos, Harlequins, goddesses, historical figures, and more, "Certain disreputable members of the lower orders—thieves, sharpers, and prostitutes—were thought ... to infiltrate ... in order to ply their trades under the cover of secrecy."[7] Castle also notes that "Much of the fear the masquerade generated throughout the century is related to the belief that it encouraged female sexual freedom, and beyond that, female emancipation generally."[8]

The world normally inhabited by Mrs. Sinclair and her associates, as well as by the other rogues and whores whom Lovelace uses in his deceptions, is one that is closely akin to carnival: It is a highly sexualized world, and it is one where the individuals routinely engage in activities deemed amoral, immoral, illegal, or even criminal by the rest of society. However, in his attempts to seduce Clarissa, Lovelace inverts the traditional masquerade world. Instead of dominos and exotic dress, everyday dress is assumed. Instead of female sexuality being loosed, it is now confined. When Clarissa first enters Mrs. Sinclair's residence *cum* place of business, all sexual activity at the brothel is abruptly put on hold, the business of selling female sexuality summarily preempted. Other disreputable activities are also abruptly halted; for instance, the forgery activities of Patrick McDonald are suspended while he plays the part of Captain Tomlinson. Of course, they are perpetrating a scam on Clarissa, yet this scam requires that they perform the parts of respectable citizens. It is still masquerade, as it is still a topsy-turvy world, yet it is a desexualized, seemingly moral, everyday world. Ironically, although Lovelace has set up this elaborate masquerade in order to seduce Clarissa mentally and emotionally, this desexualized world keeps Lovelace from seducing her physically. As Bakhtin writes, "While carnival lasts, there is no other life outside it,"[9] and each and every participant is forced to live his or her role, which, in this instance, requires the guise of unimpeachable respectability. It is only when the masks have been dropped, and the true faces revealed, that Lovelace and his vile associates can carry out the rape of Clarissa.

In London, and at Lovelace's instigation, Clarissa has taken rooms in what appears to be the respectable household of Mrs. Sinclair, a widow of "an officer in the guards" (3:179), and her two nieces by marriage, Sally Martin and Polly Horton. Mrs. Sinclair has obligingly provided Clarissa with a maidservant, named Dorcas Wykes, the pseudonym of one "Deb. Butler" (3:284). Yet the house is a brothel; Mrs. Sinclair, a madam; and the nieces and maidservant, prostitutes. Clarissa takes an instant disliking to them all, though she can find nothing wrong with their appearance, nor, technically speaking, with their manners and mode of behavior.

While no mention is made of the outer garments worn by the denizens of Mrs. Sinclair's house, in keeping with Richardson's desire to demonstrate that their dress is superficial and artificial, their costume appears in character for the widow of a retired army officer, her nieces, and her servants. Mrs. Sinclair is a fat woman with coarse features and "a *masculine air*" (3:179); nonetheless, "the appearance of every-thing about her, as well house as dress, carries the marks of such good circumstances, as require not abasement" (3:297). The clothing of Polly and Sally is seemingly so appropriate as not to garner any comment on the part of Clarissa or Lovelace. "Dorcas is a neat creature, both in person and dress" (3:285). (Of course, Richardson reveals the true nature of these women after Clarissa's death, at Mrs. Sinclair's own deathbed, where they are displayed in all their tawdriness and filth while in *dishabille*, in severe contrast to the earlier portrait of Clarissa in *dishabille*, in her clean white shift and underpetticoat.)

However, for dress to be effective as art, as disguise, it must also be accompanied by appropriate performance. Just as revelers at a masquerade must not only look their parts, but act their parts, so too must the women at Sinclair's brothel take on their assumed characters, though the nuances of these roles are often difficult to master. Dorcas must attempt a role similar to that of Clarissa's beloved Hannah, the part of trusted servant and confidant. However, when Dorcas tries to act modestly, something to which she is evidently unaccustomed, she

"*Over-did* it a little, perhaps!" (3:285); she also appears "too genteel indeed ... for a servant" (3:289). Mrs. Sinclair takes on the character of surrogate aunt and mother to Clarissa, yet her "respectfulness seems too much studied, ... for the London ease and freedom" (3:289); indeed, she treats Clarissa with greater respect "than should be from distance of years, as she was the wife of a gentleman" (3:297). Yet, with time, Mrs. Sinclair and Dorcas apparently improve their performances: Clarissa pronounces Mrs. Sinclair "*tolerable*" (3:326) and "*Dorcas* stands well in her Lady's graces" (4:140). While Mrs. Sinclair lacks the pedigree, graciousness, and elegant physical presence of Mrs. Harlowe or Aunt Hervey, she nonetheless becomes a parodic conflation of those two women, in her role as "mother" and in her willingness to force a young female (Clarissa), living under her protection, into an unwanted liaison with a male suitor. Similarly, Dorcas appears like the loyal, trustworthy Hannah, but is, in reality, closer to the grasping Betty Barnes.

Once ensconced in the brothel, Clarissa finds herself uneasy in the company of Polly Horton and Sally Martin—"But with those two Nieces of the Widow I never can be intimate—I don't know why" (3:300)—yet they seem quite successful in their assumed roles, as masquerade versions of Dolly Hervey and Arabella Harlowe respectively. Polly, like Dolly, appears sweet-tempered and a sincere admirer of Clarissa. Clarissa writes to Anna that "Miss Horton ... seems to have taken a great liking to me, and to be of a gentler temper and manners, than Miss Martin" (3:311–2). At Rowland's, Sally later taunts Clarissa, "Miss Horton is below: She was once your favourite" (6:264). Sally herself is a marvelous carnivalesque version of Arabella Harlowe. As Margaret Anne Doody comments:

> Sally in particular is tormented by a jealousy whose depths Lovelace himself does not understand. Once he tells Sally that there is absolutely no hope he will ever sleep with her again, she can hardly bear to see him and Clarissa together, and plots Clarissa's downfall on her own account. Sally's jealous desire to be in Clarissa's place emerges several times in odd plays of disguise and mimicry not ordained by Lovelace.[10]

In many respects, Sally and Bella are mirror images of each other: Both have had prior relationships with Lovelace; both have been supplanted by Clarissa in Lovelace's affections; both are jealous of Clarissa and plot revenge against her; both taunt and tease Clarissa. In one particularly eerie moment, Sally even asks Clarissa her "opinion of some patterns of rich silks" (3:341) for wedding garb, just as Arabella had earlier displayed "patterns of the richest silks" (1:281) intended for Clarissa's wedding clothes.[11] As with Dorcas and Mrs. Sinclair, Clarissa's initial misgivings of Sally and Polly are ultimately conquered, possibly because they represent known character types: Clarissa soon finds them to be "very courteous and obliging; ... we are now in a tolerable way" (3:311–2).

Despite the apparent correctness of their outward apparel and behavior, and, indeed, the correctness of their overall performance, all four of the women—Mrs. Sinclair, Dorcas Wykes, Sally Martin, and Polly Horton—reveal their inner corruption, the true condition of their heart, through their eyes. As Lovelace later comments, "The *Eye*, thou knowest, is the *Casement*, at which the *Heart* generally looks out. Many a woman, who will not shew herself at the *Door*, has tipt the sly, intelligible *wink* from the *Windows*" (6:344). Indeed, Mrs. Sinclair has "an odd winking eye"; Dorcas, "a strange sly Eye" (3:289); and Sally and Polly, eyes that fall under Clarissa's "ocular notice ... as if they could not stand its examination" (3:300). As with masquerade, the eyes are one of the few clues to the face behind the mask. Terry Castle has noted that "Masks had always carried risqué associations. Conventional wisdom held that someone donning a mask, especially a woman, experienced the abrupt loss of sexual inhibition. Anonymity, actual or stylized, relaxed the safeguards of virtue."[12] However, in Lovelace's topsy-turvy world, masks inhibit sexuality, and the eyes alone show the true nature of these vile women, as they are "windows to the soul."

In addition to the prostitutes at Mrs. Sinclair's brothel, Lovelace introduces Clarissa to the Irish rogue, the "honest Patrick McDonald," a man with an "ingenious knack of Forgery" (4:313). Dressed in the riding clothes of a country gentleman, Patrick McDonald is transformed into Captain Antony Tomlinson, a former army captain retired into country life, and the new-found friend and emissary of John Harlowe, Clarissa's elder uncle. Clarissa, desperate for reunion with her family, is eager to believe Captain Tomlinson is the agent of her uncle, "healing breaches, and reconciling differences" (4:313) between her and her family. Clarissa describes Tomlinson as "a grave good sort of man" and "a genteel man, of great gravity, and a good aspect; ... upwards of fifty years of age" (4:317). She confides to Anna that she "liked him ... as soon as I saw him" (4:317).

Patrick McDonald, as Captain Tomlinson, always appears in riding dress, though the specific details of his outfit remain vague. When he first arrives at Mrs. Sinclair's, on May 28, he comes with riding whip in hand, "booted and spurred" (4:297). He explains his attire to Lovelace, saying, "Be pleased to excuse my Garb. I am obliged to go out of town directly, that I may return at night," unsure whether he was to have found the *"time to do myself this honour"* (4:287) of meeting with Lovelace. (Clarissa listens to the ensuing conversation in an adjoining room.) Tomlinson returns at seven the next morning, again "ready equipped for his journey" (4:305); this time he and Clarissa meet. On June 10 Tomlinson again appears, this time summoned by Lovelace to Mrs. Moore's, whence Clarissa has fled, after the nighttime fire. Again, he appears with riding whip in hand (5:196). Clarissa never sees Tomlinson again, as she effects her second escape from Sinclair's on the very day he is supposed to meet her; however, for this meeting, Lovelace had advised Tomlinson that "Your Riding-dress will do for the first visit. Nor let your Boots be over-clean. I have always told you the consequence of attending to the *minutiæ*, where Art (or *Imposture*, as the ill-mannered would call it) is designed—Your Linen rumpled and soily, when you wait upon her—Easy terms these" (6:83).

As costume, the riding dress presents Tomlinson as extremely manly, particularly with spurs upon his boots and riding whip in hand, as becomes a retired army captain who reveres "a brave man" (4:290). His clothes also suggest that he is a sensible man, more concerned about business affairs and family matters, rather than outward appearance. In riding dress, he appears to be in charge, unwilling to rely on the services of a coachman, or anyone else, when he might do the job as well, if not better, himself. In addition, Tomlinson appears to be always journeying, in town with Clarissa one moment, then back to Uncle John Harlowe the next; he seems a steady, reliable, and direct link to those whom she loves best, her family. In combination, his clothing and his age make him seem someone to be trusted and to be relied upon. Indeed, his disguise is that of another uncle to Clarissa, and she is easily taken in.

Patrick McDonald is reasonably well-educated, having attended Dublin University prior to his expulsion, and he is apparently of good birth. Thus, although he needs a change of costume in order to act the part of the retired captain, now a country gentleman, his mannerisms and behavior are suited to his role. If anything, he is perhaps too well-bred for his part, as Lovelace advises him to act slightly more coarsely and authoritatively than he would otherwise, perhaps with more of Uncle Antony Harlowe in his performance:

—Remember (as formerly) to loll, to throw out your Legs, to stroke and grasp down your Ruffles, as if of significance enough to be careless. What tho' the presence of a fine Lady would require a different behaviour, are you not of years to dispense with Politeness? You can have no design upon her, you know. You are a father yourself of daughters as old as she. Evermore is *parade* and *obsequiousness* suspectable: It must shew either a foolish head, or a knavish heart. Assume airs of *consequence* therefore; and you will be treated as a *man* of consequence.

(6:83–4)

Lovelace (apparently an early proponent of the method school of acting) has coached Patrick McDonald into a seamless and utterly convincing performance as Captain Antony Tomlinson. Because of an overheard conversation in which Captain Tomlinson drops "a hint in commendation of the people of the house" (4:297), Clarissa remains at Mrs. Sinclair's establishment, conquering her former qualms, secure in the respectability of the "widow" and her "nieces." Upon Captain Tomlinson's insistence that her Uncle John wishes it so, Clarissa continues the pretence of being Mrs. Lovelace, something that works to her severe disadvantage when she is discovered at Mrs. Moore's. As she says to Tomlinson, "It was true … [that] she *had* given her consent to such an expedient, believing it was her *Uncle's*" (5:177). With Mrs. Moore, Miss Rawlins, and the Widow Bevis believing that she is married to Lovelace, Clarissa appears simply to be suffering from a severe case of early marital jitters, rather than from genuine fear of being raped. The man playing Captain Antony Tomlinson, then, becomes a masquerade version of Clarissa's two uncles: He pretends to act on behalf of Uncle John Harlowe, while playing the part of Uncle Antony Harlowe (and, surely, the pseudonym Antony Tomlinson is not coincidental). Clarissa is deceived by McDonald/Tomlinson because of his likeness to her uncles, but Tomlinson's actions also reflect poorly on the uncles, in turn. Clarissa is not so much duped by the dress, gestures, and words of these rogues and whores, but by their resemblance to members of her family, even though her family members have dealt with her harshly and unfairly.

Although Lovelace insists that he prefers to conduct his love intrigues with little outside interference—"As little foreign aid as possible in my amorous conflicts has always been a rule with me; tho' here I have been obliged to call in so much" (5:64–5)—he nonetheless requires the services of yet two more individuals in order to effect the return of Clarissa to Mrs. Sinclair's house, after her initial escape. The two new recruits are Bab Wallis and Johanetta Golding. Under Lovelace's skillful hand (and apparently this is not the first time they have acted the part of fine ladies), Bab Wallis is transformed into his aunt, Lady Betty Lawrance, and Johanetta Golding into his cousin, Miss Charlotte Montague.

Previously, Lovelace had assigned his confederates—Mrs. Sinclair, Polly, Sally, Dorcas, and McDonald—to play characters (the stern, yet admiring aunt and mother; the sweet, adoring cousin; the jealous, spiteful sister; the faithful, honest maidservant; the gruff, concerned uncle) reminiscent of those found in the Harlowe household. He now takes the masquerade one step further, by having his new associates impersonate his own kinswomen.

Lovelace explains his choice of women for these roles: "Both have wit at will. Both are accustomed to ape Quality. Both are genteelly descended. Mistresses of themselves; and well educated—Yet past pity.—True *Spartan* dames; ashamed of nothing but *detection*—Always, therefore, upon their guard against that. And in their own conceit, when assuming top parts, the very Quality they ape" (5:276). As usual, Lovelace pays close attention to the minutiae of their dress:

And how dost think I dress them out?—I'll tell thee.

Lady Betty in a rich gold Tissue, adorned with Jewels of high price.

My Cousin Montague in a pale pink, standing an end with silver flowers of her own working. Charlotte, as well as my Beloved, is admirable at her needle. Not quite so richly jewel'd out as Lady Betty; but Ear-rings and Solitaire very valuable, and infinitely becoming.

Johanetta, thou knowest, has a good complexion, a fine neck, and ears remarkably fine—So has Charlotte. She is nearly of Charlotte's stature too.

Laces both, the richest that could be procured.

Thou canst not imagine what a sum the Loan of the Jewels cost me; tho' but for three days.

(5:276–7)

In this instance, Richardson has provided the most detailed description of artful dress, primarily because the reader needs to be convinced that these two high-class whores can successfully beguile Clarissa in the roles of Lady Betty and Miss Montague; however, there is little of the specificity with which Clarissa's clothing is treated. Instead of a "pair of diamond snaps in her ears" (3:28) or "a rose-diamond ring" on her finger (5:27), the pretended Lady Betty wears only "Jewels of high price" and the pretended Miss Montague, "Ear-rings and Solitaire" of indiscriminate origin. Instead of a gown of "pale primrose-coloured paduasoy: The cuffs and robing curiously embroidered ..., in a running pattern of violets and their leaves; the light in the flowers silver; gold in the leaves" (3:28), the pretended Lady Betty wears "a rich gold Tissue" and the pretended

Miss Montague wears "pale pink" with unspecified "silver flowers." The description provides enough information to imagine the clothing of these two women, yet it lacks specificity and, thus, suggests its imitative, artificial, and tinsel-like nature.

Lady Betty is a member of the aristocracy, and the rich dress of "gold Tissue" that her pretender wears is extraordinary costly, yet in keeping with Lady Betty's rank and wealth. The rich linens and costly jewels are also in keeping with her rank, as well as her age and marital status. This is an outfit intended to awe—and it does—yet it lacks any personal touches which the real Lady Betty might be expected to add. The outfit of the pretended Charlotte Montague is comparable to what Clarissa might have worn for a similar occasion. The pale, pastel pink of the gown is appropriate for a young, unmarried girl. As with Clarissa's own dress, the embroidery on the gown would demonstrate the young wearer's skill and domesticity, as well as the availability of leisure time, a sign of wealth. Simple, yet expensive, jewelry attests to her wealth and her youth. Yet, again, there is nothing unique in this outfit; it lacks the small, yet unusual details that make Clarissa's own dress so distinctive. However, because the style of this ensemble is extremely similar to Clarissa's own style of dress—indeed, it seems deliberately imitative—it suggests that the pretended Miss Montague is of similar mind, morals, and taste, something that must reassure the badly frightened and confused Clarissa.

Although Bab Wallis and Johanetta Golding are "accustomed to ape quality," they require some additional coaching for their roles, as they must act like real individuals, with known mannerisms. Lovelace urges them, to be "Easy and unaffected!" (5:278) and to have "Airs of superiority, as if *born* to rank—But no overdo!" (5:277). The pretended Lady Betty is admonished to show "Less arrogance" and "More significance," to be a "little *graver*" (5:278). The pretended cousin Montague is "a little too frolicky" and her "Leer" is "Too *significantly* arch!" (5:278). They practice curtseying, the pretended Charlotte advised to "courtesy low," while the pretended Lady Betty is warned that her curtsy is "too low, too low, ... for your years and your quality" (5:279). At last, Lovelace proclaims them to be "Charming!" (5:279). However, like the lower-end members of their profession, their true nature can still be discerned by their eyes. Lovelace repeatedly cautions them: "—Once more, what-a-devil has your heart to do in your eyes?" (5:278) and "be sure to have a guard upon your Eyes" (5:279).

Clarissa is unsuspecting, though she notes that "in some respects (tho' I hardly knew in what) they fell short of what I expected *them* to be" (6:156). She later reports to Anna Howe on their appearance and dress: "Such were these impostors; and having never seen either of them, I had not the least suspicion, that they were not the Ladies they personated; and being put a little out of countenance by the richness of their dresses, I could not help (fool that I was!) to apologize for my own" (6:150). The "richness of their dresses" confounds her, clouding her judgment. She returns to town, on the false Lady Betty's insistence, and, once there, is left at Mrs. Sinclair's for the unmasking of Mrs. Sinclair and Lovelace, a move that necessarily must precede Clarissa's rape. This introduction of the false Lady Betty and the false Charlotte Montague, involved as they are in returning Clarissa to the brothel, begs the question: To what extent does Richardson hold Lovelace's relatives responsible for Clarissa's rape? To be sure, they have used words, in writing and in person, to urge Lovelace to marry Clarissa, yet, as Lord M. himself reminds us, "*Words are wind; but deeds are mind*" (6:212).

The rape of Clarissa has been pre-arranged: She is returned to Mrs. Sinclair's residence, deserted by the pretended Lady Betty and Miss Montague, and drugged. The unmasking of Mrs. Sinclair, that is, the revealing of her true nature, seems to have been intended "to frighten" (6:173) Clarissa into submission, at least, that is what Clarissa believes. Of course, this recalls the Harlowe's attempts to frighten Clarissa into marrying Solmes, as well as Mrs. Harlowe's command that "you think of being Mrs. Solmes" (1:97) and her severing of communications with Clarissa, when she refuses to comply. Mrs. Sinclair, with "masculine air, and fierce look" (5:290), soon becomes a terrifying version of the entire Harlowe family melded into a single frightening form:

> The old dragon straddled up to her, with her arms kemboed again—
> Her eye-brows erect, like the bristles upon a hog's back, and, scowl-
> ing over her shortened nose, more than half-hid her ferret eyes. Her
> mouth was distorted. She pouted out her blubber-lips, as if to bellows
> up wind and sputter into her horse-nostrils; and her chin was curdled,
> and more than usually prominent with passion.
> With two *Hoh-madams* she accosted the frighted Fair-one.
>
> (5:290)

Terry Castle writes, "And yet it was the very fluidity of carnival—the way it subverted the dualities of male and female, animal and human, dark and light, life and death—that made it so inimical to the new 'atomizing' sensibility that heralded the development of modern bour-geois society."[13] In this moment of transformation, Mrs. Sinclair is both feminine and masculine; both human and animal; both respectable widow and hideous whore. She is the Harlowes, and she is the whore-house madam. However, with the unmasking of Mrs. Sinclair, all need for pretence and disguise is gone; the masquerade has ended, and Mrs. Sinclair's house becomes a brothel once more. In this highly sexualized environment, Clarissa may now be raped—and she is.

Interestingly, when Clarissa later relates the horrors of this night to Anna Howe, she does not dwell on Mrs. Sinclair's unmasking, but on Lovelace's, which occurred just slightly earlier, and which is the true cause of Clarissa's terror and alarm:

> He terrified me with his looks, and with his violent emotions, as he gazed upon me. Evident *joy-suppressed* emotions, as I have since rec-ollected. His sentences short, and pronounced as if his breath were touched. Never saw I his abominable eyes look, as they then looked—Triumph in them!—Fierce and wild; and more disagreeable than the womens at the vile house appeared to me when I first saw them: And at times, such a leering, mischief-boding cast!
>
> (6:171)

His eyes, the windows to his heart and soul, reveal Lovelace to be a more hideous and vile creature than his whores and rogues could ever be. Indeed, an earlier unmasking has revealed the true nature that lies beneath Lovelace's Protean exterior.

Earlier in the novel, while at Mrs. Moore's, Lovelace had donned the costume of "an antiquated beau" (5:75), a hobbling, gouty old man, in order to gain access to his terrified prey, as Clarissa is fearful of "Every well-dressed man I see from my windows, whether on horseback or on foot" (5:54). (Compare the description of "antiquated beau" to that of Clarissa's elderly father, who suffers from "frequent gouty paroxysms" (1:134).) Yet at the moment of unmasking, Lovelace's devilish nature is revealed:

> I saw it was impossible to conceal myself longer from her, any more than (from the violent impulses of my passion) to forbear manifesting myself. I unbuttoned therefore my cape, I pulled off my slapt slouched hat; I threw open my great coat, and, like the devil in Milton [an odd comparison though!]
> *I started up in my own form divine,*
> *Touch'd by the beam of her celestial eye,*
> *More potent than Ithuriel's spear!*—
>
> (5:83)

One of Mrs. Moore's servants is convinced that Lovelace is evil incarnate: "she would have it, that I was neither more nor less than the devil, and could not keep her eye from my foot; expecting, no doubt, every minute to see it discover itself to be cloven" (5:84). Of course, this is precisely what Lovelace's handsome looks and elegant dress conceal, and perhaps this is what the gout-ridden frame of Clarissa's father hides, once he treats his daughter as something to be bartered and sold.

Thus, combined with artful performance, dress as artful expression proves highly successful: Until the fire, Clarissa believes that Mrs. Sinclair and her associates are who and what they purport to be, respectable members of society, just like her own family. Only after the rape does Clarissa realize the deception of the pretended Lady Betty and Miss Montague, as well as that of the "vile Tomlinson" (6:158). Of Mrs. Sinclair, Polly, Sally, and Dorcas, Clarissa writes, "altho' I liked not the people," she had little suspicion of them "till the Wednesday night before, that they offered not to come to my assistance, altho' within hearing of my distress (as I am sure they were) and having as much reason as I to be frighted at the fire, had it been real" (6:158). Of course, the irony is that Clarissa's family "offered not to come to my assistance." No Harlowe mother, sister, aunt, or servant offers aid to Clarissa, with the exception of those too powerless to offer real help, like young Dolly or Hannah. As to the pretended Lady Betty and Miss Montague, Clarissa notes: "Never were there more cunning, more artful impostors, than these women. Practiced creatures, to be sure: Yet genteel: and they must have been well educated—Once, perhaps, as much the delight of their parents, as I was of mine" (6:157). While Lovelace's female relatives are not culpable of active malice, they may be indicted for passive virtue, for not actively securing Clarissa's physical safety and moral reputation. (As will be clearly demonstrated in the chapters on *The History of Sir Charles Grandison*, Richardson strongly condemns passive virtue.) Yet, of all of Lovelace's associates, Clarissa reserves her greatest contempt for "that detested Tomlinson; whose years, and seriousness, joined with a solidity of sense and judgment, that seemed uncommon, gave him, one would have thought, advantages in villainy" (6:157). As a masquerade version of her beloved uncles, Clarissa feels the most betrayed by this middle-aged, seemingly kindly and caring man.

Thus, Richardson, through the trope of masquerade, reveals the falseness and perfidy of Lovelace and his associates, and, in doing so, reveals the falseness and perfidy that exists at Harlowe Place. Of course, Arabella Harlowe is not a prostitute, nor is Mrs. Harlowe a madam, nor Uncle Antony a rogue, yet Richardson, through his use of masquerade, insists that certain comparisons be made, not only in how Clarissa is treated, but in the way in which a forced marriage is akin to prostitution. Strong governance and guidance of the young is needed, precisely because they are young, because they lack the knowledge and experience of the world to read through the masks that others wear in order to conceal the contents contained within "the Shop of our Minds." However, tyranny of any sort, particularly on the part of those whose duty it is to protect, is never acceptable.

Part IV Refashioning the World with *Sir Charles Grandison*

Introduction

In a letter to Lady Bradshaigh, thought to have been written in either November or December of 1749, Samuel Richardson responded to her request that he compose a novel based on a "good man." He writes, "To draw a good man—a man who needs not repentance, as the world would think! How tame a character? Has not the world shewn me, that it is much better pleased to receive and applaud the character that shews us what we are . . . than what we ought to be?"[1] Yet Grandison is that man, and, in *The History of Sir Charles Grandison*, Richardson fashions a world in which a single individual, a "good man" singularly attuned to the nuances and niceties of social relations, makes a real and positive difference in a society that seemed, at least to Richardson and many of his contemporaries, debauched and depraved.[2] In doing so, Richardson presents his readers with a lesson-book on proper governance of self, which, in turn, should lead to proper governance in all things. By refashioning oneself, so *Grandison* argues, one can refashion the world.

Sir Charles Grandison epitomizes the domestic ideal; his scrupulous honesty, strict moral code, concern for others, selflessness, attention to duty, sensitivity, and, yes, chastity render him without compare. Nancy Armstrong has detailed the attributes of "domestic woman": She is "a wise spender and tasteful consumer." In her unmarried form, she possesses "modesty, humility, and honesty," though her virtue tends to be passive in nature. Once married, domestic woman becomes a model of active virtue, an "efficient housewife" responsible for "household management, regulation of servants, supervision of children, planning of entertainment, and concern for the sick." Most importantly, "domestic woman executes her role in the household by regulating her own desire."[3]

Sir Charles, as we know, manifestly possesses all these characteristics and more. Like unmarried domestic woman, he is modest and humble concerning his own considerable charms and accomplishments, he is obedient and dutiful to his parents, and he remains a virgin until his wedding night. Yet he also excels in active virtue, in ways similar to or surpassing those of married domestic woman. His father has squandered estate and household resources, yet Sir Charles introduces some economies that render the estate profitable and prosperous again, such as the selling of his father's "racers, hunters, and dogs" and the felling, then selling, of estate timber "which would be the worse for standing" (1:379). (Of course, he plants a seedling for every tree felled.) His household is efficiently run; his servants industrious and content. Sir Charles himself is the preferred guardian for young Emily Jervois, rather than her own mother, and he educates her in the arts of domesticity through discussion and example. He tenderly cares for the wounded Jeronymo; he secures the restoration of Clementina's sanity, through the ministrations of Dr. Lowther. And, in his desire to render all households as happy and productive as his, Sir Charles espouses the benefits of domestic ideology, instructing others in the arts of domestic bliss, such as Sir Harry and Lady Beauchamp, Lord W., and the young Danbys. Sir Charles emphasizes private, domestic life, not public life, and, in his democratic desire to secure domestic bliss for all, he arranges more marriages than any matchmaker could. In sum, as Charlotte notes, Sir Charles "was one of the busiest men in the kingdom, who was not engaged in public affairs; and yet the most of a family-man" (1:279). Note that he is "*not* engaged in public affairs"[emphasis mine], that he is "a family-man." Although "Sir Charles is noted for his great dexterity in business" (1:361), it is always and ultimately in service of domestic life.

Yet, is Sir Charles merely domestic woman in drag? Or, is he the literary manifestation and articulation of the bourgeois masculine ideal, an amalgamation of morally reformed gentleman, successful economic man, and man of feeling? I think both. The middle station gained cultural hegemony partly by professing its moral superiority (regardless of whether or not it possessed it in actuality), and the characteristics associated with domestic woman, all of which have moral value and intent, are also those associated with and valued by the middle station, as a whole. The ideal domestic woman combines all those attributes esteemed by the lesser gentry and upper middle class, yet, as woman, even as a "perfect" idealized woman, she is always defined in reference to the "perfect" idealized man. As Erin Mackie writes, "*The Tatler* and *The Spectator* bear ample witness to a kind of domestication of masculine virtue that emerges with more fanfare later in the century in the fuller expression of sensibility and sentimentality. In a sense, the bourgeois male can afford this intimacy with domesticity as long as his value as a legitimately masculine man is guaranteed by his essential difference from the effeminate homosexual man." Mackie continues, "For it is the white, middle-class, *male* individual who must stand—universalized, departicularized, unmarked, and unconstructed—as the central icon of bourgeois subjectivity. He becomes this icon largely through what his identity repels: the bad feminine and, related closely to this, the effeminate, modern homosexual."[4] In addition, as a man and a gentleman, possessed of wealth, property, and social status, Sir Charles enjoys agency and independence in ways that no woman or member of the lower stations could, allowing him countless more active opportunities to promote virtue and engage in acts of goodness. And, because Sir Charles is male, even passive virtue becomes active, as his duty, obedience, and chasteness are viewed as choices, not culturally imposed sanctions or "natural" feminine traits.

That the domestic ideal and domestic ideology become most fully realized through the masculine or male figure becomes clear when analyzing dress in *Sir Charles Grandison*. In the novel, clothing becomes a primary indicator of morality, yet moral dress is always defined in relation to the clothing choices made by Sir Charles or through his sartorial pronouncements. Immoral or inappropriate dress is always associated with the female, the feminine, or the feminized, suggesting that "natural" and "authentic" dress is the province of the male. Of course, within the novel, a woman may dress appropriately, as do Clementina and Harriet (at least most of the time), and a man may dress inappropriately, as male characters do, but a gendered model of dress underlies and informs the depiction of dress throughout Richardson's third and final novel.

In *Grandison*, appropriate attire indicates attentiveness to duty and obligation, to social responsibility, and to active engagement with virtue; inappropriate attire, instead, expresses self-involvement, irresponsibility, passive morality, or willful immorality. With the former mode of dress, a conversation with others transpires: The wearer acknowledges his or her role in society, dresses in a manner becoming to this role, yet examines the attire of others and adjusts his or her own accordingly, in order to avoid giving pain or embarrassment, always shunning self-pride and self-aggrandizement in favor of the greater good of the community. With the latter, a dialogue with self alone ensues: The wearer engages with others only as the means to confirm her or his own sartorial splendor, to hear words of praise repeated about the self; society exists merely as a mirror, in which the self-besotted wearer views herself or himself, endlessly primping and preening, blind to those who stand outside the reflection of the mirror's gilded frame. Appropriate attire, in this novel, becomes an integral part of etiquette, manners, and morality, and, thus, is instrumental in creating social harmony. In contrast, unsuitable attire of any sort—whether masquerade or disguise, or merely bad taste—succeeds only in creating discord.

This gendered model of dress entered into English culture in the late seventeenth and early eighteenth century, along with the related notion that women manifest "*innate* frivolity and fashion-mad foolishness," yet this model became naturalized and ubiquitous by mid-century.[5] What is curious is that Richardson did not employ this model until *Grandison*. In other respects as well, *The History of Sir Charles Grandison* presents several paradoxes and conflicts in terms of his earlier novelistic renderings of dress: First, the novel functions as Richardson's most thorough articulation of his philosophy of dress, yet it contains only one detailed description of dress. Second, the single detailed description of dress is of Harriet Byron's masquerade costume, which is an artful construction, not a natural expression of self, and providing a detailed description of artful dress is a tactic inconsistent with Richardson's treatment of dress both in *Pamela* and in *Clarissa*. In addition, unlike *Clarissa*, where artful clothing confounds and confuses, where artifice and imposture easily mimic the genuine and true, *Grandison* suggests that, when viewed by the educated eye, clothing can—and does— disclose the true personality of the wearer. Finally, the novel expresses a marked longing for an idealized gentrified past, a longing remarkably inconsistent with the social aspirations and ambitions of Richardson's earliest protagonist, Pamela Andrews, as well as a desire for clearly delineated class markers, expressed primarily through the return of sumptuary legislation, undercutting *Clarissa*'s emphasis on personal style.

These major alterations in treatment of dress appear to generate from Richardson's struggle to contain and control signification, both sartorial and novelistic. Perhaps seeking what appeared to be stable textual and didactic models, *Grandison* shows evidence of a vigorous return to the conduct book and the *Spectator*. Both provide approaches to dress similar to that which Richardson employs in his final novel, as *The History of Sir Charles Grandison* depicts the "Seeds and Principles of an affected Dress, without descending to the Dress it self."[6] Thus, Richardson's concern in *Grandison* appears to be the articulation of the "Principles" of dress, both affected and non-affected, without the need for "descending to the Dress it self."

In *Grandison*, Richardson achieves some stability in terms of sartorial signification, by eliminating detailed descriptions of appropriate and natural dress, explicating only "Principles," and by aligning appropriate dress with the masculine and male. Detailed descriptions of dress are inherently problematic, as Richardson learned in *Pamela*, partly because they call attention to dress, making simple attire appear ornate, making modesty and humility in dress seem false. This problem is compounded when providing detailed descriptions of feminine dress, as female fashion was associated with shopping, consumption, frivolity, and display, all of which could undermine masculine authority if engaged in to excess, threatening financial ruin or encouraging female promiscuity. Instead, Richardson utilizes the instability associated with detailed feminine dress by associating it with the unruliness of masquerade. By definition, masquerade dress is "unnatural" dress. And, if masquerade is "the World Upside-Down," it is also a world that eighteenth-century English men and women believed "encouraged female sexual freedom, and beyond that, female emancipation generally."[7] Masquerade inverts the "natural" heterosexual patriarchal order, and, thus, becomes associated with the female, the feminine, the feminized, and the effeminate. Interestingly, Richardson can only stabilize sartorial signification in his novels by confining—or hiding— all forms of unstable, unruly, and inappropriate dress under the hooped petticoat of masquerade attire.

Thus, Richardson describes Harriet's Arcadian princess costume with several purposes in mind: First, it allows readers to interpret Harriet's dress, within the known context of masquerade. Some readers view the outfit as indicative of willfulness and at least a small measure of sexual licentiousness. Others judge the costume based on the court of public opinion: Everyone attends masquerades, and the Arcadian shepherdess costume is a perpetual favorite, so this must make the costume acceptable, even favorable, attire. However, it also allows readers to discern Sir Charles's lightning-quick ability to judge others based on their dress and other external appearances: While Harriet's costume testifies against her, her genuine distress argues for her innate modesty and morality. Above all, Harriet's costume indicates a flaw in her character, albeit a small one. She wears the costume, not because she likes it, but because she is passive, and passivity is never prized in *Grandison*, even in the unmarried female. Harriet changes in the course of the novel, as Richardson no doubt hoped his readers would, and she does so by exchanging passive virtue for active virtue of the kind practiced by Sir Charles (though it is always at a lesser level than that of Sir Charles and it is always performed with an eye to his approval). Thus, Richardson's avoidance of all detailed descriptions of dress, with the exception of Harriet's masquerade gown, continues to advance his didactic program, and it allows for some containment of meaning.

Another seeming aberration from or rupture with Richardson's former ideology of dress stems from the novel's claim that artificial dress of any sort may always be detected, a claim that *Clarissa* belies. In *Clarissa*, one of the central problems is how to tell the artificial from the real, based on external signs, such as dress, body, gestures, words, and history. Clarissa, of course, fails in her ability to discern the fine distinctions between the impostor and the real thing, until it is too late. In contrast, *Grandison* claims that the impostor can always be identified, through careful and close examination of outward signs. In this, *Grandison* aligns itself with the majority of eighteenth-century periodicals, poems, conduct books, and more, in suggesting that dress accurately reveals the mind. In a pretend letter to the editor of the *Connoisseur*, one Eutrapelus Trim writes, "We may know the disposition of man by his apparel," and he suggests that he "can discover impudence flaring from the bold cock of a *Kevenhuller*, frugality skulking in a darned stocking, and foppery dangling from a shoulder-knot."[8] (A Kevenhuller is a large, cocked hat, which mimics military headgear.) Fordyce's *Sermons to Young Women* similarly assumes that a "manifest difference" exists between "the attire of a Virtuous Woman" and one who is not, so much so that "It were indelicate, it is unnecessary to explain the difference," though "it is sufficiently discerned by the eye of the public."[9] Thus, impudence, frugality, foppery, and virtue are presumed to be discernable, by most observers, from outward dress. If so, then Clarissa's failure seems even more inexplicable, except when understood in terms of her youth, naivety, inexperience, and femaleness.

Clarissa herself is "transparent," that is, her exterior dress and person exactly mirror her inner self, and her own transparency appears to render her naïve in terms of reading others. In addition, her family actively engages in metaphoric masquerade, covering up their weaknesses and flaws under the domino-like cloaks of wealth and respectability. (Remember, too, that Lovelace's confederates masquerade as Harlowe family members.) Clarissa's youth also pleads in her behalf, as she is still at the age where parental advice and guidance is deemed necessary. And, finally, Clarissa allows herself to be blinded by Lovelace's pleasing exterior precisely because she is female—or so it would seem. She knows his history, and she can see small, yet telling indications of his inner corruption, such as his pride in his person and dress and his inadvertent gestures that reveal delight at Clarissa's plight. Nonetheless, Clarissa believes that she can reform Lovelace. Clarissa conforms to eighteenth-century English notions concerning female vulnerability in regards to dazzling exterior appearances and the supposed tendency of the female sex to give preference to rakes, libertines, fops, and fancy-dressed fellows. As John Essex writes, in *The Young Ladies Conduct*, "I cannot but look back with Concern, at the unaccountable Humour, or rather Foible of the Sex, in being taken and seduced with every thing showy and meer outside; after reflecting on the numberless Mischiefs that have befallen them, from this light fantastical Disposition of theirs."[10]

Although Sir Charles is transparently good, like Clarissa, with exterior and interior in harmony, he is older, wiser, and wary of female rakes. Sir Charles has benefited by the wise governance of his mother and Dr. Lewen, and he is twenty-seven years old, not nineteen. His education and experience also make a difference. The "cabinet" of his mind contains sufficient information to allow him to decipher accurately dress, behavior, words, and more. As a male, Sir Charles presumably is not as easily swayed or seduced by exteriors, particularly in dress. A better comparison may be made between Harriet Byron and Clarissa Harlowe, rather than Clarissa and Sir Charles. Like Clarissa, Harriet Byron is virtuous. Unlike Clarissa, Harriet is slightly older and possesses a loving, caring family that has provided her with a strong moral education. However, for all this, Harriet lacks the final touches to her education, and she makes a single error that could easily have led her into Clarissa's own situation. And, so, *The History of Sir Charles Grandison* argues, in Lockean fashion, for education and experience, as the means to refine and polish the mind and soul, yet, paradoxically, much of this needed education and experience always remains unavailable to women: women with experience, women who are older and wiser, are frequently those women deemed unvirtuous by society.

The final paradox or problem of dress in *Grandison* centers on the novel's seeming longing for an idealized gentrified or aristocratic past, expressed most directly through Sir Charles's desire for the reinstatement of sumptuary legislation. Yet constant calls for the return of sumptuary legislation were made during the eighteenth century, as Jennie Batchelor notes: "In response to the seemingly vertiginous powers of dress to encrypt the social hierarchy and generate false or multiple meanings, many writers suggested the return to some form of sumptuary legislation."[11] Ironically, the seemingly contradictory ideas that dress could reveal the mind and that dress could disguise the mind happily coexisted in eighteenth-century English culture and texts. Thus, Sir Charles merely restates ideas widely in circulation during that time period.

Yet rather than merely being a mouthpiece for sartorial clichés, Sir Charles both represents and reveals the ultimate goal behind all conduct-book literature, addressed both to females and males—the reformation of the gentry, or more specifically, the gentleman himself. It is possible to infer from all of Richardson's novels that preoccupation with self, with individualistic (and possibly eccentric) expression, with pursuit of personal desires inconsistent with societal good, were deemed attributes of the upper station, a sign of the supposed debauchment and debasement of the aristocracy, a disease which had spread down through the gentry and even into the middle station. Mr. B. initially wants Pamela, simply to fulfill his own lustful desires. Lovelace operates from far more complex motives, including a love of plotting and intrigue, yet his unconcern at—and, indeed, his delight in—seducing myriad young women, solely because he can, suggests his immorality and self-interest. However, in creating the character of Sir Charles Grandison, Richardson refashions the gentry, summoning up older notions of nobility (*civilitas, fidelitas, gentilesse, virtus*) and imbuing them with the energy, industriousness, economic savvy, and religious and moral enthusiasm of the middle station.

Ingrid H. Tague had identified Allestree's *The Ladies Calling* (1673) as the most influential early conduct book on "the later development of the genre," and she cites Fenela Childs's finding that Allestree's text functioned "as a source for another eight works between 1694 and 1753."[12] Yet this influential book was mere companion piece to *The Gentleman's Calling* (1660) in which Allestree, a Anglican minister and ardent Royalist, blamed the deprecations experienced by gentry during the Civil Wars and under the Commonwealth and Protectorate governments, as directly attributable to the gentleman's indulgence in "Lust" and "Intemperance," even going so far as to suggest that the "Punishments" endured during the Interregnum were "but the results of sins."[13] For Allestree, the reformation and reinvigoration of the gentry relies upon their adoption of Christian and bourgeois morality. Allestree understands that the incorporation of middle-class morality may be deemed insulting or threatening to the gentry, so he takes pains to assure his gentleman readers that this is not "a Levelling project," yet he insists that a reformed gentry "will be the best Humane means to recover this sinful Nation."[14] A gentleman is looked up to, and, thus, provides an example for all, so the idea goes. Sir Charles Grandison functions in this capacity. Sir Charles represents the new gentry; his father, the old.

Conduct books for women were based on the underlying assumption that women may influence masculine behavior: Allestree writes, "if after a successful Attempt upon the more impregnable Masculine part of the Gentry, I now essay the Feminine, whose native Softness and Gentleness may render them less apt for that resistance of good Counsel, wherein too many Men place their Gallantry."[15] It was thought that women possessed a civilizing influence over men, and, thus, the morally inclined domestic lady may reclaim the gentleman from certain ruin. Strangely enough, inherent in this concept is the idea so often condemned by eighteenth-century texts, including Richardson's own—that a good woman may reform a rake—and, therein, of course, lies the promise of *Pamela*, as she functions as the instrument by which Mr. B.'s reformation is effected. *Instructions for a Young Lady* (1773) laments that "So numerous have been the unhappy victims to the ridiculous opinion, that a reformed libertine makes the best husband,"[16] yet the libertine and rake is the unreformed gentleman or aristocrat, the debauched but still beloved societal ideal, which must be reclaimed and restored to former goodness and glory.

The following chapters explore these ideas more fully. Chapter 9 discusses the philosophy of dress espoused by the three main characters in the novel—Sir Charles and his two great loves, the charming, deprecating, young Englishwoman, Harriet Byron, and the beautiful, pious Bolognese aristocrat, Clementina della Poretta. All three characters function as moral exemplars of sorts, and their attitudes towards dress display Richardson's own concerns with the relationship between dress and responsibility to self, to family, to friends, to community, to country. The garments worn by Clementina demonstrate honor and obeisance to her parents; by Harriet, sensitivity to those less fortunate; by Sir Charles, respect for his father, concern for his country and his religion, and acknowledgement of the demands of society. The frivolity and foolishness of "the fops, foplings, and pretty fellows" (3:247), "the gaudy insects" (1:229), with their craving for foreign fashions, is also analyzed, as overly elaborate and ornate dress serves only to conceal foolishness or inner baseness, and undue love of foreign goods is shown to be irreligious and unpatriotic.

Masquerade and disguise play an essential part in all of Richardson's novels, and, in *Grandison*, it is Harriet's abduction from a masquerade ball that introduces Sir Charles into the story, as anti-masquerade hero. Chapter 10 analyzes Harriet's masquerade outfit, that of an "Arcadian Princess" (1:115), which is described in sensuous detail in the novel: It hugs her waist, emphasizes her hips; the bugles, bangles, and bracelets, the flowers and feathers, that bedeck her outfit—all call attention to Harriet's exquisite beauty and form, as well as to the debased nature of a society that enjoys the pleasures of masquerade. Richardson has culled this outfit from Sir Philip Sidney's *Arcadia*, specifically the cross-dressing garb of Pyrocles, as Amazon, not the simple shepherdess dress of Sidney's Arcadian princess, Pamela. In its association with sexual licentiousness and transvestism, Harriet's masquerade garb conjures up images of illicit sexual conduct, irrationality, deception, and disguise—and it suggests moral weakness in Harriet herself. The theme of masquerade continues throughout the novel, with a large assortment of characters (Sir Hargrave Pollexfen, Lady Olivia, Everard Grandison, Camilla, and even Clementina herself) at one time, or another, donning disguise, suggesting that everyone (with the exception of Sir Charles) inevitably engages in concealment of some kind, as the means to mask moral weakness, uncontrolled passion, or egregious vice.

Chapter 11 discusses color as it relates to clothing and accoutrement within the novel, and of the importance of dress color in social relations, as it functions as a primary means of communication regarding the moral and emotional status of the wearer, revealing the childishness of an elderly woman, the virtue of a bride, the mental confusion and despair of a young female depressive. Pale pink, primrose yellow, and brilliant white, all hues previously worn almost exclusively by the aristocracy or gentry of either sex, take on more nuanced social meaning by Richardson's day, with pink and yellow, the favored hues for young girls and young unmarried women; with white, the color of choice for the gown of any virgin bride, regardless of social station; and, with all shades of dress, functioning as psychological, emotional, and moral indicators.

9
"A Conformist to Fashion": Dressing for Duty

Sylvia Kasey Marks calls *Sir Charles Grandison* "a new species of conduct book," and, while Richardson's novel is certainly more than that, it is also true that the novel attempts to educate its readers, precisely in the manner of conduct-book literature. Marks writes:

> In many ways *Grandison* harks back to an older aristocratic tradition in which the nature of nobility, the formation of the young man, his education and recreation, and his larger responsibilities to his family and the state were important. At the same time, we see the same emphasis on duty and on the responsibilities one has to one's superiors, peers, and inferiors found in the conduct books directed toward a more general audience.[1]

With such a didactic emphasis, it should come as no surprise that *Grandison*'s treatment of dress also conforms to the conduct-book model, not only in its attention to social aspects of attire, but also in its emphasis on general principles of dress, rather than on specific articles of dress. For instance, *The Spectator*, with its emphasis on the reformation of mores, morals, and manners, similar to conduct-book literature, addressed itself to the "Seeds and Principles of an affected Dress, without descending to the Dress it self."[2] Or, in Fordyce's conduct book, "a lovely Modesty and graceful Simplicity of Apparel" is recommended, though any specific details of dress are avoided.[3] In *Grandison*, consistent with conduct-book methodology, only one outfit, Harriet's masquerade costume, is described in any detail—and this for specific reasons, as will be made evident in a subsequent chapter.

Of all of Richardson's novels, *Grandison* most fully articulates a comprehensive philosophy of dress, with guidelines, rules, and examples, a conduct guide and etiquette manual guaranteed to smooth all manner of sartorial and social relations. Sir Charles functions as author of this fashion-based guide to manners and mores, expounding upon fashion's intricacies and subtleties, philosophizing about its consequences and implications. Harriet and Clementina, earnest proselytes and practitioners both, affirm the wisdom of following such sage, sartorial advice through the general conformity of their own clothing choices to Sir Charles's fashion-based principles; both demonstrate the ill consequences that attend avoidance or neglect of these tenets through the occasional fashion folly.

In dress, as in every thing, Sir Charles follows "the laws of reason and convenience" (1:137), and the novel's fashion policy purports to be founded upon these cornerstones of common sense and good taste. As noted in the *Female Spectator*, "In effect, nothing can be called a true taste, that is not regulated by reason, and which does not incline us to what will render us better and wiser."[4] Singularity in dress is a fashion *faux pas*, as "Singularity is usually the indication of something wrong in judgment" (3:124). Harriet muses that singularity in dress is "a fault to which great minds are perhaps too often subject" (1:230); however, it also provides evidence of a mind too preoccupied with self, too eccentric, too narrow in perspective. Odd or eccentric dress is impolite, as it demonstrates disdain for societal conventions. Often, such idiosyncrasy stems from "a Sowrness and Spirit of Contradiction," and such deliberate avoidance of fashion is often "not sincere," generating instead from "mere Obstinacy,"[5] or, perhaps, from "Fickleness, or vanity, or ambition."[6] Sir Charles, of course, avoids singularity in his own dress: As Harriet writes, "*he* is so much above it" (1:230), possessed of "such an easy, yet manly politeness, as well in his dress, as in his address (no singularity appearing in either)" (1:181). To avoid singularity, fashion should be followed, though not slavishly. Again, Harriet notes, "Something is due to fashion in dress, however absurd that dress might have appeared in the last age (as theirs do to us) or may in the next" (3:100). One should "modernize a little" (1:230). Specifically, one should dress like Sir Charles: "He uses the fashion, without abusing it, or himself, by following it" (2:498). (Singularity in dress differs from uniqueness in dress, as exemplified by Clarissa, in a very specific way: Singular dress means something in the attire appears odd or out-of-place, inconsistent with social custom, time, or place, or incompatible with a person's age, gender, social station, and more. Clarissa's clothing sense is unique, in that she does not follow fashion slavishly, and she alters or moderates specific styles to accommodate her own unique person.)

In addition, dress is language, a means of communication with others, and, as such, it should be a dialogue, not a soliloquy. Those who pay too close attention to their appearance, obsessed with self-image and self-representation, are egotistical, engorged with pride and self-love, desirous of serving only their own self-interests. Women of this variety are "Butterflies, and other gaudy insects" (1:229); men of this sort, "fops, foplings, and pretty fellows" (3:247). Each is "a dear Lover of his person" (1:20) or hers. In *Grandison*, among this brilliant and dazzling company, are Sir Hargrave Pollexfen, in "his gaudy dress" (1:44); Everard Grandison, "at the *head* of the fashion, as, it seems, he thinks" (1:231); Lord G., "a gay-dressing man" (1:399) who "seems a little too finical in his dress" (1:230); as well as an assortment of minor characters, such as Mr. Somner, "very affected, and very opinionated . . . tho' he was very gaily dressed" (1:20); Mr. Barnet, a fop who "dresses very gaily" and relishes the "sound of his own voice" (1:20); and Sir Walter Watkyns, who "outdoes" Lord G. "in Foppery" (1:230). Not all of these men are villains; some, like Lord G., are merely foolish, focused on "Moths and Butterflies, Shells, China, and such-like trifles" (2:436–7), rather than on other human beings. (Notably, once Lord G. has married Charlotte Grandison, he presents his collection of shells to Sir Charles's young ward, Emily Jervois, and his collection of butterflies and moths, to a friend; one assumes that, in time, Lord G. will also leave behind his fondness for foppish dress.) Yet, whether villainous, insufferably vain, or merely foolish, all those who dress "too finical" or too foppishly prove neglectful of social duties and responsibilities.

Of all the characters in this novel, Sir Hargrave Pollexfen most fully demonstrates what *not* to do in matters of dress. Harriet's description of him is telling, a portrait of extreme narcissism:

> But he would, in my opinion, better become his dress, if the pains he undoubtedly takes before he ventures to come into public, were less apparent: This I judge from his solicitude to preserve all in exact order, when in company; for he forgets not to pay his respects to himself at every glass; yet does it with a seeming consciousness, as if he would hide a vanity too apparent to be concealed; breaking from it, if he finds himself observed, with an half-careless, yet seemingly dissatisfied air, pretending to have discover'd something amiss in himself. This seldom fails to bring him a complement: Of which he shows himself very sensible, by affectedly disclaiming the merit of it.

> (1:45)

This is an amusing portrait of a conceited fop whose constant self-surveillance reveals unparalleled vanity and self-absorption. Surrounded by others, Sir Hargrave repeatedly pays his respects to himself; encircled by lovely young women, Sir Hargrave finds himself gazing in admiration at his own reflection in the glass. However, Richardson views this seemingly comic self-absorption as dangerous to self and to others. To view such behavior as comical is not to distinguish it for what it truly is—an expression of extreme egotism, self-centeredness, and pride. As Harriet writes, "Could you have thought, my Lucy, that this laughing, fine-dressing man, could have been a man of malice; of resentment; of enterprise; a cruel man?" (1:63). Someone who dresses only for self cares nothing for others, and Sir Hargrave Pollexfen's actions throughout the novel confirm this: For instance, in his abduction of Harriet, though Harriet's distaste for him is apparent; in his repeated challenges to duel with Sir Charles, solely to assuage wounded pride; in his mortification over his ruined looks, while paying no heed to mind or morality; in his attempt at debauching a married French woman, solely to engage in dissipation; in his painful, self-pitying fear of death, while continuing his profligate lifestyle—all express his unhealthy need for self-gratification at all costs, irregardless of others.

Yet, if one does not dress for self, then for whom? And, once this is known, how does one dress to suit? The Reverend Wetenhall Wilkes, in *A Letter of Genteel and Moral Advice to a Young Lady*, suggests that "Social Duties" are owed to "King and Government," to "Clergy," to "Parents and Relations," and to "Friends," and this essentially sums up sartorial duties as well.[7] To begin with, the individual should dress in a manner that demonstrates respect to "Parents and Relations." Sir Charles, a man who admittedly prefers conformity in dress and "who builds nothing on outward appearance," nonetheless admits, "I rather perhaps dress too shewy." However, as Sir Charles explains, "But my father loved to be dressed. In matters which regard not morals, I chose to appear to his friends and tenants, as not doing discredit to his magnificent spirit . . . In a word, all my father's steps, in which I could tread, I did" (3:124). His father, Sir Thomas Grandison, a magnificently dressed man, whose "delights centred in himself" (1:312), was notably lacking in moral principles; but because Sir Charles feels obligated to demonstrate duty and respect towards his deceased father, he chooses dress, the one thing at which Sir Thomas excelled, as the means by which to do so. Similarly, Clementina dresses to honor her parents and relations—at least most of the time. She says, "My father and mother loved to see me dressed. I dressed many a time to please them more than to please myself" (3:334).

For Clementina to be "dressed," is for her to wear clothes befitting her aristocratic background, dress suitable for the daughter of a Marchese and Marchesa, for the sister of a General and a Bishop. However, when she disobeys the dictates of parents and brothers, fleeing to England without permission, against their express wishes, Clementina comes "with very few cloaths, and they were not the best" (3:334). The clothes she brings to England embarrass her, as does her behavior in coming there. Demonstrating filial duty through dress means wearing garments that respect the taste, the social position, and the desires of parents and relatives; one dresses in a manner that pleases them in order to indicate outwardly the duty, honor, and affection that most eighteenth-century English men and women thought was *due* to parents and relations, regardless of their faults and follies. However, it is important to note that son and daughter must *choose* to dress in this manner, not merely allow themselves to be dressed, as attire must be considered appropriate by the wearer, as well as by parents and guardians.

However, in the art of socially responsible dressing, acknowledgement of parents is but the first step. One must also dress for other individuals, whether they be "Friends," acquaintances, business associates, or strangers. This requires a wardrobe that always suggests "ease and dignity in the person, in the dress" (1:11). Mr. Reeves, upon first meeting Sir Charles, comments upon the way in which Sir Charles has set him at ease, made him feel comfortable, even though Reeves and his cousin Harriet owe a considerable, almost burdensome, debt to Sir Charles: "Sir Charles appears to be one of the most unreserved of men, as well as one of the most polite. He makes not his guests uneasy with his civilities" (1:146–7). True politeness comes from making others comfortable, not in perfunctory attention to punctilio. Politeness in dress comes from the same source; it should set others at ease, not make them conscious of their own sartorial shortcomings. It is dress that sets others before self, and, in doing so, suggests the confidence of the wearer and compels the ease of those around him/her. Sir Charles possesses "an easy, yet manly politeness, as well in his dress, as in his address" (1:181). On Sir Charles's wedding day, Lucy Selby writes of his "native dignity and ease, and that inattentiveness to his own figure and appearance, which demonstrate the truly fine gentleman, accustomed, as he is, to be always elegant" (3:252). Harriet, too, possesses "ease and dignity" in dress, as her admirer Greville relates: "there is so much ease and dignity in the person, in the dress, and in every air and motion, of Miss Harriet Byron, that fine shapes will ever be in fashion where she is, be either native or foreigner the judge" (1:11). Clementina, as well, prior to her madness, dresses with "unaffected elegance" (2:524). Ease in dress should not be mistaken for sloppiness or slovenliness, both of which indicate disrespect for others. Starchiness, stiffness, and stuffiness in dress—all are incompatible with true politeness, as are negligence, neglect, and indifference. As the *Spectator* notes, "The Medium between a Fop and a Sloven is what a Man of Sense would endeavor to keep."[8]

Reason, ease, and dignity are general guidelines for tasteful dress on most occasions, but, in specific circumstances, something more may be demanded of the wearer. Sometimes, the wearer must alter her own dress in order to spare the dignity of others. Dressing for others requires scrupulous sensitivity to the feelings of others, particularly those in distress, and Harriet possesses this thoughtfulness and compassion in bountiful supply. For her wedding, Harriet shuns ostentation, saying, "Humility becomes persons of some degree. We want not glare: We are *known* to be able to afford rich dresses; need them not, therefore, to give us consequence" (3:172). A silvered gown, one woven with threads of silk and silver, might serve to acknowledge Harriet's wedding in fine fashion, yet would needlessly remind Harriet's young friends, like Miss Orme, the "two Miss Nedhams, Miss Watson, Miss Barclay, the two Miss Holles's" (3:210), of their perhaps less happy financial circumstances. Harriet also shows great compassion when dressing for her first encounter with Clementina della Porretta, the beautiful Italian, Sir Charles's first love. Harriet chooses a simple outfit, *sans* ornamentation or jewels, in consideration of Clementina's wounded pride, her embarrassment, and her relative poverty of dress, occasioned by her mad-cap flight to England. Harriet proudly notes:

> Sir Charles approved my dress, as he passed by me to go to Mr. Lowther in the Study. He snatched my hand, and pressed it with his lips: My ever-lovely, my ever-considerate Harriet, you want no ornaments: But I was sure you would not give yourself any but those that flowed from a compassionate yet generous heart, when you were to visit a Lady who at present is not in happy circumstances; yet is intitled by merit, as well as rank, to be in the happiest.
>
> (3:352)

Others might be inclined to dress richly and ostentatiously, to lord over a fallen rival with costly jewels and silky knots and ribbons; Harriet instead allows kindness and compassion to guide her choice of attire, possessing genuine politeness in manner and dress.

Yet socially conscious dressing requires a great deal more from the willing practitioner, as something is also due to social station and community, both of which are inextricably entwined in Richardson's novel, as social station determines the role that the individual plays within the community. Wearing clothes appropriate to social station apprizes others of the individual's position within the community, which, in turn, determines the level of social responsibility: The higher the rank, the greater degree of responsibility that attends it. Sir Charles "regards the heart, rather than the head, and much more than either rank or fortune, tho' it were princely; and yet is not a leveller, but thinks that rank or degree intitles a man who is not utterly unworthy of both, to respect" (3:241). To whit, Sir Charles values individual merit over rank, but, where merit and high rank meet, in a single individual, then this person is indeed worthy of the highest esteem, as being capable of performing the most good. As Sir Charles tells his ward, Emily Jervois, "See, child . . . what it is in the power of people of fortune to do" (2:312). A "great fortune" may be a "blessing to multitudes" (1:64); "large and independent fortunes" can prove "beneficial to the world," particularly in the hands of those "who have the hearts and understanding to use them as they ought" (3:408).

Sartorial choices also depend upon fortune, as well as degree. Harriet writes of Sir Charles, "Does he not say, that he always consults fortune, as well as degree, in matters of outward appearance?" (3:136). Wearing attire beyond one's financial means places burdens on family and community, as it directs funds away from worthier causes, keeping tradespeople from receiving their pay, impoverishing laborers and servants who work the estate lands, and forcing the "the honest poor" (1:97) to rely on others for relief. A profligate master or miserly mistress of an estate starves the land and, subsequently, the surrounding community. Dressing below one's fortune is equally problematic, suggesting lack of self-respect, disrespect toward family and community, and the possible eschewing of duty. *Spectator* No. 150 discusses this at some length: "few things make a Man appear more despicable, or more prejudice his Hearers against what he is going to offer, than an aukward or pitiful Dress. . . . This last Reflection made me wonder at a Set of Men, who, without being subjected to it by the Unkindness of their Fortunes, are contented to draw upon themselves the Ridicule of the World in this Particular." As "an handsome suit of Cloaths always procures additional Respect," the *Spectator* questions why a person would be found "walking in Masquerade," that is, "appearing in a Dress so much beneath his Quality and Estate."[9]

For Sundays and for ceremonial occasions, such as weddings, funerals, and the like, one dresses as much for community, as for self and others. In Harriet's country village, a crowd of rustic laborers gathers each Sunday "to see the gentry go in and come out" (3:224), and, for Harriet's wedding, the churchyard is packed with admiring rustics, the church, with "Ladies and well-dressed women of the neighbourhood" (3:225). Although Harriet desires a simple wedding gown, she nonetheless must dress in a way not to dishonor the locals, whether gentry or laborers. The Selbys and Mrs. Shirley, Harriet's relatives, are among the major landowners in the community, and, as such, Harriet's wedding holds importance, as a way for the rustics to acknowledge the beneficence and goodness of these families, to celebrate the good fortune of Miss Byron and her family, and to seek assurance of future prosperity. Later, for Harriet's first public appearance after her wedding, an equally, if not more, important occasion in terms of eighteenth-century English culture, she chooses a richer and more costly gown, as befits her new role as Lady Grandison. She writes to Sir Charles's sisters, "Something must be done, I grant, on our *appearance*; for an appearance we must not dispense with here in the country, whatever you women of quality may do in town" (3:172).

Finally, one must, as the Reverend Wilkes suggests, dress for "King and Government," that is for country. Dress is political in nature. Every article of clothing and accoutrement, each ribbon, each jewel, each gown or silk stocking, is brought about by labor—and, of course, it is the conditions of labor that render garments political. While trade with foreign countries was encouraged—Defoe, for instance, expresses his admiration of England's extensive export and import trade[10]—fear nevertheless existed that love of foreign goods would predominate, at the cost of English laborers, servants, and trades-people. This is a primary reason why Sir Charles desires a return of sumptuary legislation, as sumptuary laws sought to protect English trade and manufacturing. (A fuller discussion of sumptuary legislation and its importance in *Sir Charles Grandison* can be found in Chapter 11). Sir Charles, though a "Citizen of the World," nonetheless views it as his patriotic and religious duty to wear English-made goods: "on a double Principle of Religion and Policy, he encourages Trades-people, the Manufactures, the Servants, of his own Country" (3:263). When Sir Charles and Lady G. engage in "lively debate" (3:263) on the subject of foreign fashion, his viewpoint is made quite clear:

> The Error . . . is growing too general, is authorized by too many persons of figure, not to make one afraid of fatal consequences, from what in its beginning seemed a trifle. Shall any one pretend to true Patriotism, and not attempt to stem this torrent of Fashion, which impoverishes our own Countrymen, whilst it carries Wealth and

Power to those whose National Religion and Interest are directly
opposite to ours!

(3:264)

For Sir Charles, loyalty to country and religion takes precedence over
"those Elegancies in Dress and Appearance" (3:263) that come from
wearing foreign goods.

Thus, the act of dressing is not a simple one: It requires attention to
the duties and responsibilities owed to parents and to relatives; to
friends, to acquaintances, to associates, to strangers; to social station and
to community; to country and to religion. But what does one owe to
self? The novel does not say outright, but suggests that perhaps neatness,
cleanliness, dignity, and elegance in dress are what the individual can
claim as her due. These attributes foster self-respect on the part of the
wearer; they force others to treat the wearer with respect. And respect, for
self and for others, is perhaps what matters most in Sir Charles's refashioning of the world.

10
"A Mighty Glitter": Seeing through the Veil

Critics have long noted the connection between Sir Philip Sidney's *Arcadia* and Richardson's *Pamela*;[1] however, a connection also exists between *Arcadia* and *Grandison*, through Harriet's masquerade costume. Jocelyn Harris identifies Harriet's costume of "Arcadian Princess" as "a favourite masquerade habit, in imitation of the princesses in Sidney's *Arcadia* who disguised themselves as shepherdesses."[2] Yet Harriet's costume is highly unlike the rustic garb of Sidney's Arcadian princess/shepherdess, Pamela, or even the rustic garb of Richardson's own Pamela. Instead, Harriet's masquerade outfit shows marked similarities to the attire worn by Sidney's Amazonian princess, Zelmane, the cross-dressing disguise of the beautiful young prince, Pyrocles, as well as to the "*Amazonian* Hunting-Habit for Ladies," a form of feminine dress deemed "masculine" in nature.[3] The swapping of costumes—Amazonian drag instead of Arcadian rusticity—articulates several interrelated themes important to *Grandison*: That masquerade, disguise, and unsuitable dress of any sort are symptomatic of irrationality and unreason; that vice and moral laxity must be cloaked and concealed by dress; and that dress unsuitable to one's sex, specifically, the respective attire of "a masculine woman, and an effeminate man" (3:247), is not only a form of disguise, but an indication of a topsy-turvy world, a masquerade world, wherein "the distinguishing characteristics of the two Sexes" (3:247) are reversed or inverted.

For those unfamiliar with Sidney's pastoral romance, a simple summary of a highly complex plot must suffice: Basilius, Duke of Arcadia, has received the following, somewhat ambiguous prophecy from the oracle at Delphi:

> Thy elder care shall from thy careful face
> By princely mean be stol'n, and yet not lost;

Thy younger shall with nature's bliss embrace
An uncouth love, which Nature hateth most.
Both they themselves unto such two shall wed,
Who at thy bier, as at a bar, shall plead
Why thee (a living man) they had made dead.
In thy own seat a foreign state shall sit.
And ere that all these blows thy head do hit,
Thou with thy wife adult'ry shall commit.[4]

Basilius believes that, by remaining at court, he will lose wife, daughters, throne, and life. Attempting to avoid his fate, Basilius abandons court, seeking refuge in the Arcadian woods with his wife, Gynecia, and daughters, Pamela and Philoclea. As the oracle has intimated that the elder daughter, Pamela, will "By princely mean be stol'n," Basilius places Pamela in the custody of an ignorant goat-herd, Damætas, and his family; as shepherdess, Pamela will not meet a prince, or so Basilius thinks. As the oracle has also proclaimed that the younger daughter will indulge in "uncouth love," Basilius keeps Philoclea, at home, in the care of his wife and himself, presumably safe from advances by "uncouth" suitors.

Alas, as so often happens with prophecies, attempts to avoid fate, merely aid in fulfilling it. Soon, two young princes, two cousins, Musidorus and Pyrocles, journey to Arcadia, and find themselves entranced by Basilius's daughters. Musidorus, disguised as the shepherd Dorus, woos the virtuous Pamela and elopes with her, though they are captured before they can wed. Pyrocles, dressed as the Amazon Zelmane, obtains access to Basilius's household, where he wins the love of Philoclea. Unfortunately, both Basilius, who believes Pyrocles to be a woman, and Gynecia, who knows Pyrocles to be a man, fall violently in love with him as well. Pyrocles separately arranges for Gynecia, dressed in Pyrocles' own Amazonian habit, and Basilius to meet him for an evening rendezvous of love, from which Pyrocles himself is absent. In the darkness of a cave, Basilius and Gynecia commit adultery, with each other, while Pyrocles consummates his love with Philoclea, in Basilius's lodge. In the morning, a distraught Basilius accidentally drinks a love potion that Gynecia has brought to the cave—and dies. Thus, the oracle's prophecy has come to pass: Pamela has eloped with a prince; Philoclea has indulged in "uncouth love"; Basilius and Gynecia have committed adultery, with each other; the duke himself is dead, with no son to inherit the throne. Gynecia, horrified by the death of her husband and her own wickedness, confesses her role in his death. Pyrocles is arrested for defiling Philoclea; Musidorus, for eloping with Pamela. Gynecia, Pyrocles, and Musidorus are sentenced to death by Pyrocles' own father, but are saved when Basilius revives from the love draught. All ends well, with Musidorus and Pyrocles marrying Basilius's daughters, with Basilius and Gynecia reconciled.

From the start, the costume of Arcadian shepherdess was a popular one, once masquerades were introduced into England, from Italy, in the early eighteenth century. *The Spectator*, no. 14, comments, "There is not a Girl in the Town, but let her have her Will in going to a Masque, and she shall dress as a Shepherdess. But let me beg of them to read the *Arcadia*, or some other good Romance, before they appear in any such Character."[5] According to Aileen Ribeiro, "From the beginning of the 18th century some of the most popular costumes at masquerades were ... rustic habits of characters such as shepherds and shepherdesses."[6] It was a simple costume to make, comprised of "a simple satin gown and often with 17th century features of dress such as front lacing, or Van Dyck cuffs worn with a dress decorated with gauze. The usual accessories were a crook and a flowered straw hat."[7] As Harriet Byron specifically terms her outfit as that of "Arcadian princess," she is ostensibly meant to be dressed in the mode of Sidney's Pamela, an Arcadian princess dressed in "shepherdish apparel, which was but of russet cloth cut after their fashion, with a straight body, open breasted, the nether part full of pleats, with long and wide sleeves,"[8] a modest enough outfit. However, upon receipt of her masquerade outfit, Harriet complains to Lucy Selby, "They call it the dress of an Arcadian Princess: But it falls not in with any of my notions of the Pastoral dress of Arcadia"—and she is correct. Harriet describes the costume as follows:

> A white Paris net sort of cap, glittering with spangles, and incircled by a chaplet of artificial flowers, with a little white feather perking from the left ear, is to be my head-dress.
>
> My masque is Venetian.
>
> My hair is to be complimented with an appearance, because of its natural ringlets, as they call my curls, and to shade my neck.
>
> Tucker and ruffles blond lace.
>
> My shape is to be consulted in this dress. A kind of waistcoat of blue satten trimm'd with silver Point d'Espagne, the skirts edged with silver fringe, is made to fit close to my waist by double clasps, a small silver tassel at the ends of each clasp; all set off, with bugles and spangles, which make a mighty glitter.

But I am to be allow'd a kind of scarf of white Persian silk; which, gathered at the top, is to be fastened to my shoulders, and to fly loose behind me.

Bracelets on my arms.

They would give me a crook; but I would not submit to that. It would give me, I said, an air of confidence to aim to manage it with any tolerable freedom; and I was apprehensive, that I should not be thought to want that from the dress itself. A large Indian fan was not improper for the supposed warmth of the place; and that contented me.

My petticoat is blue satten, trimm'd and fring'd as my waistcoat. I am not to have an hoop that is perceivable. They wore not hoops in Arcadia.

(I:115–16)

Indeed, Harriet's assessment of the outfit is correct: "it falls not in with any of my notions of the Pastoral dress of Arcadia."[9] This glittery costume possesses little resemblance to Pamela's "shepeardish apparell," fashioned from plain "Russet cloth."[10]

As Zelmane, Pyrocles wears a "doublet of sky-colour satin covered with plates of gold, and as it were, nailed with precious stones,"[11] very much like the "kind of waistcoat of blue satten trimm'd with silver Point d'Espagne" worn by Harriet. Similarly, draped over his doublet, Pyrocles/Zelmane wears a cloak, "a certain mantle, made in such manner that, coming under her right arm, and covering most of that side, it had no fastening of the left side, but only upon the top of the shoulder where the two ends met and were closed together with a very riche jewel."[12] Harriet's cloak resembles "a kind of scarf of white Persian silk; which, gathered at the top, is to be fastened at the shoulders, and to fly loose behind me." Harriet's terminology (a "kind of waistcoat," "a kind of scarf") suggests her unfamiliarity with the actual garments she is wearing, something that might occur if she were wearing a doublet and mantle. Pyrocles, as the Amazonian Zelmane, arranges his hair in an artful shower of curls, atop of which is perched a coronet of pearls and feathers: "the hanging of her hair in fairest quantity, in locks, some curled and some as it were forgotten, with such a careless care ..., the rest whereof was drawn into a coronet of gold, richly set with pearl, and so joined all over with gold wires and covered with feathers of divers colours that it was not unlike to an helmet, such a glittering show."[13] Harriet's hair tumbles down her back in "ringlets," while her head is crowned with a cap of "white Paris net," adorned with spangles and a single white feather. Some differences do exist between Harriet's "Arcadian

Princess" habit and Pyrocles' Amazonian attire (for instance, Harriet wears a petticoat; Pyrocles, crimson velvet buskins), yet the similarities are striking: the sky blue doublets, the mantles, the loose curls, the spangles, jewels, and feathers. However, why would Richardson choose to dress Harriet like Pyrocles, a prince in Amazonian drag, rather than as Pamela, the prim Arcadian shepherdess?

Eaves and Kimpel suggest the possibility that Richardson's knowledge of *Arcadia* came solely via Steele's *The Tender Husband,* and this may explain this disjuncture between the dress of an Arcadian shepherdess and a cross-dressing prince; however, this explanation seems unlikely given the two-line mention of Pamela and Musidorus (and no mention of Pyrocles) in Steele's play, as well as Richardson's detailed knowledge of Pamela and other characters in *Arcadia.*[14] More likely, this is a sly wink at those who dress for masquerades, without regard for, or understanding of, the implications of costume. As a remorseful Harriet later says, "What would my good grandfather have thought, could he have seen his Harriet, the girl whose mind he took pains to form and enlarge, mingling in a habit so preposterously rich and gaudy, with a croud of Satyrs, Harlequins, Scaramouches, Fauns, and Dryads; nay, of Witches and Devils" (1:427). In addition, Harriet's Pyroclean masquerade garb emphasizes the licentiousness of masquerades, which many associated with the loss of reason: Pyrocles, as Amazon, sings a "dittie," whose lines demonstrate his obsession with Philoclea and intimate his now-fallen nature: "Transformed in show, but more transformed in mind" the song begins. Other lines reveal the overthrow of reason, the betrayal of self:

> For from without came to mine eyes the blow,
> Whereto mine inward thoughts did faintly yield;
> Both these conspired poor reason's overthrow;
> False in my self, thus have I lost the field.
> Thus are my eyes still captive to one sight;
> Thus all my thoughts are slaves to one thought still;
> Thus reason to his servants yields his right[15]

When viewed in terms of Richardson's novel, the allusion to Pyrocles suggests enslavement of mind, loss of reason, giving over all for passion—and this, of course, is what Richardson's novel condemns. For Richardson, a masquerade is the site of irrationality and immorality. As Harriet remembers, "I whispered to my cousin Reeves more than once, O madam! this is sad! This is intolerable stuff! This place is one great Bedlam! Good Heaven! Could there be in this one town so many creatures devoid of reason, as are here got together?" (1:426). She mentions "the wild, the senseless confusion," yet also "the common freedoms of the place"; she concludes, "No prude could come, or if she came, could be a prude, there" (1:427).

Harriet's outfit also suggests her own faultiness, a failure that stems from passivity, from not engaging actively in warding off evil, but, instead, allowing others to determine her activities and her dress, against her own intuition, feelings, and better judgment. Prior to attending the masquerade, she writes, "I wish the night were over. I dare say, it will be the last diversion of this kind I ever shall be at; for I never had any notion of Masquerades" (1:116). Later, she notes, "Indeed I had no opinion of the diversion, even before I went. I knew I should despise it. I knew I should often wish myself at home before the evening was over. And so indeed I did" (1:426). Regardless, Harriet attends, out of courtesy to her cousins, certainly, but also because she has always relied on others in matters concerning her morality and her honor. Harriet also allows Lady Betty Williams to choose her masquerade costume, nor does Harriet refuse to wear the outfit, once received, though she dislikes the choice of costume: "Our dresses are ready. ... But I by no means like mine, because of its gaudiness: The very *thing* I was afraid of" (1:115). She later pleads her innocence in wearing the costume, saying, "This vile appearance was not my choice. Fie upon me! I must thus be dress'd out for a Masquerade. Hated diversion!" (1:132). Although Harriet is indeed a virtuous, innocent creature, Richardson's novel promotes active morality, not simply passive acceptance of the offerings of life, suggesting Harriet's folly in agreeing to attend a masquerade and to wear a costume so obviously unsuitable to a young, virtuous-minded woman. An older, wiser Harriet sadly regrets the inadequacy of her moral education: "Surely, surely, I have *had* my punishment for *my* compliances with this foolish world. False glory, and false shame, the poor Harriet has never been totally above. Why, was I so much indulged? Why was I allowed to stop so many miles short of my journey's end, and then complimented, as if I had no farther to go?—But surely, I was past all shame, when I gave my consent to make such an appearance as I made, among a thousand strangers, at a Masquerade!" (1:183).

Harriet's masquerade costume is a highly sexual one, simultaneously encouraging attention from men and mimicking masculine attire. The hooped petticoat was perceived as a sexual garment, either protecting the female sexual organs, or allowing easier access to them, and the lack of a noticeable hoop under Harriet's costume is highly suggestive, as it makes her ensemble distinctly different from the *status quo*, the style of her outfit emphasizing the natural curves of her hips, a rarity at the time. In fact, the style of dress suggests female riding attire, considered a "mannish" form of dress, or, as John Gay described it, "Hermaphroditical," in its combining of masculine and feminine fashion.[16] *Spectator* No. 104 describes the dress of "a certain Equestrian Order of Ladies" as follows, which also shows a remarkable resemblance to Harriet's masquerade costume (note that the "he" described is really a she): "He had a Coat and Wast-coat of blue Camlet trimm'd and embroider'd with Silver, a Cravat of the finest Lace, and wore, in a smart Cock, a little Beaver Hat edg'd with Silver, and made more sprightly by a Feather." Again, the blue camlet trimmed in silver, the lace cravat, and, most significantly, the single feather describe Harriet's outfit perfectly. *The Spectator* describes the outfit as an "*Amazonian* Hunting-Habit for Ladies" and notes that the "Petticoat is a kind of Incumbrance upon it; and if the *Amazons* should think fit to go on in this Plunder of our Sex's Ornaments, they ought to add to their Spoils, and compleat their Triumph over us, by wearing the Breeches." *The Spectator* further worries that "these occasional Perplexities and Mixtures of Dress" might become more frequent, "turning out publick Assemblies into a general Masquerade."[17] This is the very gender-bending that Sir Charles condemns:

> Can there be characters more odious than those of a masculine woman, and an effeminate man? What are the distinguishing characteristics of the two Sexes? And whence this odiousness? There are, indeed, *men*, whose minds, if I may be allowed the expression, seem to be cast in a Female mould; whence the fops, foplings, and pretty fellows, who buz about your Sex at public places; *women*, whose minds seem to be cast in a masculine one; whence your Barnevelts, my dear, and most of the women who, at such places, give the men stare for stare, swing their arms, look jolly; and those married women who are so kind as to take the reins out of their husbands hands, in order to save the honest men trouble.
>
> (3:247)

Sir Charles believes that "there is a natural inferiority in the faculties of the one Sex" (3:246), to use the words Charlotte puts in his mouth, and fears the overturning of this "natural" order, with women attempting to take on masculine roles, with men becoming increasingly foppish and effeminate in dress and mannerisms. While this sentiment seems archaic, even laughable to twenty-first century minds—especially when

Sir Charles speaks of "The surly bull, the meek, the beneficent, cow" (3:247)—the blurring of gender roles was nonetheless a concern to eighteenth-century English men and women, many of whom feared that slippage in gender roles would render individuals incapable of performing duties and responsibilities, both public and private.[18] As responsibility and duty are of primary importance in *Sir Charles Grandison*, Harriet's masquerade outfit suggests a disregard for her role in society, a disdain for feminine modesty, a desire to compete with men, though, indeed, Harriet herself is innocent of such attitudes and behavior.

In addition, the richness, the sparkle, the sheer gaudiness of Harriet's costume marks it as attire intended to attract sexual attention: "Gay and costly apparel directly tends to create and inflame lust," John Wesley preached.[19] Jocelyn Harris notes that "to the moral eye Harriet is inviting disaster by the vanity of her ostentation."[20] Harriet's "waist-coat of blue satten" is "trimm'd with silver Point d'Espagne." Presumably, the Point d'Espagne would have run along the edgings of the waistcoat where it fastened in front. Point d'Espagne "was in fact neither gold nor silver lace, nor 'needlepoint,' nor guipure, but a very fine and delicate fabric, known to this day in Andalusia as *punto de aguja*."[21] This fine, delicate, and spidery silver fabric, sewn along the front closure of the sky blue waist-coat, as well as on portions of the petticoat, is complemented by the clasps of the waist-coat, each with its own "small silver tassel" and by the silver fringe, running along the bottom edges of waistcoat and petticoat. To further add to the glare, bugles and spangles have been sewn onto the waistcoat and petticoat of Harriet's outfit. Bugles, tubular glass beads, came in black, white, or blue; spangles, an early version of sequins, were "Small discs of shining metal."[22] Harriet's headdress is comprised of a small cap, made of white net, encrusted with additional spangles and encircled with artificial flowers, with a single white feather dangling over her left ear; like Pyrocles' headgear, "it was not unlike to an helmet, such, a glittering shew." Harriet urges Lucy to "think ... how many Pretty-fellows you imagine, in the dress, will be slain ... by *Your* HARRIET BYRON" (1:116). As Harriet admits, this "tinsel dress" (1:427) makes "a mighty glitter" (1:115), guaranteed to attract the attentions of the opposite sex.

When Harriet is abducted, her masquerade outfit further suggests her complicity in illicit behavior; her garments suggest lack of respect for self, and, thus, allow others to treat Harriet with disrespect. It is an immodest outfit, and, as *The Female Spectator* suggests, only modesty can secure respect for women: "it is the fountain-head as well as the guardian of our chastity and honour. ... she who forfeits it is liable to fall."[23] The servants assisting Sir Hargrave Pollexfen in the abduction are informed that

Harriet is "an heiress, and had agreed to go off from the Masquerade with her lover" (1:123); her outfit convinces them of the truth of this assertion. When stopped by Sir Charles, Sir Hargrave Pollexfen attests that Harriet is his own wife, attempting "to elope from me at a damn'd Masquerade!" (1:139). Sir Pollexfen pulls aside the cloak that Harriet wears, saying, "See! ... detected in the very dress" (1:139). Luckily, for Harriet, Sir Charles "had not leisure to consider her dress," though he himself admits that he was "struck" by "her figure" (1:141).

In Figure 10.1, Johann Michael Stock's illustration of Sir Charles's rescue of Harriet, Harriet's masquerade outfit seems both feminine and modest by twenty-first century standards; however, as "read" through the lens of eighteenth-century English culture, the long doublet is highly reminiscent of the masculine waistcoat. If one considers that Stock has given Harriet a more voluminous petticoat than described in the novel (her hoop is un-perceptible, remember), the silhouette is more in tune with masculine attire, than feminine. Her glaring, glittering white cap, decorated with artificial flowers and the single white feather, and her lose ringlets are also decorously covered in Stock's illustration, by Sir Hargrave's "scarlet cloak" (1:139); just a hint of feather shows.

Harriet's masquerade costume poses yet one additional disadvantage, from a moral standpoint: It is fashioned from textiles and accoutrement of foreign, rather than English, Scottish, or even Irish manufacture. The net is from Paris; the fine, lacey trim from Spain; the mantle, silk from Persia; the fan from India; the mask, Venetian in origin. Jocelyn Harris comments, "to the patriot the wearing of foreign goods was provocative."[24] As noted previously, Sir Charles views a love of foreign dress as unpatriotic and irreligious. Thus, Harriet's passivity, innocently, yet ignorantly, encourages immorality and social injustice. A simple masquerade outfit, presumably that of an "Arcadian Princess," yet, in reality, that of an Arcadian transvestite reveals itself as an inherently debauched ensemble, associated with "uncouth love," illicit sexual liaisons, and uncontrolled passions; with irrationality, unreason, and folly; with ostentation and pride; with immodesty and lack of self-respect; with anti-English sentiment; with moral weakness and passivity.

Yet, lest the reader think too harshly of Harriet, on this occasion, the trope of masquerade and misrule carries throughout the novel, with numerous other characters engaging in some form of disguise, a signal that some form of unbecoming behavior has been indulged in, such as folly, lust, or disobedience. All individuals who sanction Harriet's attendance at the masquerade, and who accompany her (her cousins Reeves, dressed as a hermit and a nun, and Lady Betty Williams, dressed as an abbess) are implicated in folly, particularly as they are older and, presumably, wiser. After Harriet's abduction, all vow never to attend masquerades in the future: Mr. Reeves notes that "Sir Charles seems not to be a friend to Masquerades," adding, "I think, were I to live an hundred years, I never would go to another. Had it not been for Lady Betty ... And she also declares (so much has she been affected with Miss Byron's

Figure 10.1 Johann Michael Stock (1737–73). Plate II, from *Geschichte Herrn Carl Grandison*. Leipzig: M. G. Weidmanns Erben und Reich, 1780. Cropped, computer-scanned image. Book in collection of K. M. Oliver

danger, of which she takes herself to be the innocent cause) that she will never again go to a Masquerade" (1:143).

Lust must also disguise itself: Harriet's abductor, Sir Hargrave Pollexfen, dressed as Harlequin (1:117), proves himself in thrall to excessive sexual passion, as does the violent, indiscreet Lady Olivia, who visits Sir Charles clandestinely, while "in disguise" (2:238). Everard Grandison, "dressed like a Sea-officer, and skulking, like a thief" debauches "another fool of our Sex" (2:441). In Italy, "A Lady, less celebrated for virtue than beauty" becomes the illicit love of the Barrone della Porretta; when Jeronymo, "in disguise" while "pursuing his amour!" (2:121) is brutally beaten by "Brescian bravoes" hired by "one of the Lady's admirers" (2:120), Sir Charles must save him.

Disobedience also requires disguise: Clementina's woman, Camilla, twice disguises herself to visit Sir Charles: The first time, the cloaked Camilla comes without the permission or the knowledge of her employers: "O, Sir, said she, what a distracted family have I left! They know not of my coming hither; but I could not forbear this officiousness" (2:184); the second time, she comes at the "Marchioness's connivance" and the "command of Signor Jeronymo" (2:199), but against the commands and wishes of the senior members of the household, the Marchese, the General, and the Bishop. Both times, Camilla provides Sir Charles with unwelcome information; as he says to her, "I hope you have eased your own heart; but you have loaded mine" (2:186). Clementina, too, disguises herself in her maidservant's clothes, attempting to visit Sir Charles against her family's wishes; however, she is caught in the act (2:202). Even Sir Charles's sisters, Charlotte and Caroline, engage in trickery and disguise, in order for Caroline to meet with Lord L., a suitor of whom Sir Thomas Grandison hardily disapproves, simply for his lack of fortune. Charlotte admits, "Once or twice did I change dresses with her. In short, I was a perfect Abigail to her in the affair" (1:275). Although Sir Charles calls Italy "the land of masquerades" (1:426), it is nonetheless clear that disguise must exist everywhere, regardless of locale, that its close associate, morally reprehensible behavior, is present. As Harriet writes, "Does not concealment always imply somewhat wrong?" (1:333).

Sir Charles changes not one whit during the course of the novel, but Harriet does. A good girl and a lovely one, possessed of admirable frankness, Harriet learns that concealment of any kind is inconsistent with true virtue. Her masquerade costume, all tinsel and glitter, forcibly reveals to her the shallowness of her own goodness, her excessive pride in, what to all intents and purposes, is essentially passive virtue, reliant upon the thoughtfulness, morality, and good behavior of others. In attending a "detested masquerade" (1:425), in wearing such "tinsel dress," Harriet learns, to her great pain and humiliation, that her physical virtue owes little to her own morality and much to a man whose constant and active pursuit of virtue engages his interest in the affairs of others. The outfit of "Arcadian Princess" articulates the discourse of both passive virtue and active vice: Instead of a pure-minded princess, dressed in the simple russet gown of a shepherdess, Harriet's masquerade attire is that of a cross-dressing prince, who incites "uncouth love" on the part of others and who indulges in "uncouth love" himself. It is "tinsel dress," all display, all glitter, all show; it is not the true dress of an Arcadian shepherdess, just at it is not the display of true virtue. Sir Charles, in contrast, possesses a virtue so innate, so true, that no concealment, no disguise, has ever been necessary. Harriet writes, "Nothing but the conscious integrity of his own heart, above disguises or concealments, as his ever was, could thus gloriously have carried him thro' situations so delicate" (3:456). Conscious virtue, active virtue, alone is able to withstand the forces of a debauched and depraved world; it alone can make a difference. This is what Harriet learns.

Throughout the course of the novel, Harriet's growth in morality, in active virtue, and in self-assertion is revealed through her dress: The gown in which she weds Sir Charles has been "left to her own choice" (3:214). Although Lady G. and Lady L. have suggested "flowered silver," Harriet resists, saying to Lady G., "Don't, my dear, let me be a bride in a masquerade outfit. ... Simplicity only can be elegance. Let me not be gaudy: Let not fancy, or art, or study, be seen in my dresses. ... But let me not, I beseech you, or as little as possible, be marked out for a *luster*" (3:172). She weds in a simple white gown. Harriet's virtue, like her wedding gown, is no longer merely "tinsel dress," all surface glitter with no inner depth. It is simple, unadorned, yet genuine.

To live as Sir Charles lives, as Harriet learns to live, as Clementina can/must learn to live, is to live a life dedicated to others, not to self. With the exception of Sir Charles, every character in the novel may be said to engage in some form of masquerade or disguise, whether it be a temporary lapse in judgment, or a prolonged sojourn in personal indulgence. To live without disguise means rigorous self-examination, an activity in which Sir Charles regularly engages, as well as scrutiny of the motivations of self and others; it also means actively pursuing good, without ceasing, without rest, without consideration of self. Lack of disguise means nothing can or must be hidden; no place to hide must exist;

all thoughts and actions must be transparent and transparently good. In return, one achieves the "Eternal sunshine of the spotless mind!" with "Desires composed, affections ever even."[25] *The History of Sir Charles Grandison* is Richardson's version of the quest narrative—not a quest for the Holy Grail, nor for lost cities of gold, nor for long forgotten manuscripts, but a quest for the transparent, spotless self. As Richardson wrote to Lady Echlin, "A good Character is a Gauntlet thrown out,"[26] and he invites his readers to begin the quest themselves.

11
"Dressing in Colours": Changing the Guard

"In the article of personal appearance, I think that propriety and degree should be consulted, as well as fortune," Sir Charles Grandison informs his beloved Harriet Byron, in the weeks preceding their wedding, adding, almost as an afterthought, that he has long "wished for the revival of Sumptuary Laws" (3:124). Sir Charles expresses his yearning for a time when dress was legislated, when the lines between social classes were clearly demarcated, a wish remarkably inconsistent with the social ambitions and mixed wardrobe of Richardson's earliest protagonist, Pamela Andrews, the vivacious and virtuous young servant girl.[1] In a moral world such as Sir Charles envisions and actively seeks to create, clothing should clearly and distinctly express the age, gender, nationality, and social station of the wearer, allowing no possibility for misreading, no opportunity for deceit, a means to differentiate the good, the moral, from the bad and the immoral.

Sumptuary laws, those sartorial-, gustatory-, and game-restricting acts of legislation of which Sir Charles desires a revival, were drafted for three purposes—to protect and encourage English wealth and trade; to enforce and encourage morality; and to reinscribe demarcations between social stations.[2] However, most scholars agree that the primary intent behind sumptuary legislation was "the desire to preserve class distinctions, so that any stranger could tell by merely looking at a man's dress to what rank in society he belonged."[3] The last passage of sumptuary legislation in England occurred during the reign of Elizabeth I. As Marjorie Garber notes:

> The medieval and Renaissance sumptuary laws ... appear to have been patriotic, economic, and conservatively class-oriented; they sought to restrict the wearing of certain furs, fabrics, and styles

to members of particular social and economic class, ranks, or "states." While protecting, at times, such native industries as the wool trade or the linen trade, and purporting, at least, to guard the public morality against excess and indulgence, these statutes (which also governed food and drink and the playing of sports or games, but were in the main directed at apparel) at the same time attempted to mark out visible and above all *legible* distinctions of wealth and rank within a society undergoing changes that threatened to blur or even obliterate such distinctions.

She continues, "The ideal scenario—from the point of view of the regulators—was one in which a person's social station, social role, gender and other indicators of identity in the world could be *read*, without ambiguity or uncertainty."[4] Aileen Ribeiro concurs, stating, "Sumptuary laws in England aimed to protect native English textile industries ... but the main purpose was to enforce class distinctions in dress."[5] To this end, specific types of furs (black jennets, luzernes, ermine), fabrics (silk, satin, velvet, damask, taffeta, grosgrain), adornment (embroidery, buttons, studs), accoutrement (jewels, stockings, caps), specific styles of dress, and specific garment lengths were prescribed for some, proscribed for others. The most expensive articles of clothing and accoutrement— expensive due to rarity of materials (silk, ermine, jewels, precious metals, rare dyes), or to the time, labor, and craftsmanship involved (jewelry, embroidery, swords)—were reserved for the upper members of society; notably, most of these articles of dress involved importation of materials from foreign countries. Inexpensive articles of dress, made from goods native to England (in particular, wool and, later, woad), that required less rigid standards of craftsmanship, or less time or labor to manufacture, were the province of the lower stations.

Sir Charles admires sumptuary legislation in all its myriad aspects, despite the fact that more than one hundred and fifty years have elapsed since their last passage. He avidly supports English trade and manufacturing; he actively works to effect change (for the better) in the morals of those he knows; and he advocates clothing indicative of social station and economic fortune, as it provides evidence of the wearer's role within the society. Yet, the colors of dress, as presented in the novel, render Sir Charles's professed desire for the return of sumptuary laws slightly problematic: Prior to the eighteenth century, dress color possessed either class, professional, or ceremonial associations—something of which Sir Charles would no doubt approve; however, Sir Charles's opinions aside, the novel itself uses clothing color to articulate age, gender, virtue, and emotion, attributes unrelated to social status, occupational status, or ceremonial occasion. Although clothing color remains consistent with the novel's emphasis on the social nature of dress, it nonetheless communicates the wearer's moral, emotional, and psychological status, not his/her social station.

This change is significant, as the cultural alteration in how clothing color is understood and interpreted reflects the beginnings of the transfer of power from upper to middle stations in English society, as well as the transition from an older model of society concerned with emblematic (outward) meaning, to a newer model, concerned with moral and psychological (inner) meaning. As Norbert Elias, in *The Civilizing Process*, demonstrates, a long-term development occurs in early modern European culture, driven by the increasing political stability of countries, as well as from the "pacification" of nature, from understanding (and fearing) the external world to understanding (and fearing) the inner self.[6] This is also, in Foucauldian manner, a movement away from the visible, outward expression of state power, to the discreet, inward internalization of discipline.

Thus, in eighteenth-century England, two cultural meanings associated with color could and did coexist: An older aristocratic model in which color signified external factors (she is a duchess; he is a judge; he/she is a member of the upper station in mourning), and a newer model in which color signified internal traits (he is foolish; she is un-virtuous; he/she is melancholy). Both models are political in nature: The former is expressive of a political culture in which the upper station dominated; the latter, of a political climate in which the middle station gained predominance through the exercise of moral self-control and the internalization of shame. Nancy Armstrong has suggested that domestic fiction challenged the cultural hegemony of the upper station, by redefining the notion of what constitutes the female and the feminine— in essence, by displacing class struggle onto the figure of the female, by (re)defining sexuality.[7] A similar act of displacement occurs with color and its meaning: The older class-oriented and ceremonially-based associations with dress color, which had served to solidify and protect the social predominance of the upper station for centuries, were rewritten by the middle station, through displacement of class onto age, gender, virtue (virginity), and emotion. Thus, Richardson's novel captures a specific moment in English culture, when attempts to reinscribe older class markers are simultaneously challenged (through displacement, replacement, and redefinition). Although Sir Charles desires a return of sumptuary legislation, a means to identify the social position of the wearer, the novel itself shows evidence that assigning moral and emotional attributes to dress and dress color proves an equally powerful means of enforcing desired and desirable sartorial and social behaviors.

Numerous scholars and critics have commented upon the morally restrictive nature of this new mode of dress, comparing it to sumptuary legislation. Michael McKeon notes, in the early eighteenth century, "the impulse to enforce difference by dress did not disappear in the modern world. Sumptuary laws were replaced by less formal means of social regulation, by polemic rather than legislation."[8] Again, discussions of the moral nature of dress may be traced to conduct-book literature, as Nancy Armstrong illustrates: "female conduct books changed the ideal of what English life ought to be when they replaced the lavish displays of aristocratic life with the frugal and private practices of the modern gentleman"[9]; to whit, feminine attire now revealed virtue through lack of display, rather than through ostentatious display. Other attempts at sartorial regulation were made through lifestyle periodicals like *The Tatler* and *The Spectator*, as Erin Mackie notes: "The absence of formal modes of social regulation makes the job of self-styled cultural watchdogs like Addison and Steel all the more decisive," and "The regulation of taste and consumption practices through more informal means is crucial at this time when there is an explosion of goods on the market and yet no sumptuary legislation on the books and little active taboo to regulate their consumption."[10] Jennie Batchelor also notes that "arguments in favour of a return to sumptuary legislation often thinly veil other motives, more closely aligned with sexual regulation than with social control,"[11] and, of course, the sexual behavior most often regulated was that of women. In the discussion that follows, I trace the color of dress as moral regulator and indicator in *Sir Charles Grandison*; interestingly, all three instances in which dress color is invoked involve some sort of moral commentary on female character.

In order to understand the significance of color in *The History of Sir Charles Grandison* some background on sumptuary laws and the reasons behind their lapse is necessary. Sumptuary restrictions regarding dress color derived, at least initially, from costliness of materials or dyestuffs. For instance, gold and silver thread was made in England and in continental locales, "by twisting long narrow strips of gold [or silver] round a line of silk or flax"; gold and silver cloths were actually woven from these finely spun threads, though often intermixed with additional silk or linen; fabric was sold by weight, the heavier fabrics containing greater amounts of gold and silver.[12] Thus, during the reign of Elizabeth I, gold and silver cloth was restricted to members of the royal family, to "Earls and above that rank," and "Countesses and all above that rank."[13] Similar restrictions included the wearing of "Crimson, Scarlet or Blewe" velvet (Proclamation of 20 October 1559) and "Silke of purple color" (Proclamation of 6 July 1597).[14] In these instances, restricted garments combined expensive and/or imported fabrics (velvet, taffeta, damask, or silk) with rare dyestuffs.[15] Although purple dye was no longer as rare as it had once been, when made from the minuscule dye sacks of Mediterranean mollusks,[16] it still retained its long-held association with "high birth and dignity" and the dyestuffs used to create the color purple were largely from non-native species;[17] during Elizabeth's reign, purple dye was made by combining the leaves of woad (a plant native to Russia, but later grown in England), with roots of the madder plant (from Southern Europe and Asia Minor) or with kermes. Crimson and scarlet dyes could be made from madder, or from cochineal, kermes, or lac (all small-scale insects, from Mexico, from Southern Europe and the Near East, and from Southeastern Asia respectively).[18] The proscription against wearing "blewe" velvet in Elizabeth's proclamation most certainly relates to the time when woad was imported at great cost; later, when woad was grown in England, the proscription appears to have been lifted.[19] A specific shade of blue "was the mark of servitude," worn by liveried servants, orphans, apprentices, and other individuals dependent upon the goodwill of others; other shades of blue appear to have had royal or aristocratic associations.[20]

In contrast, the colors of dress worn by those from the lower station coincided with the natural colors of un-dyed native textiles (the pale brownish-white of unbleached wool, or the soft greenish-brown of woven flax), or of native dyestuffs, made from indigenous plant materials (roots, bark, nuts, seed pods, flowers, leaves, seaweed, even onion peels), minerals (iron, steel, clay, copper, soot, saltpeter, etc.), or other assorted natural and local by-products, such as honey, eggs, urine, and more.[21] "Nankin" or "buff" linen could be—and was—made by "soaking old horseshoes, nails, etc. in home-made vinegar, and for alkali an infusion of wood ashes."[22] The colors worn by those from the laboring and middling classes tended to be more muted and softer in tone than those worn by the upper station, and the colors tended to fade more easily: Imported dyestuffs produced more intense or purer colors, accounting for their desirability, as did the more complex mordants (chemicals used to affix color) used by commercial dyers. Fabric also affected color, as dyestuffs and mordants reacted differently with wool, linen, silk, and cotton. Silk and cotton, because imported and therefore costly, were primarily worn by members of the upper station; all stations wore some sort of linen or wool, though "a great range of quality, of weight and texture of cloth" existed.[23] Even up into the eighteenth century, as Anne Buck notes, "at one extreme, in the clothes of the fashionable woman, the fabrics were almost entirely imported; other groups wore a decreasing proportion of imported fabrics, until in the lower ranks of the common people clothing was entirely home-produced, that is produced in Great Britain."[24]

Differences in fabrics (silk, cotton, wool, linen); differences in mordants (alum, tannin, cream of tartar, vinegar, for example); differences in quality, quantity, and source of dyestuff; and differences in the complexity of specific dye processes—all produced different color variants, which, in turn, produced some disparity in the color of dress worn by different social stations. A red silk gown, worn by a fashionable lady, might be a deep, rich, shimmering crimson; a red cloth cloak, "a traditional garment of the English countrywoman"[25], a berry-bright scarlet; and a red wool waistcoat, worn by a rustic laborer, a warm reddish-brown. Other than cost of fabric, mordant, and dyestuffs, other considerations for members of the lower station included the durability of the garment (coarser fabrics were often less color-permeable); practicality (dirt and grime were less readily apparent on dark-hued clothing); and lack of access to soap (a highly expensive commodity) and hot water (necessary for the soap to work). Although the upper station had virtually unlimited access to soap, hot water, and servants, many of the silks, satins, and velvets worn by the upper station could not be washed at all, but were kept fresh looking by regular brushing, damp-wiping, stain-removal, and repair by valet or lady's maid, a luxury unavailable to the lower orders.

By the eighteenth century, sumptuary legislation was largely a thing of the distant past, though restrictions on importation of certain materials and dyestuffs continued to occur, dependent upon the political and economic climate.[26] On the whole, however, increased international trade and the establishment of plantations in British colonies made silk and cotton more readily available, and once rare dyestuffs, such as madder, cochineal, kermes, and indigo, became relatively commonplace throughout England. Differences still existed in styles, fabrics, and colors of dress among different social stations, but rigid distinctions were being blurred, and, perhaps because of this, and other cultural changes, color in dress began to accrue other, newer meanings.

Pink and yellow, though never restricted under sumptuary legislation, had generally been associated with upper-class garments, for many of the reasons stated: the expensiveness of imported dyestuffs (cochineal, kermes, or madder for pink; weld, saffron, safflower, or turmeric for yellow), susceptibility to soiling and staining, difficulty in cleaning, problems in attaining permanency of color. Of course, many shades of pink and yellow existed, from palest pink to deepest carnation; from onion-peel buff, to primrose yellow, to deep, orange-gold saffron, but the most prized pinks and yellows (the blush and carnation pinks, the Van Dyck and primrose yellows, and such) were produced with silk and cotton, rather than with wool and linen. For those from the upper stations, pink and yellow ranked among the most popular clothing colors of the eighteenth century. Aileen Ribeiro writes, "Pink was the eighteenth-century colour *par* excellence for women's dress; in different shades, from peachy pink, coral pink, sugar pink and a dark pink, in portraits and in surviving costume, it testifies to the popularity of a colour which suited most women, flattering and warming their complexions. ... Pink was especially in vogue during the period from the 1740s until into the 1770s."[27] Certainly, Mary Granville Pendarves (later, Mrs. Delany), found pink damask an extremely attractive choice for a gown, as she wrote to her sister Anne, in 1731: "yesterday I bought a pink-coloured damask for seven shillings a yard, the prettiest colour I ever saw for a night-gown."[28] Yet fashionable men enjoyed wearing pink clothing and accoutrement as well. Ribeiro cites the following examples: Prince Frederick's "Vandyke costume of white satin," trimmed with "pink puffs and knots"; a young man attending a Vauxhall masquerade, dressed in "Pink Sattin with silver Pods"; and young master Nicholls of *Pink Boy* fame, wearing a pink suit.[29] Indeed, for summer wear, most men from the upper station wore silk suits, in such "pale colours as pink, light blue, buff, and lilac."[30]

Yellow was also much in vogue, particularly during the 1740s and 1750s. Eliza Haywood, in *The Female Spectator*, describes it as "yellow, the colour so rever'd in Hanover, and so much the mode in England in the present."[31] *The Inspector*, in 1751, writes of a "Dandy" wearing "yellow velvet breeches."[32] Of course, Richardson's most fashionably dressed heroine, Clarissa, wears a pale primrose-colored gown when she is abducted from Harlowe Place.

In *Sir Charles Grandison*, pink and yellow are mentioned but few times, but these references are significant, as all indicate an age-specific and gender-specific, rather than class-specific, interpretation of dress color. Within Richardson's novel, the few references made to pink and yellow relate to older, unmarried women, "stale virgins" all—and these older women are gently chided for their "girlish" fondness for "spring-like" colors, more suitable, so the references imply, to young women.[33]

Eleanor Grandison, the aunt of Sir Charles and Charlotte, a "good, plump, bonny-faced old virgin" (2:443), is humorously derided for her passion for pink and yellow ribbons. When the engagement of Sir Charles and Harriet is announced, Aunt Nell greets the news with a flurry of ribbons: "Aunt Nell prank'd herself, stroked her ribbands of pink and yellow, and chuckled and mumped for joy" (3:22). Waiting for an invitation to join the wedding party, Aunt Nell sits at home, her outfit ready for the summons: "Pink and yellow, all is ready provided" (3:198).[34] Later on, after the wedding, Nancy Selby muses about the "dreary unconnected Life of a single woman in years"; Nancy says, "I thought of poor Mrs. Penelope Arby. You all know her. I saw her in imagination, surrounded with parrots and lap-dogs!—So spring-like at past fifty, with her pale pink Lustring, and back head. Yet so peevish at girls!—" (3:397). These "young-old" (3:407) women, dressed in "spring-like" colors, are reproached for their spinsterish foolishness in attempting to cling to youth. As Lady G. writes to Harriet, "these old virgins! they do so love to be thought useful. ... I always think, when I see those badgerly virgins fond of a parrot, a squirrel, or a lap-dog, that their imagination makes out husband and children in the animals—Poor things!" (2:654). In a society that believed "a woman is most likely to find her proper happiness in the married state" (3:408), pink and yellow ribbons, surrounding a worn and wrinkled face, were both laughable and pitiable.

As noted, two meanings for the same colors could and did coexist in eighteenth century England, without apparent questioning. Prince Frederick could wear "pink puffs and knots," and a 57-year-old Horace Walpole could waspishly complain, "If I went to Almack's and decked out my wrinkles in pink and green like Lord Harrington, I might still be in vogue."[35] However, during the same time period, most individuals became conscious of the unsuitability of older persons, particularly women, wearing pastel colors: "For women there was very much a sense of what was suitable for their age, thirty being the onset of middle age when the frivolities of fashion, such as pastel colours, feathers and flowers, should be abandoned."[36] Ribeiro notes, "the acid Princess Royal of Prussia remarked on her great-aunt in 1731 that 'she tricked herself off like a young person. She wore her hair in large curls with pink ribbands of a shade somewhat lighter than her face."[37] In 1754, Lady Jane Coke wrote: "One thing is new, which is, there is not such a thing as a decent old woman left, everybody curls their hair, shews their neck, and wears pink, but your humble servant. People who have covered their heads for forty years now leave off their caps and think it becomes them."[38]

In poking gentle fun at Aunt Eleanor and the seemingly perpetual girlishness of unmarried women, expressed through a love of pink gowns and yellow ribbons, Richardson's novel documents the socio-political transformation occurring in England, as the reading of pink and yellow as gender-specific and age-specific indicates a more-modern, more-bourgeois perspective. Pink gowns and yellow ribbons *should*, under this new interpretation, identify a young adolescent woman eager to enter into her life's duties—all of which center around the institution of marriage. As Richardson's novel notes, "it is a duty" for women to enter into marriage, and "a kind of faulty *indulgence* and self-ishness, in order to avoid these cares and troubles, to live single" (3:411). As Harriet Byron comments, "I remember what my Uncle once averr'd: That a woman out of wedlock is half useless to the end of her being. How indeed do the duties of a good Wife, of a good Mother, and a worthy Matron, well performed, dignify a woman!" (1:25). Sympathy is given to those who, without choice, without suitors, must live single; but for those who *choose* to live single, admonishments are due for refusing "to be called out into active life" (2:547), that is, into married life. (Even Clementina is chided for her desire to be come a nun, par-ticularly when the attractive and sympathetic Count of Belvedere per-sists in his desire to wed her.) Active duty is always preferable to passive duty, in Richardson's novel. On young, single women, pink and yellow ribbons signify acceptance of this duty, the eagerness to attract a mate and enter into a life filled with and fulfilled by duty; on older, unmar-ried women, the same ribbons indicate a "halt useless" life, as well as possible neglect of or deliberate avoidance of duty. These elderly virgins masquerade as actively dutiful young women, wishing to be thought useful; however, the pink and yellow ribbons (instead of the matronly cap), the lap dogs, tabby cats, and parrots upon which they lavish all their care and attention (instead of husband and children) indicate self-love and self-involvement.

Similarly, a man wearing these same colors begins to be deemed remiss in fulfilling his social obligations and duties. Sober businessmen do not wear pink suits, nor do earnest shopkeepers dress in pale yellow waistcoats (buff, yes; primrose, no). Part of this reform begins as early as 1666 with the introduction of the three-piece suit, an ensemble designed "to teach the nobility thrift," a form of "sartorial renunciation ... opposed to the presumed luxury and extravagant dress of decadent courtiers and middle-class social climbers."[39] This trend continued throughout the eighteenth century; as Ribeiro notes, "The 1770s was in fact the last time that men would wear colourful costume, and this was a taste limited to the macaronis and those who imitated their extreme fashions"; "men's dress seems to move inexorably towards dull conformity."[40] The pastel-colored silks worn by male members of the upper station translate to effeminacy, a dislike of dirty hands and hard work, when viewed through the ideological lens of the lesser gentry and the middle station; for many from the upper station, a disdain for pastel silks demonstrated "good taste,"[41] a way to differentiate oneself from the *nouveau riche* or the highly effeminate fop.

Although Sir Charles expresses interest in maintaining class distinctions, he is more concerned with maintaining (or creating) gender distinctions, as indicated by his horror of "an effeminate man" and "a masculine woman" (3:247). To a large extent, this morally based interpretation of dress color becomes as effective as sumptuary legislation, as social disapproval exists as a highly effective means of enforcing dress codes and prescribing/proscribing specific sartorial and social behaviors.

Richardson's novel also provides evidence of how dress, interpreted in a morally based manner, can serve as a means to restrict sexual conduct. An all-white wedding gown becomes the means of encouraging morality, specifically by attempting to curtail premarital sexual activity, though, in fact, white clothing (primarily white formal dress) had long been associated with the upper station. The wedding of Sir Charles Grandison and Harriet Byron is celebrated in grand fashion: The church is packed with well-wishers; Harriet and her attendants wear white gowns; four little village girls strew flowers about the bride and groom; a lavish reception follows. However, eighteenth-century weddings, on the whole, were relatively simple affairs, particularly in London and other urban environs. A church ceremony was preferred, though a civil ("clandestine") wedding was also acceptable, particularly for those who wished for more privacy.[42] The latter, these "chamber-marriages," were increasingly considered "neither *decent*, nor *godly*" (3:193). Afterwards, an informal reception might take place, with music and dancing. This is the case when Charlotte Grandison marries Lord G.: Although Charlotte prefers a civil ceremony, conducted in the privacy of her chambers, she nonetheless concedes to the wishes of others for a church ceremony. The ceremony is a simple one, with immediate family and friends in attendance. Afterwards, Charlotte and Lord G., Sir Charles, Harriet, Lord and Lady L., Lord W., Emily Jervois, Mr. Beauchamp, and some other close intimates join in an informal concert, with dancing, though "We were not company enough for country dances" (2:345). A midnight supper concludes the festivities. Charlotte's wedding gown is not described.

Wedding gowns, *per se*, did not exist in eighteenth-century England, though most brides, regardless of social class, preferred a new gown (new, at least, to them) to be married in, as a sign of good luck and prosperity in the future marriage. For instance, in Daniel Defoe's *Colonel Jack*, the thrice unlucky-in-love Jack tries to talk Moggy into marrying him, upon the spur of the moment: "she laugh'd, and told me it was not lucky to be married in her old Cloaths"; once Jack presents Moggy with "a new Morning Gown of my Wife's, that she had never worn above two or three Times," Moggy agrees to wed.[43] Similarly, Richardson's Pamela weds Mr. B. in "rich white Sattin Night-gown, that had been my good Lady's" (287). However, if new clothes were not available, then Sunday best was considered suitable. *The Connoisseur* confirms that the "happy couple are drest in their richest suits."[44]

For those from the upper stations, wedding garments consisted of a number of complete suits of clothing (gowns, petticoats, stays) that were detailed in the articles of settlement between the bride's family and the groom, not merely a single gown or a single ensemble. For instance, if Clarissa had agreed to marry Solmes, her parents would have provided her with six complete suits of clothing as part of the agreement: "Your Father intends you six Suits (three of them dressed Suits) at his own expence. You have an entire new Suit. ... As the new Suit is rich, if you chuse to make That one of the six, your Father will present you with an hundred guineas in lieu" (1:281). Quite frequently, as is the case with Solmes, Mr. B., and Sir Charles, the prospective groom was responsible for gifting the bride with jewelry appropriate to her new station. From all the various suits of new clothing, some made prior to the wedding, others afterwards, the bride might choose two outfits to commemorate her marriage: The first, a gown to be worn during the actual wedding ceremony; the second, a more elaborate gown for wear during the first public appearance together of the newly married couple, an event that most often took place the Sunday after the wedding. For instance, upon the return of Mr. B. and Pamela to Bedfordshire, Pamela attends church services wearing a "Suit ... of White flower'd with Gold, and a rich Head-dress, and the Diamond Necklace, Ear-rings, &c" (399). Similarly, Harriet wears a simple white gown for her wedding and a more elaborate gown for her first public appearance as Lady Grandison.

All wedding garments were meant to be worn on numerous other occasions, and, thus, had to prove serviceable for other events, which, for those of the upper stations, were most often full dress occasions. As Phillis Cunnington and Charles Beard note, male wedding attire "had been merely a ceremonial 'full dress' suit,"[45] and female wedding attire was essentially the same. Because wedding and presentation gowns were worn on other occasions, they were often in cheerful, fashionable colors, sometimes white, but, as often as not, yellow, blue, or silver.[46] Cunnington and Beard suggest that, prior to the nineteenth century, most wedding dresses were "usually white,"[47] though this fact is disputed by other fashion scholars. Karen Baclawski notes, "Until the nineteenth century, the clothes of both the bride and bridegroom were likely to be coloured, although references to brides wearing white may be found as early as the fifteenth century. These clothes were generally fashionably cut and made of the richest fabrics available to the couple. In the eighteenth century, many brides began to wear gowns of silver, white or blue."[48] These favorite color choices ("silver, white or blue") for wedding gowns appear an extension of Elizabethan color symbolism, originally associated with heraldic blazons. In 1583, an English translation of an Italian treatise on color symbolism was published, authored by Sicile, Herald to the King of Aragon, and translated by Richardson Robinson, entitled *A Rare True and Proper Blazon of Coloures and Ensignes Military with theyre Peculiar Signification*. As Linthicum writes, "According to Sicile, white indicated faith, humility, and chastity; ... silver, purity; yellow, hope, joy, magnaminity; ... green, love, joy; blue, amity."[49] Although white wedding gowns came to represent the presumed virginity of the bride, the original symbolism was slightly more complex, suggesting more than chastity. For instance, Edmund Spenser's Una, a symbol of the "True Church," rides "a lowly Asse more white than snow, / Yet she much whiter ..." (I.i.4.2–3); her gown is "All lilly white, withoutten spot ..." (I.xii.22.7).[50] Una is the embodiment of truth, chastity, and faith. Of course, Elizabeth I, the "Virgin Queen" to whom Spenser dedicated his epic and who herself was an astute observer and manipulator of the nuances of representation and attire, also dressed in white, as the occasion warranted.[51] It is important to note that Elizabethan color symbolism was largely restricted to upper-class dress, as those from the middling or lower stations possessed limited clothing choices, constrained either by economic considerations or sumptuary legislation. In addition, Elizabethan color symbolism tended to represent abstract concepts, such as truth, fidelity, hope, for instance, rather than to display the moral, emotional, or psychological status of the wearer.

Furthermore, because white formal dress garments were almost always silk or satin, rarely wool or linen, white gowns, petticoats, waistcoats, and pants must undoubtedly have been worn only by those from the upper stations. Pure white cloth of any sort was difficult to achieve: Wool must be "scoured" to remove lanolin and oils, a process that involves boiling the wool in water and urine, and the wool, even then, would most often attain an off-white color, rather than pure white. Silk must also be "scoured" in soap and boiling water in order to remove its natural "gum or varnish" as well as the yellow gum preservative in which it was packed for import. Cotton, which could vary in natural color from "a deep yellow to a white," must be bleached.[52] White linen was the most labor intensive to make: The cloth must first be steeped in a bath of lye and warm water, allowed to ferment, then rinsed, washed, dried; placed again in a bath of lye, water, and salts, where the linen is "squeezed down by a man with wooden shoes"; it is then taken out and spread on the grass, where it is repeatedly watered; the last process is repeated "ten to sixteen times," after which the linen is finally ready for scouring and washing.[53] (White linens, of course, were associated with the gentry and aristocracy, an indication of the wearer's access to numerous changes of linen and prodigious amounts of soap and hot water). As with pink and yellow, white fabric stained and soiled easily, and, thus, would not have been a practicable color choice for long-term wear, among the lower stations, even as Sunday attire. White gowns, on the whole, did not become highly popular for general wear until "the law banning the importation of all cotton fabrics [into England] was lifted,"[54] in 1774.

Richardson, however, prefers his heroines in white. Pamela wears white, both for her wedding and her first public appearance as Mrs. B. Clarissa, after her rape, wears "a white damask night-gown" (5:321). Harriet, more happily, dresses "All in Virgin White" (3:219) for her wedding to Sir Charles. As many scholars have noted, Clarissa's gown most assuredly relates to the gowns worn by the heroines of stage tragedies, particularly by the heroines of the so-called "she-tragedies." White is a solemn color, as evidenced by the fact that it could be worn for half-mourning, the period after deep mourning was concluded,[55] and it retains its Elizabethan associations with "faith, humility, and chastity," and, thus, would be an appropriate choice for Clarissa. The solemnity associated with white would also fit with Richardson's notions of marriage being "an awful rite," "a joyful solemnity" (2:347). The irrepressible Lady G. specifically relates white wedding gowns to virgin sacrifice: "After all, Lady L. we women, dressed out in ribbands, and gaudy trappings, and in Virgin-white, on our Wedding-days, seem but like milk-white heifers led to sacrifice" (3:236). She reiterates these thoughts, saying, "Ah silly maidens! If you could look three yards from your noses, you would pity, instead of envying, the milk-white heifer dressed in ribbands, and just ready to be led to sacrifice" (3:358). (One assumes that the "milk-white heifer" later becomes "the meek, the beneficent cow," upon marriage.) White was also deemed an angelic color, and, angels, as we all know from *Paradise Lost*, do not engage in sexual relations, or, at least, allow no "Flesh to mix with Flesh" (VIII.629). Clementina, dressed in "plain white satten ... looks like an Angel" (2:561). Harriet, too, appears in heavenly hues: "All in Virgin White. She looks, she moves, an Angel!" (3:219).

For Harriet, a member of the lesser gentry, a white gown would be considered unexceptional attire for both wedding and for future wear, particularly as she has chosen a morning gown, a moderately informal style that could be worn to Sunday services. However, Richardson's insistence on pure white gowns for all his heroines suggests a larger, symbolic significance: It is not Harriet's social station that entitles her to wear white, but her virtue. She is an angel, a virgin to be sacrificed on the altar of marriage, aware of the solemnity of the event, yet willing, even shyly eager to perform her duty.

Every young female, regardless of social station, could relate, could aspire to become like Harriet, to be as happy in her choice of chosen spouse as Harriet. The elaborate wedding church ceremony, the lavish reception, the ceremonial accoutrements, including seven female and seven male attendants (all orchestrated by Harriet's Uncle Selby, whom Lady G. terms "Earlmarshal Selby" (3:219), the earliest literary mention of a wedding planner), serve to create a literary event of some importance (after all, up until the last minute, Sir Charles's prospective bride might as easily have been Clementina), but, also, to celebrate and elevate the institution of marriage, particularly marriage between two such worthy individuals. The *coup de grace* is the four little flower girls, daughters of tenant farmers, whose innocence comments upon and complements the proceedings:

> Four girls, tenants daughters, the eldest not above Thirteen, appeared with neat wicker-baskets in their hands, filled with flowers of the season. Chearful way was made for them. As soon as the Bride, and Father, and Sir Charles, and Mrs. Shirley, alighted, these pretty little Flora's, all dressed in white, chaplets of flowers for head-dresses, large nosegays in their bosoms, white ribbands adorning their stays and their baskets; some streaming down, others tied around the handles in true lover's knots; attended the company, two going before, two other here and there, and every-where, all strewing flowers: A pretty thought of the tenants, among themselves.
>
> (3:224)

The fact that the daughters of tenant farmers possess white gowns, no doubt linen gowns for Sunday wear, suggests the prosperity that the Selby and Shirley families have brought to the region. These cherubic young "Floras" appear, as if from nowhere, almost as if heaven itself was acknowledging the event, celebrating marriage between two chaste and morally upright individuals. (Sir Charles, if one recalls, is a virgin, "virtuous, even, ... to chastity?" (2:497)). The strewing of flowers symbolizes the fruitfulness and prosperity that will attend such a union, and the fact that these are tenants' daughters also suggests the importance of the marriage to the continued prosperity and health of the community.

The Connoisseur suggests that country marriages among members of the gentry were often highly festive affairs: "In the Country, when the squire, or any other person of distinction is married, the Honey-Moon is almost a continued Carnival: and every marriage is accounted more or less likely to be prosperous, in proportion to the number of deer, oxen, and sheep, that are killed on the occasion, and the hogsheads of wine and tuns of ale, with which they are washed down."[56] However, the wedding of Sir Charles and Harriet appears more elaborate than most, replete with bridesmaids, groomsmen, flower girls, and the like, and it presages the elaborate weddings and receptions of the nineteenth, twentieth, and twenty-first centuries, which emphasize and attempt to elevate the institution of marriage.[57] The white gown and petticoat, formerly symbolic of upper-class purity, truth, chastity—and wealth—becomes, instead, a maker of morality, an outward sign of the virginity of the bride, a sign which presumes her continued chastity upon marriage, her continued attention to her wedding vows. Although sumptuary legislation sought to control the moral behavior of those from the middling and lower stations, keeping extravagance in clothing, food, and fun to a minimum, the new moral symbolism associated with the white wedding gown proves a highly effective social regulator.

Finally, in *Grandison*, the color of dress relates to the emotional and psychological status of the wearer. The color of Clementina's numerous outfits becomes the medium through which she communicates her deepest inner emotions, those passions and sensations inexpressible through mere words. This specific use of color is subtly different from the way in which color of dress was used in the past. The Elizabethans utilized color emblematically, assigning specific colors to certain abstract attributes—for instance, "obscure grey" designated patience, silver meant purity[58]—and, as the occasion warranted, the upper-class wearer selected specific colors in order to signify his patience or her purity, regardless of whether or not the wearer was indeed patient or pure. To a great extent, the color of dress was related to performance: One dressed the part of a patient person, or a pure person. Queen Elizabeth I insisted "that her six Maids of Honour should wear a white and silver costume when at court" to indicate their purity, chastity, humility, and faithfulness, yet she did not require that these maids be pure, chaste, and humble (though faithfulness to the Queen went without saying).[59] Meaning remained external to the individual wearer. However, in *Grandison*, clothing color is presumed to express the inner passions and innate attributes of the individual; in this system, the internal imposes meaning upon the external. Although color meaning frequently remained the same (grey still symbolized patience), the impetus to wear grey appears to come from within, rather than from without. The individual is patient; therefore, the individual wears grey, as no other color can express this innate attribute of the wearer.

In *Grandison*, Clementina's mental illness and confusion expresses itself through her attire: The wearing of deepest black signals her despair, melancholy, and madness; bright colors suggest a manic turn of mind; pure white suggests momentary emotional tranquility, a return to knowledge of self. The frequent changes in Clementina's dress color provides evidence of her overall emotional instability and her psychological fragility, and, because Clementina is never allowed to speak directly for herself, as all her words are transcribed into Sir Charles's letters or the letters of her family, her clothing becomes a seminal means of communication.

In European fashion, black clothing has long been associated with solemnity and dignity, with wealth and prosperity. Aileen Ribeiro writes:

> Black has always been a colour of immense significance in the history of dress. Black clothes were expensive, for the dyes used were costly; a poor-quality dye produced cloth of uneven colour which quickly faded, but a good dye enhanced the lustre of fine cloth, whether of silk or wool. Throughout history, black clothes usually indicated rich but unostentatious consumption. ... Black created an impression of gravitas; it was the colour of officials and dignitaries; it was the colour of the ruling castes such as the élite of the city-state of Venice and the merchant oligarchy of The Netherlands. Black was the colour worn by clerics, by lawyers and academics as part of a collective wish by society that sobriety should mark its formal dealings.[60]

The English association of black with death and mourning appears to have begun in 1200s, as Rosemary Horrox relates:

> Wearing black had been a feature of elite funerals from at least the late thirteenth century. In 1281 the executors of Cecily Talmache paid for black gowns for her funeral, and since they were furred, albeit not lavishly, they were probably for elite mourners—distinguishing them from

the poor candle-bearers clad in white. By the fourteenth century, however, it was usual to put the poor into black, and the provision of such gowns is a common element in contemporary wills.[61]

(One assumes that the "poor candle-bearers" wore coarse white linen or white wool garments.) In Elizabethan heraldry, black "signified grief and constancy,"[62] and black bile, of course, was the bodily humor associated with melancholy.

Black becomes an exceedingly popular dress color in late eighteenth-century England, associated with the cult of sensibility: Horace Walpole, in a letter to George Montagu, dated 14 October 1760, writes, "As I never dress in summer, I had nothing upon earth but a frock, unless I went in black, like a poet, and pretended that a cousin was dead, one of the Muses."[63] As Ribeiro comments, "black in particular, with its context of mourning, emphasized the man of sorrows, the intellectual, the writer. Byron, for example, liked to wear black; it made him look slimmer, made his skin appear whiter and added the air of romantic melancholy appropriate for a fashionable poet with a scandalous private life."[64] England, lest we forget, was a country that prized itself on the melancholy nature of its inhabitants. Dr. George Cheyne's 1724 treatise, *An Essay on Health and Long Life*, celebrated the English predisposition towards gloom: "*Thoughtful* People, and those of good Understanding, suffer most by the *slow*, and *secretly consuming* Passions."[65]

Clementina, thus, is a character of the moment, a child of melancholy and sorrow. No one has died, yet Clementina wears deepest mourning. Clementina's madness stems from extreme emotional distress: Clementina loves Sir Charles, but views him as an English heretic, and the conflict between her faith and her love for Sir Charles, a conflict which she internalizes, a conflict about which she never speaks, translates into madness. Her black flowing robes, her black veils, her black gown, whose hem drags along the floor—all indicate profound depression, melancholy, and despair. She chooses black because she sees herself as burnt and scorched by Grandison: She translates the Canticles from Latin: "*Look not upon me because I am black, because the sun hath looked upon me*" (2:247). Sir Charles is the sun. The profundity of Clementina's despair becomes signaled through her dress: "Just then entered the sweet Lady, leaning upon Camilla, Laura attending. Her movement was slow and solemn. Her eyes were cast on the ground. Her robes were black and flowing. A veil of black gause half covered her face. What woe was there in it!" (2:469). In Clementina, we find an early precursor of the Romantic and Gothic tragic heroine.

In Stock's illustration of this scene from *Grandison*, as shown in Figure 11.1, the gloominess of Clementina's attire is heightened by the light-colored dress of the other characters. Even the attire of Clementina's brother, the Bishop (the figure in the upper-left corner, with the crucifix around his neck), appears lighter, less weighty than Clementina's own attire. The black gown, petticoat, and veil are relieved

Figure 11.1 Johann Michael Stock (1737–73). Plate XIII, from *Geschichte Herrn Carl Grandison*. Leipzig: M. G. Weidmanns Erben und Reich, 1780. Cropped, computer-scanned image. Book in collection of K. M. Oliver

only by the whiteness of her neckerchief and linen, a sign of her high social rank and a symbol of her inner purity. While most eyes are upon Clementina, she herself looks down and away.

Grief and constancy are a part of Clementina's madness and melancholy, as are dignity and solemnity, yet her somber clothing is also an outward indication of her resistance to internalizing specific societal and sartorial rules. To a large extent, she has internalized the rules of the Catholic Church, regarding Sir Charles as a heretic, yet her desire to have what she wants, rather than what her family wants, also indicates a degree of self-interest and willfulness, a disregard for others, inconsistent with Sir Charles's worldview. Her madness, one might argue, generates from the conflict between self-interest and duty towards family; she struggles to internalize rules that are inconsistent with her personal desire.

Later, when some semblance of sanity returns, Clementina's numerous outfit changes reflect her continued emotional fragility. Clementina's maid informs Sir Charles that "My young Lady is dressing in colours, to receive you. She will no more *appear* to you, she says, in black" (2:523). However, Sir Charles, an astute observer of dress, is dismayed by Clementina's appearance: "Clementina appeared exceedingly lovely. But her fancifulness in the disposition of her ornaments, and the unusual lustre of her eyes, which every one was wont to admire for their *serene* brightness, shewed an imagination more disordered than I hoped to see; and gave me pain at my entrance." He recalls, "Clementina, when her mind was sound, used to be all unaffected elegance" (2:524). Now, of course, the "fancifulness" displayed in her dress expresses the disorder of her mind. The bright colors suggest her desire to appear youthful and desirable to Sir Charles; again, self-interest, personal desire still appear to possess Clementina, more than a sense of filial duty. However, as Clementina begins to regain control of her mind and emotions, to internalize societal rules, her clothing demonstrates the return of tranquility and serenity, when she chooses to wear an all-white gown: "She was not to be pleased with her dress. Once she would be in black; then in colours; then her white and silver was taken out: But that, she said, would give her a bridal appearance: She at last chose her plain white satten. She looks like an Angel" (2:561). She has waged war with her own emotions, finally gaining control, by conquering both her melancholy and mania, by rejecting extremes in the passions, by forgoing self-interest in lieu of responsibility to family, to country, to religion.

From the hellish black of despair, to the bright colors of mania, to the angelic white of serenity—the color of Clementina's attire functions as a barometer of her mental, emotional, and psychological state, and it indicates her struggle to internalize rules that directly conflict with her own desires. Clementina doesn't wear black because an external event—the death of another—has occurred, or because she wishes to appear dignified, melancholic, or somber, but because a death of sorts has occurred in her mind. She doesn't wear blue, or yellow, or green to indicate friendship, hope, or love, but because all these emotions are tumbled together within her own psyche. She doesn't wear white because she wishes to appear chaste, humble, faithful, and pure, but because she is indeed so, because she has once again reclaimed mental control and cleansed her mind of its emotional distress, leaving it blank, transparent, spotless. The color of Clementina's attire reflects her emotional and psychological status, and, above all, her moral conflict—her attempt to gain control over passions, emotions, and mind, her struggle to regulate self, without the interference of confessor, parents, brothers.

Although color exists as a minor element in the descriptions of dress in *The History of Sir Charles Grandison*, a few phrases or sentences only in an immensely long novel, it nonetheless demonstrates Richardson's sophisticated, subtle, and intuitive use of color to portray the inner traits and emotions of his characters: the silly foolishness of Aunt Nell, the chaste morality of Harriet, and the mental and emotional distress of Clementina. The color of dress communicates important social messages about the wearer, and it also provides evidence of literary and cultural change in eighteenth-century England, where meanings assigned to objects and colors, to dress and the colors of dress, were forever changed by the increasing cultural dominance of the middle station and of the genre of the novel itself.

Conclusion

"What ... is the boasted characters of most of those who are called HEROES, to the un-ostentatious merit of a TRULY GOOD MAN? In what a variety of amiable lights does such a one appear? In how many ways is he a blessing and a joy to his fellow-creatures" (3:462). So ends the penultimate paragraph of *The History of Sir Charles Grandison*. Each of Richardson's three fictional histories depicts a life of exemplary virtue: The first, the story of a little servant girl who reforms her naughty master, and, as reward, becomes his wife; the second, the tragic tale of a young woman from the highest and wealthiest ranks of the middle station whose attempts to avoid a forced marriage allow her to become the prey of an accomplished rake; the third, the celebratory account of a young gentleman whose pious actions and strict attention to duty secure him the admiration of all and the love of not one but two virtuous young women.

The two novels with happy endings are those that start—or end—with a virtuous gentleman; the one novel with the unhappy ending, with the rape and subsequent death of the virtuous young heroine, suggests the failure of patrician honor, as it currently exists, a system in which marriages are based on convenience, rather than companionship, and with gentlemen engaged in pursuits of pleasure, rather than of duty. All three of Richardson's novels attempt to render legible the domestic feminine ideal, with Pamela, Clarissa, Harriet, and Clementina representing this ideal in various forms and fashion, yet surely an underlying narrative of all three novels is the education, the reformation, and, ultimately, the domestication of the male gentry. The differing social ranks of Pamela (servant class), Clarissa (middle station), Harriet (lesser gentry), and Clementina (aristocracy) suggest the relative instability associated with the domestic feminine ideal, an instability generated by the culture's tendency to categorize women based on their relationships to and with men, allowing women some measure of social mobility through marriage, but also by the fact that women were, first and foremost, defined by their female sex, with all the attendant cultural associations of femaleness with frailty, with contradiction. However, all three of Richardson's male protagonists are members of the gentry; the positive (or negative) outcomes of each novel rest upon gentlemanly potential for domestication.

Is *Pamela; or Virtue Rewarded*, then, really all about Mr. B.? Was Richardson, through his novels, attempting to render legible the domestic masculine ideal, rather than the domestic feminine ideal? And, on a cultural level, was the female conduct book, in which the domestic feminine ideal was replicated over and over, and which Richardson used as a model for his own narratives, merely a Trojan horse of sorts from which a new form of patriarchy stole forth?

While I do not believe in a cultural conspiracy, I do think that female conduct-book literature promoted a new type of patriarchal order, one in which the gentleman and the gentleman-tradesman gained cultural hegemony, replacing the former alliance between gentleman and aristocrat. Several reasons may exist as to why conduct books for women readers proliferated in eighteenth-century England, and why the publication of conduct books for women greatly surpassed that for men: They include the overall explosion of printed materials upon the lapse of the 1695 Licensing Act; the increase in female literacy during this time period, from an estimated 25 percent of all English women in 1714 to approximately 33 percent by 1750, with at least 56 percent of the female inhabitants of London able to read and write by the 1720s;[1] the limited types of literature deemed "suitable" for female readers; the overall cultural message that the attributes embodied in the domestic feminine ideal were those most prized in women; and, finally, the fact that the domestic feminine ideal could never be realized, as any ideal, by its very nature, assumes a level of perfection generally beyond the capabilities of real individuals, and because any ideal undergoes constant, if small, revision rendering it as elusive and as addictive as fashion itself.

I like to think that Richardson began his novelistic project with the intent of proving that a servant girl may possess virtue equal to that of a gentlewoman—or a princess—and a belief that a virtuous woman of any social station may have an improving effect on men. Yet the instability of signification associated with Pamela (and her clothes), coupled with the fact that eighteenth-century English culture itself deemed marriage to a gentleman the highest reward for feminine virtue, forced Richardson on a quest to stabilize meaning. With *Clarissa*, instability associated with the heroine's social station is erased, yet difficulties in stabilizing meaning continue to exist, largely because the character of Lovelace, the unreformed, unrepentant gentleman, continues to fascinate and allure. Ultimately, a cultural truth reveals itself—that the gentleman, rakish or reformed, urbane or domesticated, exists as the "dominant social ideal" in eighteenth-century England. With *Grandison*, Richardson presents his readers with a reformed, domesticated vision of the gentleman, a vision that depends upon the gentleman embracing the values of the middling sorts, while eschewing the degenerate habits associated with the aristocracy. The domestic feminine ideal also reveals her true self with Richardson's final novel: Although the domestic feminine ideal (as expressed through the characters of Harriet and Clementina) indeed embodies those attributes associated with feminine virtue, she nonetheless is prone to slight slips in behavior, and, in order to achieve ideal feminine perfection, she requires the steadying influence of a "TRULY GOOD MAN," a Sir Charles Grandison. Beneath the voluminous hooped petticoat of domestic woman the true object of desire for eighteenth-century English culture lies hidden—domestic man.

Notes

Introduction

1. Anne Laurence, *Women in England, 1500–1760: A Social History* (London: Weidenfeld and Nicolson, 1994), 227.
2. Letter to Aaron Hill, 26 January 1746/7. In *Selected Letters of Samuel Richardson*, ed. John Carroll (Oxford: Clarendon Press, 1964), 82. In Carroll's edition of Richardson's correspondence, brackets (< >) and daggers (†) respectively represent deletions and additions to letters, as made by Richardson.
3. See Nancy Armstrong, *Desire and Domestic Fiction: A Political History of the Novel* (New York and Oxford: Oxford University Press, 1987), and "The Rise of the Domestic Woman," in *The Ideology of Conduct: Essays on Literature and the History of Sexuality*, eds. Nancy Armstrong and Leonard Tennenhouse (New York: Methuen, 1987), 96–141.
4. Jennie Batchelor, *Dress, Distress and Desire: Clothing and the Female Body in Eighteenth-Century Literature* (Basingstoke: Palgrave Macmillan, 2005), 151.
5. See Armstrong.
6. Clair Hughes, *Dressed in Fiction* (Oxford and New York: Berg, 2005), 5.
7. Susan B. Kaiser, *The Social Psychology of Clothing: Symbolic Appearances in Context*, 2nd ed. revised (New York: Fairchild Publications, 1998), 1.
8. Claude Lévi-Strauss, *The Origin of Table Manners: Introduction to a Science of Mythology*, vol. 3, trans. John and Doreen Weightman (London: Cape, 1968), 130, 131.
9. Malcolm Barnard, *Fashion as Communication* (London and New York: Routledge, 1996), 39–40.
10. Karl Marx, "The Fetishism of Commodities," in vol. I of *Capital: A Critique of Political Economy*, trans. Samuel Moore and Edward Aveling, ed. Frederick Engels (1887; Moscow: Progress Publishers, 1954), 77.
11. Marx, 78.
12. Herbert Marcuse, *One-Dimensional Man: Studies in the Ideology of Advanced Industrial Society* (Boston: Beacon Press, 1964), 9.
13. Erin Mackie, *Market à la Mode: Fashion, Commodity, and Gender in The Tatler and the Spectator* (London and Baltimore, MD: The Johns Hopkins University Press, 1997), 15.
14. Mackie, 6.
15. Mackie, 15.
16. Kaiser, 145. The original quote is in italics.
17. Barnard, 30.
18. Kaiser, 549.
19. Barnard, 26. Notably, Alison Lurie, in *The Language of Clothes* (New York: Henry Holt and Company, 1981), claims that clothing possesses "a vocabulary and a grammar like other languages" (4).
20. Roland Barthes, *The Fashion System*, trans. Matthew Ward and Richard Howard (Berkeley and Los Angeles: University of California Press, 1990), 8.

21. Terry Castle, *Masquerade and Civilization: The Carnivalesque in Eighteenth-Century English Culture and Fiction* (Stanford, CA: Stanford University Press, 1986), 55–6.
22. Joanne Entwistle, *The Fashioned Body: Fashion, Dress and Modern Social Theory* (Cambridge: Blackwell Publishers, 2000), 71.
23. Entwistle, 9.
24. Castle, 117–8.
25. Castle, 120.
26. Castle, 125. Catherine Craft-Fairchild, *Masquerade and Gender: Disguise and Female Identity in Eighteenth-Century Fictions by Women* (University Park, PA: The Pennsylvania State University Press, 1993), 2.
27. Mackie, 2.
28. Mackie, 5.
29. Batchelor, 12.
30. Batchelor, 15, 16.
31. Batchelor, 16.
32. Armstrong, *Desire and Domestic Fiction*, 59.
33. Armstrong, *Desire and Domestic Fiction*, 5.
34. Batchelor, 177.
35. Robert Markley, "Sentimentality as Performance: Shaftesbury, Sterne, and the Theatrics of Virtue," in *The New Eighteenth Century: Theory, Politics, English Literature*, eds. Felicity Nussbaum and Laura Brown (New York and London: Methuen, 1987), 211–2.
36. Juliet McMaster, *Reading the Body in the Eighteenth-Century Novel* (Basingstoke: Palgrave Macmillan, 2004), x.
37. McMaster, xi.
38. McMaster, xii.
39. Aileen Ribeiro, *Fashion and Fiction: Dress in Art and Literature in Stuart England* (London and New Haven, CT: Yale University Press, 2005), 3.
40. Hughes, 6.
41. Armstrong, "The Rise of the Domestic Woman," 103.

Part I   The Body and Dress of Thought

Introduction

1. Samuel Richardson, *Clarissa; or, the History of a Young Lady*, ed. Angus Ross (1747–8; London: Penguin, 1985), 543. This will be the only use of the Penguin edition of the text, which reproduces the first edition.
2. Samuel Richardson, *Clarissa; or, the History of a Young Lady*, reprint of 3rd ed. (London: S. Richardson, 1751; New York: AMS Press, 1990), 3:332. All further quotes are taken from this edition of the novel, and all subsequent references are documented parenthetically.

1   Dress and the Discourses of the Mind

1. Roy Porter, *Flesh in the Age of Reason* (New York and London: W. W. Norton, 2003), 20–6. See also Christopher Fox's *Locke and the Scriblerians: Identity and Consciousness in Early Eighteenth-Century Britain* (Berkeley: University of California Press, 1988).

2. Samuel Richardson, *Pamela; or Virtue Rewarded*, in *The Complete Novels of Samuel Richardson* (London: William Heinemann, 1902), IV:83, IV:84, IV:84. All quotes from *Pamela*, Part Two, are taken from the Heinemann edition, and all subsequent references to *Pamela*, Part Two, are documented parenthetically.

3. Janet E. Aikins argues that, in *Pamela*, Part Two, Richardson utilizes Locke's *Thoughts Concerning Education* in order "to argue for improved female education" (92). Aikins continues: "Through the palpable depiction of Mrs. B.'s narrative encounter with a book presented by her husband, Richardson critiques gendered social roles and explores the complex metaphoric relations between human 'generation' and the powers of language" (93). See Janet E. Aikins, "Pamela's Use of Locke's Words," *Studies in Eighteenth-Century Culture* 25 (1996): 75–97.

4. Leslie Richardson demonstrates how *Clarissa* engages with Locke's *Second Treatise of Government*. In her essay, Leslie Richardson investigates Locke's idea of "possessive individualism," the notion that every individual has a right to his own body, and how, paradoxically, this philosophy works to deny women ownership of their own bodies. As L. Richardson writes, Clarissa "must be dependent upon men's protection from the violence of other men. Clarissa must die to substantiate her claim that she values her virtue above her life; but I would argue that the right of self-definition, for which she has struggled throughout the novel, is not simply the right to maintain this virtue, but more fundamentally the right to control her own sexual body" (153). See Leslie Richardson, "Leaving Her Father's House: Astell, Locke, and Clarissa's Body Politic," *Studies in Eighteenth-Century Culture* 34 (2005): 151–71.

5. John Locke, *An Essay Concerning Human Understanding*, 2 vols. (New York: Dover, 1959), I:407 (ii.xxiii.17); I:444 (ii.xxvii.7). Parenthetical information refers to Book, Chapter, and Section(s) of *An Essay* and will be used, in addition to volume and page number(s) throughout.

6. Locke, *An Essay*, I:409 (ii.xxiii.22).

7. George Cheyne, *The English Malady*, ed. Roy Porter (1733; London and New York: Tavistock/Routledge, 1991), 4–5. Cheyne's view of the body as machine can be traced to Descartes' 1649 *The Passions of the Soul: Les Passions de Lame*, ed. and trans. Stephen Voss (Indianapolis and Cambridge: Hackett Publishing, 1989). For instance, in Article 7, Descartes refers to "the machine of our body" (21).

8. Cheyne, 5.

9. Joseph Addison and Richard Steele, *The Spectator*, 5 vols., ed. Donald F. Bond (Oxford: Oxford University Press, 1965), V:51. (*Spectator* No. 600, Wednesday, September 29, 1714).

10. Locke, *An Essay*, I:448 (ii.xxvii.10).

11. Locke, *An Essay*, I:465 (ii.xxvii.27).

12. Locke, *An Essay*, I:48 (i.i.15); II:211–12 (ii.xi.17).

13. Locke, *An Essay*, I:465 (ii.xxvii.25).

14. Porter, 72–9, 94–109.

15. Addison and Steele, II:571 (*Spectator*, No. 275, Tuesday, January 15, 1712).

16. Addison and Steele, II:573 (*Spectator*, No. 275).

17. Jonathan Swift, *A Tale of a Tub*, in *Gulliver's Travels and Other Writings*, ed. Louis A. Landa (Boston: Houghton Mifflin Company, 1960), 284.

18. [Bonnell Thornton and George Colman], *The Connoisseur by Mr. Town, Critic and Censor-General*, No. LXXVII (Thursday, July 14, 1755): 458. See also

No. LXXV. Harriet Guest's essay, entitled "Sterne, Elizabeth Draper, and Drapery," *The Shandean* 9 (November 1997): 9–33, provides an interesting discussion of the female consumption as it relates to the mind as shop metaphor.
19. Samuel Richardson, *The History of Sir Charles Grandison*, ed. Jocelyn Harris, 3 vols. (London: Oxford University Press, 1972; Otago, Dunedin, New Zealand: Otago University Print, 2001), III:343, III:126. All quotes are taken from this edition of the novel, and all subsequent references are documented parenthetically.
20. Samuel Richardson, *The Apprentice's Vade Mecum* (1734; reprint, Augustan Reprint Society, Nos. 169–79, Los Angeles: William Andrews Clark Memorial Library, 1975), 55.
21. Richardson, *The Apprentice's Vade Mecum*, 58.
22. Richardson, *The Apprentice's Vade Mecum*, 58.
23. Addison and Steele, I:381 (*Spectator* No. 90, Wednesday, June 13, 1711).
24. Addison and Steele, IV:72–3 (*Spectator* No. 447, Saturday, August 2, 1712).
25. Addison and Steele, IV:72.
26. Locke, *An Essay*, I:37 (i.i.1).
27. *Selected Letters of Samuel Richardson*, 151.
28. Letter to Lady Bradshaigh, 26 Oct. 1748, in *Selected Letters*, 95.
29. Letter to Lady Bradshaigh, 15 Dec. 1748, in *Selected Letters*, 115.
30. Addison and Steele, I:457 (*Spectator* No. 111, Saturday, July 7, 1711).
31. McMaster, x.
32. Addison and Steele, I:367 (*Spectator* No. 86, Friday, June 8, 1711).
33. McMaster, 25.
34. McMaster, 67.
35. McMaster, 69.
36. McMaster, 69.
37. McMaster, 69.
38. Locke, *An Essay*, II:8 (iii.ii.1).
39. Locke, *An Essay*, II:9 (iii.ii.2).
40. [Thornton and Coleman], *The Connoisseur*, No. 120 (Thursday, May 13, 1756), 722.
41. Locke, *An Essay*, I:409 (ii.xxiii.22).
42. Sarah Fielding, *The Lives of Cleopatra and Octavia*, ed. Christopher D. Johnson (Lewisburg: Bucknell University Press; London and Toronto: Associated University Presses, 1994), 54.
43. Locke, *An Essay* 1:121–2 (ii.1.2).
44. Addison and Steele, II:501 (*Spectator* No. 257, Tuesday, December 25, 1711).
45. Addison and Steele, II:501.
46. Addison and Steele, II:399 (*Spectator* No. 231, Saturday, November 24, 1711).
47. Richardson, *Grandison*, I:45.

2 Dress in 18th-Century English Life and Literature

1. Aileen Ribeiro, *The Art of Dress: Fashion in England and France, 1750 to 1820* (London and New Haven, CT: Yale University Press, 1995), 38.
2. *The Ladies Library*, published by R. Steele (London: Jacob Tonson, 1714), I:70. *Eighteenth Century Collections Online*.

3. Eliza Haywood, *The Female Spectator*, 4 vols. (1744–1746; London: A. Millar, W. Law, and R. Cater, 1775), I:122–3. Microfilm. Ann Arbor, MI: Xerox University Microfilms, 1973. *Early British Periodicals*, film PR 268, reel 48.

4. Anne Buck, *Dress in Eighteenth-Century England* (New York: Holmes & Meier, 1979), 179; and Elizabeth Ewing, *Everyday Dress, 1650–1900* (New York and Philadelphia: Chelsea House Publishers, 1984), 90.

5. Peter Earle, *The Making of the English Middle Class: Business, Society and Family Life in London, 1660–1730* (Berkeley and Los Angeles: University of California Press, 1989), 281.

6. Frances Elizabeth Baldwin, "Sumptuary Legislation and Personal Regulation in England," in Series XLIV, *Johns Hopkins University Studies in Historical and Political Science* (Baltimore, MD: The Johns Hopkins Press, 1926), 250.

7. Paul Langford, *A Polite and Commercial People: England, 1727–1783* (Oxford: Clarendon Press, 1989), 2.

8. Langford, 2.

9. Daniel Defoe, *The Complete English Tradesman* (1726; Gloucester: Alan Sutton, 1987), 8.

10. Earle, 290.

11. Addison and Steele, IV:344. (*Spectator* No. 518, Friday, October 24, 1712).

12. *The Ladies Library*, 81.

13. Aileen Ribeiro, *Dress in Eighteenth-Century Europe, 1715–1789* (London and New Haven, CT: Yale University Press, 2002), 6.

14. Jane Ashelford, *The Art of Dress: Clothes and Society, 1500–1914* (London: National Trust Enterprises and Laura Ashley, Ltd., 1996), 123–4.

15. Jessica Munns and Penny Richards, "Introduction: 'The Clothes That Wear Us,'" in *The Clothes That Wear Us: Essays on Dressing and Transgressing in Eighteenth-Century Culture*, eds. Jessica Munns and Penny Richards (Newark: University of Delaware Press; London: Associated University Presses, 1999), 13–14.

16. Defoe, *The Complete English Tradesman*, 86.

17. Paula Backscheider, *Daniel Defoe: Ambition and Innovation* (Lexington: University of Kentucky Press, 1986), 197.

18. Garber has written extensively about this in *Vested Interests: Cross-Dressing and Cultural Anxiety* (1992; New York: Routledge, 1997).

19. Janet E. Aikins, "Richardson's 'Speaking Pictures,'" in *Samuel Richardson: Tercentenary Essays*, eds. Margaret Anne Doody and Peter Sabor (Cambridge: Cambridge University Press, 1989), 147, 148. Margaret Anne Doody has also note the pictorial nature of certain scenes in Richardson's novels, particularly in *Clarissa*. See Margaret Anne Doody, *A Natural Passion: A Study of the Novels of Samuel Richardson* (London: Oxford University Press, 1974), 16–40.

20. M. Channing Linthicum, *Costume in the Drama of Shakespeare and his Contemporaries* (New York: Hacker Art Books, 1972).

21. Tita Chico, *Designing Women: The Dressing Room in Eighteenth-Century English Literature and Culture* (Lewisburg: Bucknell University Press, 2005), 82, 83, 83.

22. *The Bath, Bristol, Tunbridge and Epsom Miscellany* (London: Printed by T. Dormer, for the author, and sold by the booksellers in town and country, 1735); Alexander Pope, "An Epistle to a Lady," in *Alexander Pope: A Critical Edition of the Major Works*, ed. Pat Rogers (Oxford and New York: Oxford University Press, 1993), 350–8.

23. Backscheider, *Daniel Defoe*, 197.

24. John Milton, *Eikonklastes*, in *John Milton: Complete Poems and Major Prose*, ed. Merritt Y. Hughes (1957; Indianapolis/Cambridge: Hackett Publishing Company, 2003), 793.

Part II   Dressing for Success with *Pamela*

Introduction

1. Samuel Richardson, *Pamela; or, Virtue Rewarded*, Eds. T. C. Duncan Eaves and Ben D. Kimpel (Boston: Houghton Mifflin, 1971), 45, 160, 162, 144,. I use Eaves and Kimpel's Riverside Edition for *Pamela*, Part One, and the 1902 Heinemann edition for *Pamela*, Part Two. The Riverside edition reprints the first (1740) edition of *Pamela*, with Richardson's typesetting largely intact; the Heinemann edition reprints the sixth (1742) octavo edition of *Pamela* (the first time that Parts One and Two were printed together), though this is technically the third edition of *Pamela*, Part Two. The Heinemann edition modernizes Richardson's typesetting. All quotes are taken from these two editions of the text, and all subsequent references are documented parenthetically.

2. For a history of Anti-Pamelism and Pro-Pamelism, see Bernard Kreissman's *Pamela-Shamela: A Study in the Criticisms, Burlesques, Parodies, and Adaptation of Richardson's Pamela* (Lincoln, NE: University of Nebraska, 1960), and Catherine Ingrassia's introduction to *Anti-Pamela and Shamela*, ed. Catherine Ingrassia (Toronto: Broadview, 2004).

3. *Pamela Censured* (1741; Los Angeles: William Andrews Clark Memorial Library, University of California Press, Augustan Reprint Society, 1976), 36.

4. Letter from Aaron Hill to Samuel Richardson, [December 29, 1740]. As quoted in *Pamela*, eds. Eaves and Kimpel, 12.

5. Works that discuss Pamela's clothing include the following: Jennie Batchelor, "Seeing through Pamela's Clothes," in *Dress, Distress and Desire: Clothing and the Female Body in Eighteenth-Century Literature*, 19–51; Patricia C. Brückman's "Clothes of Pamela's Own: Shopping at B-Hall," *Eighteenth-Century Life* (Spring 2001): 201–13; Anne Buck's "Pamela's Clothes," *Costume: The Journal of the Costume Society* 26 (1992): 21–31; Terry Castle's "The Recarnivalization of Pamela: Richardson's *Pamela*, Part 2," in *Masquerade and Civilization*, 130–76; Caryn Chaden's "Pamela's Identity Sewn Into Clothes," in *Eighteenth-Century Women and the Arts*, eds. Frederick M. Keener and Susan E. Lorsch (New York: Greenwood Press, 1988), 109–18; Sheila C. Conboy's "Fabric and Fabrication in Richardson's *Pamela*," *English Literary History* 54.1 (Spring 1987): 81–96; Tassie Gwilliam's *Samuel Richardson's Fictions of Gender* (Stanford, CA: Stanford University Press, 1993), 31–7; Mark Kinkead-Weekes's *Samuel Richardson: Dramatic Novelist* (Ithaca, NY: Cornell University Press, 1973), 7–19; Carey McIntosh's "Pamela's Clothes," *English Literary History* 54.1 (Spring 1987), 75–83; Ann Rosalind Jones and Peter Stallybrass, *Renaissance Clothing and the Materials of Memory* (Cambridge: Cambridge University Press, 2000): 274–77; Michael McKeon's *The Secret History of Domesticity: Public, Private, and the Division of Knowledge* (Baltimore, MD: The Johns Hopkins University Press, 2005), 649–56; and William B. Warner's "The Pamela Media Event," in *Licensing*

Entertainment: The Elevation of Novel Reading in Britain, 1684–1750 (Berkeley, Los Angeles, and London: University of California Press, 1998), 176–230. Other discussions of Pamela's clothing no doubt exist.

6. Gwillliam, 15.
7. McKeon, *The Secret History of Domesticity*, 649, 653.
8. Batchelor, 16.
9. McKeon, *The Secret History of Domesticity*, 652.
10. Batchelor, 42.
11. Warner, 176–208; James Grantham Turner, "Novel Panic: Picture and Performance in the Reception of Richardson's *Pamela*," *Representations* 48 (Autumn 1994), 70–96.

3 Ladies, Gentlemen, and Servants: Virtue and the Domestic Ideal

1. J. C. D. Clark, *English Society, 1660–1832*, 2nd ed. (Cambridge: Cambridge University Press, 2000), 164.
2. McKeon, *The Origins of the English Novel*, 131.
3. Laurence, 19.
4. Donald Greene, *The Age of Exuberance: Backgrounds to Eighteenth-Century Literature* (New York: McGraw-Hill, 1970), 36, 37.
5. Henry Fielding, *The History of Tom Jones, a Foundling*, 2 vols., ed. Fredson Bowers (Oxford: Oxford University Press, 1975), I:149. The character described, of course, is Squire Western.
6. Richard Allestree, *The Gentleman's Calling* (London: T. Garthwait, 1660), unnumbered page (ii) of Preface. *Early English Books Online*. In *Origins of the English Novel*, McKeon has an excellent discussion of honor and virtue as relates to Mr. B. and Pamela, 364–9.
7. McKeon, *The Origins of the English Novel*, 156, 212.
8. Markley, 218.
9. Clark, 228.
10. Clark, 229.
11. F. L., *The Virgin's Nosegay; or, The Duties of Christian Virtue* (London and Belfast: F. Joy, 1744), microfilm, *The History of Women* (New Haven, CT: Research Publications, 1975), reel no. 563, 20.
12. James Bland, *The Charmes of Women: Or a Mirrour for Ladies. Wherein the Accomplishments of the Fair Sex are Impartially Delineated* (London: E. Curll, 1736), 70. *Eighteenth-Century Collections Online*. Gale Group.
13. Clark, 165, 165–6.
14. Quoted in Clark, 166.
15. John Wesley, Sermon 98, "On Visiting the Sick," in *Sermons on Several Occasions* (Grand Rapids, MI: Christian Ethereal Library, n.d.), 659. Calvin College, http://www.ccel.org/ccel/wesley/sermons.html. Reprint of 1872 edition, ed. Thomas Jackson. The sermon, "On Visiting the Sick," has been dated 23 May 1786, according to Timothy L. Smith, "Chronological List of John Wesley's Sermons and Doctrinal Essays," *Wesleyan Theological Journal* 17.2 (Fall 1982), 88–110.
16. Bland, 75.

17. Samuel Johnson, *The Rambler*, 3 vols., eds. W. J. Bate and Albrecht B. Strauss (London and New Haven, CT: Yale University Press, 1969), II:6. (No. 70, Saturday, 17 November 1750).

18. Thomas Gisborne, *An Enquiry into the Duties of the Female Sex* (London: T. Cadell Junior and W. Davies, 1797), 15–16, 21–2.

19. Richard Allestree, *The Ladies Calling* (Oxford: Printed at the Theatre, 1673), unnumbered Preface (vii and viii), 2.

20. Gisborne, 32.

21. Amanda Vickery, "Golden Age to Separate Spheres? A Review of the Categories and Chronology of English Women's History," in *Women's Work: The English Experience, 1650–1914*, ed. Pamela Sharpe (London, New York, Sydney, Auckland: Arnold, 1998), 314, 315.

22. Daniel Defoe, *The Fortunes and Misfortunes of the Famous Moll Flanders*, vols. I and II of *The Shakespeare Head Edition of the Novels and Selected Writings of Daniel Defoe* (Oxford: Basil Blackwell; Boston and New York: Houghton Mifflin Company, 1920), I:59.

23. Ingrid H. Tague, *Women of Quality: Accepting and Contesting Ideals of Femininity in England, 1690–1760* (Woodbridge, Suffolk: Boydell Press, 2002), 28.

24. Allestree, *The Ladies Calling*, 2.

25. John Essex, *The Young Ladies Conduct; or Rules for Education under Several Heads* (London: John Brotherton, 1722), xxxviii.

26. Reverend Wetenhall Wilkes, *A Letter of Genteel and Moral Advice to a Young Lady* (London: C. Hitch, 1748), 134.

27. Gisborne, 93–4.

28. Defoe, *The Complete English Tradesman*, 201.

29. Allestree, *The Ladies Calling*, unnumbered page (xii) of Preface.

30. Gisborne, 7.

4 "So Neat, So Clean, So Pretty!": Dressing Up Virtue

1. Aileen Ribeiro, *Dress and Morality* (New York: Holmes & Meier, 1986), 12.

2. As Anne Buck, in "Pamela's Clothes," notes, the calico nightgown is "working dress" for Pamela as lady's maid, though "Printed linen or cotton gowns like this were common to mistress and maid" (26). Many English gentlewomen wore calico gowns in the morning to breakfast and to perform household duties, such as giving orders to the servants, planning meals, and reviewing household accounts. Under no circumstances should such a gown be worn to receive visitors or dine in. In *Dress in Eighteenth-Century England*, Buck writes, "Dresses of printed linen or cotton were general mourning wear in the households of country gentry. ... The mistress of the house kept certain tasks to herself and her morning dress was to this extent a working dress" (72).

3. E. S. Turner, *What the Butler Saw: Two Hundred and Fifty Years of the Servant Problem* (London: Penguin, 1962), 121–32; and Isabella Beeton, *Mrs. Beeton's Book of Household Management* (1861; Oxford: Oxford University Press, 2000), 419–30.

4. In "Everybody's Business is Nobody's Business," 5th ed. (1725; Baltimore, MD: Blackmask Online, 2001), Daniel Defoe, using the pseudonym of Andrew Moreton, complains about the high wages of London servant maids,

who demand "six, seven, nay, eight pounds per annum and upwards"; in contrast, a country maid-servant could be acquired for the price of "fifty shillings, or three pounds a year" (2). By 1825, Samuel and Sarah Adams, in *The Complete Servant*, estimated the average salary for a lady's maid at 20 guineas per annum, as quoted in E. S. Turner (113).

5. Pamela A. Sambrook, in *The Country House Servant* (Phoenix Mill: Sutton Publishing, in association with the National Trust, 1999), writes that even in the early part of the twentieth century, "young girls ... went into service on the great estates at the bottom of the house, laundry or kitchen hierarchy, aged a mere thirteen years, working for little or even no wages, serving unofficial apprenticeships" (9).

6. Phillis Cunnington and Catherine Lucas, *Occupational Dress in England: From the 11th Century to 1914* (New York: Barnes and Noble, 1967), 195. See also Diana de Marly, *Working Dress: A History of Occupational Costume* (London: B. T. Batsford, 1986), 70–5.

7. Cunnington and Lucas, 196. *The Spectator*, no. 107, Tuesday, July 3, 1711, argues against the custom of presenting clothes to servants: "There is another Circumstance in which my Friend excels in his Management, which is the manner of rewarding his Servants: He has ever been of Opinion, that giving his cast Cloaths to be worn by Valets has a very ill effect upon little Minds, and creates a silly Sense of Equality between the Parties, in Persons affected only by outward things" (I:444).

8. Jonathan Swift, *Directions to Servants* (1745; London: Hesperus Press, 2003), 60.

9. Turner, 121; Buck, *Dress in Eighteenth-Century England*, 110.

10. Defoe, "Everybody's Business," 3.

11. Swift, *Directions to Servants*, 60–1.

12. Richardson, *The Apprentice's Vade Mecum*, v.

13. Defoe, "Everybody's Business," 3.

14. Defoe, "Everybody's Business," 4, 5.

15. Defoe, "Everybody's Business," 6.

16. Defoe, "Everybody's Business," 3.

17. Defoe, *The Complete English Tradesman*, 230.

18. Earle, 1.

19. Earle, 9; Defoe, "Everybody's Business," 6.

20. It should be noted that most lower-level servants, particularly those whose duties required them to be frequently in the public eye, wore livery. As Jones and Stallybrass write, "Livery was a form of incorporation, a material mnemonic that inscribed obligations and indebtedness upon the body" (20).

21. Ribeiro, *Dress and Morality*, 113.

22. *The Connoisseur*, No. 117, 704.

23. Beverly Lemire, *Dress, Culture and Commerce: The English Clothing Trade before the Factory, 1660–1800* (Basingstoke: Palgrave Macmillan, 1997; New York: St. Martin's Press, 1997), 96, 98, 99–100.

24. See Anne Buck, *Dress in Eighteenth-Century England*, 114–15. Also, in Richardson's *Clarissa*, the eponymous heroine presents a gown and petticoat to a maidservant, for Sunday wear, saying, "I will give you ... a quilted coat, which will require but little alteration, if any; ... But the gown I will give directions about, because the sleeves and the robings and the facings must be altered for your wear, being, I believe, above your station" (6:92).

25. Beeton, 419.
26. Defoe, *The Complete English Tradesman*, 86.
27. For more detailed information on marriage settlements and their impact on women, see Laurence, 230–4.
28. McKeon, *The Origins of the English Novel*, 131.
29. Buck, "Pamela's Clothes," 24.
30. Gwilliam, 32.
31. John Wesley's sermon "On Dress," notes that "Cleanliness is, indeed, next to godliness" (658), though this phrase, the earliest known version in print according to the *OED*, is in quotation marks within the sermon, suggesting an originary source other than Wesley.
32. Chaden, 111.
33. Chaden, 112, 111. Defoe, in "Everybody's Business," remarks on the transformation in dress of a country maid once she arrives in London: "Her neat's leathern shoes are now transformed into laced ones with high heels" (3). "Neat's leathern" is leather made from oxen.
34. Chaden, 112–13.
35. *Pamela Censored*, 34–5.
36. Sir Philip Sidney, *The Countess of Pembroke's Arcadia: The New Arcadia*, ed. Victor Skretkowicz. (Oxford: Clarendon Press; New York: Oxford University Press, 1987), 83.
37. *Arcadia*, 336.
38. *Arcadia*, 83.
39. *The Ladies Library*, I:92.
40. *Arcadia*, 83.
41. Milton, *Eikonklastes*, 793.

5 Quaker, Rustic, and Fool: Masquerading with Mrs. B.

1. Castle, 130–1.
2. Ribeiro, *Dress and Morality*, 97.
3. Rosemary Moore, *The Light in Their Consciences: Early Quakers in Britain, 1646–1666* (University Park, PA: The Pennsylvania State University Press, 2000), 118, 119.
4. Moore, 115–28.
5. Allestree, *The Gentleman's Calling*, unnumbered page (ii) of Preface.
6. *Ladies Library*, 79.
7. Marcia Pointon, "Quakerism and Visual Culture, 1650–1800," *Art History* 20.3 (September 1997): 408.
8. Batchelor, 136.
9. Batchelor, 138.
10. Daniel Defoe, *Roxana, or The Fortunate Mistress*, ed. David Blewett (Harmondsworth, Middlesex; New York: Penguin, 1982), 252, 254, 256.
11. Hughes, 28.
12. Langford, 73. Langford notes, "The vast majority of gentry were, nominally at least, members of the Church of England. Within landed society only a dwindling minority of Roman Catholics, and a still tinier residue of that once extensive class, the Puritan gentry, declined to conform. Middle-class religion

presented a more diverse and complicated picture. Dissent was in decline in the countryside, though in some regions, for instance the old Puritan heartland of East Anglia, it retained a significant rural presence. But in the towns it proved both more resistant to decay and readier to respond to opportunities for expansion, particularly in the second half of the century" (73–4).
13. E. I. Watkin, *Roman Catholicism in England, from the Reformation to 1950* (London: Oxford University Press, 1957), 105–6.

Part III   Window-Shopping the Essential Self with *Clarissa*

Part III first appeared as "Clarissa Harlowe and the Language of Dress" in *The Eighteenth-Century Novel*, 2:45–90 (©AMS Press, Inc., New York, 2002). Used with permission.

Introduction

1. Terry Castle, in *Clarissa's Ciphers: Meaning and Disruption in Richardson's "Clarissa"* (Ithaca and London: Cornell University Press, 1982), notes the association of Nature with Clarissa and Art with Lovelace (54–55).
2. Joseph M. Levine, *Between the Ancients and the Moderns: Baroque Culture in Restoration England* (London and New Haven, CT: Yale University Press, 1999), x.
3. Edward Young, *Conjectures on Original Composition: In a Letter to the Author of Sir Charles Grandison* (London: A. Millar and R. and J. Dodsley, 1759; reprint, Toronto: University of Toronto, 1996), 12. *Representative Criticism On-line*, ed. Ian Lancashire, http://www.g7.utoronto.ca/utel/rp/criticism/conje_il.html.
4. See Jonathan Swift, "A Full and True Account of the Battel Fought last Friday, Between the Antient and the Modern Books in St. James's Library," in *Gulliver's Travels and Other Writings*, ed. Louis A. Landa (Boston: Houghton Mifflin Company, 1960), 366, 368.
5. John Dryden, "To the Pious Memory of the Accomplished Young Lady Mrs. Anne Killigrew," in *John Dryden: A Critical Edition of the Major Works*, ed. Keith Walker (Oxford and New York: Oxford University Press, 1987), 310–15, lines 71–6.
6. It does not seem that Richardson wished to associate Clarissa with the ancients, nor Lovelace with the moderns, by making the respective dress of one "natural" and the other "artful." (If anything, it is possible that Clarissa may be an early precursor of Romanticism, in her fierce sense of individualism, in her value—and the novel's value—for personal experience, etc. Of course, that early pre-Romantic writer, Edward Young, was a friend and correspondent of Richardson.) Instead, Clarissa's dress is natural as it is unstudied and apparently does not rely on others—past or present—for its style. (Of course, Clarissa does indeed wear clothing suitable to her sex, age, and social position, as not to do so would render her outside her place and time, yet she invests these garments with her own unique style, expressive of her own unique nature.) In contrast, the dress of Lovelace and his confederates is artful in that it has been carefully studied, and imitative, in that it has been based on careful observation of what individuals of specific social background and in specific social situations wear.

7. Caroline Weber, *Queen of Fashion: What Marie Antoinette Wore to the Revolution* (New York: Henry Holt and Company, 2006), 101.
8. To Lady Bradshaigh [1750], in *Selected Letters of Samuel Richardson*, 170.
9. James Grantham Turner, "Lovelace and the Paradoxes of Libertinism," in *Samuel Richardson: Tercentenary Essays*, eds. Margaret Anne Doody and Peter Sabor (Cambridge: Cambridge University Press, 1989), 73.
10. In *Clarissa's Ciphers*, Terry Castle notes Lovelace's obsession with "dress as costume—as disguise for, rather than revelation of the inner person" (103).
11. Again, Terry Castle's brilliant reading of *Clarissa* notes that Sinclair is "a more nightmarish version of Mrs. Harlowe, the original non-mothering mother in *Clarissa*" (*Clarissa's Ciphers*, 98).
12. To Aaron Hill, 29 Oct. 1746, in *Selected Letters of Samuel Richardson*, 71.
13. Leslie Richardson, "Leaving Her Father's House: Astell, Locke, and Clarissa's Body Politic," 160.
14. To Frances Grainger, 21 Dec. 1749, in *Selected Letters of Samuel Richardson*, 139.
15. Michael McKeon, *The Secret History of Domesticity*, 642.

6 Virtuous Stays and Sexual Hoops: The Social Self

1. Alison Carter, *Underwear: The Fashion History* (New York: Drama Book Publishers, 1992), 27–8; C. Willett Cunnington and Phillis Cunnington, *The History of Underclothes* (1951; New York: Dover Publications, 1992), 87–8; Elizabeth Ewing, *Underwear: A History* (New York: Theatre Arts Books, 1972), 35–6; Norah Waugh, *Corsets and Crinolines* (1954; New York: Theatre Arts Books, 1970), 36–45, 153–5.
2. William Hogarth, *The Analysis of Beauty*, ed. Ronald Paulson (London and New Haven, CT: Yale University Press, for the Paul Mellon Centre for British Art, 1997), Chapter IX, 48, 49.
3. Cunnington and Cunnington, *The History of Underclothes*, 88.
4. Ibid., 88–91. See also Karen Baclawski, *The Guide to Historic Costume* (New York: Drama Book Publishers, 1995), 127–8; Buck, *Dress in Eighteenth-Century England*, 27; Carter, 25–6; Ewing, 39; Waugh, 46–9.
5. Buck, 121–2, 143–4, 146; Carter, 27.
6. Ribeiro, *The Art of Dress*, 54.
7. Kimberly Chrisman, in her essay entitled "Unhoop the Fair Sex: The Campaign Against the Hoop Petticoat in Eighteenth-Century England," *Eighteenth-Century Studies* 30.1 (1996), 5–23, quite rightly notes that "female servants were likely the first of the lower classes to wear hoops, as they often copied their mistresses' wardrobes or inherited their castoffs." She continues, "A country-bred maid might pass on the idea—or, very likely, the actual garment—to a rustic relation. The hoop's visibility made it a convenient symbol for lower-class (specifically, female lower-class) pretensions to gentility" (17). Contemporary texts of the time (as cited in Chrisman's essay) confirm this notion, as does an American conduct book, published in 1836. *The Young Lady's Friend* (Boston: American Stationer's Company, 1836), written by the ubiquitous "A Lady" (in actuality, Mrs. John Farrar), puzzles that the fashion for hoops was once "so universal in London, that maid-servants were seen

washing down the door steps in hoop-petticoats!" (96). However, it is important to note that clothing passed down from mistress to maid was either
unwanted by the mistress (which means that it was no longer fashionable
and could not be refashioned to make it so), or it was given to the maid as a
reward for service, which often meant the clothing most normally would
have been altered to make it suitable to the maid's rank (as when Clarissa
gives Mabell the brown lustring gown and quilted petticoat). Thus, most
maidservants were most probably wearing hoops of unfashionable shapes
and/or sizes. As such, social position and class could still be ascertained.

8. Kimberly Chrisman writes, "By widening the hoops while accentuating the
small, tightly corseted waist, the hoop suggested both fertility and virginity,
two characteristics universally valued in women" (19), arguing that the hoop
itself combines attributes of "both fertility and virginity"; however, it is the
"small, tightly corseted waist" that is the indicator of virginity, and, thus, it
is the stays that signify virginity, not the hooped petticoat.

9. Wilkes, 188.

10. Ribeiro, *The Art of Dress*, 59.

11. Ewing, 38–9.

12. Addison and Steele, *The Spectator*, IV:246. (*Spectator* No. 492, September 24, 1712).

13. A. D. Harvey, *Sex in Georgian England: Attitudes and Prejudices from the 1720s to the 1820s* (New York: St. Martin's Press, 1994), 22.

14. Mackie, 111.

15. Chrisman, 20.

16. Mackie, 135.

17. Addison and Steele, II:6. (*Spectator* No. 127, July 26, 1711).

18. As quoted in Waugh, 59.

19. Anne Hollander, *Sex and Suits* (New York: Alfred A. Knopf, 1994), 140.

20. Ibid.,141.

21. Chrisman, 22.

22. Kaiser, 234–6. Kaiser is referring to studies mentioned in N. M. Henley's *Body Politics: Power, Sex, and Nonverbal Communication* (Englewood Cliffs, NJ: Prentice Hall, 1977).

23. Mackie, 125. Mackie is using *Tatler* 113 as a source.

24. Henry Fielding, *The Covent-Garden Journal* (1752), ed. Gerard Edward Jensen, 2 vols. (New York: Russell & Russell, 1964), I, 348; Saturday, May 9, 1752, number 37.

7   "Of Her Own Invention": Revealing the Self

1. Young, 42.

2. It is in Clarissa's will that she mentions that the silver suit had never been worn and that it had been newly made up just prior to her confinement at Harlowe Place; throughout the novel, only *one* suit of clothing is said never to have been worn. In reconstructing when the silver suit is mentioned, I have relied both on its specific mention, as well as on the mention of the new suit of clothing and/or of the suit of clothing that had never been worn.

3. Buck, 71.

4. Ibid., 13–15, 18. See also Ribeiro, *Dress in Eighteenth-Century Europe*, 136.

5. Although hoops were as wide as eleven feet during the 1740s, it is unlikely that Clarissa's hoops would have been quite so large, as the largest hoops were reserved for Court wear.

6. For information on the *sacque*, see Baclawski, 93–4, 172–4; Buck, 26–7, 40; C. Willett Cunnington and Phillis Cunnington, *Handbook of English Costume in the Eighteenth Century* (Boston: Plays, Inc., 1972), 124–7; Ribeiro, *Dress in Eighteenth-Century Europe*, 32–7. Note: After 1750, robings extended from the bodice to the hem of the skirt, rather than to the waist.

7. Ribeiro, *Dress in Eighteenth-Century Europe*, 33.

8. It is curious that Clarissa's gown is specifically referred to as a "morning-gown," whereas two other gowns of the basic same construction—the brown lustring and the white damask—are specifically referred to as "night-gowns." The difference in terminology may simply be due to the *time* of day when a particular outfit was worn, or some subtle differences in *style* may exist between morning gowns and nightgowns, which are no longer discernable to twentieth- and twentieth-first century eyes. If anything, the morning-gown may have been even more informal than the nightgown, which could be worn out in public. If such is the case, Clarissa's outfit pleads her innocence in eloping that much more strongly.

9. Baclawski, 153; Buck, 43–4; Cunnington and Cunnington, *A Handbook of English Costume*, 118–9, 278–83; Ribeiro, *The Art of Dress*, 64; Ribeiro, *Dress in Eighteenth-Century Europe*, 37–8; Jane Tozer and Sarah Levitt, *Fabric of Society: A Century of People and Their Clothes, 1770–1870* (Carno, Powys, Wales: Laura Ashley Limited and City of Manchester Cultural Services, 1983), 49–50.

10. Haywood, *The Female Spectator*, III:160.

11. Ribeiro, *Dress in Eighteenth-Century Europe*, 118.

12. Baclawski, 172; Cunnington and Cunnington, *A Handbook of English Costume*, 304–5. When travelling, Clarissa most probably wears a riding habit. When alighting at the inn at St. Albans, during the elopement, Lovelace comments, "She cast a conscious glance, as she alighted, upon her habit, which was *no habit*; and repulsively, as I may say, quiting my assisting hand, hurried into the house" (3:50).

13. C. Willett and Phillis Cunnington, in *A Picture History of English Costume* (New York: The Macmillan Company, 1960), specifically state that embroidered robings were rare prior to 1750 (page 74, illustration number 213). In *A Handbook of English Costume*, the Cunningtons state that "Until *c.* 1750 the robings ended at or just below waist level, and were usually plain, rarely embroidered before 1745 except for Court wear" (107), and that "Trimming or embroidery to robings usual from 1750" (266).

14. Baclawski, 149–50; Cunnington and Cunnington, *A Handbook of English Costume*, 177; Ribeiro, *The Art of Dress*, 78–9, and *Dress in Eighteenth-Century Europe*, 114.

15. Cunnington and Cunnington, *Handbook of English Costume*, 177.

16. Baclawski, 145.

17. Ibid., 62–4; Carter, 15, 23, 28–9; Cunnington and Cunnington, *The History of Underclothes*, 82–3, 92–4; 98, 111.

18. According to A. D. Harvey, "During the eighteenth century, and for some hundreds of years previously, it had not been customary for lovers or even married couples to see each other naked" (21). As Harvey also notes, "even

an experienced courtesan like Fanny Hill" finds it odd that one of her clients strips her stark naked (23).

19. Richardson responded to the charges of "indecency" with a eleven-page pamphlet, entitled *An Answer to the Letter of a Very Reverend and Worthy Gentleman*, dated 8 June 1749. According to Eaves and Kimpel, this gentleman was probably Philip Skelton, an Irish clergyman. See T. C. Duncan Eaves and Ben D. Kimpel, *Samuel Richardson: A Biography* (Oxford: Clarendon Press, 1971), 289–90.

20. Leslie Richardson also links this scene to rape. She writes, "The long struggle between Clarissa and Lovelace is fought over control of her body and her identity. Lovelace admits to desiring mastery, *possession*, rather than sexual pleasure, and both characters represent the rape as a crime against property. A rape, like the theft of an heiress, subverts the traditional system of exchange among men, depriving the father of his right to dispose of his daughter in marriage; indeed, the crimes were indistinguishable, in the eyes of the law, for centuries" (162–3).

21. Ribeiro, *The Art of Dress*, 64.

22. Ribeiro, 65.

23. "Carnation," *OED*, A.1.a. and A.1.b.

24. All of Clarissa's outfits have flowers associated with them: the "silver-*flower*ed suit"; the embroidered *violets* on the robings of her *primrose*-colored paduasoy; the brown lustring gown with *carnation*-colored petticoat; and the white damask gown.

25. One other instance of this occurs early in the novel, when Clarissa is to be forcibly wedded to Solmes. Her mother insists to her that "you think of being Mrs. Solmes"; Clarissa feels a "dagger" to her heart, swoons, and must have her laces cut (1:97).

8   "Where ... Art is Designed": Concealing the Self

1. To Lady Bradshaigh [1750], in *Selected Letters of Samuel Richardson*, 170.

2. To Lady Bradshaigh [1750], in *Selected Letters of Samuel Richardson*, 170.

3. Kaiser, 3.

4. Richardson, *Sir Charles Grandison*, I:427. Harriet, of course, is referring to her own masquerade costume.

5. Margaret Anne Doody, "Disguise and Personality in Richardson's *Clarissa*," *Eighteenth-Century Life* 12.2 (May 1988): 18. In this article, Doody chronicles the myriad deceptions that occur throughout the novel, not only by Lovelace and his gang of rogues and whores, but also by Clarissa herself.

6. Castle, 6.

7. Castle, 31.

8. Castle, 33.

9. Mikhail Bakhtin, *Rabelais and His World* (Bloomington, IN: Indiana University Press, 1984), 7.

10. Doody, 23.

11. See *Clarissa*, I:319–20, for the scene between Clarissa and Arabella.

12. Castle, 39.

13. Ibid., 103.

Part IV Refashioning the World with Sir Charles *Grandison*

Introduction

1. Samuel Richardson to Lady Bradshaigh [1749], *Selected Letters of Samuel Richardson*, 133.
2. In a letter to Frances Grainger, dated 29 March 1750, Richardson writes, "'Where shall we meet with undepraved nature?' you ask. I answer, no where, but I hope we may frequently meet with a repentant heart; a heart that will not persevere in a fault and take its example from hearts more faulty than good." In *Selected Letters of Samuel Richardson*, 151.
3. Armstrong, "The Rise of Domestic Woman," 97, 104, 104, 120.
4. Mackie, 169. Mackie views the "the worldly, fashionable, libertine whore" (counterpart to domestic woman) as a residual leftover from the older, aristocratic model of society (166). However, I would argue that this negative counterpart is equally at home in bourgeois culture, and, in fact, is a necessary element in the construction of bourgeois domesticity, as new domestic woman required both new domestic man and worldly woman in order to define herself.
5. See Mackie, 164, 170.
6. Addison and Steele, I:70 (No. 16, Monday, March 19, 1711).
7. Castle, 89, 33.
8. *The Connoisseur*, No. LXXVII (Thursday, July 17, 1755), 460.
9. Fordyce, 46–7.
10. Essex, 96.
11. Batchelor, 10.
12. Tague, 28. Tague refers to Fenela Childs's dissertation, entitled "Prescriptions for Manners in English Courtesy Literature, 1690–1760, and Their Social Implications." D. Phil. Thesis, University of Oxford, 1984, 267.
13. Allestree, *The Gentlemans Calling*, Preface, articles 3 and 4.
14. Allestree, *The Gentlemans Calling*, Letter to Mr. Gathwait.
15. Allestree, *The Ladies Calling*, 2.
16. *Instructions for a Young Lady, in Every Sphere and Period of Life* (Edinburgh: A. Donaldson, 1773), 47. microfilm. *History of Women* (New Haven, CT: Research Publications, 1975).

9 "A Conformist to Fashion": Dressing for Duty

1. Sylvia Kasey Marks, *Sir Charles Grandison: The Compleat Conduct Book* (Lewisburg: Bucknell University Press; London and Toronto: Associated University Presses, 1986), 65, 70. Marks mentions the role of dress in conduct book literature only briefly (two paragraphs), though she admits that "Taste in dress" is "another subject treated by conduct-book writers" (74).
2. Addison and Steele, *The Spectator*, I:70 (No. 16, Monday, March 19, 1711).
3. Fordyce, 50.
4. Haywood, *The Female Spectator*, III:113.
5. Addison and Steele, *The Spectator*, II:526 (No. 264, Wednesday, January 2, 1712).
6. Gisborne, 123.

7. Wilkes, 115–21.
8. Addison and Steele, *The Spectator*, II:91. (No. 150, Wednesday, August 22, 1711).
9. Addison and Steele, *The Spectator*, II:90, 91, 93. (No.150, Wednesday, August 22, 1711).
10. Defoe, *The Complete English Tradesman*, 212–22.

10 "A Mighty Glitter": Seeing through the Veil

1. Eaves and Kimpel note, "Pamela's then unusual name goes back to Sidney's *Arcadia*, perhaps via Steele's *Tender Husband*" (116). In T. C. Duncan Eaves and Ben D. Kimpel, *Samuel Richardson: A Biography* (Oxford: Clarendon Press, 1971). Also, in *Pamela*, Part II, the lawyer *cum* gentleman, Turner, refers to Mr. B. as Musidorus, a way for Turner to intimate his knowledge of Pamela, as Sidney's romance pairs Musidorus with the Arcadian shepherdess, Pamela. In addition, Gillian Beer writes, Richardson's "firm printed the fourteenth edition of Sidney's *Works*," which included *Arcadia*. Jacob Leed demonstrates the correspondences between Richardson's *Pamela* and *Arcadia*, while Beer reveals how Richardson's *Pamela* is a "revisionary reading and rewriting of *Arcadia*." Gillian Beer, "*Pamela*: Rethinking *Arcadia*," in *Samuel Richardson: Tercentenary Essays*, eds. Margaret Anne Doody and Peter Sabor (Cambridge: Cambridge University Press, 1989), 23, 25; and Jacob Leed, "Richardson's Pamela and Sidney's," *Journal of the Australasian Universities Language and Literature Association* 40 (1973), 240–5.
2. Harris, *Sir Charles Grandison*, 1:473, footnote 2, to page 115. Harris refers the reader to *Spectator*. No. 14, and *Tatler*, no. 139.
3. Addison and Steele, *The Spectator*, I:435 (No. 104, Friday, June 29, 1711).
4. Sidney, *Arcadia*, 295–6. (Book Two).
5. Addison and Steele, *The Spectator*, I:63. (No. 14, Friday, March 16, 1711).
6. Aileen Ribeiro, *The Dress Worn at Masquerades in England, 1730 to 1790, and Its Relation to Fancy Dress Portraiture* (New York and London: Garland Publishing, 1984), 253.
7. Ribeiro, *The Dress Worn at Masquerades in England*, 253.
8. Sidney, *Arcadia*, 83. (Book One).
9. In *The Art of Dress* and elsewhere, Aileen Ribeiro has hinted that Harriet's masquerade outfit is indeed an eighteenth-century version of "Arcadian Shepherdess," which often proved to be a "hybrid" mixture "of the fashionable with elements of the historical" (200); in essence, such an outfit combined some elements of the immensely popular "Ruben's wife" costume with some additional pastoral accoutrement, such as a straw hat, a crook, a basket of flowers, etc. (194–200). No doubt Ribeiro is correct regarding historical masquerade costume, yet the association of Harriet's masquerade outfit with Amazonian attire, both as described in Sidney's *Arcadia* and in *The Spectator*, is quite evident.
10. Sidney, *Arcadia*, 35. (The First Book: Philanax. His Letter to Basilius).
11. Sidney, *Arcadia*, 68. (Book One).
12. Sidney, *Arcadia*, 69. (Book One).
13. Sidney, *Arcadia*, 68. (Book One).
14. Richard Steele, *The Complete Plays of Richard Steele*, Ed. G. A. Aitken (London: T. Fisher Unwin; New York: Charles Scribner's Sons, 1894. *The Spectator*

Project: A Hypermedia Research Archive of Eighteenth-Century Periodicals. Rutgers University, http://www.tabula.rutgers.edu/spectator), 223. In Steele's *The Tender Husband; or the Accomplished Fools,* the sole reference to *Arcadia* comes from an exchange between Captain Clerimont and Biddy Tipkin, in Act II, Scene I. Captain Clerimont says, "Do you believe Pamela was one-and-twenty before she knew Musidorus?" Biddy replies only with an aside, in regards to Clerimont, that "I could hear him ever".

15. Sidney, *Arcadia,* 69 (Book One).
16. John Gay, *The Guardian,* No. 149, 1713. As quoted in Janet Arnold, "Dashing Amazons: The Development of Women's Riding Dress, *c.* 1500–1900," *Defining Dress: Dress as Object, Meaning and Identity,* eds. Amy de la Haye and Elizabeth Wilson (Manchester and New York: Manchester University Press, 1999), 20.
17. *The Spectator,* I:434–5 (No. 104, Friday, June 29, 1711).
18. See G. J. Barker-Benfield, Chapter 3, "The Question of Effeminacy," *The Culture of Sensibility: Sex and Society in Eighteenth-Century Britain;* and Michèle Cohen's *Fashioning Masculinity: National Identity and Language in the Eighteenth Century* (London and New York: Routledge, 1996).
19. John Wesley, "On Dress," in *Sermons on Several Occasions,* 660.
20. Harris, *Sir Charles Grandison,* page 473, footnote 1, to page 116.
21. Bernard and Ellen M. Whishaw, "Punto de Aguja and Point d'Espagne: Part I," *The Connoisseur,* vol. 26 (1910), 51. *On-line Digital Archive of Documents on Weaving and Related Topics.* 20 November 2003. University of Arizona, College of Engineering, http://www.cs.arizona.edu/patterns/weaving/weavedocs.html.
22. C. Willet Cunnington, Phillis Cunnington, and Charles Beard, "Bugles" and "Spangles," *A Dictionary of English Costume, 900–1900* (London: Adam & Charles Black, 1960), 28, 200–1.
23. Haywood, *The Female Spectator,* I:243.
24. Harris, *Grandison,* 1:473, footnote, page 116 (1).
25. Alexander Pope, "Eloisa to Abelard," *Alexander Pope,* 137–47, lines 209, 213.
26. Richardson, letter to Lady Echlin, 10 October 1754. In *Selected Letters of Samuel Richardson,* 315.

11 "Dressing in Colours": Changing the Guard

1. According to Aileen Ribeiro, "Sumptuary legislation, which in England existed from the fourteenth to the seventeenth centuries had as its avowed aim the protection of native textile industries, but the real purpose was to enforce class distinctions which it was felt were being eroded by dress; in addition, certain styles of dress, notably those which were too tight or revealing, were thought of as wicked and harmful to the morals of the people." From Aileen Ribeiro, *Dress and Morality,* 15.
2. Baldwin, 10.
3. Baldwin, 10.
4. Garber, 25–6.
5. Ribeiro, *Dress and Morality,* 46.
6. Norbert Elias, *The Civilizing Process: Sociogenetic and Psychogenetic Investigations,* trans. Edmund Jephcott, eds. Eric Dunning, Johan Goudsblom and Stephen Mennell (Oxford: Blackwell Publishers, 2000), 414–21, 451–83.

See also "Gendering the Civilizing Process: The Case of Charlotte Smith's *Emmeline, the Orphan of the Castle,*" in Diane Long Hoeveler's *Gothic Feminism: The Professionalization of Gender from Charlotte Smith to the Brontës* (University Park, PA: The Pennsylvania State University Press, 1998), 26–50.

7. Armstong, *Desire and Domestic Fiction*, 110.
8. McKeon, "Historicizing Patriarchy: The Emergence of Gender Difference in England, 1660–1760," *Eighteenth-Century Studies* 28 (1995), 305.
9. Armstrong, "The Rise of Domestic Woman," 109.
10. Mackie, 22.
11. Batchelor, 11.
12. M. Jourdain, "Gold and Silver Lace: Part II," *The Connoisseur* 17 (1906), 94. See also, M. Jourdain, "Gold and Silver Lace: Part I," *The Connoisseur* 17 (1906), 9–12. *On-line Digital Archive of Documents on Weaving and Related Topics.* 12 June 2003. University of Arizona, Department of Engineering, http://www.cs.arizona.edu/patterns/weaving/weavedocs.html.
13. Royal Proclamation of Elizabeth I, 6 July 1597. As quoted in Baldwin, 228–9. Gold and silver cloth "mixed or embroidered with gold or silver" could be worn by Barons and Baronesses and "all above that rank"; gold or silver lace could be worn only by Barons's sons, daughters, and the wives of Barons's eldest sons, and "all above that rank." Interestingly, from the perspective of sumptuary legislation, the *point d'espagne* trim on Harriet's masquerade costume, would be in violation of the law during Elizabeth's reign.
14. Baldwin, 217–8, 228. The Proclamation of 20 October 1559 reinstated "the statutes of 1 and 2 Philip and Mary and parts of 24 Henry VIII."
15. In fact, prior to the seventeenth century, most English "cloths were sent to Holland, to be dressed and dyed." From "Dyeing," *Ree's Cyclopaedia,* 1819. *On-line Digital Archive of Documents on Weaving and Related Topics.* 22 June 2003. University of Arizona, College of Engineering, http://www.cs.arizona. edu/patterns/weaving/weavedocs.html.
16. Arnold and Connie Krochmal, *The Complete Illustrated Book of Dyes from Natural Sources* (Garden City, New York: Doubleday & Company, 1974), 15–16.
17. "Dyeing," *Ree's Cyclopaedia,* 1819.
18. Krochmal, 5–19. See also Jenny Balfour-Paul, *Indigo* (Chicago and London: Fitzroy Dearborn Publishers, 1998), 89–113, and Robert Chenciner, *Madder Red: A History of Luxury and Trade: Plant Dyes and Pigments in World Commerce and Art* (Richmond, Surrey, England: Caucasus World, 2000), 28–52.
19. In 1579, a dyer named Morgan Hubblethorne journeyed to Persia, instructed by Richard Hakluyt "to fixe and make sure the color to be given by loggewood; so shall we not need to buy woad so dear, to the enrichment of our enemies." From Richard Hakluyt, *Voyages,* iii 249 seq., as quoted in Linthicum, 9. However, by 1580, Elizabeth I "forbade the planting of woad within eight miles of the royal residences" (3–4), due to its malodorous aroma during fermentation.
20. Linthicum, 27.
21. An American publication, *The Domestic Dyer, Being Receipts for Dyeing Cotton and Linen, Hot and Cold* (New England: 1811), urges the use of indigenous materials for home-dyeing cotton and linen. For yellow, the author recommends that the reader "Take two pounds of leaves or peelings of onions that are clean and clear from dirt" (6). *On-line Digital Archive of Documents on*

Weaving and Related Topics. 11 April 2004. University of Arizona, College of Engineering, http://www.cs.arizona.edu/patterns/weaving/weavedocs.html.

22. Charles E. Pellow, "Mediæval Dyestuffs," *Bulletin of the Needle and Bobbin Club*, vol. 2 (1918): 6. *On-line Digital Archive of Documents on Weaving and Related Topics.* 11 December 2003. University of Arizona, College of Engineering, http://www.cs.arizona.edu/patterns/weaving/weavedocs.html.

23. Buck, *Dress in Eighteenth-Century England*, 187.

24. Buck, *Dress in Eighteenth-Century England*, 186.

25. Buck, *Dress in Eighteenth-Century England*, 130.

26. See Baldwin, 248–75.

27. Ribeiro, *The Art of Dress*, 65.

28. *The Autobiography and Correspondence of Mrs. Delany* (Revised from Lady Llanover's Edition), ed. Sarah Chauncey Woolsey, 2 vols. (Boston: Roberts Brothers, 1879), I:113.

29. Ribeiro, *The Art of Dress*, 208. The masquerade outfit in "Pink Sattin with silver Pods" is described in *Vauxhall Garden Scrapbooks*, 5 vols. (London: British Library), I:77.

30. Ribeiro, *Dress in Eighteenth-Century Europe*, 208.

31. Haywood, *The Female Spectator*, III:160.

32. As quoted in Cunnington and Cunnington, *Handbook of English Costume in the Eighteenth Century*, 217.

33. Charlotte refers to Aunt Nell as "the stale virgin" (2:519).

34. Apparently, the pink and yellow ribbons allude to a private joke between Richardson and Lady Bradshaigh, though the particulars remain unknown. See Richardson's letter of 4 January 1754, in *Selected Letters*, 268.

35. Horace Walpole, Letter to Lady Ossory, Saturday, 19 February 1774. In *The Yale Edition of Horace Walpole's Correspondence*, ed. W. S. Lewis, 48 vols. (London and New Haven, CT: Yale University Press, 1937–83), 32:191.

36. Ribeiro, *The Art of Dress*, 170.

37. Ribeiro, *The Art of Dress*, 170.

38. Lady Jane Coke, *Letters to Her friend Mrs. Eyre at Derby*, ed. Mrs. Ambrose Rathborne (London: Swan Sonneschein, 1899), 134–5.

39. David Kuchta, *The Three-Piece Suit and Modern Masculinity: England, 1550–1850* (Berkeley, Los Angeles, London: University of California Press, 2002), 4.

40. Ribeiro, *The Art of Dress*, 211.

41. Kuchta, 110.

42. Laurence, 41–4.

43. Daniel Defoe, *The History of the Remarkable Life, and Extraordinary Adventures, of the Truly Honourable Colonel Jaque, vulgarly call'd Colonel Jack*, vols. III and IV of *The Shakespeare Head Edition of the Novels and Selected Writings of Daniel Defoe* (Oxford: Basil Blackwell; Boston and New York: Houghton Mifflin Company, 1920), IV:78.

44. *The Connoisseur*, Number XCV (Thursday, November 20, 1755), 571.

45. Cunnington and Beard, "Wedding Suit," *A Dictionary of English Costume*, 233.

46. Linthicum, in a footnote, tells of a "curious tract," entitled "Fifteen Comforts of Marriage," which explains "how various colours were discarded when a selection was made for the bride. Violet, signifying religion, was considered too grave; popingay, meaning wantonness; flesh colour, meaning lasciviousness; willow, meaning desertion; sea-green, meaning inconstancy, were

likewise rejected. Finally, blue, peach colour, and orange-tawny were selected for the favours; flame, straw, grass-green, and milk-white chosen for the knots, and gold for the garters" (24).
47. Cunnington and Beard, "Wedding Clothes," 233.
48. Baclawski, 224.
49. *Le Blason des couleurs en Armes Liurées det deuises*, 1526, trans. R[ichard] R[obinson] with the title *A Rare True and Proper Blazon of Coloures and Ensignes Military with theyre Peculiar Signification*, 1583, quoted in M. C. Linthicum, 17. See also Ashelford, 31, and Jeanne Arnold, *Queen Elizabeth's Wardrobe Unlock'd* (Leeds: W. S. Maney and Son, 1988), 90–1.
50. Edmund Spenser, *The Faerie Queene*, ed. Thomas P. Roche, Jr. (Hammondsworth, Middlesex, and New York: Penguin, 1984).
51. Jeanne Arnold's *Queen Elizabeth's Wardrobe Unlock'd* provides a fascinating look at Elizabeth I's attire, as presented in portraiture and in the "Inventories of the Wardrobe of Robes prepared in July 1600." In addition, Ashelford provides evidence of Elizabeth I's interest in color symbolism of dress by the Queen's "insistence that her six Maids of Honour should wear a white and silver costume when at court" (31).
52. "Dyeing," *London Encyclopedia*, 1829. *On-line Digital Archive of Documents on Weaving and Related Topics*. 17 July 2003. University of Arizona, College of Engineering, http://www.cs.arizona.edu/patterns/weaving/weavedocs.html.
53. "Bleaching," *Encyclopedia Brittanica*, 1st ed., 1771. *On-line Digital Archive of Documents on Weaving and Related Topics*. 9 March 2004. University of Arizona, College of Engineering, http://www.cs.arizona.edu/patterns/weaving/weavedocs.html.
54. Ribeiro, *The Art of Dress*, 70.
55. Buck, *Dress in Eighteenth-Century England*, 60–63.
56. *The Connoisseur*, No. 95, 571–2.
57. As *The History of Sir Charles Grandison* was an extremely popular novel, it is quite possible that the wedding of Sir Charles and Harriet influenced the wedding preferences of many young English women.
58. As quoted in Linthicum, 17.
59. Ashelford, 31.
60. Aileen Ribeiro, *Ingres in Fashion: Representations of Dress and Appearance in Ingre's Images of Women* (London and New Haven, CT: Yale University Press, 1999), 107.
61. Rosemary Horrox, "Purgatory, Prayer and Plague: 1150–1380," *Death in England: An Illustrated History*, eds. Peter C. Jupp and Clare Gittings (New Brunswick, NJ: Rutgers University Press, 2000), 107–8.
62. Ashelford, 31.
63. Walpole, 9:305. Letter to George Montagu, 14 October 1760.
64. Ribeiro, *The Art of Dress*, 101–2.
65. George Cheyne, *An Essay of Health and Long Life*, reprint edition (New York: Arno Press, 1979), 171.

Conclusion

1. David Cressy, *Literacy and the Social Order: Reading and Writing in Tudor and Stuart England* (Cambridge: Cambridge University Press, 1980), 145–7.

Works Cited

Addison, Joseph, and Richard Steele. *The Spectator.* 5 vols. Ed. Donald F. Bond. 1711–12. Oxford: Clarendon Press, 1965.

Aikins, Janet E. "Pamela's Use of Locke's Words." *Studies in Eighteenth-Century Culture* 25 (1996): 75–97.

———. "Richardson's 'Speaking Pictures.'" In *Samuel Richardson: Tercentenary Essays.* Eds. Margaret Anne Doody and Peter Sabor. Cambridge: Cambridge University Press, 1989.

Allestree, Richard. *The Gentleman's Calling.* London: T. Garthwait, 1660.

———. *The Ladies Calling.* Oxford: Printed at the Theatre, 1673.

Armstrong, Nancy. *Desire and Domestic Fiction: A Political History of the Novel.* New York and Oxford: Oxford University Press, 1987.

———. "The Rise of Domestic Woman." In *The Ideology of Conduct: Essays on Literature and the History of Sexuality.* Eds. Nancy Armstrong and Leonard Tennenhouse. New York: Methuen, 1987. 96–141.

Arnold, Janet. "Dashing Amazons: The Development of Women's Riding Dress, c. 1500–1900." In *Defining Dress: Dress as Object, Meaning and Identity.* Eds. Amy de la Haye and Elizabeth Wilson. Manchester and New York: Manchester University Press, 1999.

Arnold, Jeanne. *Queen Elizabeth's Wardrobe Unlock'd.* Leeds: W. S. Maney and Son, 1988.

Ashelford, Jane. *The Art of Dress: Clothes and Society, 1500–1914.* London: Laura Ashley, Ltd., and National Trust Enterprises Limited, 1996.

Backscheider, Paula. *Daniel Defoe: Ambition and Innovation.* Lexington: University of Kentucky Press, 1986.

Baclawski, Karen. *A Guide to Historic Costume.* New York: Drama Book Publishers, 1995.

Bakhtin, Mikhail. *Rabelais and His World.* Bloomington, IN: Indiana University Press, 1984.

Baldwin, Frances Elizabeth. "Sumptuary Legislation and Personal Regulation in England." In vol. xliv, *Johns Hopkins University Studies in Historical and Political Science.* Baltimore, MD: The Johns Hopkins University Press, 1926. 1–282.

Balfour-Paul, Jenny. *Indigo.* Chicago and London: Fitzroy Dearborn Publishers, 1998.

Barker-Benfield, G. J. *The Culture of Sensibility: Sex and Society in Eighteenth-Century Britain.* Chicago: University of Chicago Press, 1992.

Barnard, Malcolm. *Fashion as Communication.* London and New York: Routledge, 1996.

Barthes, Roland. *The Fashion System.* Trans. Matthew Ward and Richard Howard. Berkeley and Los Angeles: University of California Press, 1990.

Batchelor, Jennie. *Dress, Distress and Desire: Clothing and the Female Body in Eighteenth-Century Literature.* Basingstoke: Palgrave Macmillan, 2005.

The Bath, Bristol, Tunbridge and Epsom Miscellany. London: Printed by T. Dormer, 1735.

Beer, Gillian. *"Pamela:* Rethinking *Arcadia."* In *Samuel Richardson: Tercentenary Essays.* Eds. Margaret Anne Doody and Peter Sabor. Cambridge: Cambridge University Press, 1989. 23–39.

Beeton, Isabella. *Mrs. Beeton's Book of Household Management.* 1861. Oxford: Oxford University Press, 2000.

Bland, James. *The Charmes of Women: Or A Mirrour for Ladies.* London: E. Curll, 1736.

"Bleaching." *Encyclopedia Brittanica.* 1st ed. 1771.

Brückmann, Patricia C. "Clothes of Pamela's Own: Shopping at B-Hall." *Eighteenth-Century Life* 25 (Spring 2001): 201–13.

Buck, Anne. *Dress in Eighteenth-Century England.* New York: Holmes & Meier, 1979.

———. "Pamela's Clothes." *Costume: The Journal of the Costume Society* 26 (1992): 21–31.

Carter, Allison. *Underwear: The Fashion History.* New York: Drama Book Publishers, 1992.

Castle, Terry. *Clarissa's Ciphers: Meaning and Disruption in Richardson's "Clarissa."* London and Ithaca, NY: Cornell University Press, 1982.

———. *Masquerade and Civilization: The Carnivalesque in Eighteenth-Century English Culture and Fiction.* Stanford CA: Stanford University Press, 1986.

Chaden, Caryn. "Pamela's Identity Sewn Into Clothes." In *Eighteenth-Century Women and the Arts.* Eds. Frederick M. Keener and Susan E. Lorsch. New York: Greenwood Press, 1988. 109–18.

Chenciner, Robert. *Madder Red: A History of Luxury and Trade: Plant Dyes and Pigments in World Commerce and Art.* Richmond, Surrey: Caucasus World, 2000.

Cheyne, George. *An Essay of Health and Long Life.* Reprint edition. New York: Arno Press, 1979.

———. *The English Malady.* Ed. Roy Porter. 1733. London and New York: Tavistock/Routledge, 1991.

Chico, Tita. *Designing Women: The Dressing Room in Eighteenth-Century English Literature and Culture.* Lewisburg, PA: Bucknell University Press, 2005.

Childs, Fenela. "Prescriptions for Manners in English Courtesy Literature, 1690–1760." D. Phil. Thesis. University of Oxford. 1984.

Chrisman, Kimberly. "Unhoop the Fair Sex: The Campaign Against the Hoop Petticoat in Eighteenth-Century England." *Eighteenth-Century Studies* 30.1 (1996): 5–23.

Clark, J. C. D. *English Society, 1660–1832.* 2nd ed. Cambridge: Cambridge University Press, 2000.

Cohen, Michèle. *Fashioning Masculinity: National Identity and Language in the Eighteenth Century.* London and New York: Routledge, 1996.

Coke, Lady Jane. *Letters to Her Friend Mrs. Eyre at Derby, 1747–1758.* Ed. Mrs. Ambrose Rathborne. London: Swan Sonneschein, 1899.

Conboy, Sheila C. "Fabric and Fabrication in Richardson's *Pamela." English Literary History* 54.1 (Spring 1987): 81–96.

Craft-Fairchild, Catherine. *Masquerade and Gender: Disguise and Female Identity in Eighteenth-Century Fictions by Women.* University Park, PA: The Pennsylvania State University Press, 1993.

Cressy, David. *Literacy and the Social Order: Reading and Writing in Tudor and Stuart England.* Cambridge: Cambridge University Press, 1980.

Cunnington, C. Willett, and Phillis Cunnington. *Handbook of English Costume in the Eighteenth Century.* Boston, MA: Plays, Inc., 1972.

————. *A Picture History of English Costume.* New York: Macmillan, 1960.

————. *The History of Underclothes.* 1951. New York: Dover, 1992.

Cunnington, C. Willett, Phillis Cunnington, and Charles Beard. *A Dictionary of English Costume, 900–1900.* London: Adam & Charles Black, 1960.

Cunnington, Phillis, and Catherine Lucas. *Occupational Dress in England: From the 11th Century to 1914.* New York: Barnes and Noble, 1967.

Defoe, Daniel. *The Complete English Tradesman.* 1726. Gloucester: Alan Sutton, 1987.

————. "Everybody's Business is Nobody's Business." 5th ed. 1725.

————. *The Fortunes and Misfortunes of the Famous Moll Flanders.* Vols. I and II of *The Shakespeare Head Edition of the Novels and Selected Writings of Daniel Defoe.* Oxford: Basil Blackwell; New York and Boston, MA: Houghton Mifflin, 1920.

————. *The History of the Remarkable Life, and Extraordinary Adventures, of the Truly Honourable Colonel Jaque, vulgarly call'd Colonel Jack.* Vols. III and IV of *The Shakespeare Head Edition of the Novels and Selected Writings of Daniel Defoe.* Oxford: Basil Blackwell; New York and Boston, MA: Houghton Mifflin Company, 1920.

————. *Roxana, or The Fortunate Mistress.* Ed. David Blewett. Harmondsworth and New York: Penguin, 1982.

Delany, Mrs. *The Autobiography and Correspondence of Mrs. Delany.* Revised from Lady Llanover's Edition. Ed. Sarah Chauncey Woolsey. 2 vols. Boston, MA: Roberts Brothers, 1879.

de Marly, Diana. *Working Dress: A History of Occupational Costume.* London: B. T. Batsford, 1986.

Descartes, René. *The Passions of the Soul.* Trans. Stephen Voss. Cambridge and Indianapolis, IN: Hackett Publishing Company, 1989.

Doody, Margaret Anne. *A Natural Passion: A Study of the Novels of Samuel Richardson.* London: Oxford University Press, 1974.

————. "Disguise and Personality in Richardson's *Clarissa*." *Eighteenth-Century Life* 12.2 (May 1988): 18–39.

Dryden, John. *John Dryden: A Critical Edition of the Major Works.* Ed. Keith Walker. Oxford and New York: Oxford University Press, 1987.

"Dyeing." *London Encyclopedia,* 1829.

"Dyeing." *Ree's Cyclopaedia,* 1819.

Earle, Peter. *The Making of the English Middle Class: Business, Society and Family Life in London, 1660–1730.* Berkeley and Los Angeles: University of California Press, 1989.

Eaves, T. C. Duncan, and Ben D. Kimpel. *Samuel Richardson: A Biography.* Oxford: Clarendon Press, 1971.

Elias, Norbert. *The Civilizing Process: Sociogenetic and Psychogenetic Investigations.* Trans. Edmund Jephcott. Eds. Eric Dunning, Johan Goudsblom, and Stephen Mennell. Oxford: Blackwell Publishers, 2000.

Entwistle, Joanne. *The Fashioned Body: Fashion, Dress and Modern Social Theory.* Cambridge: Blackwell Publishers, 2000.

Essex, John. *The Young Ladies Conduct; or Rules for Education Under Several Heads.* London: John Brotherton, 1722.

Ewing, Elizabeth. *Everyday Dress, 1650–1900.* New York and Philadelphia, PN: Chelsea House Publishers, 1984.

————. *Underwear: A History.* New York: Theatre Art Books, 1972.

F. L. *The Virgin's Nosegay; or, The Duties of Christian Virtue.* London and Belfast: F. Joy, 1744.

[Farrar, Mrs. John]. *The Young Lady's Friend*. Boston, MA: American Stationer's Company, 1836.

Fielding, Henry. *The Covent Garden Journal*. Ed. Gerard Edward Jensen. 2 vols. New York: Russell & Russell, 1964.

———. *The History of Tom Jones, A Foundling*. 2 vols. Ed. Fredson Bowers. Oxford: Oxford University Press, 1975.

Fielding, Sarah. *The Lives of Cleopatra and Octavia*. Ed. Christopher D. Johnson. Lewisburg, PA: Bucknell University Press; London and Toronto: Associated University Presses, 1994.

Fox, Christopher. *Locke and the Scriblerians: Identity and Consciousness in Early Eighteenth-Century Britain*. Berkeley, Los Angeles, London: University of California Press, 1988.

Garber, Marjorie. *Vested Interests: Cross-Dressing and Cultural Anxiety*. New York: Routledge, 1997.

Gay, John. *The Guardian*. 1714.

Gisborne, Thomas. *An Enquiry into the Duties of the Female Sex*. London: T. Cadell, Jr. and W. Davies, 1797.

Greene, Donald. *The Age of Exuberance: Backgrounds to Eighteenth-Century Literature*. New York: McGraw-Hill, 1970.

Guest, Harriet. "Sterne, Elizabeth Draper, and Drapery." *The Shandean* 9 (November 1997): 9–33.

Gwilliam, Tassie. *Samuel Richardson's Fictions of Gender*. Stanford, CA: Stanford University Press, 1993.

Harvey, A. D. *Sex in Georgian England: Attitudes and Prejudices from the 1720s to the 1820s*. New York: St. Martin's, 1994.

Haywood, Eliza. *The Female Spectator*. 4 vols. 1744–1746. London: Printed for A. Millar, W. Law, and R. Cater, 1775.

Henley, N. M. *Body Politics: Power, Sex, and Nonverbal Communication*. Englewood Cliffs, NJ: Prentice Hall, 1977.

Hoeveler, Diane Long. *Gothic Feminism: The Professionalization of Gender from Charlotte Smith to the Brontës*. University Park, PA: The Pennsylvania State University Press, 1998.

Hogarth, William. *The Analysis of Beauty*. Ed. Ronald Paulson. London and New Haven, CT: Yale University Press, for the Paul Mellon Centre for British Art, 1997.

Hollander, Anne. *Sex and Suits*. New York: Knopf, 1994.

Horrox, Rosemary. "Purgatory, Prayer and Plague: 1150–1380." *Death in England: An Illustrated History*. Eds. Peter C. Jupp and Clare Gittings. New Brunswick, NJ: Rutgers University Press, 2000. 90–118.

Hughes, Clair. *Dressed in Fiction*. Oxford and New York: Berg, 2005.

Ingrassia, Catherine. Introduction. *Anti-Pamela and Shamela*, by Eliza Haywood and Henry Fielding. Ed. Catherine Ingrassia. Toronto: Broadview, 2004.

Instructions for a Young Lady, in Every Sphere and Period of Life. Edinburgh: A. Donaldson, 1773.

Johnson, Samuel. *The Rambler*. 3 vols. Eds. W. J. Bate and Albrecht B. Strauss. London and New Haven, CT: Yale University Press, 1969.

Jones, Ann Rosalind, and Peter Stallybrass. *Renaissance Clothing and the Materials of Memory*. Cambridge: Cambridge University Press, 2000.

Jourdain, M. "Gold and Silver Lace: Part I." *The Connoisseur* 17 (1906): 9–12.

———. "Gold and Silver Lace: Part II." *The Connoisseur* 17 (1906): 92–6.

Kaiser, Susan B. *The Social Psychology of Clothing: Symbolic Appearances in Context.* 2nd ed. revised. New York: Fairchild, 1997.

Kinkead-Weekes, Mark. *Samuel Richardson: Dramatic Novelist.* Ithaca, NY: Cornell University Press, 1973.

Kreissman, Bernard. *Pamela-Shamela: A Study in the Criticisms, Burlesques, Parodies, and Adaptation of Richardson's Pamela.* Lincoln, Nebraska: University of Nebraska, 1960.

Krochmal, Arnold, and Connie. *The Complete Illustrated Book of Dyes from Natural Sources.* Garden City, New York: Doubleday & Company, 1974.

Kuchta, David. *The Three-Piece Suit and Modern Masculinity: England, 1550–1850.* Berkeley, Los Angeles, London: University of California Press, 2002.

Langford, Paul. *A Polite and Commercial People: England, 1727–1783.* Oxford: Clarendon Press, 1989.

Laurence, Anne. *Women in England, 1500–1760: A Social History.* London: Weidenfeld and Nicolson, 1995.

Leed, Jacob. "Richardson's Pamela and Sidney's." *Journal of the Australasian Universities Language and Literature Association* 40 (1973): 240–5.

Lemire, Beverly. *Dress, Culture and Commerce: The English Clothing Trade Before the Factory, 1660–1800.* Basingstoke: Macmillan; New York: St. Martin's Press, 1997.

Lévi-Strauss, Claude. *The Origin of Table Manners: Introduction to a Science of Mythology.* 3 vols. Trans. John and Doreen Weightman. London: Cape, 1968.

Levine, Joseph M. *Between the Ancients and the Moderns: Baroque Culture in Restoration England.* New Haven, CT: Yale University Press, 1999.

Linthicum, M. Channing. *Costume in the Drama of Shakespeare and His Contemporaries.* New York: Hacker Art Books, 1972.

Locke, John. *An Essay Concerning Human Understanding.* 2 vols. New York: Dover, 1959.

Lurie, Alison. *The Language of Clothes.* New York: Henry Holt and Company, 1981.

Mackie, Erin. *Market à la Mode: Fashion, Commodity, and Gender in "The Tatler" and "The Spectator."* Baltimore, MD: The Johns Hopkins University Press, 1997.

Marcuse, Herbert. *One-Dimensional Man: Studies in the Ideology of Advanced Industrial Society.* Boston, MA: Beacon Press, 1964.

Markley, Robert. "Sentimentality as Performance: Shaftesbury, Sterne, and the Theatrics of Virtue." In *The New Eighteenth-Century: Theory, Politics, English Literature.* Eds. Felicity Nussbaum and Laura Brown. New York and London: Methuen, 1987. 210–30.

Marks, Sylvia Kasey. *Sir Charles Grandison: The Compleat Conduct Book.* Lewisburg, PA: Bucknell University Press; London and Toronto: Associated University Presses, 1986.

Marx, Karl. *Capital: A Critique of Political Economy.* Trans. Samuel Moore and Edward Aveling. Ed. Frederick Engels. 1887. Moscow: Progress Publishers, 1954.

McIntosh, Carey. "Pamela's Clothes." *English Literary History* 54.1 (Spring 1967): 75–83.

McKeon, Michael. "Historicizing Patriarchy: The Emergence of Gender Difference in England, 1660–1760." *Eighteenth-Century Studies* 28 (1995): 295–322.

————. *The Origins of the English Novel, 1600–1740.* Baltimore, MD: The Johns Hopkins University Press, 1987.

————. *The Secret History of Domesticity: Public, Private, and the Division of Knowledge.* Baltimore, MD: The Johns Hopkins University Press, 2005.

McMaster, Juliet. *Reading the Body in the Eighteenth-Century Novel.* Basingstoke: Palgrave Macmillan, 2004.

Milton, John. *John Milton: Complete Poems and Major Prose.* Ed. Merritt Y. Hughes. Reprinted 1957. Cambridge and Indianapolis, IN: Hackett Publishing Company, 2003.

Moore, Rosemary. *The Light in Their Consciences: Early Quakers in Britain, 1646–1666.* University Park, PA: The Pennsylvania State University Press, 2000.

Munns, Jessica, and Penny Richards. "Introduction: The Clothes That Wear Us." In *The Clothes That Wear Us: Essays on Dressing and Transgressing in Eighteenth-Century Culture.* Eds. Jessica Munns and Penny Richards. Newark: University of Delaware Press; London: Associated University Presses, 1999. 9–32.

Pamela Censored. 1741. Los Angeles: William Andrews Clark Memorial Library, University of California Press, 1976. Publication Number 175 of the Augustan Reprint Society.

Pellow, Charles E. "Mediæval Dyestuffs." *The Bulletin of the Needle and Bobbin Club,* vol. 2 (1918): 3–11.

Pointon, Marcia. "Quakerism and Visual Culture, 1650–1800." *Art History* 20.3 (September 1997): 397–431.

Pope, Alexander. *Alexander Pope: A Critical Edition of the Major Works.* Ed. Pat Rogers. Oxford and New York: Oxford University Press, 1993.

Porter, Roy. *Flesh in the Age of Reason.* New York and London: W. W. Norton, 2003.

Ribeiro, Aileen. *The Art of Dress: Fashion in England and France, 1750 to 1820.* New Haven: Yale University Press, 1995.

————. *Dress and Morality.* New York: Holmes & Meier, 1986.

————. *Dress in Eighteenth-Century Europe, 1715–1789.* New York: Holmes & Meier, 1985.

————. *The Dress Worn at Masquerades in England, 1730 to 1790, and Its Relation to Fancy Dress Portraiture.* New York and London: Garland Publishing, 1984.

————. *Fashion and Fiction: Dress in Art and Literature in Stuart England.* London and New Haven, CT: Yale University Press, 2005.

————. *Ingres in Fashion: Representations of Dress and Appearance in Ingres' Images of Women.* London and New Haven, CT: Yale University Press, 1999.

Richardson, Leslie. "Leaving Her Father's House: Astell, Locke, and Clarissa's Body Politic." *Studies in Eighteenth-Century Culture* 34 (2005): 151–71.

Richardson, Samuel. *The Apprentice's Vade Mecum.* 1734; Los Angeles: William Andrews Clark Memorial Library, University of California, 1975. Augustan Reprint Society. Publications Nos. 169–70.

————. *Clarissa; or, the History of a Young Lady.* Ed. Angus Ross. 1747–8. London: Penguin, 1985.

————. *Clarissa; or, the History of a Young Lady.* Reprint of 3rd edition. London: S. Richardson, 1751; New York: AMS Press, 1990.

————. *The History of Sir Charles Grandison.* Ed. Jocelyn Harris. 3 vols. 1753–4. London: Oxford University Press, 1972; Dunedin, New Zealand: Otago University Print, 2001.

————. *Pamela; or, Virtue Rewarded.* Eds. T. C. Duncan Eaves and Ben D. Kimpel. Boston, MA: Houghton Mifflin, 1971.

————. *Pamela.* 4 vols. In *The Complete Novels of Samuel Richardson.* London: William Heinemann, 1902.

————. *Selected Letters of Samuel Richardson.* Ed. John Carroll. Oxford: Clarendon Press, 1964.

Roulston, Christine. *Virtue, Gender, and the Authentic Self in Eighteenth-Century Fiction.* Gainesville, FL: University Press of Florida, 1998.

Sambrook, Pamela A. *The Country House Servant.* Phoenix Mill: Sutton Publishing, in association with the National Trust, 1999.

Sidney, Sir Philip. *The Countess of Pembroke's Arcadia: The New Arcadia.* Ed. Victor Skretkowicz. Oxford: Clarendon Press; New York: Oxford University Press, 1987.

Smith, Timothy L. "Chronological List of John Wesley's Sermons and Doctrinal Essays," *Wesley Theological Journal* 17.2 (Fall 1982): 88–110.

Spenser, Edmund. *The Faerie Queene.* Ed. Thomas P. Roche, Jr., with the assistance of C. Patrick O'Donnell, Jr., Harmondsworth: Penguin, 1978.

Steele, Richard. *The Complete Plays of Richard Steele.* Ed. G. A. Aitken. London: T. Fisher Unwin; New York: Charles Scribner's Sons, 1894.

Swift, Jonathan. *Directions to Servants.* 1745. London: Hesperus Press, 2003.

————. "A Full and True Account of the Battel Fought last Friday, Between the Antient and the Modern Books in St. James's Library." In *Gulliver's Travels and Other Writings.* Ed. Louis A. Landa. Boston, MA: Houghton Mifflin, 1960. 355–80.

————. *A Tale of a Tub.* In *Gulliver's Travels and Other Writings.* Ed. Louis A. Landa. Boston, MA: Houghton Mifflin Company, 1960.

Tague, Ingrid H. *Women of Quality: Accepting and Contesting Ideals of Femininity in England, 1690–1760.* Woodbridge, Suffolk: Boydell Press, 2002.

The Domestic Dyer, Being Receipts for Dyeing Cotton and Linen, Hot and Cold. New England, Printed for Domestic Uses, 1811.

The Ladies Library. Published by R. Steele. London. Jacob Tonson, 1714.

[Thornton, Bonnell, and George Colman]. *The Connoisseur by Mr. Town, Critic and Censor-General.* London: 1754–5.

Tozer, Jane, and Sarah Levitt. *Fabric of Society: A Century of People and Their Clothes, 1770–1870.* Carno, Powys, Wales: Laura Ashley Ltd. and City of Manchester Cultural Services, 1983.

Turner, E. S. *What the Butler Saw: Two Hundred and Fifty Years of the Servant Problem.* London: Penguin, 1962.

Turner, John Grantham. "Lovelace and the Paradoxes of Libertinism." In *Samuel Richardson: Tercentenary Essays.* Eds. Margaret Anne Doody and Peter Sabor. Cambridge: Cambridge University Press, 1989.

————. "Novel Panic: Picture and Performance in the Reception of Richardson's *Pamela.*" *Representations* 48 (Autumn 1994): 70–96.

Vickery, Amanda. "Golden Age to Separate Spheres? A Review of the Categories and Chronology of English Women's History." In *Women's Work: The English Experience, 1650–1914.* Ed. Pamela Sharpe. London, New York, Sidney, Auckland: Arnold, 1998. 294–332.

Walpole, Horace. *The Yale Edition of Horace Walpole's Correspondence.* 48 vols. Ed. W. S. Lewis. London and New Haven, CT: Yale University Press, 1937–1983.

Warner, William B. *Licensing Entertainment: The Elevation of Novel Reading in Britain, 1684–1750.* Berkeley, Los Angeles, London: University of California Press, 1998.

Watkin, E. I. *Roman Catholicism in England, from the Reformation to 1950.* London: Oxford University Press, 1957.

Waugh, Norah. *Corsets and Crinolines.* 1954. New York: Theatre Arts Books, 1970.

Weber, Caroline. *Queen of Fashion: What Marie Antoinette Wore to the Revolution.* New York: Henry Holt and Company, 2006.

Wesley, John. *Sermons on Several Occasions.* Grand Rapids, MI: Christian Classics Ethereal Library, n.d. Calvin College.

Whishaw, Bernard, and Ellen M. "Punto de Aguja and Point d'Espagne: Part I." *The Connoisseur,* vol. 26 (1910): 51–5.

Wilkes, Reverend Wetenhall. *A Letter of Genteel and Moral Advice to a Young Lady.* London: C. Hitch, 1740.

Young, Edward. *Conjectures on Original Composition: In a Letter to the Author of Sir Charles Grandison.* London: A. Millar and R. and J. Dodsley, 1759.

Index